BESIDE THE MUSIC

BJ KNAPP

Hi Cassandra —
It was a pleasure to meet you at the Big E. I hope you like my book. Thank you for your support!
All my best —
BJ

Copyright 2015 BJ Knapp

PRINT ISBN 978-0692729632
EPUB ISBN 0692729631

BJ Knapp

Praise for Beside the Music

BJ Knapp creates for her witty and endearing protagonist, Brenda Dunkirk, a mix tape of the pleasures and perils of serving as a musician's muse. Besides the Music is a smart, humorous look at the compromises of marriage, art, and career-- and the power of rock 'n roll to rock the soul.
---Céline Keating, author of Layla and Play for Me

Beside the Music is a real treat from first-time author BJ Knapp. Her writing style is warm and witty and her characters are engaging and totally authentic. I loved this book from beginning to end.
---Gail Ward Olmstead, author of Jeep Tour, Guessing at Normal and Driving on the Left

Knapp has spun a story full of wit and realistically drawn characters who dare to ask if heroes can rise again and if new dreams can rival old.
---Nicole Waggoner, author of Center Ring and The Act

The whole idea of all of this is quite unique--if you're looking for a quirky and funny tale than I strongly suggest picking this one up. It was a breath of fresh air for me because the read is light yet fun. I can't wait to read more books by the author in the future as she clearly has a knack for writing!
---Pretty Little Book Reviews

Beside the Music

For Todd, my best friend, accomplice and dive buddy--the best husband a girl could have. Without you, none of this would have ever happened. I love you more than everything.

BJ Knapp

Chapter 1

I AM IN THE ONE PLACE in Westwood, Rhode Island that reeks of possibility: the public library. I take in the papery smell of the books lined up on the shelves and detect just a hint of mildew. Possibility extends beyond smell; it also includes sounds like the hushed whispers of teenagers huddled over their textbooks and their suppressed giggles. I can hear Peggy at the front desk chatting to patrons as she checks out their books—do those people get as excited as I do about devouring their new finds? I hope so.

This is the one place where time slows down for me. I have never been one of those people who runs in here and grabs anything to check out. I take my time. I browse. It's a spa for my brain. I am strolling through the K section at the library, running my fingers down the spines lined up on the shelf to my right; so many of them I haven't read yet. Right now I am obsessed with tell-all memoirs written by '80s rock stars. I've read all of them I can get my hands on: Ozzy Osbourne, Stephen Tyler, Neil Peart from Rush, and Motley Crue, to name a few.

But today I am searching the stacks for the latest in a series written by Amy Kulpepper. When I am not reading rock star tell-all memoirs, Amy's work is my favorite escape: a period dramatic series about an '80s metal band on the verge of hitting it big. Apparently, I am not the only one in Westwood, Rhode Island who is obsessed with the rise and fall of Amy's band, Pound of Flesh: all of her books have been checked out.

1

Just before I decide to give up on Kulpepper, I find another book I hadn't noticed on the same top shelf. It has a white dust jacket with its title in light-gray font: *Colors Fade*. In a font a shade lighter is the name of the author: Keith Kutter. I slide the book off the shelf and look at his picture. He's almost as I remember him, though his hair is now shorter and more modern, not the mullet I remember from the '80s. Then I examine the inside dust jacket blurb—*Keith Kutter's journey to hell and back,* it reads tantalizingly. My heart beats just a bit faster as I gaze at his photo. The hint of age on his face makes him hotter than he was back then. Now he looks like a man who has it all figured out. It had been Keith Kutter's face that I'd plastered all over my room when I was a teenager. He has a few more lines around his piercing blue eyes, but I still feel like he's staring deep into me from in front of the camera. When I was fifteen, I had entire conversations with his photos; right now, I feel like I could tell him anything.

Keith Kutter was the bassist from the multi-platinum metal band Hydra. I wish I could stand here in the K aisle and spill my deepest darkest feelings to his photo. I feel like he'd understand. But since I got married, I've allowed myself to lose the ability to confide in someone who isn't my husband, Tim. Sometimes my deep, dark feelings are about Tim.

He's waiting in the car for me outside the library, and I hope he hasn't gotten too impatient. I grab *Colors Fade* and head up to Peggy at the checkout desk.

"Hi, Brenda," she says, looking over the cover. "Another rock star memoir, huh? Man, you are hooked on these things. Are they really that good?" Apparently my rock star memoir binge is trending.

"Peggy," I ask her, "you know how some people are into history? Like my dad will read anything about World War II that he can get his hands on? Well, to me, this is art history. I grew up listening to these guys." I point to Keith Kutter's face on the back cover. "And now I get to learn about what their lives were really like back then, while they were making all that music. It's fascinating." Peggy nods, but I can tell she's not interested. It's like when my dad talks about World War II: I just smile politely, the way Peggy's doing now. I don't think Peggy's the rock-and-roll type. But I am. It's why I became a publicist in my professional career. Maybe someday I'll get to work on a band's PR. But for now, I'm working in corporate public relations at Amanda Dixon PR, which provides me the occasional opportunity to work on a local personality's image. But I am hoping I can convince my boss, Amanda, that she needs to expand the company's reach into the local music industry—and that I am the one who should head up that division.

When I get out to the car, I notice that Tim has moved to the passenger seat so that I can drive. He's got his Bluetooth in his ear and Skype on his iPhone. I can see Aria Kendall's long, salon-perfect blonde hair filling the screen. *How is it that Aria can look like a supermodel while Skyping?* When I use my phone to

Beside the Music
do that, my skin looks both gray and greasy. Aria is Tim's campaign manager. He's running for state Senate, and it's completely taken over his life. Every day, he's either meeting or Skyping with Aria. By the time he is done with that, he's already told someone else—Aria—all about his day, and he's all talked out.

"Aria," Tim is saying, "I'm glad that you agree about door-to-door campaigning. It would be a huge waste of time. Nobody wants me walking up to their front door, right?" As I'm listening, I realize that I agree with Tim on that point, too. The truth is I've closed our front door—which we rarely use—on many candidates for this or that office and instantly forgotten them the moment I'd locked the door again.

I have my own opinions about Aria as a person, which I wouldn't ever share with Tim, but I think she's a good campaign manager. Tim met Aria at one of his mother's over-the-top expensive fundraisers. I suspect that Portia, Tim's mom, had really been trying to fix Tim up with Aria, but they'd hit it off anyway after they got to talking about local politics. I am not sure that Aria's intentions are completely pure when it comes to Tim; but she really hasn't given me a solid reason to be suspicious. Yet.

"Can we film a TV spot at the shop?" Tim asks her. Tim is also a mechanic, and he owns an auto repair shop in town. "I want to put up a big campaign sign out in front, too. There's a lot of traffic on Orchard Street. It'll be free exposure."

Now he's talking my language. I've asked Tim if there was any way I could help with the campaign, seeing as how PR is my job, but he's told me that he doesn't want to burden me with it. "I want you focused on getting your promotion at work," he said. And he's probably right. Amanda has been dangling a vice president's role in front of me for about half a year now. I want it so bad that I work late just about every single night, and sometimes on weekends. And while I work, Tim and Aria are plotting to take over Rhode Island with his Senate campaign.

The truth is I don't really know where I would fit in, as Aria is running everything for him. Of course, I am interested in what Tim is doing, and I'd love to talk to him about it more. But by the time he gets home, he doesn't want to talk about the shop or his campaign anymore. What else is there for him to talk about? I don't know... Are we just going through the seven-year itch? We've certainly been married that long; have we run out of things to talk about? *Am I not interesting enough anymore?* Aria, I am sure, is fascinating, with her connections in business and government all over the state.

As Tim continues with his conversation, I pull the car out of the parking lot and head toward home. I reach over and take his hand. I give it a slight squeeze, and he squeezes back briefly, then he lets go. That's how it's been between us lately. These mini-moments of affection, kind of like, "Oh yeah, we're supposed

3

to make loving gestures to each other in between all the stuff we have going on."

Lately, I've been wondering what the next step is for Tim and me as a couple. I can't help thinking we aren't as aligned in our goals as we had been, that maybe we're going too far off on our own individual tracks. I want us to embark on an adventure together, to get us back to being a team. A baby would be just the thing to get us focused as a family again. Right now I feel like we're both on our own separate orbits, with me trying to get promoted at work and him trying to get elected. When will it ever be the right time to start our family? For me, there's no time like the present. But for Tim, there's always some goal we need to reach first, like our bank balance getting to a certain amount, or his getting elected, or me getting my promotion. Just thinking about the situation gets my jaw working and my teeth grinding as I drive—and as my husband discusses his campaign talking points with some other woman. I decide, then, that we have got to do something to break out of this rut.

When we get home, I head to my computer to look up a travel site on the Internet. "Hey, Tim?" I call to him from my desk. "I just found a great deal for flights to Orlando next week. How about we get away for a few days? You know, before things really heat up heading into the election? I don't know about you, but I could use some fun." Okay, it's probably not the right time. It's never the right time. But that's what makes a spontaneous trip exciting—going anyway, even if you're feeling overwhelmed with life at home.

From where I sit, I can see Tim pick up his phone and swipe over a couple of screens, probably to his calendar. He furrows his eyebrows. He's about to say no, I just know it. "When is the last time you and I just packed up and went on a long weekend trip?" I ask him. "We need this. Let's go. Please."

He ambles toward me, looking troubled. "Bren, I just don't think…"

"Come on. We'll fly out on Thursday night and come back on Monday by noon. It's only a day and a half off from work."

I see him weighing the pros and cons of taking the time off; I start to tap my foot on the parquet floor, knowing eventually the tapping will make him nuts.

"Okay, fine," he sighs. "You win. Let's go to Orlando."

I jump into his arms, but they feel rigid to me. I know getting away from work can be hard for him; I'll have to reschedule a few things at the office, as well. I have the Smile Airlines product launch coming up soon, and I am in the thick of it with coordinating ad spots in the local media and organizing the redesign of the airline's website. But a little romantic trip will be just the thing to get us back to having fun together again, I just know it.

Chapter 2

TIM AND I ARE AT THE GATE, waiting to board our plane to Orlando. I am psyched that he agreed to this spontaneous trip. We are way overdue for some fun, but so far it's been anything but that. Right after we got through security, he implanted his Bluetooth into his ear so he can wrap up last-minute business before he has to turn off the phone. So much for having a conversation about all the plans I've made for us in Orlando.

Tim is pacing and speaking urgently into his cell phone. "Make sure you process Mrs. Keene's insurance paperwork first thing in the morning. They've been giving her the runaround, and I want to help her out." He's going to be bummed when he has to turn the phone off. I leave him in the waiting area and walk over to the newsstand to get some snacks for the flight.

When I get back to the gate, Tim's still on the phone. "A debate with Mitch Goldstein on NPR? Hell yeah, I'll do it." I figure he's talking to Aria again. "Wait," he says, "that's the day after I get back from Orlando. I don't know if I'll have time to prepare." He paces and runs a hand through his red hair. I can tell he regrets going on this trip already. "It's only April, and the election isn't until November. Why does it have to be now?" I hold out the bottle of Coke I bought for him; he waves me off, turns his back on me, and keeps talking. I know he's tense, but this stings me a little. A moment later, though, he seems to realize what he's done and turns to face me again. He holds out his hand, and I put the Coke into it. He shakes his head and takes my hand, instead. He kisses the back of it and apologizes with his eyes. I smile at him while he opens the Coke and takes a sip. He mouths, "Thank you" to me. I nod in response and then sit down.

We haven't started boarding yet. Tim likes to get to the airport insanely early, so we usually end up sitting around by the gate for nearly an hour before we board. Judging by how things look, he'll probably be on the phone the entire time. That's okay; I can dig into Keith Kutter's book.

I remember exactly when I first fell in love with Hydra. I was in eighth grade

5

and getting ready for school; my clock radio with the tinny speakers was on. I was sitting on my bed facing the dresser with the mirror on it. I'd purposely arranged my room that way so that the bed and dresser would serve as a vanity table, and I had all my various hair products and makeup strewn all over the surface. The doily that my mom insisted on keeping on the dresser had been irreparably stained from spilled eye shadow and from my compact exploding in a flesh-colored powder bomb one time when I'd dropped it.

I was smudging my black eyeliner as fast as I could, because I was chronically in danger of missing the bus. WYNH, the radio station out of New Haven, which was my source for new music at the time, was surprisingly clear in its broadcast from sixty miles away. First, I heard the bass drum beating over the last few seconds of the traffic report. It was like the song was bursting in and didn't need any introduction. The cliché had always been to make it sound like a beating heart—like in that Huey Lewis song about the "heart of rock and roll." But this drummer didn't do that. It was a simple four beats in eighth notes. *Bah-BUMP bah-BUMP.* A silence followed for a moment—almost like an intentional affront to 'ol Huey. Then, right after the bass drum pounded out the four beats again, Keith oozed in on his bass guitar and took over. It obscured the bass drum, until the lead guitar burst in and whipped tension into the melody with its gritty distortion. I was captivated from the first four beats. The introduction to this song was so dramatic that I had to set the eyeliner down and listen with my full attention. The vocalist, whom I'd never heard before, described a soldier returning from a battlefield, where he'd learned that the generals had intentionally sent the army into a losing fight. The singer described the blood and the wailing mothers and widows. And then the song faded out. Whoa.

"New guys from down under hitting the scene," the DJ shot out over the last few notes. *"That was 'Battleground Zero,' by Hydra. Remember, you heard it here first on WYNH, because they are going to be hot, hot, hot in the next few weeks."* I scribbled down the band's name on the doily with my black eyeliner.

"Brenda, you're going to be late," my Mom said, bursting into the room. "What are you doing?" I was sitting there with my mouth hanging open, eyeliner on only one eye; she probably thought I looked like a spaz. She switched off the radio, spotted my writing on the doily, and shook her head. "Brenda, it's a doily, not a notepad." I wished I had thought to tape the song off of the radio; I knew I'd need to hear it again and soon.

"Mom! Wait! That was Hydra!"

"Who cares? You have school. March!" She pointed to the door.

"But I have to finish getting ready," I said. I picked up my eyeliner, now dull from using it as a pencil. "I can't go like this," I said, pointing to my eyes.

"Five minutes, Bren. I mean it." She turned on her heel and walked out of the room. I drew a heart around the word Hydra with the hot pink Clinique freebie lipstick I never used. It was at that point I became Hydra's biggest fan at East Windsor Middle School and began buying every single thing they released.

6

Beside the Music

My bedroom soon became plastered with Hydra posters, pictures torn from magazines, really anything I could apply Scotch tape to. Keith Kutter never looked directly at the camera in any of the pictures—even in the liner notes—which added to his mystique. I scoured the teeny bopper mags for some secret about his life that nobody else would notice. I learned his birthday from *Heavy Beats* Magazine—January seventh. From *Rock Insider*, I learned his favorite flavor of ice cream—mint chocolate chip. And *People* Magazine told me he had a Dalmatian named Winston. But everyone else knew those secrets. What about his really dark secrets? In which closet would I find his skeletons?

The teeny bopper mags didn't have to publish his skeletons; Keith Kutter eventually published them on his own. I thought I'd heard about him publishing his memoir, but by then I hadn't given it much thought. Of course, my sixteen-year-old self would have devoured the book the moment I'd gotten home. But my thirty-five-year-old self merely packed it into my carryon bag for the plane so I could have that forced inactivity of a plane ride to devour it properly.

While I wait for Tim to finish his call, I fish out *Colors Fade* from my carryon and thumb through the pictures in the center pages. Whenever I read a memoir, I always try to wait until I've read to that point before looking at the pictures in the middle, but I always end up giving in to the temptation to peek. Keith didn't include any pictures of Hydra, as this book isn't about the band. It's about the tragic accident that tore his family apart. First, there's a wedding picture of him and his wife Tamsen, then baby pictures of his son Damien. Even in the baby pictures, I can see Keith's dimpled chin and square jaw in Damien's face. I wonder what our baby will look like, if Tim and I ever get around to having one. I always picture our daughter as a red-haired little girl named Zoe, because I'd rather our daughter have Tim's vibrant hair than my drab brown. I look at the rest of the photos: there's a picture of the destroyed car and one of Damien, drowsy on painkillers, in traction.

By the time I got to college, I'd stopped listening to Hydra. I volunteered at the campus radio station and even had my own radio show. Hydra slipped away from me the moment I encountered the seemingly endless stacks of CDs at WRIU. I used to run my fingers along the shelves and count to seven. Whatever CD was under my finger when I arrived at seven was the one I played on my show. I discovered some really bad music that way—but I also found some hidden gems that I still have on my iPod. I knew that the band had put out a few albums since I'd stopped listening to them, but I never bought them, and I never really noticed when they were played on the radio. I had stopped paying attention, with the result that, today, I don't know whether Hydra has become one of those aging metal bands who started calling their music "art" as they get older. I hope they haven't.

In my mind they are still wearing the same tight spandex pants and barely buttoned billowing shirts they wore in their videos on MTV. They had big, permed hair that flowed in the fan's air current in their videos, but they weren't into eye makeup, the way Poison or even Motley Crüe were. I know that their reputation has taken a hit as the band has declined into semi-obscurity. I've seen a few Twitter hashtags about them behaving rudely to their fans. In one instance, I dug into it a bit more and found an article, written by a blogger, recounting how she'd met Keith Kutter in person. She'd said hello to him, and he'd responded by snarling at her. The blog entry had gone viral. I guess a band that was that big in the '80s doesn't always have the sense to worry about what is said about them on today's social media. I would love to formally pitch them as a client at work. I know that, if I were their publicist, I could fix Keith's reputation, and there would be no negative blog entries about him snarling at anyone.

While I dug into the gossip about Hydra's reputation, I also Googled the story behind Keith's memoir. I learned that he and his family had been driving back from a barbeque at which Keith had had too much to drink. He'd lost control of the car, and as a result of the crash, his twelve-year-old son, Damien, had been rendered a quadriplegic. Keith had broken his collar bone. His wife, Tamsen, had been banged up but was otherwise uninjured.

After the accident, Keith went on a pharmaceutically-induced bender. Tamsen kicked him out after she'd found him raiding his son's medication bottles. She was afraid of what he would do while under the influence and frankly didn't want to take care of Keith on top of taking care of Damien. I don't think anyone can say they blamed her.

I vaguely remember the media outrage at the time over why Keith hadn't been thrown in jail over the accident; after all, he'd been drunk while driving. Later, I stumbled on a YouTube video of a rare interview with him on one of those *Where Are They Now?* shows on VH1 or MTV. Tears streamed down my cheeks as I listened to Keith describe the guilt he felt for stealing his son's life. That was the only interview Keith had done since the book came out, and he declared the topic officially closed to the media. That's understandable. Why would he want to rehash that, over and over, in each interview? Still, I would think that he could find a way to use the media as a way to move the world past its outrage. I know that, if I were his publicist, that's what I would do. Still, talk about a publicity disaster.

I flip back to the beginning of Keith's book and devour the first chapter before it's finally time to get on the plane. People approach the counter beside the gate, trying to score a last minute seat upgrade. Tim checks his boarding pass and his watch; his knee bounces impatiently.

I reach out to still his leg. "Hey, what are you thinking?"

"Bren, I don't know why I agreed to this trip. There is just too much going on."

"That's the point, Tim. We barely spend any time together anymore."

"What do you mean? We have dinner together every night."

8

Beside the Music

"Yeah, in front of the TV. We're in the same room, but we're not really in the same place." It's not just his fault—I am guilty, too.

"Can we please not do this right now?" he asks.

"Then when, Tim?"

He doesn't answer. His phone rings. I see it's Jimmy from the shop. And now I've lost him again. "Shit," he says. "I completely forgot that *Rhode Island List* is coming to the shop today." He glares at me as if to say, *If I wasn't going on this trip, I'd be on top of it.* His shop was recently voted the number one small business in *Rhode Island List Magazine.* As a result, business has been pouring in—which is great. "Call Aria," he says into the phone. "She has photos of me in the shop that you can give to them to use for the magazine story."

Aria has photos of him in the shop? Just how much time is she spending there?

Don't get me wrong. I am proud of what Tim has accomplished with the shop. But the downside is that he's working around the clock and never gets the chance to unwind. That's the dilemma when it comes to being married to a small-business owner. He needs a vacation to recover from the stress, but it's often the vacation that causes even more stress.

I am hoping that this will be one of those trips where we'll just forget everything at home and have fun. I've managed to get us signed up for a habitat tour at SeaWorld, as well as a few other activities. Then maybe we'll have one of those nights where we sit up all night talking. I can't remember the last time we did that.

Tim hangs up his phone, and I watch his jaw clench and unclench. When he's ready to unwind, he will. I can't force him, so why pick a fight? After we finally board the plane and are settled into our seats, I squeeze his thigh, which I hope he'll take as a relaxing gesture. I wait a few moments for him to respond and then I allow myself to get sucked back into the book.

The writing style Keith used is dreamlike, which perfectly expresses the drug-induced haze he was living in immediately after the accident. I can feel the raw emotion coming through the early part of the book, and my heart pounds as I burn through the pages. By the time we land in Orlando, I am at the part where he's failing miserably at rehab. Then, as the plane pulls up to the gate, Keith has checked himself out of rehab and set off on his sailboat for months on end to heal himself on his own. *That's an interesting way to kick a drug habit*, I think to myself. *Go out to sea, and don't bring any drugs with you.* Although I do wonder how safe it would be to detox while alone and offshore. I am picturing him going stir-crazy for the first few weeks, while the drugs work their way out of his system—just like in the movies, when people try to kick the habit. I imagine him scratching at his arms and talking to people who aren't there. I really hope that

9

sort of behavior is over-dramatized for the movies, because I think it would be a horrible thing to experience while alone and surrounded by ocean.

"So, is this one any good?" Tim says to me, gesturing to my book as I shove it back into my carryon. "You barely looked up from it for the entire flight." Tim had had his headphones on, watching a movie on his iPad. I like to read on planes; he likes to watch movies. So we usually don't talk the whole time. Sometimes we hold hands, but during this flight, we didn't.

"It's one of the guys from Hydra," I say to him.

Tim pulls the book from my bag. "I remember this guy. He's the one who was drunk and broke his son's arms and legs in a car accident." He snorts as he thumbs through the pictures. "And now he gets to write a book to glorify how irresponsible he was?"

"It's more than that, Tim. He's recovering from an addiction to painkillers and trying to figure out how to cope after a traumatic event like that."

"He has to learn how to cope? What about his kid? Does *he* get to write a book, too?" He points to the picture of Damien in traction.

"It's still an interesting story. I grew up listening to this band."

Tim always laughs at me when an old Hydra song comes on the radio. I still know all the words to those oldies. "Plus, all the proceeds from his book are going to the Rainbow House—they help families with kids who ended up quadriplegic like Damien. At least he's trying to make it right, you know? He's still not allowed to see his son, so he's trying to help other kids." I think that's pretty cool of Keith Kutter. It's a step in the right direction to improve his reputation, if he tries to make something positive out of a bad situation that he actually caused.

Tim and I make our way off the plane then wind our way to baggage claim. While I wait for the bags, he goes to the rental car counter.

Tim comes back to the baggage claim just as our bags are sliding onto the carousel. He smiles as he jingles the keys at me. "Free upgrade. Convertible." He tosses the keys at me. I catch them and smile back at him. Maybe this weekend getaway will be just the ticket for us after all.

Chapter 3

"AREN'T YOU COMING IN?" Tim calls to me from the pool. I'm sitting in a lounge chair finishing Keith Kutter's book. "The water is amazing. Come on, Bren! You need to come and play with me."

Tim's pretty high-strung, and it usually takes a day or so for him to uncoil and enjoy the vacation. While he is in this uncoiling period, I usually spend that time reading—so I've gotten the chance to read most of Keith's book already. Now he's fully uncoiled and ready to have fun, but I am trying to read to the end. Bad timing.

"Just a few more pages," I tell him. "I'm almost finished."

"You've had your nose buried in that book all weekend," he says, playfully splashing me.

Like he's even noticed. He's had his phone glued to his ear, frantically checking in with the shop and with Aria. I know that a minute on the phone is better than him constantly wondering what's going on back home without him. Still, I am pretty pissed that I went to the trouble of planning this whole trip and he hasn't seemed to enjoy any of it. He answered his phone three times during the habitat tour at SeaWorld yesterday. Even the tour guide started to get annoyed. And he cancelled the couple's massage this morning because he stayed too long on the phone with Aria. Now it's like he's just remembered that he has a wife who has been wanting his attention for the last two days.

Tim has completely missed the point of this trip, which was to get away from the grind at home and relax. I know he'll be an awesome state senator, and I know he's a great mechanic. His shop's reviews on Yelp are all positive; they absolutely gush about his honesty. But I have to admit: sometimes it's hard to stay supportive when I feel like I have to take the back seat. This trip is not at all what I planned. For example, we were just about to get onto a roller coaster when his mom called. We'd spent forever waiting in line for it at SeaWorld, but we had to let the people behind us take our seats so he could finish talking to her. I don't know what they

11

talked about, but why couldn't he just tell her he'd call her back later? I am pretty tired of being the last person on his list. His mother, Portia, doesn't like me, so it makes me feel even worse, knowing he'll talk to her before he'll talk to me.

When Tim and I first met, he'd been on track to go to medical school and then to take over his dad's very successful ocular surgery practice. Tim's father was the first surgeon in the state to perform Lasik surgery, and he'd made an absolute fortune off of his practice. Naturally, Portia had wanted Tim to take over the business and continue his dad's legacy. But Tim hadn't been passionate about medicine. Instead, his real love had always been cars. He's the kind of guy who can fix just about anything. He finally made the decision to become a mechanic instead of a surgeon, and now his mother thinks that I "white-trashed" him. Never mind the fact that Tim's shop is very successful and we are comfortable—not only because of his excellent reputation as a mechanic, but also because of my budding career as a publicist. And now she probably thinks I am extra trashy because I took him to an amusement park in Orlando instead of some exclusive spa in West Palm Beach. But Tim loves roller coasters. He'd rather spend a day riding them than getting massaged and buffed with sugar scrubs.

Just before we came out to the pool, Tim said, "It's the last day of the trip. I am leaving this thing behind so I can get some sun." Then he'd plugged the phone into the charger and left it on the bedside table. He raised his eyebrows when I took the book with me; I think he'd hoped I would also leave it behind. But I couldn't bear to; I am so close to the end.

"Come on," he says, splashing me again. "I left my phone in the room. You should have left the book."

"Last page! *Shhhh*!" I wave him off. He rests his head on the side of the pool and whimpers like a puppy until, a few minutes later, I finally close the book. His red hair is shining in the sun, and he's sprouted a few new freckles on his shoulders during this trip. "You're worse than Vito." I laugh, stepping into the pool. The cool water is refreshing against my hot skin. We left Vito, our beagle, in a kennel near the airport back home; he'd whimpered as the attendant took his leash and dragged him to his home for the weekend, trying to dig in, but hadn't been able to get a grip on the slippery linoleum floor. Betrayed by his paws, he'd gone with the pull on the leash. When the attendant opened the door to the room with the kennels in it, I could hear the deafening racket of dozens of dogs barking at once. Vito looked back with an alarmed look on his face. Hopefully he's made some friends while he's been in the doggie slammer, as Tim calls it. Maybe he'll learn a trade and get a prison tatt.

"*Aaaahhh*, this is nice." I float on my back and feel the warm sun on my face, trying not to think of Vito howling from inside his cage.

I like to call Vito our trial baby, at least until we have a human one. We got Vito from a beagle rescue organization in order to settle my urge to be a mom

Beside the Music

until Tim decides it's the right time.

"So, how did it end?" Tim asks, nodding toward the book I've left on the chaise.

"I kinda feel like the story didn't really end," I say. "Keith doesn't see his wife or his kid, as far as I know. Where is the big Hollywood ending where he gets forgiven and gets his family back?"

"Well, based on what you told me at dinner last night, why would they want to see him? He tore that family apart."

Okay, I know I've been complaining, but dinner last night with Tim really was pretty great. In fact, it was how I'd hoped the whole trip would be: no Aria; no shop. Just the two of us talking about what we had going on. We even got into a debate about whether Keith should have been arrested for driving drunk. I bet it was one of those situations where his manager did some fast talking and got the charges cleared. Maybe the chief of police was a big fan.

We used to have debates like that when we first got together; nothing too competitive, just friendly discussions about particular issues. They were a lot of fun, and I always learned something new. Until last night, we hadn't had one for quite a while, and I'd missed it. At dinner, it was as if we were back in the initial stages of our relationship. We learned a lot about each other from the debates back then. Now that we've been married for a while, I wonder if we can ever learn something new about each other again.

"It was a moment of weakness," I argued at dinner.

"Even in a moment like that, you are still supposed to know right from wrong," Tim shot back. "You don't get behind the wheel with your kid in the car after you've been drinking. And you sure as hell don't take your son's painkillers," he insisted. "Not cool. Plus, if his wife hadn't got rid of him, that boy would have had nothing but trouble, with a drug-addicted dad. I don't blame her for not allowing Keith near her son anymore. I'd probably do the same thing."

"I'm just saying that you haven't walked a mile, you know? He's telling his side of the story..."

"And which side is that? The side where an irresponsible drunk got behind the wheel and nearly killed his family? The side where a drug addict couldn't stand to be the father of a quadriplegic? I feel no sympathy for the guy. It sounds like the whining of a has-been rock star to me. He should have been tossed into jail for driving drunk. He's a selfish prick for having gotten behind the wheel in the first place." He paused to take a sip of his wine. I wish I liked wine; it has this exotic mystique to me, and I'm fascinated about how people describe the different flavors of what are really just crushed grapes. To me, it all tastes the same. Bad.

"And another thing," he said, dabbing a bite-sized chunk of his prime rib in the au jus. "He gets to take off on his yacht while his poor wife is left to care for

13

this kid on her own. Must be nice, not to have to deal with the consequences." Then he popped the steak into his mouth.

Today in the pool, the debate continues. I hold the tiled side and let my legs float out behind me. "Yes," I say, "he made some poor decisions. So many people do. But I think he's trying to make it better. He donates all that money from the book to the Rainbow House. I am sure he's got round-the-clock care and the best of everything for Damien. I think he's looking for a second chance." I pause for a moment to let that sink in before I go further. "Aren't you always saying that everyone deserves a second chance if they are truly sorry for what they did?"

"But how do you know if he's truly sorry?" Tim asks me.

"Because I just finished a three hundred page book where his guilt is spilled on every single page. He gets it. He knows he screwed up."

"I don't know, Bren. Guys like that are too big for their own good."

"But you haven't read the book at all. How can you possibly say that?"

"Obviously, he fast-talked his way out of going to jail for committing a crime. He should have been thrown in jail."

"So, the only way to show that you're sorry is to go to jail? I'll bet that every day Keith regrets getting behind the wheel. That's still kind of like a jail, isn't it? At what point does he finally get forgiven?" I pause to wet my hair. "What about Jimmy?" I ask. "You gave him keys to the shop, even though he's gone to jail for stealing cars. How can you possibly trust him?"

"Jimmy's changed," Tim said. "He's not that punk kid anymore. He wants to move forward, and you think anybody's going to hire him with his record? He's a great mechanic, and he never would have gotten the chance to make a living from it." Jimmy's story is a pretty interesting one. He came out of jail armed with car mechanic skills but couldn't get a job. What shop owner in his right mind would give a car thief a job, right? But Tim recognized Jimmy's talent and hired him. One of Tim's reviews on Yelp actually said that Jimmy is the car whisperer. And it's true. That guy can fix just about anything.

"So, Jimmy wanted to change," I said. "I think Keith does, too. You were quick to give an ex-con a second chance, Tim." One of Tim's most important issues on his campaign is the problem of finding jobs for people who get out of prison. So many ex-convicts go back to committing crimes because they have no other way to survive. Tim wants to set up a formal state-run program to change that.

"You know, you're right, Bren." Tim runs his fingers over the surface of the pool and makes small ripples. "I think that I have a bad attitude about this guy because he's so famous. I hold people like that to a higher standard because I think they should be doing more with the position they have. Sure, he donates the money from the book, but what else has he done lately?"

I would love to know the answer to that question, too. I can't stop thinking about Keith and his image problem. If someone like Tim—who's not a fan—is barely convinced that Keith is really trying to be a good guy after having made some unfortunate choices, then how will the rest of the world ever be convinced? I would love to sit Keith down at my kitchen table and have a long talk about his behavior. Where is his publicist? Why aren't they doing anything to quash the negative stories going around?

"I'm surprised that they just didn't get another bass player and move on," Tim says. He leans his back against the side of the pool and lets his legs float out in front of him. "Sounds to me like he has too much drama."

"But he also writes the lyrics," I remind him. "And these guys are like a family. You don't turn your back on someone when they're having hard times, right?"

"I guess. But there comes a time when you have to break up with a friend when they start dragging you down, you know?"

I don't answer him. At that moment, a couple with a toddler comes into the pool area, distracting me. The mom lays down an enormous tote bag filled with everything the little girl could possibly need. I can just picture Tim doing that. He would have our child's snacks alphabetized in the tote bag. Maybe he'd fashion a belt with holsters that would contain something to eat, something to drink, wet wipes, Purell, toys—nothing frivolous, only educational or nutritious. I smile as I watch the family settle in at the other end of the pool. The toddler stands waist-deep in the kiddie pool and smacks her palms against the surface, beaming into the sun. The dad snaps a picture, and I wonder if it'll get framed and put up in their house. I would totally frame a picture like that.

I'm sure that Tim has caught me staring, so I turn my gaze to him and see that I am right. It comes out before I can even stop it: a longing sigh.

"Bren, come on. We've talked about this."

"I know. But it doesn't change the fact that I'm ready for that." I point to the family. The mom and dad are sitting in the shallow kiddie pool, trying to teach their daughter to put her face in the water and blow bubbles.

Here we are again: the Dunkirk family impasse. Though, lately, with how busy we both have been, who would parent this kid? What I really want is for us to be that family in the kiddie pool. The mom and dad are laughing and splashing with their daughter and working together to teach that little girl how to interact with the world. I want that to be Tim and me, an infallible wall of family. But will it really be like that? I'd wanted just one weekend for the two of us to reconnect, and he couldn't even do that. Maybe he's right: it's not the right time. Tim and I are just not on the same page. Hell, we're not even in the same book right now. Sometimes I look at him when I come home from work and think, *Who the hell is this guy? I don't even know him anymore.*

"Can we please talk about this after the election?" Tim asks. "I just have way too much on my plate right now."

"Why would the election matter? It's not like you're going to have morning sickness while you're campaigning. It's not like you'd have to take maternity leave from the state Senate. Getting pregnant won't really affect you, Tim. Why is it all about what's on *your* plate?"

"You have a lot on your plate, too," he says. "How the hell do you expect to become a vice president in your firm if you're just going to turn around and immediately go out on maternity leave? Vice presidents of PR firms don't leave work right at five to pick up the baby from daycare." He swirls his fingers through the water. "It's one more thing to think about, one more thing to worry about. I've got a lot going on, between the shop and the election. And what about your job? Won't it stress you out, knowing that our kid is in daycare?"

"So, what you're saying is that women who have executive level jobs can't have children? It won't stress me out that the kid is in daycare, Tim. That's just what people do—it's a part of life. When you have a family you find a way to make things work. It looks to me as if you aren't even interested in trying to become a family. You've been on the phone this whole trip, and frankly, I've mostly had to sit around and wait for you to pay attention to me."

"Bren, come on. You know I have a lot going on."

"I do, too, Tim. The difference is, even with as hard as I work at my job, you are still number one on my list. Where am I on yours?"

I see the stricken look on Tim's face; I think I need to stop. This disagreement won't get resolved today. I just hate waiting around for him to make a decision that will affect my life. I feel like he's not hearing me lately, and I hate that, too. I don't want to turn into some nagging wife who has to beg her husband to pay attention to her. We float in silence for a few moments, not knowing how to change the subject. I don't want to change it, because I want his answer to change. He probably won't move on from the conversation because he probably thinks he'll look insensitive. Then there's the awkward pause, while we both silently try to decide when would be an appropriate moment to move on. I decide I can put us out of this misery right now. Radical subject change.

"When we get back," I announce, "I want to see if I can find any underground copies of the album that Hydra tried to write without Keith Kutter." I recall having read that they'd tried to produce something new but then scrapped it because it just wasn't the same without him.

Tim smiles at me, looking relieved but trying not to show it, and pulls me close at the side of the pool. He kisses me deeply, but it still feels like a mercy kiss. "So," he says, "are you now going off on one of your research projects?" He knows me well enough to know that I am heading toward one of my full-blown mini-obsessions. I get that way sometimes: I investigate the hell out of a particular topic until I make myself sick of it. Then he gets to hear about every single piece of new information I uncover along the way. He's usually pretty supportive while

Beside the Music

I bombard him with it all, but I am sure that gets annoying after a while. Still, it's nice to have a new hobby while he's on the campaign trail.

Colors Fade came out a few years ago. What I want to know is what has happened since then. The way it stands right now, Keith isn't in contact with his family, and the world hates him for driving drunk and being rude to his fans. There's got to be more to the story than that. Is he just donating to the Rainbow House because it makes him look good? Or is he actually out there *doing* good? Based on the band's lousy reputation, how can they ever hope to fill an arena again? I doubt I am the only inquiring mind that wants to know, but maybe I can be the one to find a way to change the world's mind about Keith Kutter.

Chapter 4

WHEN WE GET BACK FROM FLORIDA, I start with a Google search—normally I get home from work before Tim, so I have time to research uninterrupted for at least an hour. I find an article about the accident in Australian *People*. There's a picture of the car; it's completely mangled, and the telephone pole he hit is splintered and looks like it'll break in half and fall at any second. The article states that Keith was escorted from the scene by a private security detail. It's interesting that he wasn't arrested on the spot, despite the fact he refused to take a breathalyzer test. The comments at the bottom of the online version of this article are scathing; there's even one that calls him an attempted murderer. I think that goes a little too far. Yes, he did something very careless by getting behind the wheel that night and not letting Tamsen drive. But to call it attempted murder? Talk about a stretch. But these are the comments that the readers notice.

In a later article, I learn that another Australian celebrity who was pulled over for drunk driving is said to have "pulled a Kutter." After the outrage died down, Keith Kutter became a punchline on late-night talk shows. Then I saw Twitter hashtags about non-celebrities pulling a Kutter, and the joke spread like wildfire. It's not funny at all. I am sure it was absolutely humiliating for him to have to confront that noise every time he turned around. The accident occurred years ago, but it still comes up in more recent articles about drunken-driving incidents. I even learned that a chapter of Students Against Drunk Driving in Oregon still uses it as a cautionary tale when reminding students about drunk driving on prom night.

I wonder why his publicist didn't release a statement from Keith to defuse some of the growing indignation. What would I do if I were his publicist? I know from my job that making a comeback from any sort of scandal is very difficult. As a publicist, I've dealt with a few scandals, but nothing as intense as the lynch mob that wants Keith thrown in jail. His publicist must have realized that this was a losing battle and decided to let it blow over instead. That's usually the absolute last resort; I wish I could have been a fly on the wall in the meeting when that decision had been made.

But maybe he could make something positive out of the situation by being a willing cautionary tale. The accident happened; there's nothing he can do about it. Why not own it and be that voice that says, "Drunk driving ruined my life, don't be like me"? Instead, it looks as if he's just waiting for everyone to forget that it happened. Sure, the outrage has died down, but the jokes haven't. I mean, everyone thinks that Mama Cass died from eating a ham sandwich. The joke was that she was overweight, and the sandwich did her in. But it's not really true: it was a heart attack. Sure, people are going to joke about "pulling a Kutter," but I think he should tackle it head on instead of hiding and letting people talk trash about him all over the Internet.

It's probably gotten to the point where Keith is scared to leave his house, not knowing if some crazy person out there intends to do him harm because of his mistake. Most famous people, I think, have that fear in the back of their minds, because they just don't know what will happen to them when they go out. John Lennon didn't know, did he? He'd even signed an autograph for his killer before he was shot. I imagine it's still pretty scary to be in Keith Kutter's shoes. Never mind the fact that his wife hates him, and he'll probably never get to see his son again. I wonder if he still feels like he's wearing a bull's eye on his back. He probably still gets tons of hate mail; that must be horrible.

I stand up from my computer and pop *After* into the CD player. I'll have a chance to listen to it without interruption until Tim gets home. I set my laptop aside and lie on the couch. This was the first album they released after Keith's accident and the band's hiatus. Yet, in reading the liner notes, there doesn't seem to be any reference to the accident. And it looks as if Keith didn't write any songs about it, either. The lyrics in here are no more meaningful than any other pop album. What happened to the depth of the lyrics on the *Friendly Fire* album? That song "Almost" that he wrote for Tamsen was exquisitely raw. What happened to lines like "One look from her and I am stripped bare/tossed in the sea under her stare?" *After* is a huge disappointment. It sounds as if Hydra is trying to be younger than they are, trying to compete with the boy bands. I look up the reviews on Amazon, and sure enough, they average just two stars. Ouch. I can imagine that the supporting tour looked a lot like the movie *This Is Spinal Tap*, where nobody shows up to events or concerts.

So, the world hates Keith Kutter. Creatively, he's in a rut and doesn't know where he fits in the rock-and-roll genre anymore. This is exactly the kind of artist I'd want to take on professionally, to help him repair his reputation. If only I could convince Amanda that there is a viable revenue stream here.

I think I might have to take on a pet project like Keith so that I can build my case. A handwritten note to Keith might be just the thing to cut through the noise.

19

Do people still write fan letters? I need to stroke his ego a bit to get his attention.

I pull out some stationary that Portia had bought for me for Christmas one year. I haven't even opened it yet; I've been saving the thick, creamy paper for a special occasion.

Dear Keith,

I've been a fan of yours since I was a teenager. You were an original voice that stood out from all the others, and you wrote the words that moved me in so many ways. I've just finished reading Colors Fade *on vacation. Yeah, I know, it's not really a beach read, but it still struck a chord with me. You have been through a great deal of heartache, and experiencing it while in the public eye has, I am sure, only made it worse. I know the accident was a few years ago, and I imagine so much has happened to you since then. I hope that you have since found some peace.*

I am writing because I feel like your story is incomplete. As it stands right now, the listening and reading public was left hanging by Colors Fade. *What is happening now? You have silenced your own voice, but we want to know how the accident has changed you. How has it affected your work as a musician and lyricist? Have you made any attempts to reconcile with your wife and son?*

You are a brilliant musician and an excellent writer. Please don't let the accident define you. As a member of your fan base, I care about the music you create, and I care about your story. We are all waiting to see how it ends. Will you please tell us?

Thanks again for all the music. I've recently rediscovered Hydra. I'd forgotten just how amazing you all are. I drove way too fast to your music back then, and now I can't wait to hear what you'll put out next.

Kindest Regards,

Brenda Dunkirk

Chapter 5

IT'S TAX DEADLINE DAY; people are snaking out the post office door. I know I can't stop to think or I'll chicken out, and then the letter will end up under the seat of my car, where things like lost pieces of candy will stick to it. Unfortunately, I can't just put a stamp on this letter, since I have no idea how much postage to Australia even costs. I shuffle ahead with the line, puffing out my cheeks as I glance at my watch. This is taking forever. *Is it worth it?* I look up and see my mother-in-law passing me on her way out. She glances in my direction then quickly looks away. I can tell that she's seen me, but she's trying to make like she didn't. I kind of wish that I could dodge her, as well, but I'd have to leave the line to do that. I've already been here fifteen minutes, so I might as well wait it out.

Portia's dressed in her standard Chanel-suit uniform with her three-strand Mikimoto pearls. I imagine her closet is a tribute to Coco, with miles of Chanel suits in every color, each pressed within an inch of its life. She steps toward me resignedly and looks me up and down with that searing look that says I married well above my station. I've seen that look before; in fact, I receive it every time I see Portia. Portia and I have never really seen eye to eye on anything. She absolutely tortured me while Tim and I were planning our wedding, so much so that I finally convinced Tim to elope to Vegas. It's not like we would have even been able to have our wedding in Rhode Island anyway. We'd had three venues cancel on us; then I found out that Portia was behind those cancellations. Tim didn't believe me until she actually admitted to paying the venues to cancel.

Tim is constantly torn between his mother and me, which I am sure is a major drag for him. Portia has interrupted more intimate moments between Tim and me than I can count. I know she's lonely since Tim's dad died and all, but she's ridiculous. It's almost as if she knows when we're about to have sex, and then she calls. Our disjointed caller ID voice always mispronounces her name, *"Call... from... Por Tee Ya Dunkirk."* And then Tim drops me and runs to answer her call every time. I used to delight in the caller ID robot mispronouncing her name. Now it just pisses me off when I hear it.

"Hi, Brenda!" Portia gushes. "Don't tell me Timothy waited to the last minute to send your taxes in." She glances at the envelope in my hand, trying to see what it is. I step ahead with the line. She follows, her eyes fixed on the letter.

"Nope, he sent ours in January, just as he always does. Our return is safely in our retirement fund." *I really wish I hadn't just told her that. Why do I invite her to discuss our finances?* What I should have said was that we've used our refund to buy a couch, so we wouldn't have to sit on those starchy chaises she bought for Tim after insisting that she decorate the house.

"Good for him," she says, smiling tightly. "You never know where the future will take you." But what she actually meant was, "Your career as a publicist is flaky at best, and Tim should be saving every penny he can for when you leave him and bleed him dry."

"Well, Tim and I are a great team." I smile back at her. But what I wish I could actually say is "I am not a gold digger. I love your son, and I am not ever planning on leaving him." At last, the woman behind the counter calls to me, and I can tell that the man behind me in line is growing impatient. "Oh look, it's my turn. Gotta go! Lovely to see you, Portia." I wave with the tips of my fingers as she makes her way to the exit. *Glad that's over with.* I wish I could just tell that woman what I really think of her. But if I did, it would hurt Tim's feelings. He and his mother are very close; more so since his dad passed away. Either I get in between them and look bad, or I can be her doormat and feel bad. Either way, I can't win.

When I get to the counter, I place the envelope face down on the scale, still not wanting anyone to see who I am writing to. The woman working the counter, obviously exhausted from her long shift, huffs and turns the letter over. She punches the postal code into her computer. I hope she doesn't notice that I am sending a letter to the attention of Mr. Keith Kutter, Hydraphonic Records, Sydney, Australia. Does anyone still know who he is? Back in the '80s and '90s, he'd been on the cover of every magazine. In the mall, you could hear their songs blasting from every single store. But today, I wince, bracing myself for her judgment. Yes, I am conscious of the fact that I am a thirty-five-year-old woman mailing a letter to an '80s rock star.

"Next!" the woman calls out to the next person in line without even giving me a second look.

I press the stamps on the envelope and slide it into the slot. This is by far the dorkiest thing I've done in a while. Sending a letter to Keith Kutter feels like I am just shy of parking myself on his front lawn like some deranged groupie. I will probably never tell another living soul about this act of dorkery I've just committed. Not even on my deathbed. Maybe Keith will see the letter, maybe he won't. Either way, I just needed to reach out to him to let him know that I want to know more. Maybe his family will never forgive him, but to survive

22

professionally, he *has* to get his fans to forgive him. I think he could pull it off if he really tried to show us that he's changed.

When I get back to work, I see that I have a voicemail from Annie Wilkins, an editor at MTV News. Annie and I went to college together, and she's still a very good friend.

"Hey, Bren," she says in her usual cheerful voice. Annie is always so upbeat. I don't know how she does it, or how it's even possible, because she never drinks anything with caffeine. "So, you got any juicy news for me?"

"Let me check," I tell her, pulling up the newsfeed on my phone. Annie can rely on me for a story now and then, which I gladly provide, mostly because talking to her is just plain fun.

"Jamie Fire is doing a benefit in your neck of the woods tonight," Annie says. "Have you heard anything about any of her shenanigans?"

I swipe through the newsfeed, but it's all pretty boring. "No, nothing too interesting yet. It's still just lunchtime, though. She has an entire afternoon to do something stupid."

Jamie Fire is the latest teenage-sensation pop tart. The entire world is on the edge of their seats, waiting for her public deflowering. Until then, she's stringing them along with her virgin/whore drama. As a result, she's selling like crazy, and her impossibly flat midriff is on the cover of every magazine and in every Pepsi ad all over the world.

"So far, she and her entourage have gone shopping," I say, reading from the newsfeed. "I think she's going to Taylor Swift's house on Ocean Drive for brunch tomorrow. Sounds like she's behaving herself." I laugh. We talk for a few minutes about how we need to get together soon, but we can never seem to get our schedules to line up.

After we hang up, it's back to work for me. I have the Smile product launch in July that I need to get to work on. This project could be just the thing to propel me into management. First on the agenda is preparing for a team meeting that I'll be leading this afternoon. Joy left the mockups for the magazine ads on my desk while I was out that still need client approval. Unfortunately, the color and the font are all wrong. And I need to get with Joy to see what kind of progress she's made on the media buys. Joy is our receptionist but wants to move into a new role, so I kind of have to hold her hand while she's learning. I have seventeen new emails in my inbox, all of which came in while I was at lunch. Amanda needs me to send her some sample press releases for the pitch she's preparing for tomorrow, too.

My letter to Keith slips out of my mind just as fast as it slipped into the slot at the post office.

Chapter 6

SMILE AIRLINES HAS KEPT ME so focused that I barely notice it's now the end of June. Before I know it, the hot Rhode Island summer is upon me. I feel like Tim and I have barely seen each other in the last month. I've been working late every night, and he's up to the same old thing, working on his campaign with Aria. Lately, we haven't had dinner together at all, and putting together meals has been a bit of a free-for-all, as neither of us has really bothered to grocery shop. But today I manage to get home at a reasonable hour, and I left a message for Tim on my way home to see if he could, as well. It would be nice to reconnect with him and actually have a conversation.

There's a box in front of the garage when I get home. I don't remember ordering anything, and I don't know if Tim has, either. I am a little disappointed it's not the dog food I ordered online, as even Vito's dinners are going to suffer soon. I park the car outside the garage and take the box with me into the back door.

I peel away the packing tape, and when I pull the lid off the box, I find inside a gorgeous flower arrangement. There are roses, lilies, those lime-green puffy things that I can never remember the name of, and some gladiolas. I have an old glass vase up in one of the cupboards. I take it down and fill it with water then pull the flowers out of the tissue paper. The arrangement is almost too big to fit into the vase, but eventually I get it all in. I press my face into it and inhale deeply; the fragrance instantly revives my mood.

I put the packaging into the recycling bin out the back door, and then carry the flowers upstairs into the bedroom. I am absolutely exhausted from working so much lately, but Tim is clearly making the effort here, and so will I. I light some candles and lower the shades to block out the bright late-afternoon sun. I rifle through my dresser and pull out my special little black lacy number. I cannot even remember the last time I wore it. I spritz it with a bit of perfume so it won't smell musty on me.

It isn't long before I hear Tim come in through the front door. "Hey, I'm

24

home," he calls out. "Honey?"

I hear the door close, and then the sound of his footsteps crossing the hardwood floor to the stairs. I debate whether to stay quiet and let him find me, but then there's the risk that he'll think I went out for a run, and he'll flop down in front of the TV and stop looking. I hear him hang his keys on the hook by the door. Then I hear his footsteps as he walks back to where I'd tossed mine on the kitchen counter; back one more time to hang mine on the hook beside his. I smile, because I know that leaving my keys on the counter drives him crazy. He's stopped hassling me about it, though, ever since I pointed out it was his hang up and not mine.

"I'm up here," I call out.

Moments later, Tim comes into the bedroom, where I am sprawled across our bed in his favorite little black lace number.

"Hey, I could get used to this," he says, smiling as he stops to peel off his greasy work jeans. He looks tired. I know the feeling. Just once, I hope that he'll just fling his clothes aside and dive into bed with me. But no, he turns the pants right side out and removes the change and a folded piece of paper from the pockets which he places into the sterling silver tray—a gift from his mother—on his dresser. Then he pulls off his T-shirt and boxers and drops them with his jeans into the hamper. I know I shouldn't complain about a fastidious husband, but sometimes waiting for him kills the mood a bit. I can tell that he's dying to get a shower before joining me in our bed—he fidgets slightly. But just before I suggest we take it to the shower together, he kisses me hard—although not nearly as hard as he has in the past.

"Wow, look at you," he whispers into my ear. "You are so hot."

Is he just saying that because he thinks he should say that? Is he really not in the mood either? Why does his voice sound as if he's reading from a script?

His hands slide over the lace, but they feel rigid, which suddenly makes me feel tense, too. We used to know how to do this, and, in fact, we were pretty damn good at it. How did we get this far off the path? Sex used to be the main event for us, but now it feels like something we're just crossing off the list because we know that we should be doing it. I just need to concentrate on the mood. *When was the last time we had really hot sex*? If I can remember that, then I can get us fired up again. Was it really so long ago that I don't remember? Come on, something has to stand out. *Think!*

He starts to peel back my negligee, but it feels like he's on auto-pilot, with his hands methodically reaching for all the right places, as if he's just trying to get things over with. Is that why he sent me flowers? Just to phone in a half-assed effort?

I need to calm down. My mind is spiraling toward an unhappy place. I need

25

to focus on Tim right now. *Okay, time to make hot sex happen.* I put my mouth on his and give him one of those powerful tongue-filled kisses that will make him see stars when I am done. I flip us over and straddle him, bracing his arms over his head, then proceed to run my tongue along his ear and down the side of his neck. He frees his hands and pulls the black lace over my head and off my body. Then, just before we're about to really make something happen, he turns his head and glances at my birth control pill pack on top of my night table.

"Whoa, I saw that," I say, pulling myself out of his arms. "Did you seriously just check my pill pack?"

A few months ago, Tim freaked out after I'd forgotten to refill my prescription for birth control pills. He wouldn't even come near me until he was sure that I'd taken them every day for two weeks. I asked him if he thought I'd done it on purpose, and he didn't exactly said no.

I don't even give Tim a chance to answer. "Do you honestly think I'd stop taking them without telling you first? I feel like you think I'm trying to trap you with a baby or something. It's nice to know that you don't trust me."

"Bren, I'm sorry," he says. He sighs and runs his hands through his red hair. "It was just one of those things. I didn't even think about it."

"I know we don't agree on the baby question right now. But I would never in a million years go behind your back and stop taking my pills. It pisses me off that, somewhere deep down, you'd even think that. God, Tim. Is this what we've come to?" I watch the guilty look cross his face. I know he feels bad about all of it. He feels bad about not being ready for a baby, and he feels bad for making me feel this way.

"Honey, I am sorry." He takes me into his arms. "I am sorry I made you feel that way. I didn't mean it."

"What are we doing here, Tim? I thought that, because you sent me flowers, we were going to have a nice night together."

"What flowers?"

"The gigantic display right there. The one you walked right past when you came in here. How could you miss them?" I laugh.

"I would think you would want me to notice you instead of the flowers," he quips. He smiles at me and kisses me on the forehead. "But I didn't send those."

"Really? Then where did they come from?"

"Maybe you have a secret admirer," he says, laughing.

"Seriously, they aren't from you? I thought for sure…" I trail off. *Who would have sent me flowers?*

It's pretty clear that we are not going all the way tonight. We're both off into our own heads again. Normally a scene like this would devolve into me having hurt feelings and him feeling guilty. And then, when I'd try to remedy the situation, the moment would be over for him. Then the night would end in an awkward silence. The next morning would be weird, as we'd fumble around each other at the bathroom sink while getting ready for work, each of us not wanting to accidently bump into each other, being over-polite in the weirdest of ways. Then, an awkward kiss on the cheek before we both got into our cars and left for our respective jobs.

But is this normal? I feel like I don't have anyone to ask. Sex has become such a minefield for us lately. The baby issue is killing me. I don't want to "accidentally" get pregnant. It's a decision that I want the both of us to make together, and I am trying to be supportive. But my patience is wearing thin, and my time is running out. I don't want to be seventy at my kid's high school graduation.

After a few minutes of lying in silence, Tim says, "Okay, the mystery of the flowers then. I know you're dying over there, so let's go." He gets up from the bed, heads to his dresser, and pulls on a clean pair of shorts and a T-shirt. "Was there a box or any wrapping on these?" He's being such a good sport. I am sure I can find some way to repay him later on tonight. I rack my brain for a sexy detective joke; but I got nuthin'.

"Yeah, a box. It's in the recycling bin."

I didn't even think to look at the packaging. I just assumed they were from him. When we're downstairs, he gets the box from the recycling bin, sets it on the counter, and begins pawing through the tissue paper. "I found an envelope," he says, finally.

I pull the card out and read the note silently. I roll my eyes. "Yeah, sure, they're not from you. Listen to this." I read the note with a mocking tone: " '*Dear Brenda, thanks for your letter. It means a great deal to hear from a fan like you. Enjoy the flowers. All my best, Keith Kutter.*'" I raise my eyebrows. "Real cute, Tim." I laugh and toss the note onto the counter.

He picks up the note and reads it himself. "What letter?" he asks.

"Huh?" I pause and feel my mouth hang open. "Holy crap. I never told you about that. I wrote a letter to Keith Kutter after I read his book."

"You mean, like a fan letter? You are such a dork!" he teases. "You wrote a fan letter to a rock star?"

"Yes, I did. But I didn't think he'd actually read it. I just figured it would get caught up by an army of assistants at the record company." I read the note again. It's handwritten—but did he actually write it himself? Surely he has an assistant who handles all his correspondence. Or does he? I stare at the note a few moments longer, dumbstruck that Keith Kutter has even read my letter, never mind that he's sent me flowers. *There is no way this is really happening.*

"There's something written on the back," Tim points out. I turn it over. Sure enough, there's a series of numbers on the back of the card.

"Tim, does this look like an international phone number to you?" I hold out

27

the card to him.

"Either that or a combination to a big safe. Maybe coordinates to the hidden treasure," he replies, laughing. "I say you dial it, and see if it is a phone number." He shrugs and holds out the cordless phone we keep on our kitchen counter. Our kitchen is way bigger than two people would ever need. We have miles of white granite counter top; the only thing Tim wants on the counter is a set of white ceramic canisters which are actually empty. We don't even keep things like flour and sugar in them, like other people would. The cabinets are white, the appliances are white. I am dying to hang up a red curtain over the kitchen window. But no, that's white, too. Tim likes all the white because it always feels clean to him. Honestly, it drives me a bit stir crazy sometimes. "Worst thing that'll happen is that you won't get through, right?"

I stare at the phone for a few seconds. In my work, I've had to call up strangers hundreds of times to ask them to do things for me like offer quotes or run stories. But this time, I have no idea what to say if I do make this call. "Dial it and say what?" I ask him. "What time is it in Australia, anyway? What if it's the middle of the night?" I head to the computer and Google a time zone map. "Look, it says they're sixteen hours ahead in Sydney. It's seven o'clock here now, so…" I count on my fingers. "It's eleven in the morning there now."

"Perfect. So call. Thank him for the flowers. It's only polite, right?"

Tim's right: that *is* a great way to start the conversation. But *then* what do I say? When I call up strangers at work, I always have a plan. This time I don't.

I take the phone from Tim and walk out onto the deck. Tim follows me and sits down in one of the patio chairs. I look out over our back yard and watch a few hummingbirds buzz around the feeders, trying to collect my thoughts. *What the hell am I going to say?* I hold my finger over the keypad; really, it's now or never—just like when I sent the letter to him to begin with. I dial.

"It's ringing!" I squeal. Tim leaps up, runs inside, and grabs the other cordless extension from the living room so he can listen, then comes back out and sits down again.

"Hello?" a woman's voice with an Australian accent answers.

My mouth goes dry. "*Um,* hi?" I squeak, and then clear my throat. "Hi. I'm Brenda Dunkirk."

"Of course, Mrs. Dunkirk," she says. "How are you?"

"Honestly, I'm a bit confused." I laugh.

"I'll just put Keith on and he'll explain everything."

"What? Wait. You mean Keith Kutter?"

"Hold please." The phone clicks, and then music blares into my ear. It's the B-side to "Battleground Zero." I haven't heard this one in ages. I should see if I can find it on iTunes.

"Oh my God," I say to Tim. "She's putting Keith Kutter on."

Tim nods and smiles his encouragement, his red hair glowing in the sun.

Beside the Music

"Hello, Brenda," a male Australian voice purrs in my ear. He definitely has my attention; his voice is deep and velvety. I imagine being able to lounge comfortably inside of it on a rainy afternoon. And that accent is making my heart race. I wish I'd put more thought into this call. I am sitting here with my mouth hanging open. "Brenda? Are you there?"

"Yes, I'm here," I squeak again.

"This is Keith Kutter. I was hoping you'd call."

"*Um*, I'm sorry. I just didn't expect to ever speak to you on the phone. I'm a little flustered." I pause to collect myself. I need to get it together; I must sound like a complete loser.

I grimace at Tim, and he gestures as if to say "Keep it moving."

"Thank you for the flowers," I say. "They're beautiful?" I plant my palm against my forehead and grimace again. Okay, time to take a breath. I lean back on the wicker loveseat, also in white. I feel the wooden slats dig into my back then sit upright again and clear my throat. I can't have a serious conversation with a piece of wood jabbing into me.

"You're very welcome," Keith replies. "Thank you for your letter. It made my day."

"So, *um*, how are you?" I ask, for lack of anything better to say.

Tim chuckles and whispers, "You are so bad at this." I glare at him for a second, and he stops laughing.

"I am well," says Keith. "Listen, Brenda, I sent those flowers to you because I wanted to thank you. Nobody sends letters anymore, and the fact that you took the time to do it means a great deal to me."

"You're, *um*... welcome," I stammer.

"In the last few years we haven't been so great at showing our appreciation for our American fans. You took the time to appreciate me, so now I wanted to take the time to appreciate you. I would like to visit with you in Rhode Island, perhaps take you to dinner?"

"Really?" I need to pay more attention—there's no way he just said that he wants to have dinner with us. "Okay," I say, trying not to sound skeptical. But I am. Surely there is more to it than sending a letter to a has-been rock star and having him fly halfway around the world to take me to dinner. This probably has everything to do with all the shitty things that people are saying about them in social media. Am I expected to talk about what a cool guy Keith is at dinner and get some positive buzz out there? Is this what this feels like to the people I ask to do this sort of thing at work? I don't want to feel like he's trying to use me. What he's doing makes a lot of sense, I get that. This seems like a genuine effort to get the band to go out into the world and make good publicity happen for themselves. I need to get over the awkwardness and decide whether or not I want to be the one to help him generate that buzz. I mean, this is what I do professionally. *I can help, right?*

29

"Are you sure? You sound hesitant. It's just dinner." He laughs. "My assistant, Toni, will call you to coordinate the details.

I clear my throat. *Where the hell did this lump come from?* Why is it that, at work, I speak to strangers all the time, and I can do so competently, but then one rock star invites me to dinner and my mouth is dry? I play it cool. "Sounds good, Keith. Looking forward to it." I look at Tim, and he just shrugs his shoulders.

I click the "end" button and stare at the phone. Then I look up at Tim. I hope that I am not hallucinating this whole thing. Maybe the phone call didn't end with an invite to dinner after all. I replay it in my mind for a minute and then shake my head. "What the hell was that?"

"Sounds like you've just made a date with a rock star," Tim teases.

Chapter 7

A FEW DAYS AFTER my phone conversation with Keith, his assistant Toni calls me to coordinate the details of the upcoming dinner. She must have been his assistant for a long time: she plans every single aspect of his itinerary and doesn't leave anything to chance. But really, am I having dinner with a rock star or embarking on a covert military operation? I am actually surprised she doesn't say things like, "Keith will land at oh-nine-hundred hours." She explains that Keith will fly into Providence on July 9, but that we'll meet at the Stone Yacht Club in Newport on July 10, so he'll have a day to adjust to the time change and rest.

An hour later my phone's email notification dings. She's sent me an itinerary. It tells me what time to get to the yacht club. She's even added Google map directions from my house. Also included on the email is a list of topics that I should not bring up at the dinner. Of course, his son Damien and his ex-wife are at the top of the list. I scroll further through the email and read a list of his allergies. I wonder how many items on the list he's actually allergic to, or whether they're just foods he doesn't like. I don't think I've ever heard of anyone who is allergic to Brussels sprouts—but apparently Keith Kutter is. She has covered every single angle and then some. Though I wonder how many of the items on here are actually for his safety—I am sure that most of them are for his comfort.

Beside the Music

On one occasion at my job, I saw the list of "requirements" that a celebrity demanded while she was participating in a benefit concert in Providence. It included things like "only white flowers, only white furniture, and only white linens" in her dressing room. At the time, I'd felt guilty when I'd had to call the director of facilities at the Providence Performing Arts Center to tell them about the diva's dressing room requirements. The disbelief in his voice when he confirmed with me that yes, he had to move *all* the furniture out of the dressing room and replace it with another set in the required color, horrified me at the time. Now I can look back on it and laugh. I didn't think that stars actually had requirements like that in real life. I had heard rumors about celebrities wanting things like only red Skittles in bowls in their fitting rooms and the like, and each time I'd thought it had to be a joke. It always makes me wonder whose job it is to isolate the red Skittles out of the bag, and how long that must take. As I read Toni's emails, I imagine that Keith's list of demands has grown longer and more obscure as his popularity has risen. It probably makes Toni's job very difficult.

I close the email and call out to Tim, who is hunched over his computer on a Skype meeting with his campaign manager, "Honey? Don't make any plans for the tenth. We're having dinner with Keith Kutter."

"Who?" I hear Aria bellow through Tim's laptop speakers. "Did she just say Keith Kutter? The guy from Hydra? Why didn't you tell me you knew him? Can we get his support?"

Tim rolls his eyes at me. "Never mind" he says to Aria. "Where were we?" Soon enough, they've continued their meeting. I try to occupy myself until their meeting is over, but I'm really just reading the same paragraph over and over in a magazine. My mind keeps wandering to the meeting with Keith. *What will he really be like?* What can I eat that I won't end up getting all over me? What does one wear to dinner at a five-star restaurant with the best rock and roll bassist in the world? (Wow, I could spend days on that question!)

While I'm thinking, I watch Tim conduct his meeting. He's completely focused on the discussion; he doesn't seem at all fazed about the idea of dinner with Keith Kutter. I can't imagine how he can possibly be so calm, knowing that we are going to be meeting a rock-and-roll legend. I've already bitten three fingernails down to nothing without even realizing it.

***

The night of the tenth rolls around before I even know it. And there is nothing in my closet that I even want to wear. There's a pile of discarded clothes draped over the chair and on the bed. I haven't had time to shop because of the launch of Smile

31

Airlines at work. Product launches are what we call a "BFD" at work, meaning it's a "big fucking deal," and I, along with everyone I work with, basically have no life until the work is done.

We've been working until nearly ten each weeknight—as well as every weekend—for the last month, coordinating a press event that took place in the Marriot adjacent to the airport. I am pretty psyched about how the press event turned out. Smile Airlines set up a life-sized model of the cabin of one of their airliners in the parking lot of the hotel. The press could go inside it and see what the cabins actually look like and then report to the public about how spacious and modern they are. We had a video created that played on a loop on the seat-back screens, so the members of the press could sit in the seats, watch the video, and be served a non-alcoholic Smile-tini. Coordinating all of that meant that I had no time or energy to go to Macy's or TJ Maxx to get something new.

Tim walks in, catching me on the verge of tears as I frantically shove my clothes aside, trying to find that one perfect outfit. At least the product launch went well. Very well, actually. Amanda's been dropping hints at promoting me. The client is over the moon with their results—and I'm the one who orchestrated every single part of it. I actually got high-fived all the way from the kitchenette to my cubicle by every single one of my co-workers. Joy, the receptionist, told me not to forget the little people when I get to the top.

Why can't meeting a rock star be that simple?

"Just put something on," Tim urges. "We're going to be late."

"What the hell am I supposed to wear? Why did I agree to this?" I sit on the foot of the bed and let my face fall onto my knees. I am on the edge of hyperventilating, and the room's starting to get spinny. Why didn't I at least set aside a few outfits to pick from? Normally I prepare my outfit for big meetings at work—I iron, I brush away stray pieces of Vito's fur. As a result, I go into the meeting calm and confident. Tonight, I am going to fling entire outfits all over our bedroom and still end up hating what I wear.

"Just wear what you would normally wear to a nice dinner," Tim suggests, rifling through the clothes on my side of the closet and the pile on the chair. "Here." He holds out my vintage turquoise dress with brown flowers on it. "You look hot in this one. Put it on, let's go."

"Shoes." I hold out my hand. He hands me the brown strappy sandals I normally wear with the dress. I slip the dress over my head and let it fall over my hips. I tug at it to settle it around my waist. Tim's right: it is the perfect dress for tonight. It fits me beautifully. I catch him eying me in the mirror. *Good choice, Tim.* I hold the sandal straps in my hand and let the shoes dangle then head to the jewelry box. I paw around for a matching pair and scowl at myself for not being more organized whenever I put my earrings away. My mom used to clip her earrings together after taking them off; another habit I really should adopt.

Beside the Music

"Bren, come on. Just put something on, and let's go." He grabs the white gold hoops he bought for my twenty-fifth birthday from my jewelry box. "Wear these. Come on, we're going to be late."

On the way there, I sit in silence while Tim drives the truck over the Newport Bridge. "You okay?" he asks as he steers us down the off ramp.

"Yeah. Nervous," I sputter.

"You are freaking yourself out," Tim warns. "Just relax and be yourself. Let's just have some fun. He'll probably just talk about himself the whole time, anyway. Let's take it as an opportunity to have a fabulous meal." He takes my hand and spreads it out over his thigh, then methodically rubs the back of it with the heel of his hand. It's amazing how calming this feels. I draw in a deep breath in through my nose and blow it out in a narrow stream from my lips. Then he lightly massages my neck with his right hand while driving with his left. "Come on, Bren. Loosen up."

My mind is a terrifying blank by the time we turn onto Bellevue Avenue, where Newport's legendary mansions line the street. Some of them have been converted into museums, while others are still lived in—like Portia's very large white brick Victorian on the corner of Dartmouth Street. I've always wondered what it must be like to live in those houses day to day. I imagine enormous bedrooms, quadruple the size of the one that Tim and I share—which is still larger than most—and being able to soak in an enormous bathtub all the way up to my chin. But then I figure that the wall-to-wall marble floors must be freezing in the winter. Sure, they have the windows that were part of the original construction; some are now tinted lavender from age. But they're probably drafty as hell when the cold ocean breeze kicks up in the doldrums of February. The people who live in these houses are wealthy enough to have another house somewhere warm where they can stay for the winter. I wish Portia would do that.

As I gaze at the mansions, I am thankful for the house that Tim and I have, where our feet don't freeze in the wintertime—even if Portia did insist on decorating it for us, and I hate what she's done with the place. I mean, does she think we live in Versailles? What is with all the creepy old-guy paintings she's put up? I've moved most of them to areas in the house where we don't spend a lot of time, because I've gotten very sketched out from feeling as if eyes are following me all through the house. I would love for our house not to echo when I get home. It feels lonely with the sterile hardwood floors and dainty antique furniture everywhere. I am so tempted to buy a ratty old La-Z-Boy off of Craigslist and plop it right in between her chaise and divan.

Then my mind drifts to what Keith's house in Sydney must look like, and I wonder if it is at all as extravagant as the ones on Bellevue. I'd be willing to bet it overlooks the ocean somewhere just outside of Sydney. It probably has a wrought iron gate at the front to keep out the creepy stalker fans. Maybe, if this publicity stunt works out, his home will be featured in *MTV Cribs*. *Is that show still on?*

We turn off Bellevue and pull up in front of the Stone Yacht Club. Tim hands the keys to the waiting valet. I compare Tim's dingy pickup truck to the gleaming BMWs and Benzes in the parking lot, and for a moment I wish I'd thought to take my car. But then, I kinda like it when we take Tim's pickup to Newport; it totally rattles his mom's socialite nerves. Surely some of her friends are at the Stone tonight, and they'll report back to Portia about Tim's filthy truck pulling in. Then at least she'll hassle Tim about being unrefined for a change, and not me.

When we get into the restaurant, we play a bit of cloak and dagger. Toni instructed me to ask for Michael Andrews, apparently Keith's code name.

"Mr. Andrews is expecting you," says the hostess. "He's at the bar." She gestures toward the doorway to the right of her podium, and then immediately turns her attention to the old-money couple behind us and smiles broadly. It's a very casual snub, executed perfectly. "Of course, Mr. and Mrs. Van Marten, your usual table is ready. Right this way." She gestures gracefully to the door on the left.

I tug uncomfortably at my dress, fidget with my hair, and wonder if the Mr. Van Marten walking past me is *the* Edward Van Marten, the infamous investment banker accused of running a multi-billion dollar Ponzi scheme with his clients' money. I check out the gigantic diamonds dripping from Mrs. Van Marten's ears and her perfectly matching diamond necklace and bracelet and figure she is probably wearing about fifty carats. The amazing thing is that her carat weight fits right in at the Stone Yacht Club. I wonder what Tim's mom wears when she comes here with the ladies who lunch. I can't help but feel a bit inadequate next to Mrs. Van Marten. *I really need to snap out of this.* I can't go in to meet my lifelong hero feeling this way.

Still, I can't help whispering to Tim, "Do you think that's..." while nodding toward the Van Martens. He nods back and warns me with his eyes to keep my voice down and my mouth closed. I fidget with my dress again.

"My God," he hisses at me, "would you stop with that already?"

I stop fidgeting when we walk through the doorway into the bar. Actually, I freeze when I see him sitting on a stool at the end. He is sipping a Scotch when he looks up at me. I recognize his face from the pictures on my old cassettes, even though now he has a few more deep-set lines around the eyes and mouth. I didn't expect him to look so normal, wearing a jacket with no tie.

"I think that's him," I whisper to Tim. "I never expected him to look so—I don't know—normal?"

"Well, what *did* you expect?" Tim says. "That he'd show up in a bandana and eyeliner, looking like Keith Richards? He probably wants to fit in a bit, don't you think?" Keith Kutter is maybe ten paces away from me. After all those mornings I woke up to his face staring down at me in my childhood bedroom, now I am

Beside the Music

about to shake his hand. He sips at his Scotch at the far end of the bar, looking dignified yet still ruggedly sexy. His naturally wavy hair is pushed back, kind of like he's just been swimming in the ocean and pushed it off his face. I can picture the water streaming down his chest. *Wow, am I seriously standing here imagining Keith Kutter without his shirt on?*

I notice his eyes give me an elevator look, as my girlfriends in college used to say. They trace me up and down and up again. I am glad I wore this dress. Tim's right: I rock this dress. And I think Keith thinks so, too.

"Come on, you look like a dork standing there. Close your mouth." Tim puts his hand at the small of my back and gently guides me through the doorway. I am always amazed at how cool Tim is in situations like these. He kicks into politician mode and is suddenly invincible. I briefly imagine him shaking every hand and kissing every baby within reach while on his way to the bar, saying "Tim Dunkirk, candidate for State Senate" to each person he meets. He strides over to the bar and looks back over his shoulder at me, his eyes saying, "Are you coming?"

The butterflies in my stomach must have snorted meth. I walk behind Tim to the far end of the bar, paying attention to keep my stride casual and fighting the urge to squeal and run up to Keith. Or, even worse, squeal and run out of the restaurant. I clench my fists at my sides until Tim takes my hand and subtly straightens out my fingers. *I need to kick in to publicist mode.*

Normally I can just turn it on and be a competent professional. But right now, I can't find that "on" switch. *Where is my confidence?* Keith Kutter is sitting at the end of the bar, and my mouth has dried out. He looks even better up close. He has a trace of five o'clock shadow on his jaw line, just enough to not look grubby. He still looks like he's a sun-bleached blond, but I wonder if there's some gray mixed in there. It's winter in Australia, but he looks like he's just spent months at the beach. I can see the veins on the back of his hands, pronounced from all the years of plucking strings on his bass. He has a tattoo on his right wrist, some sort of tribal thing maybe. He's wearing what I think is his wedding ring, but it's on his right hand.

Tim is the first to speak, but only because he probably knows I'd say something scintillating like "*Woooowwww*" over and over again. "Hi, I'm Tim Dunkirk." He extends his hand to shake Keith's. "This is my wife Brenda."

"Hello, Brenda." Keith greets my breasts. *Is he seriously checking me out in front of my husband?* His bodyguard clears his throat, and Keith's eyes dart up to meet mine. "Yes, *um*. This is Greg, my bodyguard." He gestures to the wall of muscle with a shaved head standing beside him; Greg nods at me but does not extend his hand to shake mine—a classic tough-guy move.

"It's… *um*… very nice to meet you?" I like to think that what I said came out perfectly coherent, but I doubt it actually did. Tim looks at my mouth with a

35

warning look in his eyes, which I take to mean, "Close your mouth." I clench my teeth together for a few seconds just to get myself to shut up for a moment and collect my thoughts. This is going to be a long night, if I keep fumbling over every single thing I say. *I really have got to get it together.* He's just an ordinary dude, out for a nice dinner. I need to calm down.

Keith sips his Scotch while we wait for my beer and Tim's Gray Goose and grapefruit. I spaced and ordered a beer. *Why? Am I at a frat party?* I search my brain for something to say, something other than, "So, you're a big rock star. What's that like?" Nothing comes to mind.

Tim saves me with his gift for gab. "So, Keith," he says, "I read online that you are a wine collector. Did you know that the Stone Yacht Club was awarded Best Wine List in all of New England for the last five years?"

Tim read up on Keith online? When could he have possibly had time to do *that?* I take his hand and give it a squeeze. I hope he knows that I am grateful to him for doing this with me.

"Actually, that's why I selected it," Keith says, taking another sip of his drink. "I heard a rumor about there being some Henri Jayer in the cellar here. I'd love to get my hands on a bottle of '87 Richeborg."

The hostess, after seating the Van Martens, finds us in the bar and escorts us to a table.

"Would you two like to share the '87 Richeborg with me?" Keith asks, settling into his seat and picking up the wine list.

"Actually, I'm not really into wine," I reply as I skim the menu, "but you guys go ahead. Tim likes it. I'll stick with my beer." I take a sip and smile. *I should finish this,* I'm thinking, *and order a classier drink, like a martini.*

Tim leans over to look at the wine list with Keith. "Doesn't look like it's on the list," he points out.

When the waiter comes back, Keith asks for it anyway.

"That is a reserved bottle, I am afraid," the waiter says, gesturing to the wine list. It's not really a list; it's more a book. "But we have a very wide selection. I can recommend something comparable."

"Who is the bottle reserved for?" Keith asks. But before the waiter can answer, he starts in with, "Do you know who I am?" and raises his voice noticeably higher. I look over my shoulder, afraid that some of the other diners may have heard.

"I am afraid not, sir. Now, please, you may select a wine from our list. Our list is quite large—"

"I am Keith Kutter. Bass player from the band Hydra. I am here to have dinner with my friends. Now, the Richeborg, please."

"I am sorry, sir, I am afraid that's impossible." I can tell that this guy has no idea who Keith is. And that is the precise problem Keith has right now. If we'd had this conversation even ten years ago, I am sure he'd have gotten his wine. Keith's face is turning red. I wonder how many times this scene has played out in the last decade. I don't think Keith even knows that he's not famous anymore. The waiter is young, probably in his twenties, and probably has no idea who Hydra is. And now Keith is looking to cash in on his former glory, but the waiter is out of Keith's league. Keith still thinks that Hydra are rock-and-roll sweethearts. But seriously, now this waiter is going to remember Keith Kutter for his tantrum, not because he'd once been *Guitar Magazine*'s bassist of the year.

I start to feel a bit sad for Keith—until he speaks again. "How can this place possibly claim five stars," Keith fumes, "when their wine list is for shit?"

Greg fidgets with his bread plate; Tim and I exchange an awkward glance. I am bracing myself. *Is Keith going to throw the table on its side and storm out?* I want to slide under the table and hide; the conversation at the other tables has pretty much stopped. It's one glance from Greg that stops Keith in his tracks. I doubt he's ever gotten physical with Keith, but his look says, "Shut the fuck up, or I will shut you up." His glare is laser-focused on Keith until he finally relents.

"Looks like I'll have to settle for…" Keith says, turning the pages on the wine list. I don't know what he's complaining about. There's no way that he can't find something suitable to drink on that list. "I guess we'll have a bottle of Le Pin." Keith thrusts the wine list at the waiter in disgust.

Tim raises his eyebrows at me, which I take to mean that this bottle is impossibly expensive. But Keith's dejected tone when he ordered it suggests it is vinegar.

I open my menu. I've never eaten at the Stone Yacht Club and try not to appear shocked at the prices. Tim used to come here with his parents for special occasions when he was growing up. The menu is mostly written in French, with English descriptions in delicate-looking italics. To me it suggests, "If you're an idiot and can't read French, here's the English version for you uncouth Americans." The menu includes things like *confit de canard*, *escargots de Bourgogne*, and *boeuf en meurette*. I minored in French in college, so I know that these items are duck, snails, and beef. I settle on the *coq au vin*, because that is the cheapest thing on the menu. The practical side of me cannot justify ordering anything else. I wonder what the chef could possibly do to a chicken breast to make it worth ninety dollars.

A few moments later, the waiter returns with the bottle of Le Pin. He shows the label to Keith, who frowns and waves him on. We all watch as the waiter cuts and removes the foil, then deftly extracts the cork with a quiet pop, setting it on the table before Keith. He picks up the cork and makes a big deal of sniffing it before grunting and tossing it back onto the table. The waiter pours a small amount into Keith's wine glass, then waits patiently while Keith swirls the liquid around in the glass and holds it up to the dim restaurant light, inspecting it carefully. Then he brings the glass to his nose and inhales deeply before, finally, emptying the glass into his mouth. He coughs, sniffs, frowns, and sets the empty glass on the table.

"It'll be fine when it's had a chance to sit, for like an hour," he says with disgust. The waiter nods without expression and sets the bottle on the table next to Keith's glass, after which he brings out the wine list and sets it in the middle of the table, presumably in case we want to order something else.

I glance at the list and notice that the Le Pin costs two thousand five hundred dollars. *How in the hell can Keith possibly not enjoy a wine that costs that much?* I watch Tim pour himself a half glass and take a sip then I watch his face for a more realistic reaction. He closes his eyes and holds the wine on his tongue for a moment. I can tell he doesn't want to contradict Keith by outwardly enjoying the wine; but I know he is in fact enjoying it.

The waiter pulls a small leather folder out from behind him and, opening it, announces that he'd be pleased to take our orders, if we are ready.

Tim orders Wagyu short ribs, braised in a burgundy wine—one of the most expensive things on the menu. I raise my eyebrows at him. That's the thing about Tim. He'll take full advantage of a situation like this and order something spectacular, while I'll feel guilty about spending so much money on something as frivolous as a fancy meal. Tim always says that it's not about the actual chicken breast and vegetables; it's the experience of eating it and the preparation of the food that I am paying for.

That's the difference in how Tim and I were raised. As a result of Tim's dad's success, Tim routinely enjoyed the experience of expensive gourmet meals. My parents, who lived comfortably within their means, usually ate dinner out based on the price and not the presentation of the meal. They often shared their entrées to save even more money. I was relieved, when Portia first met my parents, that my mom didn't insisted on bringing a coupon to the restaurant. Dad couldn't stand the coupons; Mom had them all over the house as a constant reminder to save money. After Mom died, he threw them all away.

The other diners are speaking in dignified hushed tones to the point where I don't want to speak up and order my entrée. Instead, I point to it.

"Oh, the *coq au vin*," the waiter says to me, smiling. "A wonderful choice. It is one of Chef Emile's specialties. Madame will love it."

"Thank you, I am looking forward to it." I hand my menu back to him.

I try to relax, but, really, I feel entirely out of my element. I've eaten in fancy restaurants with clients before. But in those sorts of situations, I am there for work, so I pay more attention to remembering the purpose of the meal and staying on top of my game. But tonight, I am seated in one of the most exclusive restaurants in New England with a famous musician and the upper crust of the northeastern United States. I feel like the other diners are staring at me, after Keith's hissy fit over the wine. I take a deep breath and try to enjoy the various aromas of the steaming entrées carried past our table. I smell garlic and lemon. I look around the room and try to take it all in. I haven't been here before, and I'm in awe of the silver vases and white roses on every table. The bread plates are so delicate that I'd swear I could see light through mine if I held it up. I am sure many a dishwasher has been fired over breaking these babies.

After the waiter leaves, the silence at our table is awkward. I don't know what to say to Keith, and apparently he doesn't know what to say to me. I don't want to engage in a discussion about his obvious disappointment in his crazy expensive wine. He glances at Greg, who merely shrugs. I turn my attention to Greg and smile, and I can tell he's bored out of his mind. Tim gives me one of those "What the hell is wrong with these people?" looks. We've already chatted about Keith's flight to Providence and the fact that it is winter in Australia. *What else is left?* I rack my brain and try not to cringe at the lack of conversation.

Finally, it's Keith who speaks up. "You know, I have spent the last thirty years of my life simultaneously avoiding and seeking out my fans. I never imagined I'd randomly sit down to dinner with one."

"Is it everything you thought it would be?" I ask, then laugh and bite into a warm dinner roll.

"Well, really, it's dinner with a stranger," he says. He looks like he's choosing his words. It's one thing to be rude to the waiter; it's another to be rude to the people who are supposed to help you to become famous again.

Mercifully, our entrées arrive; now, at least, we can talk about our food. Out of habit, Tim scrapes his veggies onto my plate and takes any offending onions off of mine. I catch a faraway look in Keith's eyes and wonder if he and Tamsen shared a similar pre-dinner ritual. He's probably remembering something about her right now, but I know I can't ask. Instead, I smile at him and make eye contact for a moment. *Hello, confidence. How nice of you to return.* At that moment, the bubble of uneasiness that has been hanging over our table pops and dissipates. It's like Keith finally remembers the purpose of our dinner tonight—he's here to meet us and get to know his American fans.

Greg hands Keith a set of silverware he has stashed in his messenger bag. *Really? He brings his own silverware?* Does he think he's going to contract some disease or be poisoned by the utensils at an expensive restaurant?

"How long have you two been together?" Keith asks flatly. It's a basic question, but I feel like he's just humoring us. He probably couldn't care less about how long Tim and I have been together. Tonight is all about him. He sips his wine and grimaces. *Come on, dude, get over it and enjoy.* Greg passes Keith a quick admonishing glare. Keith's expression changes; it's as if he's just remembered that he needs to feign interest in us for his great publicity stunt to work. But at least he's trying to break the ice.

"We've been together for twelve years," I say, "but married for seven." I cut into my chicken then bite into it and slowly chew, trying to take Tim's advice and enjoy the experience of the food. He may be on to something: I've never known that chicken could actually melt in my mouth. I can't ever get chicken to come out like this without its turning to mush. And the flavors: it's like an explosion of savory spices, the tang of lemon, and something else a tiny bit sweet that I can't quite place.

"By the time Bren relented and married me, we had a house," Tim says. *A house that your mother insisted on decorating*, I want to add, but then figure it would probably tick Tim off. We've actually had a few conversations about how decorating our home has been worthwhile, something to keep Portia busy and happy, as she has so few hobbies since Tim's dad died. I maintain that, since it's our house and we live in it, it should reflect our taste, and not something she's seen in *Paris Architectural Review*.

"So, how did you two meet?" Keith asks. He'd been busy cracking his lobster; now, I notice that he puts down his utensils so that he can listen to us undistracted.

"When I was in college," I say, "I used to perform at an open mike night in a coffee house in Providence. It was there that I met the guys in Tim's band and became friends with them."

"By the time I joined the band," Tim adds, "Bren was opening for the band at almost every show. I loved her voice. She never bothered to tune her guitar very well, but her singing voice is amazing."

"I had no idea, Brenda!" Keith picks up his fork again. *Wow, this is getting to be a pretty nice conversation.*

Maybe we just got off to a bad start with the wine tantrum. I thought that Tim and I would have to kiss Keith's ass tonight, but now I actually feel like he's interested in what we have to say. I still can't help but wonder if it's a bit of an act, though. And, the way his eyes keep wandering to my breasts, I am starting to wonder if one of them is completely exposed. I can't get a read on him. *Is he some asshole rock star? Or is he a nice guy?* Greg apparently notices Keith ogling me and glares at him again.

"Then we both got dumped at the same time by our respective significant others," I say, "and ended up commiserating together. It's amazing how what you think will just be a summer fling ends up being forever." I smile at Tim and caress the back of his hand.

I once Googled the boyfriend I had before Tim. I managed to find his mug shot. Apparently, he'd tried to rob a liquor store with a baseball bat and been caught trying to run through the snow after breaking his ankle. Bullet dodged. Tim's ex-girlfriend, however, is a model and has posed for the cover of Italian fashion magazines since their breakup. I know this, because Portia keeps copies on her coffee table.

"So you aren't going to tell him the rest?" Tim asks.

"What do you mean?"

40

Beside the Music

"The part where you invited yourself to my parents' cabin in Vermont." He smiles and raises his eyebrows provocatively.

Keith sets down his fork and leans in closer. "I am a sucker for party-crashing stories. I've never been brave enough to do it on my own. Do tell."

"For what it's worth, I was *invited* to Vermont, thank you very much." I stick my tongue out at Tim. "And I still can't believe you guys call that place a cabin. You don't use the word 'wing' when talking about a section of a 'cabin.'" Keith nods in agreement. It's nice to see him on my side—although I'll bet his house in Sydney has wings.

I still remember that weekend when I arrived at the "cabin." Tim's mother had told me that I'd be sleeping in the east wing, while Tim and his parents would sleep in the west one. I should have known then how things would turn out with his mother and me, as the east wing was also where the housekeeper and the chef stayed. It's also important to note that cabins don't have housekeepers and chefs.

"Tim had gone with his parents to Vermont for the summer," I continue, "and I was living and working in Boston. He called me at work on a crappy day. I told him I was stressed out, and he said, 'You should come to Vermont. It's relaxing here.' So I did."

"Okay, so when did you crash the party?" Keith asks.

"Well," Tim interjects, "I didn't say, 'Come to my parents' house in Vermont.' I didn't explicitly invite her to visit me at the cabin. So, she wasn't invited, right? "

"Yeah," I say, "but you said, 'Come to Vermont.' I mean, if you didn't want me to visit you at the cabin, you could have said anything else, like, 'You need a vacation.' You wanted me to go there to visit you, and you know it."

Keith watches us banter back and forth until Tim asks him, "So, member of the jury, what do you think?"

"*Hmmm…* interesting." Keith strokes his chin in mock deliberation. "The evidence on both sides is compelling. But Brenda, I just have to ask, what did you say to Tim's parents after you turned up uninvited?"

"*Uninvited?* Come on! Work with me, would ya?" I ask with feigned irritation.

"*Yes!*" Tim exclaims. They high-five, and I bite into another piece of chicken, pretending to be annoyed. But I can't stay annoyed for too long: *this chicken is ridiculously good.* Keith has apparently relented and drunk half the bottle of wine, and I think he's mellowing out. After we've told Keith the story about my visit to the cabin, it's as if we're having dinner with an old friend. He makes me feel as if we actually *could* be friends after tonight. He tells us a few funny stories about being on tour with the band—run-ins with small-town sheriffs and the like. But he lets us tell him funny stories, too. The evening *isn't* all about him, apparently,

41

and that's very cool of him.

"Okay, here's one for you," Tim says, sipping his wine.

"Not the stinky car, Tim," I say and laugh. It's gross, but it's actually a really funny story.

"Yes, the stinky car," he says, laughing. He has a gleam in his eye I haven't seen in a while. "So, a guy brings his car into the shop. I get in behind the wheel to move it into the bay so we can get it up on the lift. And man, I've never smelled anything this bad. I just know something's died in that car."

"*No!*" Keith says, hooting with laughter. "How did he drive around like that?"

"That's what I wanted to know. So I call the guy up and ask him about it."

"What on earth did he say?" Keith is snickering now.

"The dude says, 'I had a head injury, and I lost my sense of smell. You mean to tell me my car stinks?'" Tim pauses so Keith can laugh. "Then he says, 'Well, shit, that probably explains why I haven't been on a second date in months.'" At this point it looks like Keith is going to fall out of his chair from laughing so hard.

"So, did you find out what made it smell so bad?"

"Yeah, a squirrel had died under the front seat."

"*Gah!* That's terrible!" Keith is wiping the tears from his eyes.

We're talking and laughing so boisterously that the other diners glare at us occasionally, but I don't care. I wish I could just say to them, "It's a restaurant, not a library. Lighten up. This is Keith Fucking Kutter." By the time we order dessert, my abs are aching from laughing so much.

This is what I wish the world could see right now. Keith is so relatable and so much fun. I am sure that tomorrow I'll get instructions from Toni about how I should talk about tonight on social media, and I am glad to do it. He really is a cool guy, once you get past the bullshit famous-rock-star exterior. I am so glad I got the chance to meet him tonight. *Would it be weird if I offered him some coaching for his next fan encounter?* He needs to know *not* to throw a tantrum over the wine list next time, and then he'll be perfect.

"I didn't quite know what to expect, coming here tonight," Keith says. "I've had such a nice time. Thank you for coming to meet me. I was so afraid that we'd end up talking about me the whole night. It's been great to have a normal night with normal people." He leans back in his chair and sighs. *Normal? Does that mean we're boring? Gosh, I hope not.* "And the meal was great. Tim, what did you think of that wine? How was it with your short ribs?"

Tim doesn't get the chance to answer, everything next happens so fast. I detect a quick movement out of the corner of my eye. I turn to look: a man wearing ratty jeans and a baseball cap is weaving between the tables, rapidly approaching ours. He pulls something from behind his back. I am frozen. *Is this what it's like when rock stars leave the house?* Does Keith constantly look around and wonder what people have in their pockets? Is every lump in a jacket a gun? My heart starts to race until I see that it's a camera and not a gun.

I turn back just in time to see Greg react; it's pure instinct in motion, and he doesn't take any chances. With one swift movement, he shoves Keith under the table. My mouth is now back to hanging open, I am so confused. A bright flash of light blinds me for a moment. Then another blinks rapidly, making me flinch every time. The flashes keep coming; I hold up my hand to shield my eyes and try to see through the glare. A crowd of photographers has materialized seemingly out of nowhere and is surrounding our table.

Between flashes, I see Keith stand and Greg take his arm. Keith tosses a wad of money on the table and hisses at me, "How could you?"

"But I didn't do anything," I say. I don't think he cares to argue the point right now, however. I don't think he even hears me. Greg holds onto Keith with his left hand; with his right, he's shoving the paparazzi out of his way and doesn't look like he even cares if he knocks anyone over. He forces himself between Keith and the crowd, and I lose sight of them just after they plow their way into the kitchen. The photographers then swarm around me and Tim and block my view. The reporters bark out questions at us in rapid fire. I can't tell who is asking what, and they come out so jumbled, I can't make sense of anything at all.

"Brenda, what did Keith...?"

"...Did he......?"

"...sober?"

I can feel my heart rate rising; this is stressful. The camera flashes are still going off all around me, and I am so disoriented, I am seeing spots. I feel as if the reporters are closing in on me and pretty soon are going to trample me with their zoom lenses. *I have to get out of here.*

I stand up from the table and straighten my back in an effort to get the crowd to fall back. It's not working, so I take a lesson from Greg and bulldoze my way through, aiming for the kitchen. I stumble and almost fall into Edward Van Marten's lap; I fumble with my apology and continue pushing my way through the wall of paparazzi. They are packed so tightly that I actually become frightened. I can hear the other diners gasping in disgust as I push my way through.

Finally, I start throwing elbows, figuring the photographers will certainly want to protect their cameras and their faces. I don't even look back to see if Tim's behind me, although I hope he's making his way out, too. I figure that, if we get separated in the confusion, we'll meet back at the truck once everything calms down.

After I've made it through the crowd, through the kitchen, and out the back door, I see Keith and Greg take off on a pair of motorcycles. I look back and see Tim still trying to push his way through the photographers who are clamoring to get my attention. The restaurant manager yells at them to get out of his kitchen. The kitchen door swings shut on Tim and the crowd, and I half-wonder if Tim will survive among the piranhas. Then the door swings open again just long enough for Tim to call out, "Bren! Wait there for me!"

It only takes a few minutes more for Tim to get around to the back of the restaurant. When finds me, I'm sitting on the back steps, looking out over the harbor. For a moment it is peaceful, until the photographers following Tim begin to spill around us again. They call my name and shout out more questions.

"Brenda, where are they staying?"

"Do you know where they went?"

How do they even know my name?

"Let's get out of here," Tim says, taking my arm. "Back off!" he barks at the paparazzi. I gaze at my husband for a moment, impressed by the way he is taking control and getting us out of here. It's actually kind of sexy.

By the time we get around to the front, we find that the valet has pulled our truck to the front door and is waiting impatiently for us to get in. The restaurant manager is standing at the front door with his arms crossed, a very pissed-off look on his face. I can't say I blame him for wanting us out as quickly as possible. The photographers have either lost interest or got their shot; they jump into their cars and speed away.

I get into the truck and watch their receding taillights from the passenger seat. I am sure a few must have followed Greg and Keith on their bikes. *Are they safe?* I imagine that riding on motorcycles away from a crowd of hungry photographers is pretty dangerous.

Just as I am about to climb into the passenger seat, I hear her shrill nasal voice: *Portia.* She has that wealthy woman's way of speaking, where she doesn't move her bottom jaw.

"Timothy. Why didn't you tell me you were dining at the club tonight? Isn't this a bit far from your neighborhood?" Portia doesn't care about geography; "neighborhood" equals "above your station," and that question was just for me. I turn around to find her striding toward us. She manages to execute the walk on the uneven cobblestone driveway perfectly in high heels. Just one more way I can tell that she's not really human: nobody can do that. "Why do you insist on driving this heap around?" She gestures to Tim's truck. I smirk a bit. "Let me call Richard on Monday, and he'll find you something more suitable." Of course, she is on a first-name basis with a luxury-car importer. She looks me up and down, and I can't help but think she's going through her mental contact list to see who can help her find a more suitable wife for Tim.

"Not necessary, mother," Tim says, air-kissing her cheek.

"Hello, Portia." I plaster a fake smile on my face and extend my hand to her. She doesn't take it.

"Well, I'd better be getting in," Portia says. She straightens the collar on Tim's shirt and artfully ignores me. "Stella and Edward are in from New York and have invited me for a digestif." Of course, she is also on a first-name basis with the Van Martens. She looks me up and down, and I can tell she disapproves of my dress—the one dress I wear when I want to feel hot and confident. Now I need to find another dress; she's ruined this one for me. I try the same up-and-down look on her probably ridiculously-expensive designer dress, but I really cannot pull off the disdain as well as she can. She's been doing it to me since Tim popped the question.

The time Tim brought me home to meet Portia was an absolute disaster. I'd Googled her and knew that, in her prime, Portia had been the "it" girl of Newport society. I learned that her debutante ball had been expected to be so well attended that she'd had hers on her own, rather than with a group of girls, the way it's normally done. Her marriage to Tim's dad was mentioned in *Time* magazine, as well, where they'd been described as the "tastemakers of Newport society."

On the night Tim drove me to his family's mansion, I brought Portia a spray of yellow roses, because Tim had told me they were her favorite. She politely thanked me and promptly handed them to the housekeeper to have them put into a vase. Then she set them on the same table where an embarrassingly large arrangement of the same flower had already been placed. Mine, a full dozen, looked pathetic next to the tower of yellow roses she already had. And she'd set mine next to hers on purpose, I just knew it.

Portia's subtlety in her efforts to make me feel inferior became more aggressive after Tim proposed. She took me to dinner soon after and handed me an envelope containing thirty thousand dollars in cash. I knew what she was doing, but I started out playing dumb.

"Oh, is this for the wedding? How generous of you." She raised her eyebrow; I'd wanted her to come right out and say that she expected me to take the money and leave Tim. I excused myself and left the cash on my bread plate. I didn't tell Tim about it, at first. It was just too bizarre. There's no way he would have believed me; I didn't quite believe it myself. Then, when she realized paying me off wouldn't work, she got a bit more creative.

A short time later, Tim and I attended a fundraiser at her mansion. We didn't know that she'd also invited a few of Tim's "more suitable" ex-girlfriends. Portia's house is an old school mansion with a ballroom on the bottom floor, where she hosts incredibly ostentatious parties that are very well attended. I learned very quickly that Portia is still very much the "it" girl of Newport high society. Get an invitation to one of Portia's parties, and you are in an exclusive club comprised of the wealthiest families in Newport. When we walked in to the party, the caterers, wearing white dinner jackets, were all bustling about with hors d'oeuvres on sterling trays. I think Portia had strategically placed young, flawless-skinned blondes all over the room, just waiting for Tim to take his pick of them. And, of course, she'd told these women that Tim was available. As a result, Tim was surrounded by impeccably dressed, ice-princess-blonde socialites, all fawning over him.

"Brenda, darling," Portia called out to me. "I need your help. I want to cut some more lemons for the bar." It didn't occur to me at the time to wonder why she would be cutting the lemons. I was more excited that she had called me "darling." So I followed her into the kitchen. She nodded at the cook and left me in there with the caterers. I'd been trying to make an impression, but before I knew it, I was chopping fruits and vegetables in Portia's steamy expanse of a kitchen while she was busy steering other women toward Tim.

Thankfully, he caught on and rescued me. For the rest of the night, Tim spun me around the highly-polished parquet wood floor; we danced underneath garlands of Portia's favorite yellow roses that were strung crisscross on the ceiling, while the socialites cooled their very high and very expensive heels on the sidelines. Portia glared at us from the head table.

I know I should stand up a bit taller; instead, I lean on the side of the truck. I need to stop letting her treat me this way. At first, Tim told me I was imagining it and asked me to just be nice. Her aversion to me is completely obvious; *why doesn't he see it?* There's no way he could have missed the way her lip curled up when she looked at me, as if I were repulsive. I know he just wants to keep the peace between me and Portia, but honestly, it's becoming increasingly difficult not to just say to her, "It's not my fault that Tim wants to perform surgery on cars and not on eyes. Get over it already." It's on the tip of my tongue, as it usually is whenever we see her. But if I say it now, after she hasn't even acknowledged me, then I know I will just look crazy.

I glance at Tim, but he's looking around, watching the photographers disperse. Portia sees him looking at them, too. "Was there some sort of excitement here tonight? Why are there so many photographers?"

Tim begins to speak, but I interrupt him. There is no way I want her to know that they were here because I'd wanted to meet Keith. "*Um,* I don't know. When we got out they were all out here." I can see the relief on Tim's face; I am glad he's on board with my lying to his mother. I feel as if he's just put a toe across the line onto my side of the fight; I'll take the small victories where I can get them. The Van Martens don't know us, so there's no way she'll be shamed by me tonight in front of her fancy friends. I think I read somewhere that Portia was roommates with Mrs. Van Marten at Radcliffe. "Honey, shall we?" I ask Tim. "We don't want your mother to keep her friends waiting." I gesture toward our truck, putting an even wider, faker smile on my face.

Tim takes Portia's hands and air kisses her one more time. "Have a lovely evening, mother," he says.

She turns her back on me and accepts the arm of the valet, who walks her to the door of the restaurant.

I am relieved as we pull out of the Stone Yacht Club driveway and back onto Bellevue Avenue. I look back to make sure we're not being followed—by Portia *or* by the photographers. *Why does she seem to show up at the most inopportune times?* Thank God she hadn't just five minutes earlier, though: she would have seen us right at the center of the crowd. And then there'd be no way that I'd ever get into her good graces.

As we ride over the Newport Bridge, I look down at a cargo ship anchored in Narragansett Bay. I can see a man walking on the deck. He looks tiny beside the ship's looming tower. I always wonder where these ships come from. This time, I wonder how long that man on deck has been away from his family. It's nice to think about something else for a moment, because I am completely freaked out about how our dinner with Keith ended. That look of complete disgust on his face keeps appearing over and over in my mind. *What must he think of me right now?*

Tim breaks the silence. "How are you?"

I groan. "I'm confused. What the hell was that? He looked really mad."

"He'll get over it. I am sure this sort of thing happens to him all the time."

"Well, it doesn't happen to *us*. We were having a nice time. He probably thinks I sold him out." I slouch down in the passenger seat, kick off my shoes, and prop my bare feet on the dashboard. "I'll probably never get the chance to tell him I didn't do it" I sigh.

"Bren, it's okay. It's not like he was going to be our friend."

"I know. But I still feel bad. Did you see the look on his face?"

"I couldn't see much with all those cameras going off."

"I know, right? That was insane." Then I laugh a little. "I'll bet the Van Martens are happy that the paparazzi weren't there for *them*."

"It probably gets pretty tiring, dealing with that bullshit all the time."

"But now he must think that I set that up. It bugs me that I'll probably never get to tell him that we had nothing to do with it. Do you think I should call Toni and explain?"

"No. I know that this will probably make you nuts for a little while. You just have to leave it alone."

"What do you mean, it'll 'make me nuts'?" I ask.

"Come on, Bren. You know how you can get sometimes—"

"No, Tim," I interrupt. "How *do* I get sometimes?" My throat is tightening, the way it usually does when we're about to get into a fight. I can taste that weird sour flavor in the back of my mouth that makes my stomach churn. I clench my fists and swallow hard, trying to get it off my tongue.

"You just get a little obsessed with dumb shit."

"Gee, it's nice to know that you find my interests dumb. Sorry I can't do something more worthwhile, like run for office." The sour taste goes away; now I am just getting mad.

"*Ugh.* That's not what I meant. Would you stop? Forget I said anything, okay?"

For the rest of the ride, we don't talk. He pulls the truck into the garage while I am still trying to calm down, but I can't. I am amped up from dealing with the paparazzi, and I am pissed off at Tim. A bad combination. We sit in the car in

47

silence, and I wonder if he can hear my teeth grinding.

Instead, we hear the telltale thud of our beagle, Vito, jumping off the forbidden couch. Tim smiles a bit and shakes his head at the sound. Even when he's not in the room, Vito can still cut the tension between us. He's interrupted more arguments than I can even count.

"Bren, if we didn't set up the photographers, then who did? And how did they know our names?"

"I don't know." Then, after a pause, I add, "But I just don't feel right with him thinking that we set that up. I don't want our meeting him to end that way."

"I know, Bren. I'm sorry about what I said earlier." We get out of the truck and walk to the inside garage door that leads into the house. But before we go inside, Tim stops and throws his arms around me. "I shouldn't have said that," he whispers into my hair. I try to tell him it's okay, but he pulls back, and I can see the thought process working its way across his face. "Keith came to meet us because the band is trying to make a bigger impression with their American fans, right? This whole thing was a publicity stunt, Bren. What the heck else do you think this was about? Keith Kutter probably doesn't want to be friends with you. He's trying to get back into the spotlight. It's even possible his manager set it up without telling him. Keith will get over it quicker when he sees that he'll profit from it. He's a businessman, after all, and he has to sell his product to survive."

"You're right," I say. "I'd just hoped it was something more than that. We started to have fun, you know?" Dejected, I walk into the house. Vito innocently wags his tail from his dog bed, trying to tell us that he's been lying there all along. I nod toward Vito. "Just wait until he figures out how to clean his fur off the couch. Then he'll be unstoppable." I bend down and absently scratch his ears as he licks my hand.

"Come on, let's go to bed." Tim hugs me, and I sigh into his chest.

I know that he's right, and I should just let it go. This was a one-time thing, and I am deluding myself if I think that I am going to be friends with Keith. Though it was kind of fun to think of hanging out with him after tonight.

Tim lets go and calls to Vito, "Let's go, buddy. *Out!*" He opens the door and lets Vito out to pee. He stands at the door and waits for him, but he's also watching me mope through the kitchen to get a glass of water. "It's going to be okay," he says, wrapping his arms around me. "I promise that the next time we meet a rock star, it'll be different."

Chapter 8

THE MORNING AFTER MEETING KEITH, I decide I need a project to distract me. I'm in the garage refinishing the coffee table and making a hell of a mess with the sander. My clothes, my safety goggles, and my mask are all covered in sawdust; the bandana I've tied around my head does little to keep my hair clean. I don't really care too much, though. I am sure I look like hell: I barely slept last night and have bags under my eyes. I kept dreaming about the photographers; Keith's voice—echoing in my head, asking me, "How could you?" over and over again—kept waking me up. I focus my attention on sanding the legs of the table and try to get my mind to go blank with the loud buzz of the sander vibrating in my hands.

Tim went into the shop to get some paperwork done, which is fine with me. I want to be alone and let the tension from last night work its way out of me. He'll come back in the afternoon, and then we'll spend the rest of the day together. Maybe we'll ride our bikes down to the town beach and go for a swim. There's a new ice cream stand that opened near there, and I'm craving a waffle cone.

When I stop to put a new piece of sandpaper on the sander, I see Tim pulling down the driveway, and he's not alone: there are two other people with him in the truck. I take off my safety glasses and rub my eyes a bit. It's not until he pulls up to the garage that I see who his passengers are: *Keith Kutter and Greg!* Tim has that "I am annoyed but trying to be polite" look on his face.

"What's going on?" I ask when they get out of the truck. Suddenly, I am embarrassed by my appearance and try to brush myself off. The cloud of dust makes Greg sneeze.

"We rented some motorcycles so we could explore today," he explains, "but mine was starting to misfire. The rental place isn't picking up, so we called Tim's shop."

"I thought they'd be more comfortable waiting here while Jimmy and I fix them up," Tim says. I take that to really mean, "These guys are driving me crazy. They belong to you, so will you please entertain them?" But it's the look on Tim's

49

face that says it all. He doesn't really like it when people stand over his shoulder and ask him all kinds of questions while he's working. I can't say I blame him.

"Keith, listen, about last night..." I begin.

"You wanted to get some notoriety out of having dinner with me," he says. "I understand." He takes off his leather jacket and flings it onto the half-sanded coffee table. Tim cringes as the jacket lands in a cloud of dust.

"No, I didn't," I shoot back. "We had nothing to do with that."

"When you live a life like I have, you become suspicious of everyone," he says, dismissing my attempt at an explanation. *Where is the Keith who laughed with us last night?* He's completely shut down.

"Well, I don't live a life like yours. I don't go around setting up paparazzi, Keith. Do you seriously think I had anything to do with that?"

"I wouldn't know what you go around doing, Brenda," he says. *Great,* I think. *So, this ass-clown is going to come into my home and insult me now? How rude.*

"Bren, did you eat lunch yet?" Tim asks, trying to change the subject. "What do you say we go inside and get some sandwiches?" I glare at Tim. I get it. He wants me to entertain Greg and Keith while he slips out the back and goes back to the shop.

I am pissed, but I figure I can at least get them inside and explain. "Come on in," I say. "Would you like a sandwich? Or are you suspicious of the cold cuts in my fridge, too?"

Greg shrugs his shoulders at Keith. He doesn't say much; he and Keith seem to have a lot of nonverbal cues. They follow me in from the garage and into the kitchen, where I fill a few glasses of ice and water. Greg gulps down half of his while Keith asks where he might wash up, and I point him in the direction of the half-bath off the kitchen.

I lay out slices of bread on the cutting board while Greg watches me from the end of the counter. He fidgets in the silence; I can tell he wants to say something to me but feels awkward.

"Here," he says, taking the bread from me. "Let me make Keith's." I shrug. "Keith insists that I prepare his food in situations like this. You never know." *Glad to see he's gotten over feeling awkward.* But I am still pretty offended. *Who the hell do these people think I am? Some media whore/assassin?*

I stand with my fists propped on my hips and my eyebrows raised. "Are you kidding me? Do you think I have a bottle of poison in the fridge, just in case the illustrious Keith Kutter stops by?"

"It's nothing personal, Brenda." *Um, yes it is.*

"Whatever," I mumble, sighing. Obviously he and Keith have a system. *Who am I to mess with it?*

"Do you have any peanut butter and jam?" he asks.

"Really? I have better things to eat here, like turkey and roast beef, tuna," I rattle off.

"I make Keith a PB&J when he's in a foul mood. It comforts him." I pull the jar of Skippy from the cupboard and hand it to Greg, along with the blueberry jam from the refrigerator. "Blueberry? That's his favorite."

"Yeah, I think I read that in the fan club newsletter," I drawl sarcastically. "I guess I figured a PB&J would be too American for Keith." *Not very gourmet.* I don't have any Chateau What-the-Fuck to pair with it.

"He fell in love with an American exchange student when he was at Uni. He got the taste for them from her." Greg puts his hand on a drawer and cocks his head as if to say, "Is your silverware in here?" I nod. He takes a knife and spreads the peanut butter onto both slices. I am surprised he's not using Keith's reserve set; maybe it's still dirty from last night.

"How long have you worked for Keith?"

"Since July of '87," he replies, spreading the jam over the peanut butter. He licks his finger and smiles. "*Mmmm...*" He glances at the label on the jar. "I'll have to pick up a few jars of this before we go back. He'll love this."

So, he knows what kind of peanut butter Keith would like. It must be a strange job, having all your waking hours consumed by the likes and dislikes of another person, entirely devoted to keeping him safe. I'll bet Keith has no idea what foods Greg prefers. "It must be an interesting job," I say to him. "How does one become a bodyguard for a rock star?"

Greg's a tall wall of muscle, the kind of guy whose arms are so muscular, he can't seem to put them down all the way. His shaved head catches the light from the window, and I can see a flame tattoo peeking above his shirt collar on the right side of his neck. I wonder if his whole body is engulfed in the flame. "Are you looking for a career change?" He laughs. "I moved to America when I was a child. My dad is Australian and my mom is American. They divorced when I was young, and I came to the States to live with her. I served in the Marines after high school and then went back to Sydney after my discharge. I lacked any other skills, so I signed on with a bodyguard-for-hire agency. I couldn't get an assignment immediately, so I took a job as a roadie at first. It was a cool way to get to see the world, when I wasn't carrying gear around. Then I got assigned onto a detail guarding Keith."

"So, you must have gotten to know him pretty well, then?"

"When you're with a man constantly, you do get to know him a bit." He laughs.

"Listen, Greg, about last night...," I begin.

"Forget it, Brenda. What's done is done."

"Yeah, it is done. But I didn't set that up."

Without responding, Greg takes the plates from the cabinet. I wonder how many times he's had to fend off rabid fans. *Does he think I am one?* Surely he

51

must know that I am pretty normal. "Do you mind?" he asks, gesturing to a bowl of apples on the counter, without even acknowledging what I've said. I see he's avoiding the subject. I nod. Greg peels an apple. "Brenda, you and Tim seem like very nice people. My job is to protect Keith. It's my responsibility to assess the situation and determine where the threats are. Last night, his safety was threatened, and it's my job to keep him safe."

Greg isn't hearing me, and I don't think I can get him to listen, but I have to try. "I get that. But I didn't set up those photographers. I am certainly not a threat to his safety. You're in my house right now, so you obviously know that I am no threat here."

Before he can respond, Tim comes in the back door, and Keith walks in from the bathroom. Greg and I set the plates on the kitchen table. While Tim scrubs his hands in the kitchen sink, Vito bounds over to Keith's feet and proceeds to sniff his boots.

"I'm allergic to dogs," Keith says, stepping back in alarm. Vito stands on his hind legs and places his front paws on Keith's thighs so he can get a better look at him. He sniffs Keith's legs.

"Vito! *Down!*" I command. "How can you be allergic to dogs? Didn't I read in *Colors Fade* that you had one?"

"Keith's allergic to dogs that aren't his," Greg jokes. Keith glares at Greg for a moment. "Am I lying?" he asks with a smile. Vito sniffs at Keith's shins, and Keith gingerly steps around him.

"Oh, please. Vito's harmless," I say, deadpan. "When's the last time you heard of a beagle mauling someone?" On cue, Vito rolls on to his back and requests a belly rub. Keith seems to warm to the idea of Vito, grins, then obediently bends down and rubs.

"Another falls victim to the beagle belly," Tim says, laughing. Keith scratches Vito's stomach and ears and chatters to him. *Did he just use the phrase "sexy beast"?* Vito has a very keen sense about people and knows precisely how to defuse an awkward situation. Keith's mood is noticeably lighter after playing with Vito.

"So, how are the bikes coming along?" I ask.

"Well, I need to go back," Tim replies. "Jimmy's gonna come pick me up in a few minutes, and we have to go down to the distributor to get some parts."

We sit at the table and start in on our sandwiches. I watch Keith's face as he takes his first bite of his peanut butter and jelly. The expression on his face softens, and his shoulders relax. Greg catches me watching and raises his eyebrows as if to say, "See? I told you." I smile and then bite into my turkey.

Now that Keith is relaxed, I can take advantage of the moment and explain that we had nothing to do with what happened last night. I want to get back to the fun Keith Kutter, not the suspicious one. But just as I open my mouth to say something, Jimmy's truck rolls down the driveway. We watch him through the window as he gets out and walks toward the door.

Keith stands and swipes his mouth with his napkin. "If you don't mind," he says, heading for the stairs, "I am going to make myself scarce while Jimmy is here."

"Keith! *Wait!*" I leap in front of him at the base of the stairs. Tim and Greg look at each other, puzzled. I can't remember if we made the bed this morning, and I frantically scramble up the stairs, practically shoving him aside. He walks into the bedroom just as I am straightening up. I grab my bra off the floor and hide it behind my back. I sidestep to the hamper and toss it in. Keith smirks at me and then assesses our bedroom. I want to ask him what his in Sydney is like. *Would that be weird?*

"Brenda, I wouldn't have cared," he says with a laugh.

"But I do. It's not every day that I have a famous person in my bedroom."

"What a shame," he says, laughing again. "I have one in mine all the time."

"Really?"

"Yeah, Angelina Jolie is a regular in my boudoir," he says, still laughing. Then he crosses the room to examine the pile of books on my bedside table. I am glad I have important-looking books there, and not some trashy novel. "What do we have here? Brenda! I am shocked. You got my book from the library? You couldn't even be bothered to buy it?" I checked it out again so that I could re-read it before the dinner.

"What can I say? I'm frugal," I say with a shrug. "Make yourself at home." I pat the corner of the bed. As I walk out of the room, Keith picks up another book off the pile and sits on my side of the bed. Inside, I squeal a little: *Keith Kutter is sitting on my bed! Reading my library books!* Yeah, I am so not returning that one.

I walk downstairs so I can say hi to Jimmy. I hope Tim offered him lunch.

When I walk in, Tim and Jimmy are deep in discussion over Keith's bike. I know nothing about inlet valves or whatever the hell else they are talking about. Jimmy's nice enough to pause and explain things to me. But it's okay: I don't really need to know. Jimmy has such an intuitive sense about engines. I watch as they continue their discussion, knowing that Jimmy will probably figure out the problem faster than Tim.

The talk about German engines versus American ones gets boring, however. Greg isn't interested, either. Tim apparently senses this and takes it as his cue to leave. He walks out the back door with Jimmy and smiles at me as he closes the door. I can tell he'll be relieved to work on the bikes uninterrupted. I feel a bit bad, though, knowing his Sunday afternoon has been derailed by work.

Greg stands and calls from the base of the stairs, "The coast is clear, princess!" I hear Keith laugh from the bedroom. A moment later, he bounds down the stairs and sits at the table.

We all sit down to lunch again, not talking at first. Then Keith looks out the window. "Oh, look at those ugly clouds."

Just as I turn my head, I hear a clap of thunder. The nasty dark clouds roll across the sky and instantly begin to dump a heavy swoosh of rain all at once. The trees sway in the wind; the sky is an ominous gray green. I leap from the table, throw aside the sliding door, then grab a clothes basket from the floor where I left it earlier and run outside to the clothesline. Of course, my clothes have been instantly soaked through. I frantically begin pulling our laundry off the pins, throwing everything into the basket. Then I look up and see Keith on the other end of the line, draping our wet clothes over his arm. My black lace bra is in his hand.

"What are you doing?" I ask, running over to him. "Give me that!" I yank the bra out of his hand, but the elastic snaps back at him, slapping him on the chin with the underwire. He chuckles then tosses the bra into the basket. It's embarrassing, though it is pretty cool of him to come out here in the pouring rain to help me take in the laundry.

"I'm helping," he says good-naturedly. "It's the least I can do, Brenda."

"Go inside," I call to him over the sound of the rain. "You're getting drenched."

"It actually feels quite nice." He tips his head toward the sky, and I watch the rain stream down his cheeks and neck. His wet shirt clings to his body, and I can see his well-defined chest and abs. I smell his sweat being washed away. I know I shouldn't stare, but I can't help it. Keith was never conventionally attractive when the band was in its heyday, but he's definitely pretty hot now, with the rain streaming down his face.

I turn my attention back to the laundry and try not to look up at him again. Then I cheat and sneak another peek. His hair, soaked with rain, clings to his forehead. He runs his hands through it and groans as he rubs the palms of his hands on his cheeks. I finish taking down what's left of the laundry, and he carries the basket back to the house for me. Of course, my one pair of granny panties is on top of the pile; as if the bra fiasco hadn't been enough.

"I'll take it from here," I say when we get to the back door, holding out my arms. He places the basket in my hands. "Thank you." I shove the panties under the other clothes, and he smirks.

I scramble through the back door, soaked, with the basket of waterlogged clothes weighing me down, but Keith doesn't come in with me. I look back and see him still there on the porch. *What the hell is he doing?* The smirk on his face is gone; I see his eyes lose their luster as he gazes at something far away, his mouth falling into an expressionless horizontal line. I crane my neck back out the door and am immediately pelted by the windblown rain. I see that he's staring at the wind chimes hanging by the back door. They are ringing rhythmically in a perfectly steady time. Keith fixes his attention on them, his eyes glazing even more as he taps his hand against his thigh.

"Keith? Are you okay?" I ask from inside the door. *Is he having a seizure?*

Beside the Music

My mind goes back to all the exacting preparations that Toni made before he flew
to Rhode Island to meet me. At the time, I'd thought it was a bit much, but now
I'm struggling to remember if there was any mention of epilepsy. He's standing
outside in the pouring rain, transfixed, but he holds up his hand to silence me and
closes his eyes. I set the basket down and watch him. I am not sure what is going
on, but it is absolutely fascinating.

"Brenda," he whispers urgently, "where's your guitar? Quick. Please."

Chapter 9

MY MOUTH IS HANGING OPEN. *How exactly has this happened: Keith Kutter ending up strumming my guitar in the pouring rain?*

Thankfully, it hadn't been a seizure: he just got an idea for a song. I listen to the guitar against the wind chimes. I never would have come up with that in a million years. I stare in awe at the complex rhythm that Keith is coaxing out of my guitar. I didn't know those rusty strings could even make that kind of sound. Reluctantly, I leave the back door. I put the clothes in the dryer and go back into the kitchen, where Greg is loading plates into the dishwasher. The counter has been scrubbed clean.

"Oh, Greg, you didn't have to do that," I chide, scrambling into the kitchen to take over. But there is nothing left to do. *Maybe,* I think, *I should have stayed out of the kitchen longer—he could have tackled the inside of the fridge.*

"It was no problem. The least I could do. We're the ones who turned up here unannounced." Greg smiles then takes Vito up on a ruthless game of tug, until Vito triumphantly carries his toy with him to his bed. Greg looks around. "Where's Keith?"

"Destroying my guitar in the rain." I gesture out the window, and Greg nods. "Does he always do this sort of thing?"

"Yup." He smiles over his shoulder as he heads for the living room, and then grabs a book off the shelf. "I'll make sure he gets you a new one."

Wow. They're just going to buy me a new guitar? Of course they are: it's Keith Kutter. I'll probably end up with some crazy expensive limited edition amazing piece of art guitar that the manufacturer is dying for Hydra to play on stage, so long as Greg is making sure of it.

I walk into the living room and pick up a magazine. I thumb through a few pages, but it doesn't hold my interest. Keith Kutter is playing my guitar right outside. I can't help but listen, but I don't want to bother him; he's obviously on a roll. I cock my ear as he blends the guitar perfectly with the wind chimes. He grunts with exasperation, apparently trying, again and again, to get the rhythm just right. I would love it if he asked me to go out there and listen. What if he gets stuck and needs me to give him some ideas? I could be on the ground floor of a brand new Hydra song, or even a Keith Kutter solo project!

He finally bursts through the back door, and I look up, expecting him to ask my opinion. I would gladly stand out in the rain all day for that. His clothes are drenched, and water is dripping off the strings into the sound hole of my guitar. "Brenda? Brenda! Do you have a tape recorder?"

"No, why?" Tape recorder? Do people still have those things? I don't think I'd even know where to buy cassette tapes. *What decade is he in?*

"I have got to get this down before I forget it," he says. "I don't care if it's a microcassette recorder. I can't lose this!"

"I have something better," I tell him, smiling as I pick up the phone and dial a number. Del picks up. "Hey, it's Brenda. What are you doing this afternoon?"

Del Riccio came into Tim's shop one day a few years ago with a '70s Ford Torino that he'd bought for $200 off of Craigslist. It was a rust bucket that didn't run; the interior was ripped to shreds. He had it towed to Tim's shop to get advice on how to get it running. Tim is a sucker for classic cars, so he spent nearly every weekend keeping the shop open so that Del could work on it, and the two of them became friends. It took nearly six months, but they managed to get the car into near pristine condition. Del is in his fifties and works as a freelance sound engineer. As a result of our friendship, the PR firm that I work for has hired him to put together a number of radio public service announcements; he also has a studio in his basement and records local bands.

While I am on the phone, Keith paces impatiently and hums to himself. He strums his empty hands against his thigh and focuses intently on some unseen object on the floor while he strides back and forth. It's like the song inside of him is a time bomb that will blow him to bits if he doesn't get it out of him on time. I don't tell Del who I am bringing to his house. He presses me a bit, and I say, "No, really, it's better this way. Trust me." I can tell Del's intrigued, and he tells me to bring my mystery guest to the studio. I hang up the phone and nod at Keith. Relief crosses his face for a moment, but he doesn't allow it to stay long, focusing once again on the floor.

"I have to get Greg," Keith says and heads for the garage door. "Hey, how attached are you to those wind chimes?"

"Take them," I tell him, sighing. Then I add, my voice heavy with sarcasm, "I certainly don't want to get in the way of genius."

"I'll buy you new ones, I promise," he says, grinning. He hops out into the rain and pulls them off of the hook. I wonder if my new wind chimes will also be some crazy-expensive work-of-art chimes. Maybe they'll be the latest in Swedish design, ergonomically balanced or some shit.

"Greg, we've got to go," Keith commands. Without questioning, Greg sets the book back on the shelf and follows Keith into the garage. I wonder how many times a scene like that has played out between them. There is probably a certain degree of strangeness that comes with being a rock star's bodyguard. There are probably a lot of things Greg doesn't question anymore.

Ten minutes later, I am watching Keith and Greg organize a spaghetti-mess of wires in Del's basement.

"Okay, explain it to me again," Del whispers. "Why is Keith Kutter in my studio?" When we showed up at his door, Del's mouth had hung open until Greg asked if we could get out of the rain. Del looked at me, puzzled; I shrugged my shoulders as we walked into his house. I admit it had been fun to surprise Del like that. He looked so awkward, standing in his front doorway, looking at Keith Kutter standing on his doorstep. I think it took Del a few minutes to fully grasp what he was seeing.

"Del, you ready?" Keith calls out to him. He's hung the wind chimes from a microphone stand, and Greg has positioned another microphone to record them. Obviously, Greg has been in enough recording studios to know exactly how to help. I pick a seat far out of the fray and watch the scene unfold in front of me. To me, this is more interesting than a sporting event or even a Broadway show. I am getting a rare opportunity to watch a world-famous musician record a new song. This is something that I will remember for the rest of my life. It's right up there with getting to watch Picasso paint or Michelangelo sculpt another masterpiece.

I look over at Del, and I can tell he's trying to mask a look of sheer awe. I smile at him, and he smiles back and shakes his head, as if to say, "I cannot believe you brought Keith Kutter to me." I flash an "I'm cooler than you" smile at him.

I turn my attention back to Keith just in time to see him examine the chimes and then rip away all but two of the bells. I wince and know that Tim will be pissed. He gave those to me after I first moved into the house. I laughed when I opened the box and found the chimes, because we knew it was something that spat in the face of the old-money décor. Buying the chimes had been an open rebellion, and it gave us the courage to redecorate—subtly, though, so as not to offend his mother. *Do they sell bug zappers anymore?* I'd love to hang one up, just to see her face.

Keith strikes the two bells in a syncopated rhythm with a drum mallet. It sounds a bit like the rhythm they sounded while swaying in the wind, when we stood near my back door. I am completely amazed at his ability to walk by a set of wind chimes, hear them for all of one second, and then make a song out of it. I've probably walked by those wind chimes thousands of times, and it's never occurred to me even once to find a song in them. I used to write my own songs compulsively when I was single; as I sit in Del's studio today, I am a bit bummed that I'd never thought to use those chimes in a song.

"Del, can you record this and play it back to me on a loop?" Keith asks, his voice stiff with intensity. After a few moments, the bells ring through the speakers. Keith puts on a pair of headphones and picks up the Taylor acoustic guitar that Del keeps in the studio and begins to play. I am glad that Keith is getting to play a guitar that is way nicer than mine. Del keeps it impeccably tuned; it's always perfect and ready to sing. Not like my crappy Yamaha, with the crack in its face that vibrates at a teeth-itching frequency anytime you strum a cord with the low E string in it. Keith drops the pick and uses the side of his thumb to pluck a complex chord pattern in time with the bells, kind of like what he was playing in the rain at my house. Only this time, it sounds more luxurious, as if the strings have been dipped in expensive dark chocolate.

As they warmly reverberate under his fingers, I cover my mouth and try to silence my breathing, afraid to distract him for even a half second. Watching a new song unfold right in front of me is unlike anything I've ever witnessed before. The instruments sit dormant until Keith coaxes them into adding a new layer to his song, and I sit on the edge of my seat, waiting for what he'll pull out next. It is pure magic, but I can tell that it's not easy at first. Keith has an idea of how it should sound in his head, and I can tell that trying to get his hands to reproduce that sound is frustrating, even for his experienced fingers.

"Dammit!" he growls, and then alters the rhythm on the guitar slightly. "Del, you getting this?" he calls out distractedly.

Del presses a button on the sound board and speaks into the intercom: "I've been recording since you walked in. Just do your thing."

There are no windows in Del's basement; they're covered up by the foam soundproofing he installed all over the walls. The first time Tim and I came down here, I watched him glance around nervously—wondering, I figured, how we'd escape if a fire broke out. It's amazing how often he thinks of things like that, and how infrequently I do.

I left my watch at home and have no concept of how long we've been down here. It doesn't feel like it, but I am sure that hours have flown by as I've watched Keith work. In that time, he's recorded a flawless acoustic guitar part and moved on to the bass line. It is unlike anything I've ever heard Hydra play. It starts out so simply, with just two notes on the bells, after which the guitar adds texture. And then the melody flows from the bass. I know he's going to write words; I am trying to imagine what the song will be about. It has a bit of a bittersweet feel to it. *Will it be about the accident?* It's the one thing he doesn't want to talk about, but *would he ever be willing to put it into a song?* I can't help feeling that the complicated, deep melancholy of this new song would be a perfect base for those lyrics.

Keith sets down his earphones and strides into the booth. Greg and I follow. It occurs to me for the first time that Greg might be bored. While this is incredibly exciting for me, Greg has probably experienced this dozens of times before. Keith sits next to Del at the board, and the song comes through the surround-sound speakers. As he listens, Keith fidgets with the dials; the bells get softer and the bass, louder. He reaches over to a vintage electric piano that Del keeps near the mixing board and selects a grand piano sound. He taps out a line that coincides perfectly with the bass. I am amazed that Keith knows how to play all of these instruments. I thought he only played the bass. He nods to Del, and Del starts recording again. Instinctively, Del loops the piano part. Keith stands and paces while he listens. "More bass here," he instructs, and Del turns a dial. "Yes! Just like that!" Keith stops pacing and listens intently. I hold my breath.

The song ends, and we all sit in silence. I am afraid to be the first one to speak, because I don't know if I am going to interrupt Keith's train of thought. But I kind of feel like this moment requires a round of applause. It would suck if I was the one who killed a brand new Hydra song because I couldn't keep my mouth shut. "Can I have a minute, guys?" Keith asks. His eyes are closed, and he's deep in thought. We clear out and go upstairs to Del's sparse bachelor kitchen. He pulls three beers out, and we sit on the stools by the counter to drink them.

"Del, is it always like this?" I ask, gushing. "Is there always a guy in the studio who just pulls a song out of thin air like that?"

"No, I can't say it's always like this. For starters," he points to the basement door, "this is Keith Fucking Kutter. Keith Kutter! In *my* studio. I still can't believe it." Del's eyes sparkle with excitement. "Usually, when bands come here, the songs have already been written and polished. Nobody writes a whole new song in the studio. Who could afford that?"

"I'm sure Keith can," I say, taking a sip of my beer and glancing at the clock over the stove. "Is the meter running?" I joke. What would one even begin to charge someone like Keith Kutter for studio time? Then it hits me: *Crap, it's 11 p.m. What should I do?* I need to go home at some point, but I am Keith's ride back to his motorcycle. I don't want to interrupt his work. But at the same time, Tim is probably home by now and worried sick. In the rush to get to Del's, I didn't even call him. I'm sure he came home to an empty house and is wondering if the rock stars have kidnapped me for their backstage entertainment.

Greg reads my mind. "Brenda, I'm sure at some point you'll want to go home. How about I call you from here, and we'll figure something out later, okay?" I move toward the basement door. "Don't," Greg instructs. "He's working. I'll tell him you said goodnight." I kiss Del on the cheek and say goodnight to Greg.

When I get back into my car, I see that Tim has left three voicemails on my cell. I don't bother to listen to them but call him, instead.

"Tim, holy crap, I just had the most incredible experience! Keith just created a whole new song right in front of me. It was amazing!"

"Where the heck are you?" he asks. "Are you guys on your way back now?"

"I'm alone. They stayed at Del's. Keith was on a roll. I wish you could have seen it—it was amazing."

"I'm sure it was," he says, dismissively. "But at least I got their bikes working again. It only took four hours, too. Man, those rental bikes are beat to shit."

Beside the Music

"I'm sorry you had to do that, Tim."

"It's just not what I had planned for today. It would have been nice to do something together. And *now,*" he says, morosely, "I get to listen to you talk about the good time *you* had with Keith."

"I'll talk to you when I get home, okay?"

Man, I hate it when he gets like this. Yes, I've been gone all afternoon, and I hope he didn't just mope around the house after he got home. I mean, I get it. Spending Sunday working sucks. Not much of a day off for him. But this exchange right here is the classic Dunkirk family clusterfuck of missed connections.

I feel as if we can't even have a normal conversation anymore. Not that telling him about Keith Kutter's prowess in the studio is normal. But I would imagine that, in a normal marriage, the husband would at least listen to the wife gush about something as mind-blowing as watching a famous musician produce a new song from nothing. And then the wife would apologize for being gone all day. Still... Maybe I'll stop on the way home and grab a pint of Ben & Jerry's for us. Okay, so we didn't ride down to the beach like we'd planned. At least I can make it up to him this way, right?

I hang up the phone and turn on the radio. Of course, "Battleground Zero" is on. I laugh and crank it up. I notice the rain has stopped, finally, and the road is steamy as the water evaporates. I roll down all the windows and gun the gas pedal, instantly transported back to cruising on the back roads in East Windsor on a hot summer night, just like this one. I have just watched Keith Kutter invent a new song right in front of my eyes! Nothing can kill this mood, not even Tim's bad one. I stick my arm out the window and wiggle my fingers in the breeze. I don't care who you are: nothing beats driving with the windows down and a great song on the radio.

"*An oldie but a goodie from Hydra,*" the announcer drones over the end of the song. Then, "*Let's all cross our fingers for Keith Kutter's safety.*" The station immediately switches over to an ad.

"What the hell?"

I press the next preset button on the radio, just in time to catch another announcer on the local alternative rock station. "*This is Rebecca Green with your entertainment news,*" she chirps. "*Bassist Keith Kutter from '80s band Hydra has been missing since last night. He was last seen having dinner with longtime fans Brenda and Tim Dunkirk here in Rhode Island.*"

Holy shit. They've just said my name on the radio. Normally that would be cool, but are they suggesting that Tim and I had something to do with Keith's disappearance? I am amazed at this: a rock star doesn't check in for one day, and everyone thinks something bad has happened.

The announcer interrupts my thoughts. "*Band manager Erik Murtaugh released the following statement."*

The man's recorded voice is heavy with an Australian accent. *"For all we know, he could be in a ditch somewhere."*

Really? Talk about overreacting. Then the announcer moves on to the next big entertainment news story of the day: pop tart Jamie Fire's twelve-hour-long Vegas marriage. But at least Keith's story came before Jamie Fire's in the news. I am sure it's nice to know that, for one day, *something* was more compelling than Jamie's public deflowering and coming of age saga.

I admit: it's pretty cool that I know something nobody else in the world knows—Keith is working on a new song. I am completely in love with that idea, though I wish I could call up the radio station and say, "Keith's fine. He's in the studio at Del Riccio's house, recording a new song. I've heard it, and it's incredible!" The last thing Del needs, though, is a crowd of fans and media on his front lawn. I laugh at the ridiculousness of the situation: his manager doesn't know where he is, and he's milking the media, trying to get some attention out of it. I've seen it before; hell, I've even *done* it before for my own clients. It'll be interesting to see how this plays out. Hydra management is crying wolf. It could make them look silly, if it's not done right.

The house is dark when I pull into the driveway. I figure Tim is in bed. I pull into the garage and hear Vito baying from the bedroom, which is probably waking Tim up right now. When I get inside, I see the "new voicemail light" blinking on the phone. *"You have eight new messages,"* the robotic voice drones. I press the play button.

"Brenda? It's Toni Wallace. I am just checking to see if you have heard from Keith. He hasn't checked in. Please call me straight away." She sounds worried.

The next is from Erik Murtaugh, whose voice I recognize from the radio interview. The rest are from Toni, each sounding more frantic than the last. I guess I should be the one to call and check in, seeing as how Keith cannot be bothered. I dial.

"Toni, it's Brenda Dunkirk," I say into the phone when she answers. "Keith's fine. He's in a studio recording a new song."

Chapter 10

I AM LATE FOR WORK and scrambling out the door when the phone rings. I debate as to whether I want to pick it up until I see Del's number on the caller ID. "Hey, Bren, listen, I have to go to New York for work. Keith and Greg are still here, and I have no idea how long they plan on staying."

"Are you serious? Del, I am so sorry!" I haven't heard from any of them in a few days. I had just assumed that Keith had found his own way back to his hotel room in Newport and moved on. I am not the only American fan he's meeting; I think he was supposed to go to Indiana next. "So what are you going to do?"

"I'm going to work. Keith and Greg have largely fended for themselves, anyway. They're actually pretty good roommates. They clean up, keep to themselves. Keith's a pretty good cook, too."

"Well, I'm glad you're having a good time at summer camp," I say with a laugh.

"Oh, and Keith called the mothership to let them know he's okay. Apparently, he's no longer bleeding in a ditch." Del roars with laughter.

"That's good news." I laugh along with him. "I was worried for a while there. God, how do these rumors get started?" I know exactly how: it all goes back to an overzealous publicist. In this case it could go horribly wrong and make Keith look like an attention whore, or it could be brilliant, and he could practically come back from the dead in the public eye. These are the things we debate in staff meetings just about every day at work—the fine line between just trying to get attention and trying to keep the world interested. Work. Crap, I'm late!

We hang up, and I peel out of the driveway and speed to the highway. The wind whips through my rolled-down windows. I slip my sunglasses onto my face and rest my elbow on the window frame. In record time, I pull into the parking lot. I know I should get inside and get to work. But how great would it be to just not show up to work and go to Del's, instead? I could sit on the basement stairs and listen to new songs unfold all day long. I could be the first one to ever hear the new songs he's working on; and then he'd take me aside and ask me what I think.

Offering my opinion on his new song is a very important job, and I'd take it very seriously. I'd sit at Del's mixing board with my eyes closed and concentrate intently on the music. And then I'd offer some incredibly insightful piece of feedback, without which the song couldn't ever possibly be a hit single. And then Keith would thank me in the liner notes on the CD. And I'd get interviewed by

Rolling Stone magazine. They'd call me the Hit Whisperer. Then other bands would hire me, and I could make a career out of making rock songs into solid gold hits. I could live a life of unbridled creativity and travel the world. I see myself storming into a studio, casting aside my luxuriously-expensive purse, taking command of the room, and everyone in it standing up and taking notice.

It's so quiet in the car, I can hear my watch ticking while I daydream; with each tick I am another second late. *No, I can't drive to Del's today.* I have a huge pitch meeting to prepare for that Amanda's letting me take the lead on. I have to report back to my clients with focus group findings on their new test campaign. *So much to do.* And I love my job, really. But what would it be like to not have to go there and, instead, be the Hit Whisperer? I take a deep breath, pull my bag off the passenger seat and glance at my watch: five minutes late. Not too bad for a Wednesday. My footsteps echo in the stairwell as I walk up the stairs to the second floor, swipe my access card in the security door, and enter my workplace.

Today is the day that I need to prove myself worthy of that promotion. The Smile Airlines product launch that I coordinated right before the dinner with Keith is proving to be amazing. Every flight out of Providence has been full, and the standby lists have been out of control. Everyone in Rhode Island and Southeastern Massachusetts is dying to fly on Smile, and it's all because of me. If I can get a few more wins like that, then Amanda will have no choice but to promote me. Amanda is normally an ice princess when it comes to work. She takes her business very seriously, and she projects a very cool, "don't fuck with me" exterior. With her white-blonde hair, freezing blue eyes, and chiseled jaw, her poker face is impermeable. But the Smile Airlines launch broke through that icy exterior. She's been smiling ear to ear, and the client has been singing our praises in the press, as well. We're sure to get some more high-profile accounts out of this.

I blow through my emails so I can clear my deck for the rest of the afternoon and begin working on the pitch for Baxter Corporation. They are a Rhode Island-based furniture manufacturer and retailer that wants to go national. They need a few solid product launches in key markets like Chicago and L.A., and Amanda wants to ride on my success with Smile Airlines.

Email is tedious as hell, though. Email leads to procrastination for me. I'd rather research for hours before I answer the fifty emails in my inbox. Before I know it, I am daydreaming at my desk about how exciting it must be to work as Keith's publicist instead of Baxter's. Improving the reputation of a rock legend is way more interesting than trying to get the nation to buy furniture that is really an Ikea knock-off. *There it is: my first order of business is to convince the world that Baxter is affordable and superior to Ikea.* Okay, time to get these emails out of my inbox and get all up in Baxter. I turn off everything else in my head and focus.

"You ready for your practice session?" Amanda asks, popping her head into my cubicle. I will be taking the lead on the Baxter pitch, and she wants to make sure I am perfect before I do. This is my second of three mock pitch sessions. She completely dismantled me in the first one, so I've been preparing like I am getting ready to defend a dissertation. I am confident that I will be bullet-proof this time.

I follow her into the conference room, trying to mimic what I call her Viking Ice Princess Walk. Her back is straight, her gaze is straight ahead, and I am convinced that her eyes will bore frozen holes into anything in her path. We walk past the row of low-wall cubes, and I can see my co-workers' puzzled expressions as two ice princesses walk by.

I close the conference room door behind me and proceed to demonstrate to her how Amanda Dixon PR will propel Baxter into the national spotlight. I whip out sample press releases, media schedules, web site mockups and an event schedule for store openings.

When I am done, I pause, waiting for her feedback. Her poker face is dead straight. *Great, does that mean I sucked?* Is she trying to figure out how to tell me that I can't pitch them? *Come on! Put me out of my misery.*

"Bren, that was…" She pauses. I lean forward in my chair. "…incredible. It was perfect. My only recommendation is to lighten up a bit. You were folding your hands on the table so tightly I thought you'd break your own fingers. Yes, you need to be dialed in to the client's agenda, but don't forget to be personable, too. Show a little pizazz with your personality. Smile, for God's sake." After she says that, I cannot *stop* smiling. I fight the urge to skip all the way back to my desk. *Vice presidency, here I come!*

The adrenaline of nailing my mock pitch courses through me. I am like a caged lion until five, and I take off right at the top of the hour.

"Night, Bren," Joy says as she's loading her coffee cup into the dishwasher in the kitchen. "You have been a complete spaz all afternoon," she jokes. "Get outside and enjoy that sunshine. Go run a marathon, for crying out loud."

I think I could. In the car, I fight the urge to go to Del's. I turn on NPR and hope that listening to *All Things Considered* will keep me from fantasizing about listening to Keith recording all night. When I get home, I spring Vito from captivity; we play outside until the phone rings. A male voice with an Australian accent introduces himself as Erik Murtaugh, Hydra's manager. His voice doesn't sound as authoritative as it was on the radio the other night. Instead, it's a bit humble, and I am suddenly curious to know why.

"Brenda, I've got a favor to ask. If it's too much of an imposition, I understand." He pauses. "As you know, Keith's been recording a new album at your friend Del's house."

"Yes, a solo album, right?"

"No, it's a new Hydra album."

"Wow, that's *fantastic*," I say, gushing.

"Yes, it is. The boys will be flying to Rhode Island to record in Del's studio next week."

"Are you *serious*?" I ask, but then I realize, of course he is. Erik is the band manager: he doesn't joke about stuff like this. "Del must be thrilled!" Why hadn't he said anything this morning? I would think he'd have wanted to shout from every rooftop.

"Yes, it's very good," Erik acknowledges, but he sounds distracted. "It's always been Hydra's policy to record in independent studios all over the world. So I am sure Mr. Riccio is thrilled to be selected this time around." *Is he reading from a press release?*

I start to speak, then decide to wait for him to continue. I am beyond excited for Del; what an awesome opportunity for him. And to have Hydra recording so close by! The idea of crashing their recording sessions and hearing all the new songs before anyone else is now closer to a reality. My name in the liner notes is looking a lot more likely right now. Maybe Keith will put some sort of inside joke in there that nobody else reading it will understand. I need to make an effort to develop that inside joke. Erik is still talking; I need to pay attention.

"See, the guys prefer to stay in a house together, in close proximity to the studio. It has also always been their policy not to live where they are working, which is why staying at Del's would not be suitable, and I understand that his house is far too small to accommodate all of us. How far is it to drive from your house to Del's studio?"

"It takes about ten minutes. He lives about five miles away—"

"And Keith tells me that your home is large enough to accommodate the boys. How many bedrooms do you have?"

"*Um…*" I stammer, realizing suddenly where this is going. "*Uh*—we have four bedrooms, two and a half bathrooms." I converted one of the bedrooms into an office, because I sometimes work from home when I want to focus on a project.

"Would you be so kind as to open your home to the boys?" he suddenly blurts out. He obviously feels nervous about asking me, a complete stranger, to house the men who he's been in charge of for decades.

"*Um…*" I stammer again. "You mean, they'll stay here?" I look around my house and try to imagine four aging rock stars sitting around my kitchen table. *What would they possibly expect out of staying in my house?* What kind of accommodations are they accustomed to? They're probably used to room service coming and going at all hours, leaving wet towels on the floor, concierges to cater to their every whim, and mints on their pillows. I could probably get a box of mints. Hell, I could even splurge for new towels, the big fluffy ones that are the size of blankets.

My mind is spiraling until Erik interrupts my thoughts. "Keith insists on staying at your home," he says, speaking noticeably faster. "The first song began there when he heard your wind chimes. He feels it is vital to the work to start and finish writing all his lyrics for a new project in the same place. Obviously, we would compensate you for the trouble and hire a housekeeper for the duration. How does fifty thousand American sound to you?" He pauses and then says, with more emphasis, "It is imperative that he resume the work on this album where it began. It's his process, and we cannot afford any disruption to that process."

"*Um…*" I stammer, yet again. "I need to discuss this with my husband first." It surprises me that Keith is so superstitious about his process.

I take a look around at our house. When Tim bought this place, Portia made sure to help Tim buy a house large enough for a family of children that could fill out a soccer team. Obviously Erik knows that we don't live in a hellhole; he probably looked it up on Google street view. *Fifty grand. Wow.* We could redecorate this entire house with that. Never mind what I could fetch on Craigslist for those stupid divans and chaises.

"Talk it over with Tim. They don't need any disruptions to their work, so you would be obligated to put them up for the duration of recording. But just know that I need an answer by tomorrow, so we can make other arrangements, if need be."

I click off the call and try to collect my thoughts, but my mind is racing. *Wow.* I mean, it was weird enough to talk to Keith on the phone and go to dinner with him. Serving him a peanut butter and jelly sandwich in my kitchen was, in my opinion, on the outer orbit of bizarre. *But to have Hydra stay in my house?* There is no way this is happening to me.

I look around my house and wonder how Tim and I can possibly accommodate a group of people who've grown so successful that they can afford to stay in—and trash—the finest hotels. Erik tried to downplay their expectations, but I am not stupid—I know they'd expect nothing short of perfect. Would the band think my house was a hellhole compared to where they live? It's going to take more than big fluffy towels and mints. Maybe I should get the fancy chocolate-dipped mints, like the ones Tim's mom finds at that gourmet chateau place where she buys all her food.

I should probably just call Erik back and say no, we can't do it. It really is a crazy idea, and we have Tim's campaign to think about. What if it gets out that Hydra is living here, while he's trying to make a name for himself politically? Will that help or hurt his campaign? I also have Tim's anxiety to think about. Tim gets edgy when we have friends stay for more than two or three days. At first, he passive-aggressively switches off the lights as our guests leave the room; then, toward the end of the visit, his jaw is clenched, and he's tossing wet towels into the hamper moments after our guests are done using them. Honestly, Tim can't deal with having others in his space for too long. How would he possibly deal with having four rock stars and their entourages around? And for how long? Erik didn't say. How long does it take to produce an album, anyway? We're expected to house them for the duration. *But what does that mean?*

I roam through the house and end up in one of our guest bedrooms. We certainly have enough bedrooms to accommodate the band, if we convert my office back to a bedroom. I sit on the bed and try to imagine how this room would look to Keith, or even to Ben Taylor, Hydra's lead singer. *Is my house even good enough?* What will they think of it when they first arrive? It's thrilling to imagine Keith sleeping here. His head would rest on this pillow, and these sheets would barely cover his naked body, night after night, just across the hall from the bedroom I share with Tim. *Again with the teenage groupie fantasy stuff.* Why am I imagining Keith sleeping naked? He has those freckles on the edge of his T-shirt, and I wonder if he has them all over his body. I run my hands over the starchy duvet, also courtesy of Portia.

The possibility of the band staying here is pretty exciting. All I can really do is flop onto the bed, press my face into the pillow, and laugh. I've pretty much made up my mind: I am *not* calling Erik back to say no.

Then I spring back onto my feet and into action. My mind starts a fresh to-do list. The house needs to be cleaned from top to bottom, and not the bullshit "hide things when company comes over" kind of clean. I am talking spotless clean. Tim-worthy clean—which is a whole new level of housekeeping. I am sure that, over the years, I have stashed all kinds of random crap in the guest room closets and my office. They all need to be cleaned out to make room for rock star clothing. I try to imagine leather jackets and black T-shirts hanging from the rods. The office bedroom needs a dresser, and I could probably move one of the end tables from the living room into it to function as a night table.

The prospect of finally buying a piece of furniture for this house on my own, without Portia's input, is delicious. For crying out loud, my name is on the deed, and I feel like I have to ask her permission to buy a piece of furniture! *That's got to stop.* I stashed a few storage bins under the guest bed with things like my wedding dress; I need to find a new home for those, as well. Maybe I can get Tim to put those into the attic for me. The ceiling in the office is dingy as hell; it needs to be painted. And I can see the dust marks around the ceiling vent. That'll take a day or so, once I get all the furniture covered. And at that point, I may as well just do the walls. *Hmmm...* yellow? I've always wanted it to be a bit brighter in here.

Then it hits me as I'm sitting on the day bed in the office bedroom: the first item on the to-do list is to convince Tim. There's no way that he'll be as excited as I am, so he needs to see why this is a good idea. I leap back into action when I realize that preparing for our rock 'n' roll house guests has to go back even further than I'd initially thought. The number one task is to make Tim's favorite meal for dinner. I know it's a cliché, but sometimes the way to a man's heart really *is* through his stomach.

I grab my keys off the kitchen counter and notice a book of fabric swatches with a Post-it note stuck to the front that says, *Timothy, pick from the colors with the paper clips on them. Kisses, Mother.* When did this get here? Does she still have a key from when we went to Florida? I thought Tim got it back from her. And is she redecorating our house? *Without my input?* I thumb through the swatches she's selected: beige, taupe, and ecru. No, no, and no—as far as I'm concerned. At least she's gotten off her all-white kick. Everything in this house is too damned white.

No time for this. I gotta get moving. I jump in the car, and soon I'm speeding down Orchard Street, careening around the corner and into the parking lot of the Stop and Shop. I frantically shove my cart down the aisles and blindly sweep items into it, like risotto, scallops, and lemons. I am sprinting down the produce aisle and nearly take out a toddler who is stooping to pick something off the floor. I mumble an apology to his mother over my shoulder as I clamp my fist onto a bag of salad; I don't even look at it to see whether it's browned. In record time, I am swiping my card in the checkout line. Then I scurry out to the car and speed all the way home, my tires squealing a little as I whip into our driveway. Tim will be home late; he has a meeting tonight with Aria after the shop closes. I glance at my watch. I have about an hour to work my mojo and make Hydra's moving in happen.

In between stirring the risotto and pan-searing the scallops, I scrub the kitchen counters, clean up my collection of shoes by the back door (I can tell the ever-growing pile is starting to annoy Tim), and re-load the dishwasher. I set the table, light candles, and fix Tim a plate. I just barely have time to swipe on a fresh coat of mascara and lip gloss and spritz on his favorite perfume before he walks in the door.

"*Mmmm*... smells good," he says. He goes upstairs to change, and I crack open a bottle of white wine that he left to chill in the fridge. He comes back downstairs, freshened up, and I hand him a glass of the wine and pop open a beer for myself.

Time to slow things down a bit. I've been frantic for the last hour. Now I need to make this evening all about him. I hand him some water crackers and brie to nibble on, while I plate dinner and carry it into the dining room.

"We're eating in the dining room tonight?" He follows me in from the kitchen. "What's the occasion?" He kisses me on the cheek before taking his seat at the table. "*Mmmm*... You smell good, too." He squeezes a fresh-cut wedge of lemon over his dish, bites into a scallop, and groans with pleasure. "I just might marry you someday," he says jokingly.

I dig in to my risotto. "How was the meeting with Aria?" I ask. I've been trying hard lately to get over my feelings about her. Nobody likes a jealous wife. I was starting to get irritated with myself, too.

"It was good. The campaign planning stuff is all going so fast. I can't keep up with her half the time. Is this how your clients feel, working with you on your publicity campaigns?"

"Probably," I say, laughing. "Amanda has two speeds. Fast and hyper-fast."

"I can see that." He bites into another scallop and smiles at me. "This is really nice, Bren. Thanks for making such a nice dinner. It really is great to come home to this. It's perfectly done."

69

I smile at him. It's nice that he noticed that I worked so hard on this dinner. But I don't think he knows I have an ulterior motive. I watch him enjoying his meal for a few minutes, trying to figure out how to start the conversation. *Maybe,* I think, *if I stare at him long enough, he'll ask me what's going on.*

But after a minute of staring, he doesn't say a word. Now I am waiting for the perfect opening, like, "So, then, how was your day?" And then I could say, "Funny you should ask. I received an interesting proposition today…" I clear my throat, and he looks up at me from his salad. He has to know I have an ulterior motive to have gone to all this trouble.

"Is there something you want to say, Bren?"

I am not sure where to begin, so I just start talking. I am doing exactly the opposite of what I did today in my mock pitch at work. Amanda would kill me if I did this in the Baxter pitch. I don't even know how long I've been talking. "…So, I'm not sure how many people on the crew they'll bring or if it'll be just the band or what. But I think we could at least fit the band members upstairs in the bedrooms. We have that daybed and the pull-out underneath it. We'll probably have to squeeze in a twin bed in the other bedroom—it might get kinda crowded with the queen in there. Maybe we could put the queen in the attic and find two twins for cheap on Craigslist." I feel like I am rambling out of control, and I know I should stop talking because, if I keep yammering on, I am going talk him out of having Hydra stay here.

He's not saying anything. I stop talking somewhere after the to-do list for the guest bedrooms. *I've probably just blown it.* He raises his eyebrows at me after I am done speaking. *Is he relieved that I am not his campaign manager?*

He spears a scallop with his fork, and I can tell he's overwhelmed by what I've been saying. Not a good start. "Whoa. Slow down," he says. "Start from the beginning. What do you mean, they want to stay here?"

He's right. Slow down. I need to step back and take another approach. I'll go for methodical this time around.

"Okay, so the band wants to record at Del's house, which, as you know, isn't far from here. They want to stay in our house, because Keith started writing the first song on the album here. He wants to write the rest of the songs here, as well, because that's an important part of his songwriting process. He does it all in one place." I watch Tim's face, trying to pick up any clues about what he is thinking. His expression is frozen on a mixture of analytical and skeptical. I need to get him off skeptical. *Okay, let's bring out the pros.*

"How long are they going to stay?" he asks. "A weekend? A few days?"

"I have no idea. But they're going to pay us $50,000 and hire a housekeeper for the duration," I say, quoting Erik.

"For the duration? And you have no idea how long that duration is," he repeats.

Beside the Music

He makes a good point. And I can see where he's going. He hates having houseguests for too long. I need to find a way to turn this around, but he interrupts my thoughts.

"Bren, I don't know about this. Don't you think this is kind of crazy? We don't know these people. What if they trash our house? Don't rock stars mess up hotel rooms all the time?" I can tell that his mind has gone right to the stereotypical '80s rock stars getting high and lobbing TVs out of high-rise hotel windows. I can also see his mind going to people being in his space for longer than three days, which, I am guessing, is precisely what is now causing that anxious crease between his eyebrows.

"But think about it. We would be part of helping Hydra create something great. What if this is the best album they've ever recorded? The album started here when he heard our wind chimes, and they want to finish it here. It messes up their process when they have to make a change, like where they're living."

"They can still record the best album ever if they aren't in our house, Brenda. I don't know. And that bit about their process is bullshit. They're professional musicians who've toured the world. There's no way that changing their living situation will mess them up that badly. This is a bad idea. Think about it. We're going to have four rock stars and their entourages coming and going at all hours. It sounds like it'll be a major pain in the ass, if you ask me." He pauses to chew. "And they're probably messy. They probably won't give a shit about cleaning up after themselves. I don't want to live on *MTV Spring Break*."

I wait for a few moments before speaking again. We've been together for a long time; I know that when he's making a big decision, he needs a few minutes to let the information sink in.

"They'll hire a housekeeper for us. We don't have to worry about the mess." I lean over my plate and try to soften my approach. "Tim, think about how awesome it would be to contribute to what could possibly be Hydra's comeback album. We could help them do that."

My mind drifts to late-night lyric writing sessions with Keith and going to Del's studio to critique their latest ideas for a song. I can barely contain my excitement. But I need to. I can't turn this into an emotional conversation. I can appeal to his more practical side—using the money to make home improvements, which will increase the value of our home. The thought of doing that without Portia's input is so liberating. Maybe I should just go for the gold and tell him how we can invest that $50,000 and diversify our investment portfolio. He loves that shit.

He meets my gaze. My knee is bouncing under the table. I know he can feel it vibrate under his own feet, which drives him crazy when we're sitting next to each other, but I can't stop doing it. "Bren, I don't know. Is this something you really want to do?"

"Yes, I do. I think it'll be an amazing experience." I set down my fork. "I

71

watched Keith pull a song out of thin air when I went with him to Del's house. It was one of the most incredibly creative things I have ever seen. And now I have the chance to experience that every day. I think this is going to be one of those things that I'll regret if I don't do it. We have the opportunity to help one of the greatest rock bands of all-time record an album. And just think of the money they're going to pay us. I mean, it's a win-win!"

"This goes against my better judgment. I think this is probably a very bad idea. But if it's what will make you happy...."

I leap from the table before he even has the chance to finish; my chair falls backward and clatters against the floor. He cringes at the noise—I've probably just dinged the finish on Portia's obnoxiously-expensive dining room chair. Then I jump into his arms. "Really? You're okay with it?"

"No. But yes," he says, sighing. "You're going to owe me. Big time."

"It'll be great, you'll see. I think this will be one of those things we'll look back on when we're old and be glad that we did it." I hug him and thank him, and he responds with a distracted "*Mm-hmmm.*"

I push a scallop around on my plate, my mind immediately going back to the supporting role I will play in the creation of this album. I look across the table at Tim and catch a brief skeptical look cross his face. I look away. I refuse to allow the thought to enter my mind that he might be right and that inviting rock stars to stay in our home may turn out to be more than we've bargained for.

Chapter 11

I PACE IN THE KITCHEN and check, again, to make sure the fridge is stocked and the counters are clean.

"What?" Tim asks after he catches me checking inventory in the pantry for the umpteenth time. "Do you think a bunch of gnomes broke in last night and ate all the snacks?"

I crack a smile. "Maybe." I can tell he's so over me right now. I am sure I am becoming annoying. I leave the pantry and walk into the kitchen where I catch Tim swiping an apple from the bowl on the kitchen table. "Tim! What the hell! Do you have any idea how long I spent arranging that bowl of fruit?" I pull it all out and start again. "It was perfect! Dammit!" He watches me arrange the fruit. Then a smudge on the front of the stove catches my eye. I grab a dishtowel and some Mr. Clean and get to work on it.

"So, my obsession for cleanliness has finally infected you. I was hoping this would happen. Maybe now you'll agree to keep the CDs in alphabetical order, like I asked."

I ignore him and focus on the stove. The band is due to arrive tonight. I've spent the last two weeks meticulously preparing everything for their stay, and I still don't feel ready. I've researched popular Australian snacks and stocked the pantry with them. When the Vegemite arrived, after I ordered a half dozen jars from the Internet, Tim and I each scooped out a spoonful of the thick brown sludge, tasted it, and promptly spat it out.

"Really?" Tim asked. "They eat this crap? What the hell is this?" He peered into the jar suspiciously. "I was optimistic, because it looked like Nutella."

"Apparently they're raised on it," I said, "the way we are with peanut butter and jelly." I screwed the cap back on the jar. "*Ugh*, not for me." I took a long sip of water to wash down the salty and bitter flavor.

"I hope they eat all of this," he said, gesturing to the line of jars in the pantry. "I don't want to be stuck with this crap. I don't think the food bank would even

73

take it..."

I am almost done buffing out the smudge when Tim pulls the dishtowel out of my hand and hangs it on the handle on the front of the oven. "Bren, you're going to be late for work." He hands me my keys and my lunch. "Get out of here."

I set them down and continue to work on polishing the stove.

"I should have taken the day off," I mutter, pacing through the kitchen and stopping to rearrange the flowers on the kitchen table again. I can't seem to get them to look right, no matter how hard I try. I step back and look at them, still not satisfied.

"And do what?" Tim says. "Climb the walls until they get here? They're not arriving until late tonight, anyway." He playfully shoves me toward the door. "You have got to get out of here. Besides, I don't think those flowers could take any more of your manhandling." He pulls a wilted daisy out of the side of the arrangement and throws it into the trash. Surprisingly, they look a lot better now, but I fight the urge to move the tall one to the back.

As I pull out of the driveway, I glance back toward my house and try to imagine how it will look to Hydra when they first arrive. From the front, it looks like your normal, oversized center-hall colonial, but yesterday, a work crew came out and erected a half dozen luxury tents in the back yard to accommodate Hydra's support crew. The strips of forest on either side of our house are fully grown in—because it's summer—and I know that our neighbors probably won't see the tents. But I wonder if they'll suspect something weird is going on at my house. Hydra's management sent us a crazy-long non-disclosure agreement. I've seen enough of these at work to know that, if we tell anyone they're here, we're pretty much screwed. And I know Tim won't want to say anything, because who knows how it'll affect his campaign if we end up with a crowd of reporters and fans on the front lawn? That scene would not make Tim a convincing pick for state Senate, would it?

Tim and I checked out the tents when we got home from work yesterday. From the inside, they don't look at all like tents. They have interior walls that offer each occupant a private space; they have electric lights hanging from the ceiling, powered by extension cords that snake to the house. Most of the tents have two beds in them, but some also have three; I am impressed that they are actual beds and not camping cots.

"How many people are coming again?" Tim asked as his eyes scanned the cluster of tents.

"Well, they have crew," I said and shrugged.

"How *much* crew do they have?" he asked, counting on is fingers. "We have six tents here, and four of them have three beds. That's twelve right there. Then the other two tents have two beds each, so we're up to sixteen...." He trailed off, deep in thought.

Beside the Music

"Well, each band member has an assistant," I began rattling off. "Then there's the band manager and *his* assistant; and we can't forget the guitar and drum techs. Toni tells me they're only bringing a skeleton crew." I laughed. "I wonder what a full-on crew is like."

We went inside the tent closest to the house.

"This is nice," I said. I ran my hands over one of the beds. Even the sheets felt luxurious. I tried to guess at the thread count and suspected it was no less than eight hundred. "Maybe we should hire this company the next time *we* go camping." I hadn't even known this sort of thing existed. *Is there really a market in Rhode Island for luxury tents?* Is this what *glamping* is? I read an article in one of the gossip mags about how "glamorous camping" is the celebrity rage right now. Tim flopped onto the bed and bounced on it, flicking his eyebrows up and down at me in mock suggestion. "Tim! Get off of there!"

He laughed in response. "Come on," he said. "How cool would it be to do it in Hydra's tent? They wouldn't even know. We could just toss the sheets in the wash, and they'd be none the wiser." He tugged at me and laughed. Then he looked down, and the skepticism came back on his face. "They're going to tear the hell out of the lawn, aren't they?" He sighed and kicked at the tent's false floor.

"It'll grow back," I replied. "Remember when Vito dug that hole over by the pear tree? Now you can't even tell it was there."

"Brenda, I am still not sure about this. I don't think we're really equipped to run a rock-and-roll bed and breakfast."

Later that night, before we went to bed, I caught him looking out the bedroom window at the tents, a concerned look frozen on his face. He probably didn't get much sleep after that, and I am pretty sure he won't get much while they're here...

He pulls the dish towel from my hand and hangs it back on the rung on the front of the oven. "You have been obsessing about this for two weeks now. You need to go. Now."

Like he noticed. I've done all the work to get the house ready, while he and Aria have been busy conspiring to take over Rhode Island with his campaign. He hasn't been home much in the evenings. And even when he has been home, he's been beached in front of the TV, while I've been painting, cleaning, and rearranging the furniture. I know that having the band move in is my pet project, but I wish he'd offered to help more.

He balked when I asked him to help me move a few boxes into the attic. "*Ugh*, no," he said "I'm exhausted. I had to push three cars into the garage today. None of the cars I worked on would start."

"Please? It would be so much easier if you could just hand the boxes up the ladder to me, so I won't have to try and muscle them up there myself." I ended up wrestling with the boxes myself and was pretty pissed about it...

Just thinking about it now on the way to work is irritating me. When I get there, I realize that I have no recollection of the drive. I sit down at my desk and get cracking on my emails. Not only did I get the house ready for rock stars, but I also totally nailed the pitch for the Baxter account at work, and they signed with us. Now I am working on their launch, and I am killing it so far.

The cable network, Innovation, is featuring them on their show Factory Tour—filming started last week. I even got to meet the host, Ed Rollins. He's been all over the place doing voiceovers on various documentaries about fishing boats, factory workers, and the like. Very cool guy. And he's taken a liking to Baxter—I think I could get him to do more for them. Amanda is psyched. I am still keeping an ear out for word on my eventual promotion. I am halfway through my emails when I notice that the clock in the corner of my computer screen only says nine o'clock. If I didn't know better, I'd swear it was running backwards.

"Hey," Joy says, popping her head into my cube and startling me so that I jump at the sound of her voice. "Oh my God, what is with you today?" She laughs. "You nearly hit the ceiling just now."

"Sorry. I didn't sleep well last night," I lie, "and I've had a lot of caffeine today." I can't tell anyone that an '80s metal band is going to invade my house tonight; and I don't know how I am going to survive however long they'll be there without being able to tell anyone.

Obviously, they know I had dinner with Keith, thanks to the army of photographers and our profession's close attention to all forms of media. My picture was all over the online gossip mags for half a day, and I got a few follow-up calls from reporters, which I declined to answer. Even Annie called me because she wanted the scoop for MTV News; of course, I gave her a bit to pad her story. *How could I not?* Joy politely asked what he was like, but she's not a fan of the band. She didn't ask again, and of course I couldn't volunteer any more information.

I just need to keep my head down and kick some serious ass on Baxter. I decide that I'll just use Baxter as an excuse for my odd behavior at work. If everyone thinks I am being uber-focused, they'll probably leave me alone.

"Well, anyway," Joy says, "I wanted to tell you that Emily from the printers came by to drop off these proofs for one last look before she does the print run. She needs an answer by noon."

"Okay, I'll take a look. Thanks." I set them aside and turn my attention back to the screen. Better yet, I need to get up and move a bit. I am way too jittery right now.

I stand up in my cube and stretch then decide I need a smoothie. I head out of the office and up the block to a café where I sit on a stool at the smoothie bar. When I take out my phone, there's a text from Annie.

Heard a rumor that Hydra is recording in R.I. Can you confirm?

Beside the Music

I am torn. She's a member of the press. Obviously I can't tell her anything, or it'll set off a group of reporters to camp out on my front lawn. Tim would kill me.

I haven't heard anything.

She responds, *Interesting. Maybe it is just a rumor.*

I hate lying to her. But over the years, I've given her a lot of tips. This time I just can't. I pay for my smoothie and walk back to the office. I have way too much work to do today, enough that I can't deal with the dilemma of helping out my friend versus keeping my sanity at home. I hope she'll just let it drop. But knowing Annie, she'll eventually find out.

When I get back to my office, I call Emily at the printer and leave her a message to go ahead with the print run on the brochures. Then I hide out in my cube and manage to bury myself in Baxter for the rest of the day. The day still goes by pretty slowly, but like every other day, it eventually ends. Then, of course, there's traffic on the highway on the way home due, apparently, to an accident. When I finally pass by the scene, I see that an eighteen-wheeler has hit a van. The van is on its side, and the paramedics are loading a person on a stretcher into the back of an ambulance. I get a little nervous and drive the speed limit the rest of the way home.

By the time I finally walk into the house, I see Vito slinking around with a guilty look on his face. Then I see why: he's shredded the leg on our Louis XIV chaise during the day. *Of course he had to pick today of all days.* He's long outgrown his puppy-chewing days; I wonder why he started up again. Maybe he senses the tension between me and Tim and feels stressed out as a result.

"*Bad dog!*" I holler at him. He slinks toward me, his tail stiff and his head bowed. I clutch his nose and press it against the damage. "No, Vito! Bad dog!" He wriggles loose and heads for the back door. He flattens himself against the floor and whimpers, which makes me feel guilty for yelling at him.

I let him out, then go out myself and throw a Frisbee for him; he's the only beagle I have ever seen that likes to play fetch. We sit on the steps, and I stroke his velvety ears. He seems to have forgotten that, just a half hour earlier, I was royally pissed off at him. I feel his warm tongue lap the back of my hand; I think he's trying to calm my nerves. He looks up at me with his dopey brown eyes, and I can't be mad anymore. I kiss him on the head, and he wags his tail. All is forgiven.

We go back inside, and I toss some kibble into his bowl. Then I put some spaghetti on for dinner and wander through the house, trying not to obsess. I make a move to rearrange the flowers, and then think better of it. I need to keep myself occupied. I pull out the mop and do the kitchen floor again.

I take a look at the shredded couch leg then try to sand out the teeth marks by hand. I manage to get most of them out, and then I paw through the junk drawer to get that stain felt-tip pen that Portia thought to buy for us when she bought the furniture. I touch up the scratches and almost can't tell that Vito chewed it up. I engage in a few more little projects, but none of them manage to keep me occupied. By the time Tim gets home, the pasta is in the colander in the sink, and I am on my hands and knees on the bathroom floor, scrubbing the grout between the tiles.

"*Um*, honey?" he asks, stepping beside me. "You need to stop."

I don't look up at first. "I'm almost done," I say. I puff the hair off my forehead.

He wrestles the brush from my hands. I open my mouth to protest. "Stop!" he commands.

"But…"

"Just stop," he replies firmly. "Do we need to go out? You're starting to go nuts."

Grudgingly, I follow him out of the bathroom. I can't believe it's already eight o'clock. I fix us each a plate of spaghetti. Just as we sit down at the kitchen table, the phone rings. I know it's them, and I know their plane must have just landed. I nearly dive over the kitchen counter to answer it. "*Hello?*"

"Brenda, it's Toni. We've just gotten through customs, and we need to get organized. We'll probably get to your place in about two hours."

I hang up and relay the message to Tim. He walks over to the kitchen window. Doubt seems to cross his face again as he gazes out at the vacant rock star encampment in the back yard. "How did I let you talk me into this again?" Is it more than just his concern for the lawn? My guess is that having Hydra in the house will be very hard for him. We always get into a fight after we have houseguests; his anxiety about our home makes him come off as very rude.

I fight the urge to say, "It'll be fine." He's been listening to me say that for weeks now, and I know he's not going to believe me if I keep saying it over and over again, even though I wish he would. The adrenaline is making my hands get all tingly, so I dump my unfinished spaghetti into a container for lunch tomorrow.

"I know this will be difficult for you. Thank you for letting me do this." I go in for a hug, but he backs off. I recognize this behavior. "You're already getting tense," I say, "and they haven't even arrived yet. You need to chill out, or this is going to be a long stay for you."

"How do you expect me to chill out? I have tents in my back yard and strangers coming into my home to stay for God knows how long. And you want me to *chill out*?" He adds an extra mocking tone to "chill out."

"Tim, come on. You *always* get bitchy when we have houseguests over. Do you remember when Annie came to visit? You practically shoved her out the door as she was leaving. What is the matter with you?" It's true. He yanked her bag from her hand and practically threw it into her trunk. She never said anything about it, but I noticed that she always has an excuse whenever I ask her to come

78

up from New York for the weekend.

"What's the matter with me is," he spouts, "that I have way too much going on to deal with this."

"Tim, you always have way too much going on. Tell me something I don't know. If you have so much going on, then maybe it's time to examine your life and cut back on a few things. Do you need to meet with Aria every single day, for example?"

"There it is. *Aria*. Brenda, there's nothing going on with her. She's my campaign manager."

"You'd better tell *her* that," I snap. "Have you seen the low-cut tops she wears when she's Skyping you? Your mother introduced you to her on purpose—and she's not only thinking about the campaign."

"And now my mother, too. Anything else you want to bitch at me about tonight?"

This is how it's been going lately. I can't bring up his mother *or* Aria. "Why are you getting so defensive? I'm worried about you because you're always so stressed out. You have a lot going on, but it's your own doing, Tim."

I walk into the living room and turn on the TV, trying to distract myself, but instead I find myself bouncing my knee and biting my fingernails. When I look down, I see that Vito is pacing on the area rug, as well. Tim and I don't talk until I finally see the headlights turn onto the driveway.

"They're here."

Chapter 12

THE CONVOY OF MINIVANS pulls into the driveway just after ten o'clock. I switch on the outside lights and step from the deck to meet our houseguests at the edge of the driveway. The van doors slide open and people pour out and stand on the lawn to stretch and shake the circulation back into their legs. One of the men asks me where the bathroom is, and Tim leads him into the house. The Australian accents flow melodically as the crew chatters to each other while they organize their belongings. I listen and am automatically drawn to the laid-back lilt of their voices. I see a crew member open the back of one of the vans and pull out beer stacked by the case. He carries the cases one by one into the house and stocks them in the fridge without saying a word.

I spot a woman yanking suitcases out of the back of the third van. She blows the hair off of her forehead and strains to lift the heavy baggage. None of the crew members asks if she needs help, as they are busy with their own tasks. I leap into place beside her to help her unload the remaining bags.

She turns to face me. "You must be Brenda," she says. "I'm Toni!" She shakes my hand and thanks me for helping her with the bags. Her blonde hair is tied in a messy ponytail, and I can tell that she is tired from traveling. She tugs a purple suitcase out of the back of the van and sets it on the ground with the rest.

"Welcome to Rhode Island!" I say, hoping I sound cheerful and not like a complete dork. "Have you ever been here before?"

"No. It's a long way from Sydney. I think it's the furthest I can get from home without falling off the face of the planet." She yawns. "What a long day."

I imagine the complication of steering a group of rock stars and their crew through customs, which is probably the equivalent of herding an entire kindergarten class through a candy store. The crowd of people around us has erupted into slight chaos as they stash bags into the tents and equipment in the garage.

"It's a shame you had to arrive at night," I say to Toni. "There's nothing like seeing a place for the first time right when you arrive."

Beside the Music

"I know, I was just thinking that on the way here. I hope I'll have some time to explore while we're here. I'd love to take a swim in the Atlantic Ocean."

Just as I am promising to take Toni to the beach, a man thrusts a clipboard into her hands and storms off. Toni shrugs at me, and I watch as she assigns members of the crew to their tents. The Bluetooth headset in her right ear chirps. "Yes, we will do the *Rolling Stone* interview, of course," she says, walking over to the tents. She points at one of them and gestures for a crew member to move some suitcases into it. She's like a rock-and-roll cruise director, but I hadn't realized that she is also the publicist.

For a moment, I allow my mind to drift off to late night PR collaboration sessions over my dining room table, in addition to the jam sessions, the critiques, and the lyric-writing all-nighters. I snap back to the present when I see Toni back at the minivan, hauling two large suitcases from it to the edge of the lawn, where she lines them up for the rest of the crew to haul to their tents. I help her pull the remainder of them out of the van. Then she proceeds to hoist a few of them up the deck stairs.

"Seriously? The big rock stars can't haul their own bags?" I ask.

"No bellman at your place?" She laughs as I help her pull the last of the luggage up the stairs and into the kitchen.

"Good lord, what the hell did they pack in here?"

"I don't know. I am sure it was worse in the '80s, when they had to pack all that hairspray and mousse." She laughs. "Though now, they're probably packing things like leg braces and Bengay." We both laugh.

Once we are in the kitchen, I put the kettle on and set out a few cups. We continue to joke around while we wait for the water to boil. Toni turns, opens the fridge, and scans the contents.

A moment later, I feel a pair of sinewy arms encircle me from behind, then warm breath on my neck as Keith whispers, "*Shhhh*" into my ear. I stand perfectly still and try not to let my heart pound through my back and into his chest. He releases me and tiptoes over to Toni, where he nuzzles her from behind and whispers in her ear as well.

Toni jumps when she hears his voice. "*Keith*! Hi!" She leaps toward him and gives him a hug. The kettle begins to whistle, and Keith picks it up from the stove then turns circles searching for a mug.

I hand him one from the cabinet and drop a tea bag into it; he empties the kettle into the mug and stirs in honey, too. As I am refilling the kettle and setting it back on to boil, the man who handed Toni the clipboard materializes at the back door. He has thinning red hair, and I can see the shine of his scalp. His belly bulges over his belt, and freckles dot his pasty face and arms. The man drags a large whiteboard through the door; it's almost as tall as he is. *Did they stop at Staples and the liquor store on the way here? Where the heck would he get such a large whiteboard at this hour?*

He barely acknowledges Keith and Toni and nods at me. "Erik Murtaugh, band manager" he says. "You must be Brenda Dunkirk." He gestures to the whiteboard. "May I hang this on that wall right there?" he asks, nodding to the wall beside the fridge. Before I can answer, he whips a power screwdriver out of his pocket and screws the board onto the wall. I recognize the screwdriver. I can see the initials that Tim carved into the handle, *TD*. Erik has raided Tim's toolbox in the garage. I'm guessing Tim is not going to be happy about that.

Tim apparently hears the whining of the power screwdriver and bolts into the kitchen. He glares at Erik as he's hanging the whiteboard. "Brenda?" he asks through gritted teeth. "A word in private please?" The moment we step into the living room and out of ear shot, Tim hisses, "Why the hell did you let him hang that thing on our wall? We just fucking painted the kitchen!"

"I, *um*, he just did it."

"What do you mean? He just walked in and started redecorating my kitchen?"

"*Um*, pretty much," I reply.

"They just got here, and they're acting like they own the place."

"Well, they are paying us. They kinda do own the place for a while."

Tim glowers at me for not taking his side. I don't know why I said that: the words just kind of fell out of my mouth. And now Tim and I are off to a great start with Hydra's visit. I need to backtrack. I reach out my hand to him; he scowls and turns his attention back to the whine of the power screwdriver.

We go back into the kitchen, and I see that a few other members of the crew have found their way to the kettle and the mugs. Tim examines the screws that Erik drove into the wall, then the screwdriver, which Erik is still holding. He snorts with disgust, and faces Erik. "Hey, that's my power screwdriver." The irritation in his voice is obvious. Erik looks at him blankly, as if not understanding why he is so upset.

"Tim," I hiss at him. "Let it go." I shoot him a look that says, 'Can we please not do this in front of everyone just after they got here?' He glares at me in response. *So much for backtracking and getting him back on my side. What the hell is wrong with me tonight?* He's probably trying to be firm with them from the get-go, so our lives won't be as disrupted, but honestly, I think he is coming off as an inhospitable jerk.

"Brenda? Tim?" Erik says. "We're going to have a crew meeting. We'd like you to listen in." Erik lifts the kettle and then sets it down, apparently disappointed that it is empty. He moves over to the sink and surveys the faucet. "No instant boiling water here? Interesting." Tim rolls his eyes in response, and I know right then that he and Erik will probably not become friends. The rest of the crew files into the kitchen. I note that a package of Oreos from the pantry has made its way onto the kitchen table; the crew members each grab a handful.

"Gee, make yourself at home," Tim mutters, watching them walk in and start rifling through the cabinets for a glass or a mug. I shoot him a quick death glare.

He really needs to chill out. *Of course* they're going to make themselves at home. This *is* their home until the new album is done. Once the crew is done getting a snack and a drink, they sit on every available surface. One of them sits on the stove.

"Hey," Tim calls out. "We prepare our food there. Will you please get your ass off my stove?" Now he's just looking for things to be pissed off about. *He needs to stop.*

"Tim!" I exclaim. He raises his eyebrows at me and challenges me to speak. I shrug in response. The crew member slides off the stove and then looks around for somewhere else to sit. He shrugs and, not looking at Tim, perches himself back onto the stove again.

"Shall we begin then?" Erik asks. "We've a lot to get through, and I know you're all tired from such a long trip." He points to the whiteboard. "The day's schedule will be posted here each morning. First, let's talk about the shower schedule." Before the meeting started, he wrote a list of names and times on the board. We have a bathroom in the hallway upstairs, as well as the one in our master bedroom. I see that our master bathroom is included as an available shower for the band. I was kind of hoping to keep them out of our bedroom; I can't imagine Tim will want the band traipsing through our bedroom at all hours. I also notice that my name is listed at ten o'clock on the shower schedule.

"Erik?" I interject sheepishly. "I'm sorry, but a ten o'clock shower time won't work for me. See, I have to be at work at eight. I need the six o'clock time."

"Well, that won't work. Ben is done with sunrise yoga then and needs to shower straight after to cleanse his vocal chords."

"Look," Tim interjects, "we agreed to let you stay here on the condition that you wouldn't disrupt our lives. A ten o'clock shower time is not practical for Brenda." The rest of the crew shifts uncomfortably. Getting off on the wrong foot has now progressed to the wrong feet.

"Tim, Ben does yoga at sunrise," Erik says.

"I don't care," Tim says, standing taller. "Why not do a sunset yoga session?"

"Erik, it's okay…" Ben says.

"No, it's not bloody okay," Erik says, glowering. "Your work is the most important thing."

"I can live with yoga at another time. Brenda and Tim need to get to their jobs."

Erik grumbles in response. I can hear him mutter, "What do I know? I've only been the band manager for thirty years." Keith fidgets with his mug, while Ben smiles at me sympathetically. Erik's muttering rant continues, something about putting the whole record in jeopardy. Even I think Erik's putting way too much stock in this yoga at sunrise thing.

He turns to the whiteboard, erases a few names on the shower schedule, and re-writes my name by the 6:00 time slot. He turns to face me as if to say, "Satisfied?" but I can tell by his sneer that he's not really concerned about my satisfaction. There are still crew members listed as showering in our bedroom, but I think we need to pick our battles. Then he moves on to assign a list of tasks to the half dozen crew members lined up against the counter. They scribble on their note pads. I look around the kitchen and see that the counter is littered with teabag wrappers and spilt milk, and the sugar bowl is tipped over. I stand in front of the mess so Tim won't see it, figuring there's no sense in making him even madder. Erik dismisses the staff, and they all move to the back door.

"Before you all go to bed, I'd just like to say one thing," Keith says. "Brenda and Tim were nice enough to take us in. Let's be sure to treat their home with respect, okay?"

Wow, that was pretty cool of him. I look around the room to see who is listening. Erik is lost inside his iPhone; everyone else is fidgeting by the door waiting for their chance to go to bed. I hear a few of them mumble "*um-hm.*" So, maybe we did get off to a rough start, but I'm thinking now that we'll be fine.

"And one more thing before you guys go to bed," Tim says, stepping to the center of the kitchen. The crew turns to face him. Tim retrieves his power screwdriver from the tray at the bottom of the whiteboard. "I use these tools to make a living. They are off limits to all of you. Do not," he says, gesturing with the screwdriver toward Erik, "help yourself to my tools ever again. Got it?" Erik snorts in response but says nothing. The crew shifts uncomfortably until they make their way out the back door.

The band members gather in the living room to discuss the recording schedule. I stand in the doorway and marvel at the fact that Keith Kutter, Ben Taylor, Jeff Gilchrist, and Gill Simms are all seated around my coffee table, sipping tea from my mugs. When I was seventeen, I never would have imagined it.

Wait—*the kitchen!* I bolt back in to tidy the mess from the crew's tea service before Tim can see it, but before I can finish, I hear Tim walking back inside from the garage, mocking Erik's posh Australian accent.

"Ben does yoga at sunrise. He has to cleanse his vocal cords." I chuckle under my breath. "Bren, it's not funny. Who do these guys think they are?"

"They're paying us to stay here. It's good money. Just let it go." I join him by the whiteboard and hug him. "Are you going to be okay?"

"And you're going to clean up their mess, too?" he asks, eying the mess on the counter. "I'm not okay with that."

"Just for tonight," I say. I reach up to smooth the tension on his temple, but he flinches and moves away from me. "Angela the housekeeper will be here tomorrow. Will you please just chill out? You're making everyone uncomfortable.

Beside the Music

This could be a lot of fun if you let it."

"I'm going to bed," he replies. "Are you coming?"

"In a bit." My eyes wander to the band sitting in the living room. I can't believe they are all in my house.

Tim follows my gaze. "Whatever, Bren. I'll be upstairs."

After cleaning up, I return to my post in the doorway to the living room. Keith is handing out printouts of the new lyrics he had written. Ben reads a few lines out loud and then says, "I can't wait to hear what this melody is like. I almost don't want to read anymore because I don't want to contaminate my brain."

I have never heard that expression before, "contaminate my brain." I think about how I can add that phrase to my day to day life. I imagine refusing to see a movie preview because I don't want to "contaminate my brain." Of course, Tim would agree with me and refuse to contaminate his own. I smile. Already life with rock stars has injected our lives with a bit more culture. I watch the band interact for a few more minutes, dying for them to notice me hovering in the doorway and to ask my opinion about the lyrics. From behind me, Toni clears her throat.

"Will you please walk me through the house so I can pick out bedrooms for Keith, Ben, Jeff, and Gill?" I nod and gesture toward the stairs, grudgingly leaving the doorway. When I pass through the kitchen, I see that Tim hasn't gone up to bed yet, and I smile meekly at him. He puffs his cheeks and exhales before going back into the garage, where he's probably locking up his tools.

"This is our bedroom," I say, pointing to the room on the left at the top of the stairs. We walk down the hall. "There's the guest bedroom with a queen sized bed, and there's another one with a double bed. Then my office, which has a daybed in it." She follows me into the office. "There's a pull-out bed under here, too." I lift the bedspread and gesture to the twin bed on wheels tucked under the daybed. "Just roll it out, squeeze the handle, and it pops up."

"Okay, Ben will take the daybed," Toni says, thinking aloud. "Keith can take the double. Jeff and Gill will take the other room."

"Toni, there's only one bed in the other room. What if Jeff and Gill took the daybed and the pullout…"

"It's alright." Toni shifts her eyes back and forth. "I'm sure they share a bed in their flat." She smiles with a hint of mischief.

"You mean… they're gay?" I gasp. *All those songs about boozing and chasing women, and fifty percent of the band is gay?* But then the lead singer from Judas Priest came out, and he had all those songs like "Turbo Lover" that made it sound like he was chasing women. *You never do know, do you?*

"They're not out to the media, just among the crew. So, if you wouldn't mind keeping it to yourself…" She pauses. "Well, I am off to my tent. The housekeeper will be in at five to cook for the day and tidy up," she reminds me. "I'll let her in

85

for the mornings." We say our goodnights.

When I get to our bedroom, Tim is lying down, furiously clicking the TV remote. The channels on the TV flip by in a way that I can't even tell what's on. "Can you believe the nerve of that asshole? 'Ben has to do yoga at sunrise,'" he says, mocking Erik in a high voice.

"I'm sorry." I sit on the bed beside him. "I know this is going to be very hard for you."

"Bren, seriously, what have we gotten ourselves into? Never in a million years would I go into someone else's house and hang up that tacky thing on the kitchen wall."

"Who knows," I quip, "maybe we'll start to like that it's there. You're always saying that I forget things too much. Maybe we can keep it there, and you can write stuff down for me so I won't forget." He responds with a snort, so I try another tack: "Jeff and Gill are gay," I blurt out, and giggle. I've learned over the years that rapidly changing the subject like that often disarms Tim.

"Gee, Captain Obvious, thanks for letting me know," he says.

"How did you know?"

"Gaydar." He points to his temple.

"Whatever." I roll my eyes. "Good night, Tim."

I switch off the light, but the room is far from dark. We never close the shades on the windows that face the back of our house, because there is only forest behind us. Nobody will catch us changing from back there, and we like having the natural light wake us up in the morning, in addition to Tim's two alarm clocks. There's a glow coming from the back yard. I look at Tim and notice that he hasn't closed his eyes; he sees it too.

"*Now* what are they doing?" he sighs.

I get out of bed, go to the window, and see what I know is sure to piss Tim off. How can I possibly explain what I'm seeing? "Bonfire." I point out the window. "In the lawn."

"What the hell are they going to do, sacrifice a goat?" Tim gets out of bed and storms to the window.

"I don't think animal sacrifices were their thing in the '80s," I say with a laugh "That was more of an Ozzy thing."

"This isn't funny, Brenda."

"Oh, come on. It is a little." I watch the crew laughing and dancing around. "It does look like fun." I turn from the window to face Tim. "Let's go out there."

"I don't think so," he grumbles and gets back into bed. "It's late, and we have work in the morning."

"Come on, Tim. When will we ever have the chance to dance around a bonfire with Hydra ever again? Don't you think this is just a little bit cool?"

"If you want to go, don't let me stop you."

Beside the Music

I pull on a hoodie over my pajamas. "Oh well, when in Rome." I smile at Tim then pause at the doorway for a moment before leaving, hoping that he'll get up and join me. His response is to roll over, away from the glow of the fire.

Once outside, I feel the cool dewy grass on my bare feet as I make my way to Tent City. I stand in front of the fire and feel its heat against my face. Keith is there; he nods at me and hands me a cold beer. He clinks his bottle neck against mine, and we both take a deep swallow. Jeff and Gill are spinning each other around on the other side of the fire, laughing.

"Gentlemen," Erik calls out, standing up and walking to a spot in front of the fire. He raises his beer in a toast: "Let's make this one the best yet." All the band members and crew cheer and raise their beers.

Spending time by Hydra's bonfire is probably the most fun I've had in a while. They all obviously know each other well; they've been together for decades. I can't imagine having this kind of bonfire with the people I work with. We'd all stand around awkwardly, and then end up talking about work, and the whole thing would end before nine PM. The band and crew reminisce about past tours and don't seem to get tired of the stories.

"Biloxi," Ben says and smiles.

"Oh, come on," Jeff shoots back. "I want to forget that one. That holding cell was disgusting. Talk about a traumatic night."

"You got arrested in Biloxi?" I ask, leaning in. "What the heck happened?"

"There was a sign on a restaurant. Gill is a sucker for shitty old signs. Our house is completely littered with them. Anyway, there was one for Gill's Crab Shack. He wanted to hang it over our bed."

"It would have been funny to hang it there," Gill protests. I have to agree.

"So, I decide to surprise the love of my life with his sign," Jeff continues. "I got half of it down, when I hear someone cocking a rifle behind me."

"*Schook-CHOOK!*" The entire crew makes the sound effect of the cocking gun, in unison.

I start to crack up. "What did you do?"

"I start running. I've got the G in my hands, the wires are tripping me, and I am just running. I don't even know where, I am so drunk. I end up in a swamp just down the road, and my feet are sticking in the mud. It was there that the cops got me."

"I couldn't get the drunk bastard out until the next morning," Erik says, laughing. "That cost me, keeping it out of the press. They're not out to the press yet, and we didn't want to take the chance at the time."

"What about now?" I ask. "Surely being gay isn't as much of an issue anymore."

"We just don't want to go there yet," Gill replies. "Maybe after the next tour."

The stories and the beer flow into the wee hours of the morning. I am a bit drunk from the four or so I drink. The fire reduces itself down to a few glowing embers, and one by one the crew make their way to their tents. The last two people left are me and Keith. We don't say much: he pokes at the embers with a stick, and I peel a label off of my last beer and toss the scraps of paper into the fire.

"What a night," I say and stretch my arms over my head. "You have a lot of history with these people." I gesture to the tents.

"I do," he says, looking up from the fire. He looks at me, but I don't think he's really registering that I am talking to him.

"You seem very pensive." I gesture to his head. "Are you cooking up new lyrics in there?"

He smiles tentatively and pokes at the embers again.

"I'd love to read some when you're done."

He doesn't look up. *Is this how it's going to be with Keith now? No more laughing with him over dinner, I guess, eh?*

I don't know what to say next, and the silence gets to be too much. My eyelids get heavy. I say goodnight and stumble across the lawn and up the stairs. From my bedroom window, I can still see Keith staring pensively into the fire. He looks up and spots me standing in the window, then quickly turns his attention back to the fire. Tim is snoring. When I settle into bed, he mumbles but doesn't wake. Vito curls up behind my knees, and we both slip into sleep. I am thankful that the room isn't spinning when I lie down. And I hope for a minimal hangover in the morning.

Chapter 13

FOR HALF THE DAY, my head pounds from the hangover. How is it that, in college, I managed to drink entire cases of beer by myself, but last night I had four and am largely incapacitated the next day?

I stumble through my day, trying to finish tasks, but I'm definitely not as productive as I normally am.

"You okay?" Amanda asks when I go into her office to update her on the Factory Tour show promos. "You seem off today." We are playing up the "Made in Rhode Island" angle on Baxter's packaging. I had a bright red icon of a Rhode Island Red rooster made by our graphic designer with the words "Made in Rhode Island" forming a circle around it. I am so proud of it: it looks awesome, and it's going on all the promotional materials as well.

"Just a really bad headache," I say, holding my hand to my head. "Excedrin won't even touch it." The last thing I want to do right now is talk about Baxter. Really, I just feel like ripping my brain out of my head and letting it dry out in the sun.

"The rooster is adorable," she says. "I love that it's so recognizable. I think we could get other companies to pick this up, as well. What else do you have for me?"

I rifle through my papers, pretending to look for something. *What does she mean, "what else"? This is all I have.*

"Nothing else?" She looks disappointed. "What about the revisions on the press releases?" Apparently an impenetrable headache is no excuse.

"I, *um*, started looking them over. I'll have them finished tomorrow." She gives me a look that says she'd expected them today. I hold my hand to my head as if to say "See? Headache."

"First thing in the morning, okay?" she asks.

I nod and walk out of her office. It's almost five, and all day long I've been daydreaming about walking in and finding the band congregated around the kitchen table working on a song. *Is that what composing a new album is really like?* Did they spend the day in my living room, lounging on Portia's chaises, exchanging ideas? I picture one of them playing a riff on a guitar, and another leaping up and saying, "That's it!" Then the rest of them sit bolt upright and play along. Once they've put the song together, they will inevitably call me in to be the first one to hear it. I will offer my opinion, which will ultimately decide if it would go on the new album.

I drive home in silence, lost in thought. When I pull into the driveway, I press the button on the garage door opener—and stop my car just short of running into a drum set. "No problem," I say to myself. "It has to go somewhere, right? Better here than in the living room, anyway."

I back out and park at the end of the driveway, so I won't be blocked in tomorrow morning. These are the sacrifices one has to make when hosting a rock band. The band's minivans aren't in the driveway; they are probably all at Del's. *No crashing a songwriting session today, I guess. Maybe tomorrow.* Until then, it might be nice to have the house to myself. I just got a new book from the library the other day; maybe I can sit out on the deck, crack into it, and enjoy the quiet before they all get home. After all, there are probably no chores to do, thanks to Angela the housekeeper—who arrived to make breakfast at *five* this morning. I imagine the house will be spotless and smell like lemons when I walk in.

Instead, I find the exact opposite. They must have had one hell of a party. Empty beer bottles cover every available surface; a half-eaten pizza is on the counter, the cold pepperoni grease staining the cheese into an unappetizing grayish color. Vito is dozing on the floor next to an empty pizza box. I have no idea how much he ate, but judging from how distended his stomach is, I'm guessing it was a lot. I feel his stomach, and he groans uncomfortably. I know that he'll probably throw up in the middle of the night, so I check under the sink to make sure we have carpet cleaner, just in case. He has no control when it comes to the smell of pizza. Not many of us do, right?

"Wanna go out, Vito?" I ask. He barely thumps his tail against the floor once and groans.

As I try coaxing my dog to go with me to the front door, I hear a dripping noise coming from the hallway off the kitchen. I step over Vito and pick up the pizza box, toss it onto the counter, and sidestep a pile of greasy paper towels that are strewn on the floor. When I throw open the door to the half bath, I see the toilet is clogged and overflowing, and there is an inch of water on the floor. The rug in front of the sink is soaked through. I pick it up and carry it down the hall to toss into the washing machine.

I steel myself as I tiptoe my way through the puddle of water, reach behind the toilet, and turn off the valve. I jump back to dry ground just outside the bathroom door then kick off my shoes and wipe them clean with a paper towel in the kitchen. I wonder whether I should throw them out and decide instead to take them outside and hose them down. From the upstairs hall closet, I grab a few beach towels and spread them on the floor, watching them become instantly waterlogged. In the kitchen, I take the phone from the counter and punch in Toni's cell number. While I wait for her to pick up, I shove the already sopping-wet towels across the floor with the tip of my toes and try to absorb as much as I can.

"Brenda, before you say anything—" Toni answers.

"*What do you mean*? You intentionally left my house this way? Toni, I have an inch of water on the bathroom floor."

"Angela is on her way, as is a plumber."

"Toni, give me one good reason why a group of grown men should have left my home in this condition."

"I am so sorry, Brenda. See, the boys were celebrating the first day of recording. It won't happen again."

"Are they going to celebrate like this every day? Didn't they celebrate enough last night?" *Gee, what happened to being respectful guests in our home*? That notion barely lasted twelve hours.

We hang up. I glance out the bathroom window and, for the first time, see the big burn mark in the grass in the daylight. I'm sure Tim already checked it out from our bedroom window this morning; I'm also sure he isn't happy about it. Then I wonder what the celebration will look like once they've *finished* recording, if this is what they do when they've just started. Will our homeowner's insurance policy even cover "act of rock star?"

I grab a few more towels and continue sopping up the puddle. A few moments later, Angela arrives at the back door, and soon after that, the plumber comes in the front. I glance at my watch and realize Tim will be home in about fifteen minutes. I start to panic. He is going to be *very* pissed off about this. I call him on his cell to try and head him off at the pass and turn on the charm.

"What do you say to dinner and a movie tonight?" I ask.

"*Hmm*... I was planning on a quiet night at home," he says, yawning. "I'm really tired."

"Quiet? With rock stars in the house? I think you'll have better luck with a quiet night out."

"Well, I *have* been wanting to see the new *Star Trek* movie."

"Okay, then, let's go."

"Bren, you hate *Star Trek*. Is something wrong?"

"No," I reply too quickly, still mopping up the bathroom floor, now with paper towels as the beach towels are over-saturated. I put them in the sink, figuring the water will at least run down the drain until we can get them into the washer. "I just figured you'd want to get away from the rock-star invasion and thought I'd take you out."

"That's nice of you," he says with a sigh. I can tell he is smiling, and that

91

makes me smile into the mirror. We agree to grab a burrito from Cilantros and then head to the theater. By the time I get off the phone, Angela has already cleaned half the kitchen in a blur of efficiency.

"I have to go keep Tim occupied," I say to her, "while you and the plumber sort this mess out. Not a word about this to Tim, okay?"

"No problem," she says. "I take it Tim won't be impressed with your house getting the rock-star treatment, *eh*?"

"*Um...* no." I ask her to wash the clump of towels in the bathroom sink. I really don't want to leave any evidence of Hydra's crimes. Then I wash my hands in the kitchen sink, generously lathering them with antibacterial soap. I suppose it could be worse. What if they had decided to throw the TV out the window or skid a motorcycle on the hardwood floors? "Will you also let Toni know that we went out and that I need everything to look normal by the time we get back?"

"Mrs. Dunkirk?" the plumber calls out from the bathroom. "Do you know what's stuck down here?" I walk down the hallway and stand at the bathroom doorway. Mr. Plumber is peering down into the toilet, apparently unsure of whether he wants to put his hand in there. *Well, I wouldn't want to put my hand in there, either.*

"I have no idea," I reply.

"I was a janitor at one of the clubs in Providence," he says, shoving a plunger up and down in the toilet and then peering inside. "I used to find used needles jammed up in the toilet. I just want to know what I'm getting into here. You've got some musicians here, right?"

"Yeah, we do," I say, sighing. "But I don't think they're into needles." I hope my tone is enough to reassure him, as he continues to peer suspiciously into the toilet.

I remember reading in Keith's book that they got into cocaine back in the '80s. Every rock band was into cocaine in the '80s, though. I wonder if they still are. I honestly hadn't thought to ask that when we made the arrangements. Everyone was more concerned about making the house suitable and making sure I wouldn't tell anyone that they were staying here.

I glance at my watch. "Oh shit, Tim's waiting. I've got to go. Good luck." I nod toward the toilet. The plumber is still jamming the plunger up and down. I don't even want to know what's in there.

I sit through *Star Trek* with Tim, but all I can think about is whether Angela and the plumber have managed to get the house cleaned up. I hope Tim hasn't noticed me constantly looking at my watch, but if he has, he probably thinks it's because I'm bored to pieces with the movie. I try to call Toni from the ladies' room, but it goes straight to voice mail. I am getting irritated. *How can she turn her phone off, when she knows that I am out keeping Tim distracted while my house gets put back together?* I pace in the ladies' room for a few minutes until I figure that, if I stay any longer, Tim will wonder where I am.

By the time we get home, Hydra is behaving in a civilized manner. They are clearing the plates from dinner, and all traces of the day's earlier festivities are gone. I breathe a sigh of relief. Tim looks at me with a puzzled expression. I shrug, and grab some lemonade from the fridge. I must ask Angela how she makes it. I doubt this is Country Time powder in here.

"Brenda," Toni says, coming into the kitchen. "I just wanted to apologize to you about today."

"What happened today?" Tim asks.

"Oh, nothing," I reply, forcing Toni to listen and, hopefully, not say anything. I'm sure she must realize that Tim can't know about this, but I can't be too careful. "They just forgot to tell me that Jeff's drum set was in the garage," I say. "I almost ran into it when I got home, and I got a little mad over it." Tim looks at me as if to say "you're lying," but doesn't say anything out loud.

Vito whines at the back door. Hopefully Angela or one of the crew members let him out while we were gone. I am sure he is still uncomfortable after eating all that pizza. Tim calls him to the front door; we decided to let him out the front for the time being, seeing as the crew wouldn't want Vito doing his business in their camp. I watch out the window while he paces uncomfortably on the front lawn, something he usually does when he needs to throw up. I hear Tim open the door and ask Vito if he's okay before stepping outside himself and closing the door.

I follow Toni into the living room; she sits beside Erik on the couch and opens her laptop. I stand.

"Brenda, how was your day?" Erik purrs.

I have a feeling he knows exactly how my day was, so I take the bait. "My day at work was fine. Coming home was another story." I pause. "The way you guys left my house was unacceptable."

"I understand," Erik replies as he scrolls through his iPhone. *I don't think he really understands or cares, but what can I say?* I turn on my heel, leave Erik and Toni in the living room, and head up to bed.

And with that, everything is fine for about a week or two. Tim and I settle in to having rock stars in the house. Tim grows less irritated with them. Basically, Tim and the band have an unspoken agreement that they will just avoid each other. That definitely makes my life more comfortable, as well. I have fun getting to know the band members and the crew.

We start to fall into a groove, where Tim and I eat with them every night; I think Tim might be enjoying himself just a little bit, too. I don't think he'll ever admit to it, and I don't want to press the issue. The friendly banter around the dinner table is contagious, and I can see why they insist on staying in a house together while recording. It must help them work together better, if they're having

93

fun together, too.

Then, two weeks into it, the band randomly breaks the peace treaty.

It's late, and Tim and I are in bed. I wake from a sound sleep to a loud crash downstairs. Vito stands at attention at the foot of the bed with his hackles raised, growling softly and cocking his ear. *How would he respond to an actual intruder in the house?* Beagles aren't often used for home security; Vito would probably try to distract a burglar with his demands for a belly rub until the police arrive.

Tim sits upright in bed. "What the hell was that?"

"I think it was rock stars," I say with a yawn. I look at the alarm clock. It's 2:30 in the morning.

"Well, they belong to you. Tell them to shut the fuck up." He rolls over and jams a pillow over his head. He's right. There is no hope of playing rock-paper-scissors to try and get out of it.

I sigh and put my robe on. When I get downstairs, I see that every light is on, and the silver candlesticks from the dining room table are missing. In the kitchen, I find Ben holding a drunken Keith upright. Ben is trying to reason with him, but Keith isn't having any of it. Keith is trying to light a joint off of one of the lit candles; Ben's trying to tell him that he's already had enough.

"Brenda!" Keith raises an empty beer bottle, and the joint falls from his lips onto the floor. "Fancy a smoke?" Ben wrenches the bottle out of Keith's hand and sets it on the counter. Then he picks up the joint and jams it into his pocket before Keith notices. Keith stumbles toward me and slips his arm around my waist.

I shove Keith off of me. "Ben, get that out of my house. Tim's going to have a cow if he knows you brought that in here."

"What do you expect?" Keith slurs. "We're rock stars, not altar boys."

Just as Keith finishes his sentence, I hear giggling coming from the living room. I face Ben but don't ask out loud. Instead, I follow the sound, while Ben tries to stop me.

"Brenda, don't go in there... *nooooo!*" He tries to grab my arm, but I slip out of his grip. He loses his hold on Keith, too, and has to lunge toward him to keep him from falling down. I storm into the living room—and see half-dressed women draped over my furniture. Two of them are older women with their cleavages shoved up in an effort to look younger. The third looks like she's barely old enough to drive. She has caked her eyes in smoky makeup, but she's so young, she looks as if she was playing dress-up in her mother's makeup before going out.

"Who are you?" I ask. *Might as well get to the point, right?*

"Hi, honey," one of the older women says. Her eyelashes look like tarantula legs under all that mascara. Her cleavage tumbles out of her skintight corset, and I can see the edge of her nipple. "Love your robe. It's very Heff." She looks me up and down. I know exactly what these women are doing here, and I am not happy about it. By the way she's checking me out, she's probably calculating how much more money she would make if I were thrown into the mix.

I look down and wonder what it is about my fuzzy magenta robe that is so "Heff." "Ben?" I ask. "What's going on in here?" Let's see what he has to say for himself.

"They're here to help us shelebrate," Keith slurs.

I turn to Keith and Ben, suddenly furious. "Are you serious? You brought hookers to my house? Come on, guys, really?" It's almost comical that they are living up to the rock star stereotype. Maybe someday I'll look back on this and laugh. Someday. Not today, though.

"Hey, we're not hookers," the other older woman pipes up. "We're escorts." She sits up straight and crosses her legs at the ankles. The way she sits reminds me of the time I went to an afternoon tea with Tim's mom. All of the women sat perched on the edge of their seats with their legs crossed at the ankle. They held their fine china teacups delicately with manicured hands and nibbled on their pastries without messing up their lipstick. I notice that this hooker was at least kind enough to set her beer on a coaster, rather than directly onto my table, and I wonder briefly about her upbringing. "We're just here to have a little fun," she says.

"Oh, Sandy, can it," the first hooker says. "Quit trying to be something you're not. The fact is we get paid to do certain things. Get over it."

Sandy sips her beer while the young hooker sitting on the other end of the couch squirms in her seat. She looks familiar, but I can't place where I've seen her. Our eyes meet for a moment until hers dart away. She turns her attention to the black-and-white photo of Vito on the wall by the couch. *Okay*, I think, *time for these bitches to go.*

"Well, I'd like it if you left," I say, opening the door. "Drive safely." I gesture outside.

The women stand up and head for the door. Surely they've seen this exact scene play out dozens of times before in their line of work.

"Bye, Keithy!" they call. "Bye Benny!"

I hold my hand up to quiet them, hoping they don't get any louder and wake Tim. The young one still hasn't said anything. She slouches behind the other girls and tugs at her skirt, pulling it down from where she'd presumably hiked it up earlier in the evening. I look closer at her face, but she is still avoiding eye contact with me, pulling her low-cut V-neck top closed to cover her meager cleavage. I know I've seen her before; it's starting to bother me.

I start to say something, but Keith lurches into action and lunges for her. "You can shtay" he slurs. "I like you."

"Keith, stop." I pull him away from her and motion for her to leave. I can't help but wonder if there's been anyone since Tamsen. Probably hookers and

95

strippers, judging by tonight. He's a good-looking guy and still semi-famous. *Why would he have to hire someone?* He's probably just going for the easy target; he doesn't want to take the time to get to know a woman before getting her into bed. A brief flicker of gratitude crosses the girl's face.

"I know you from somewhere," I say to her.

"I hear that a lot," she says, so cool she seems unfazed. She steps out the door and glances at me for a second before joining the other women already making their way to the car. I memorize the license plate and watch them drive away, but it probably won't matter: Sandy's driving. I am still trying to place the girl's face when Ben speaks up. I kind of wish I had Google in my brain, so I could look her up.

"Sorry, Brenda," Ben says. He slips between me and Keith. "Okay, you drunk bastard," he says to Keith. "Off to bed."

"If you breathe a word of this to Tim…" I hiss.

"Don't worry, Brenda," Ben says. "I don't want to piss him off, either."

I go back up the stairs and slip back into bed next to Tim. He moans softly, still half asleep. "What was that?"

"Nothing, honey. Go back to sleep." I figure the less Tim knows about hookers and weed in his home, the better off he'll be. I'm sure Aria will freak out if she learns that hookers were in our house, let alone rock stars and pot. I am not exactly thrilled about it, either, but I think this will be one of those things that I'll tell Tim about later. *Way* later.

Chapter 14

IN THE MORNING, I walk into the kitchen, surprisingly ahead of schedule seeing as how I was awake in the middle of the night. I pour myself a glass of fresh-squeezed orange juice, courtesy of Angela. Ben and Erik are at the kitchen table, poring over scattered papers, deep in discussion.

"I'm telling you," Erik is saying, "these lyrics are just too damn dark." I pause, mid-sip, and listen.

"But they go well with the feeling of the song," Ben replies.

"That's nice. But people don't give a damn about the *feeling* of the song. We all know it's the *lyrics* that sell the song."

"Brenda," Ben turns to me, "I need a second opinion. Will you please read these lyrics and tell us what you think? Erik thinks Keith's gotten dark in his old age."

Here is the moment I've been waiting for since they moved in! But the timing is a bit weird. I planned on giving them hell this morning before Tim got out of the shower. Bringing hookers around was definitely not cool.

They stare at me expectantly. *What can I say?* I'm a sucker for rock stars making album-altering decisions around my kitchen table. I feel my heart beat faster as Ben hands me the printout. I wonder how seriously they will take my opinion. *Will my input determine whether the song makes it onto the album? Will they ask me about other songs too?* Would I be crazy to think that the entire future of the new album depends on this one moment, and my feedback could change everything?

> *Twisted metal*
> *Broken glass*
> *I stumble in a haze*
> *The smell of leaking gas*
>
> *You are broken*

I can't make you whole
You are broken
Trapped inside your soul

Erik and Ben look at me expectantly. I read the lines a few more times and try to formulate a response. "Yes, it is dark," I begin. Erik raises his eyebrows at Ben as if to say, "See?" "But I think that's just what you guys need right now." Then Ben returns the same look to Erik.

"What do you mean?" snaps Erik. He leans in aggressively, as though let down that I didn't side with him. Everyone is supposed to side with Erik in all matters pertaining to the band.

It actually feels a bit good to not side with him. He totally blew me off when I tried to express my irritation about the way the band left my house the first day they were here. He hasn't exactly been a gracious house guest since then, either, the way he leaves his trash around for Angela to clean up.

I feel my stomach lurch; the butterflies are waking up, and my hands shake with an adrenaline rush. This is a big deal, and I don't want to take it lightly— someday I'll hear this song on the radio, and I'll know that it was *this moment* that gave birth to it, that I helped make it happen. I have been daydreaming about this moment since Erik first asked if the band could stay in my house.

I clear my throat and take a sip of my juice, just to slow myself down and provide the singular response that will change the direction of this song. But I can tell that I am also building the suspense: Erik and Ben are leaning in, waiting for me to elaborate. I admit it feels nice to be the center of attention and have them on the edge of their seats, waiting for me to respond. My head starts to buzz a bit with the power. I cannot remember the last time I had two grown men hanging on my every word. In fact, I don't think that has *ever* happened. This is what they must feel on stage night after night, with a crowd of adoring faces waiting to find out what song they'll play next. I wish I could prolong this sensation just a bit longer: it feels too damn good.

"Well, everyone knows what Keith's been through." I pause; they lean in closer. "It's controversial, but it's a very real part of Keith's life. I mean, we all have this image of the glamorous life of a rock star. Keith's shown us the real him, and how he responded to a tragedy that really was his fault. And everyone out there who is calling him a drunk driver and drug-addicted loser is demanding an explanation."

"So?" Erik asks.

"Well, how does the story end, Erik? At what point do we get to see that the accident affected Keith?"

"That's really not so important. I want the song to sell."

"The world still thinks Keith is a jerk," I shoot back. "People don't want to buy music from people they don't like. That's why I wrote my fan letter in the first place. I read his book, and I am waiting to see if he's grown or changed. With this song, you can win over your listeners way faster than allowing him to brood about it forever." I hear a sound and turn just in time to see Keith duck out of the kitchen doorway. "Oh shit!" I turn back to Erik and Ben. "Do you think he heard me?"

Ben nods.

"Should I go talk to him?"

"No," Erik says. He clears his throat. "Better to let that one go." He points back to the printout. "So you think the lyrics should stay?"

"Yes, I do. It's obvious that Keith still needs to get this out. And believe me, the listening public is interested in the story. That alone will sell it."

"Well, I'm still not convinced this is the right way to go," Erik says, standing. "We need something people will want to sing along to, and not his belly-aching." He walks to the back door and calls out to Toni, then heads toward Tent City. Toni, who is standing a short distance away, wrapping up a phone call on Bluetooth, holds up a finger toward him, indicating, "just one moment." *Does she sleep with that thing on?*

Ben sips his tea. "He's wrong," he says.

"Agreed."

"He needs to think it was *his* idea to let the lyrics stay. You'll see—it'll get done." He pauses to take another sip of his tea. "Listen, Brenda, I'm really sorry about last night. Did we wake up Tim?"

I sip my juice and try to formulate a response. I don't want to say it was okay, because it wasn't. As exciting as it is to have rock stars living in my house, so far Tim has been right: it's a pain in the ass. But I am trying not to let the logistical annoyances get to me. I just gave them my opinion about Keith's lyrics and their salability, and it was unlike anything I've ever done before. It is incredibly validating to have Erik, who probably never cared about what anybody else thought, lean in and make eye contact with me, absorbing my viewpoint, even if he did say he wasn't convinced. It doesn't seem to me that he does that very often. I can't wait to hear the song on the radio; I am pretty sure I just rescued it from the cutting-room floor.

"I can explain, if you like." Ben's voice brings me back from daydreaming about riding in my car with the windows down, listening to that song. "About last night," he says. I nod, although I'm already pretty sure it was just a classic case of the rock-star sense of entitlement. They wanted to party with a bunch of hookers, and it could have gone way worse. They could have brought them upstairs, and Tim and I would have heard them from our bedroom. That would have ended badly.

"Yesterday was the anniversary of the day Tamsen threw Keith out," Ben says.

"So he hires hookers to get over it? Can you imagine if Tim had seen them here last night? He would have called the cops. That would have killed the election for him, Ben."

"He tends to spend that day fucked up," he continues, apparently not stopping to consider what I am saying. "At least we're all here to keep an eye on him. But he doesn't always think through what he's doing. I'm so sorry."

I still don't want to say it's okay, but I can feel it on the tip of my tongue. I need to be strong here, and not instantly feel sorry for Keith because this is the anniversary of one of his worst days. Tim always says I am sympathetic for the wrong reasons; here I go again. I should be mad at *them* for bringing those women into my house.

I check my watch and note that it's my designated shower time and leave the kitchen. Keith is sitting on the bottom stair, writing in his journal. I sit beside him. Under normal circumstances, I'd have every right to be pissed. I should be pissed. They brought hookers and weed into my house last night. That's just what Tim and I need: for the cops to show up and arrest a bunch of prostitutes on our front lawn. To have that kind of controversy show up at our door would make Tim a laughing stock on the local news, and his chances for state Senate would be thrown out the window. But these aren't normal circumstances, and now that I know the whole story, I can't be completely pissed off, can I? Even though it's been awhile, and even though he wrote the book about his experiences, he is still hurting. *What can I do in this situation? Kick him while he's down?*

"Keith, Ben told me about the anniversary. I'm sorry."

He looks up from his journal and meets my gaze. "Thank you for saying so," he whispers. Tears fill my eyes. "It never makes sense. You know, thanking people when they say they're sorry."

"I know," I say. "I thought the same thing when I lost my mom to cancer ten years ago."

"I had no idea. I am so sorry, Brenda." He pauses. "I couldn't imagine life without my mum. I talk to her at least twice a week. She's the only one who didn't give me any shit after everything happened with Tamsen and Damien."

"At least you had someone in your corner," I say with a shrug. "I'm sure it was a chaotic time for you."

"It was. I am so appreciative of her." He pauses. "Were you close with your mum?"

"I was twenty-five when she died, and she didn't get to see me and Tim get married. I feel like I missed out on the adult relationship I could have had with her. Like, I was still in the 'just moved out of home and don't bug me' phase of my live. I wish I could have talked to her one more time, you know?"

Beside the Music

"I wonder if I'll ever have that kind of relationship with Damien." He stares out the window.

Most normal people would still be pretty mad at Keith. And I know I should be. He brought drugs and prostitutes into my home. That is definitely overstepping the line between polite houseguest and raging asshole. But he is being so human with me right now. I wish I could record this moment and show it to the world. This is what they all need to see; not the spoiled rock star who expects to have everything handed to him. I know that, if given the chance, I can be the one to help him look like a decent human being. I can be the one to help him get back into the good graces of his fans. It's not about publicity; it's so much more. Sure, I can change the public's perception of him, but what I really want to do is to change his attitude and change his life for the better.

I reach out and squeeze his arm. *Time for a bit of honesty to get him started on his new path.* "I'm not sure that acting in the way you have been for the last few days will answer those questions for you, Keith. At least Damien is still alive. You have the chance to make a relationship with Damien happen. But it's not going to happen like this. You need to make the effort here."

Without saying a word, Keith stands up and walks into the kitchen. I go after him.

"I'm sorry, Keith. Clearly, I overstepped." If I want him to listen to me, I need to not crush him like that.

He's by the back door, putting his shoes on. He stands and points an accusing finger at me. "You have no idea what I've been through," he hisses. "Just because you read my book doesn't mean you know me." Then he walks out the door, slamming it behind him.

Wow. That was a bit intense. Kind of rude, actually. I open the door again and step out onto the deck. I spot him walking toward the woods. "Yeah, Keith," I yell after him. "Maybe I *don't* know you. And that's the problem. *You won't let anyone know you.*" The crew looks up from Tent City. I am sure I look crazy, standing out here on the deck in my bathrobe, shouting across the lawn at Keith. Toni even pulls her Bluetooth out of her ear and throws me a puzzled look.

Okay, enough drama for one day. It's time to get to work; I go back inside. As I walk up the stairs, it crosses my mind that Keith didn't apologize to me for last night. I wonder how much of it he actually remembers. I wonder if he actually cares. His reaction is disappointing. I thought I could actually get through to him, but he just walked away. Maybe he's not ready for my brand of honesty. Operation Fix Keith is going to be harder than I thought, but I will not give up on him.

After I get dressed, I head back to the kitchen and find that Ben has made an egg on toast for me. "Eat up, Brenda!" he says. "Breakfast is the most important meal of the day!" He laughs.

"Thanks," I say, biting into it. "*Mmmm...* this is good. I should have sent you a fan letter, instead."

"So, have you had a good talk with Keith, then?" he asks. I am about to answer that I didn't really feel that it was a good talk at all and don't feel that he was at all sorry for last night—but then Erik walks in and grabs a banana from the rack on the counter. I clam up. I just don't feel right talking about Keith in front of Erik.

"Ben, have you done your yoga? We need those vocal chords fresh," Erik warns.

"Yes, I have."

"What are you going to sing today?" I ask. "That song we were talking about earlier?"

"Yes," Erik says, gazing out the kitchen window. "Keith's only finished writing a few of the songs, and now you've sent him on walk about." *Seriously? He's blaming* me *for Keith's little temper tantrum this morning? Wow, talk about enabling behavior.*

"Bren, you're going to be late," Tim warns, coming into the kitchen, saving me.

"Okay," I say, leaning in to give him a kiss. "Bye-bye, love. See you tonight." I turn to Ben. "Good luck today. I hope it goes well."

I am halfway to work when I realize that Ben and Keith have worked their magic on me. I never did get a chance to express my irritation over last night. Maybe I'm too easily seduced by being a rock-and-roll muse.

Chapter 15

"OH, SHIT," I MUTTER TO MYSELF as I approach our house after work. "How the hell did this happen?" I press my hand to my forehead as I pull into our driveway. I know Tim will go berserk when he gets home.

My day was bad enough. Baxter hates the rooster. They want to use a clam for the Made in Rhode Island logo. An icky gray clam with googly eyes on it. Who the hell thinks of a clam when they think of Rhode Island? Everyone thinks of Rhode Island Reds. I have the market research to prove it. But no. The client wants a shitty-looking clam on their product packaging. Nobody is going to get it—from far away, it looks like a gray lump of shit. Amanda flipped out on *me* about it, as if I can control the client's opinion. Apparently it's my job to control Baxter's thoughts.

And now, chaos reigns at home. I managed to get rid of the hookers last night, but I have no idea how the hell I am going to make this go away. Surely the neighbors have noticed, and they're probably not going to be happy about it, either. Hopefully they won't call the cops. *God, what if the press catches wind of this?*

As I pull down the driveway, a crowd of people gathers around my car. I have to stop, just to avoid running anyone over. There has to be at least twenty to thirty people clustered on my front yard. They slap their open palms on the driver's side window, trying to get my attention. I can feel them jostle the car, and I am afraid they're going to break through the glass. *How the hell did Hydra get through the '80s?* I am sure this sort of thing happened all the time back then, and there were way more than twenty or thirty people. They must have had one hell of a security detail, not to mention car windows made of shatter-proof glass.

"It's Brenda Dunkirk!" one female member of the crowd calls out. "She's an old friend of Keith's!" She holds up a picture that was taken at the Stone Yacht Club. It's not a flattering picture: my ass is sticking out because, apparently, I was halfway to standing at the time the paparazzi stormed the restaurant. Not my best side.

She called me "an old friend of Keith's?" *Really?* Then I suddenly realize: I don't really have time to reflect on the ridiculous notion that Keith and I are old friends. The group of people swarms along the driver's side. It's absolutely terrifying. *Are they going to climb on top of my car? Are they going to lift it from one side and tip it over?* I honk the horn and gesture for them to get out of the way so I can pull my car all the way in. Thankfully, they part, and I am able to drive up to the house.

"Hi, Brenda!" A woman approaches me as I'm getting out of the car. I am starting to get sick of people knowing my name without my having introduced myself. It's awkward. "Are they inside? Can I come in and meet them?"

"I don't think so." The crowd surrounds me, and my heart begins to race. I don't have the security of the car anymore. *This could get real bad real fast.* "I really think you should leave, before I call the police," I say, threatening. "This is private property."

"But I *have* to go inside with you," she insists. "Keith knows me."

I don't know what to say to this woman. Maybe Keith knows her, maybe he doesn't. It's not my place to be his bouncer. "Maybe you should call him then."

"We don't need a phone to communicate," she says. "We've transcended beyond the telephone." I consider asking, but I don't really want to know. She pulls out a copy of *Friendly Fire* on vinyl from her tote bag. "Do you know the song on side two? The one called 'Almost'? He wrote that one for me." I am pretty sure he wrote it for Tamsen. *But who am I to say?*

I turn toward the house, but she keeps walking with me and talking. I stop, because I don't want her to think that I am inviting her to follow me. My choices are to stand out here and talk to a complete psycho or have her follow me into the house. Either way, my options aren't so great.

"He talks to me through the lyrics. It's as clear as day. Look." She pulls the liner notes out of the album. "It's right there," she says, pointing. She puts her finger on the stanza about a white dress and daisies in her hair. I am pretty sure I remember seeing a photo of Keith and Tamsen on their wedding day; that's what she wore. "I wore that the first time I saw Hydra in concert. I was in the front row. It was before this album ever came out. He wrote it for me."

I swear, I've become a freak magnet. People often tell me their life story, uninvited. How do I get this woman to stop talking to me? I am getting kind of nervous: the more she talks, the more determined she gets. *What exactly will she do?* Break a window and crawl in through it so she can finally meet her soul mate? I want to tell her that I want to go inside, but she's still yammering away.

"But wait, there's more." She flips over the liner notes and points to another stanza. I need to shut her down. It's entirely possible that she's got Hydra's entire discography in that tote bag; this conversation could last for hours—and I'll never get those hours back.

Beside the Music

"I have to go now." I turn my back on her and walk into the house.

I expect her to say something like, "And now I'll burn the place down. You should have listened to me." But she doesn't. I hear her mumble, "Okay. Later, then." *Maybe she's one of those mild-mannered psychos.*

As I make my way to the back door, I hear the sound of guitar and drums from behind the garage door. Jeff and Gill have started practicing. I wonder if they know there is a crowd of fans outside. I look up and notice that the curtains are drawn in all of the downstairs windows. The band is inside; they have to know these people are outside of my house. I am kind of annoyed that they haven't done anything to get these insane people off my front lawn. Though I am not sure what can be done at this point. *Is it the right thing to call the cops? Will that wreck Tim's election prospects?*

Once the crowd hears the music, they start cheering. Thankfully, they lose interest in me. "This is a new one! We're hearing a new one before anyone else in the world!" They dance and high five as I sneak into the house and lock the door behind me.

"What the hell is going on out there?" I call out as I get inside the house. Vito is pacing in the living room; likely unsure how to handle the vibration in the floor from Jeff's bass drum. I peek out the curtains and wonder how I am supposed to walk my dog with those freaks outside. Then I see Keith, sprawled and snoring on the couch; a half-empty bottle of vodka and a glass are on the coffee table. Crumpled balls of paper litter the floor. *Gee, looks like our conversation on the stairs this morning was very inspirational and had a great impact. Not.*

I'm kind of thinking of sneaking a shot of Keith's vodka when Toni comes in. I tilt my head toward the front of the house. "Is it always like this, with people staking out the band?"

"I can't say I've ever seen that," she says. "I'm kind of scared to go outside." She pulls back a curtain and peers out. "You ought to have Greg walk Vito." She tips her head toward my dog pacing by the door. Of course, he has to go out right now, when there are rabid fans waiting to pounce on anyone coming out of the house. Nonetheless, Toni fetches Greg, and he takes Vito out.

"They want to come inside to meet the guys," I say, raising my eyebrows. "There's one out there who swears Keith is writing songs just for her."

"Trisha's out there?" she asks. "That girl gets around."

"You know her name? Aren't you concerned about safety? She's a fucking weirdo. Please tell me that you've called the police."

"No, I haven't. Erik told me not to."

"Why? Toni, I am freaked out. Those people know my name. They surrounded me when I pulled into the driveway. Do you have any idea how scary that is for me? Are they going to *sleep* out there?"

"I hope not." Toni watches the die-hard Hydra fans playing Frisbee on the front lawn. Vito chases after it until Greg calls him back. Concern crosses Toni's

105

face, and I'm pretty sure she's scared, too. "Erik said he'd handle it."

"Tim's going to be *so* mad when he gets home," I say. Then I gesture to the living room. "So, what's up with Keith? I have to say that this is the most interesting thing I've ever come home to—a crowd on my lawn, and a drunken bassist passed out on my couch." I nod toward Keith. "So, is that how he always writes lyrics?"

Toni rolls her eyes then goes to the kitchen and fills a glass under the tap. She goes into the living room and replaces the glass of vodka with the glass of water. Then, back in the kitchen, she dumps the vodka into the sink and tosses the empty bottle into the recycling bin.

Erik comes in through the back door; I can hear the crowd calling out to him until he squeezes inside and slams the door on the noise. He sets his iPhone on the counter. I'm impressed. That must mean he really wants to talk to me. "Brenda, before you say anything," he says, gesturing toward the door, "I will handle the situation outside." He turns to his phone before speaking again. "Oh, and who's Portia?"

"Why? She's Tim's mom. Did she call here?"

I've lost Erik to his iPhone, so Toni speaks up. "No, she came over here this afternoon. Does she do that much?"

"Not really," I say. "Were you here? What did she want?"

"Well, she came by to drop something off." She points to a book of fabric swatches on the kitchen table. *What the hell is she going to do to my house now?* The swatches have Antonio Diego's logo on them; he's a big shot interior designer who has his own TV show—kind of like a male, Latino Martha Stewart. *Has she hired him to redecorate our house? Just what I need. Why doesn't Tim ever tell me about these things?*

Oh, crap—*Tim!* Toni is peering out the window. I join her and watch the crowd approach Tim's truck the same way they swarmed my car. I can see his face through the truck's windshield, a blatant expression of disgust crossing his face. He gets out and forces his way through the crowd.

"It's Tim!" someone screams.

"Tim! Can we come inside with you?"

"They're in there, aren't they?"

"*Are you kidding me with this?*" Tim yells. "No, you can't *fucking* come inside. Get off my lawn!"

Out the window, I watch Tim trying to convince the crowd to leave. *Yeah, good luck, pal.* Trisha approaches Tim, and I see him glance toward the house with longing. She looks up at him with a twinkle in her eye; maybe someday she'll think his campaign trail speeches were written for her.

Erik notices Keith on the couch. "Keith's pissed, *eh?*"

"What is *he* pissed about?" I ask.

"Because he drank too much," he says slowly, as if I am intellectually challenged.

"*Huh*? Oh! Here, we say that someone's pissed when they're angry," I say.

"Well, he's that, too." Erik shrugs. "Doesn't matter, so long as he's writing."

I wonder how long Keith has been passed out on the couch and exactly how long it will take for him to write lyrics for an entire album. *Is he going to get drunk every day? Does that speed up the song writing process or slow it down?* Hydra has been in the house for about three weeks at this point, and I am starting to get a bit antsy about when they'll be done. I know Tim's definitely over it; this is especially so, now that we have a fan club on the front lawn.

Toni is writing tomorrow's schedule on the whiteboard as Tim comes in the back door and locks it behind him. "What the hell is that all about?" he asks, gesturing out the door.

"I'll take care of it," Erik replies while thumbing his iPhone screen. Not for the first time, I wonder if he does that when he doesn't want to fully participate in an uncomfortable conversation.

"You'd better," Tim says to him. "I don't want more people sleeping on my lawn." This time, I don't blame Tim for being irritated. I'm irritated, too; and I'm sure I won't hear the end of it from him tonight, when we're alone in our room.

Erik pulls out some stakes and yellow caution tape from a box in the living room then heads for the door. *Did he go to Home Depot and get that stuff today? Just how long have these jokers been on my front lawn?*

"What are you doing with that?" Tim asks.

"Now that they know where we are, they aren't going to leave," Erik says. "And God knows how many other people they've told. Over the years, I've found it easier to give them a section they can hang out in, so they won't be disruptive. Most fans are respectful of that. It's when you tell them to leave that things get nasty."

"No. I don't think you understand," Tim says. "I don't want strangers camped outside my house. What if they stampede and try to storm into my house?"

"Stampede? They're not bulls, Tim. In all my years managing Hydra, that's never happened. I've been in this situation many times. They want to be close by, but these people don't have the courage to come up to the house. If they did, they would have done it by now."

"What do you mean, they don't have the courage?" I ask Erik. "They came up to my car, and they know my name. These aren't normal people, and honestly, I'm concerned for my safety."

"Right now, they don't have any boundaries," Erik explains. "So they're roaming free out there. Once we corral them and give them some rules, you'll see that they won't be a bother." I can tell Erik is trying to comfort me, but I'm not convinced.

"So, are you suggesting that we let them stay in their little designated parking area?" Tim asks.

107

"Yes. I've learned that, in a way, you just have to give the fans some of what they want, and they're satisfied. They'll hang around for a few days, and then they'll get bored. You'll see. You won't even notice them after a while, and by next week, they'll be gone."

Tim and I exchange glances. I can tell he isn't buying it; neither am I. *But what else can we do?* We don't have experience in this kind of situation; Erik does. We pretty much have to trust him on this.

"Maybe Erik's right," I say to Tim. "I mean, if we tell them to leave, then they might trash our house. They're here now, so I don't really see what else we can do." Though now I am starting to wonder if we can ever leave the house unattended with those people out there. *What if Erik is wrong? What if, when we are at work and the band is at Del's, the fans break in and try to score some memorabilia?* What about Tent City? Nothing is secure out there. I imagine the people living in those tents will probably have to lock up their valuables in the garage, while everyone is out of the house.

"Fine," Tim says, gritting his teeth. "But when I agreed to do this, I didn't think I'd have to deal with screaming fans outside. I just thought you guys would crash here and that would be it. If they stray from their parking area just a little bit, I am calling the cops."

"Tim," Erik says to him, "you've allowed a rock band to stay in your house. What did you think would happen?" Good question—though I don't think either of us imagined this. "Trust me, calling the cops would be infinitely worse on you. If you piss off rabid fans, they get ugly. Now, may I please borrow a mallet from your toolbox?" He holds up the caution tape and stakes. "I've got some crowd control to do."

Tim turns to find the swatches on the kitchen table. "Oh, so my mother's been here. Now *she* knows that Hydra's here, too. Great. Can't wait to answer *that* phone call." He sighs.

Chapter 16

"GET OFF! *GET OFF!* GETOFFGETOFFGETOFF, you cretin!" It's morning. Sure, the mornings are pretty hectic around here, but I've yet to hear someone screeching in the living room. Are they doing an imitation of Portia? If so, it's dead on. I rush to put on my clothes and get downstairs. *What the hell is going on down there?*

By the time I get into the living room, I see Portia swinging her purse at Keith. "These raw silk cushions were imported from Paris," she continues to screech at him. "They are *not* impervious to your drool!" She swings again.

Keith groans and covers his face with his arms. His words are slurred. "*Unnnngh*... stophiddingme... crazyfurginlady."

A tall Latino man is standing next to her, dressed in impeccably-distressed jeans and a clingy black T-shirt. The sleeves can barely contain is sculpted biceps, and the sunglasses atop his head hold back sleek black waves of hair. *Holy crap. Antonio Diego is in my house.* He is glancing around my home, and I am immediately self-conscious. Somebody has left a glass and a plate with a pizza crust on the coffee table. Normally, I would rush to stash it in the kitchen sink, but I am frozen in the doorway as Portia slams Keith repeatedly with her purse, shrieking at him.

"What the hell is going on down here?" I ask Toni. But, like me, she is transfixed by the scene playing out in the living room. Portia swings her purse again and makes contact. Keith tries to sit upright but is knocked over from the weight of her blows.

"That is a Louis XIV divan," Portia spouts, gesturing to the overly-fancy couch she bought Tim and me for a wedding gift. "*Not* some beanbag in a flop house, you imbecile. Stand up from there immediately!" The divan is a white raw silk Louis XIV-style chaise. Even I won't sit on it, because I'm too afraid to mess it up. I always put down a throw blanket first.

Keith wobbles on his feet and rubs his eyes. I wonder if he even woke up from having passed out yesterday afternoon. Portia examines the side of her bag. There is a gouge in it from where it hit the studs on Keith's jacket.

She glares at me. "Brenda, I don't know why you didn't tell me that you are having house guests," she says. I can tell that she's trying to come off polite, but the tone of her voice is clipped. She's clearly pissed. Before I get the chance to say anything, she starts in again. "Get off of there! You are *filthy*!" She swings again. Keith groans and rubs at the stubble on his face, clearly trying to make sense of the situation. "*Off*!" Portia screams. "*Immediately!*"

"*Ow*! Fuck off, you crazy bitch!" he yells back at her. He moans then holds his head. "Quieter, please…" he grumbles. "…head is pounding."

I know I should just tell her right now that guests in my house are none of her business. But she barrels right over me before I can even speak. "I expect that your houseguest will replace my Birkin." *Oh, shit. That's Portia's obnoxiously expensive handbag—the one that cost her tens of thousands of dollars.* She was on the waiting list for five years for that thing. There's no way Erik will buy her a new handbag. Antonio's mouth falls open, but he has yet to say a word.

I examine the bag with her, while she continues to rant. "They'll be hearing from my lawyer. My Birkin now has a scratch in it, and I *demand* that it be replaced." I am about to tell her to calm down when I hear the front door open. It's Keith. Leaving. *Where is he going? Is he still drunk?*

Portia continues to bluster. "I have never seen such behavior in my entire life," she says, pointing her finger at me. Clearly, Keith's passing out on her divan was my fault and is the sort of behavior that perfectly illustrates just how far beneath her station I really am.

I ignore her for the moment and watch Keith out the window, willing him not to do anything stupid. The fans have all stopped what they were doing and are watching Keith stumble down the front walk. I watch as Trisha approaches him and then stops a few paces away. She is talking to him, but I can't hear what she's saying.

Portia continues, oblivious: "Well, as you know," she says, "Antonio is reupholstering the sofas to match the divan." *Really? That's news to me.* I've been thinking of putting those awful couches on Craigslist and buying something that better suits Tim and me—you know, like something we won't be afraid to sit on. *What use is a divan?* It has no back; we can't even flop onto it while we watch TV. "So, I thought I'd drop off the swatches for you and Timothy. I put paperclips on the ones that I want you to pick from. As you can imagine, Antonio Diego is a very busy man, darling. And then I saw your drunken friend sprawled upon the divan. Oh, I do hope he hasn't sullied the fabric." She bends over to inspect the surface of the divan. "Antonio, darling, what do you think?"

"I think it's fine, Portia," he says, running his fingers over the drool spot. "This'll come out with some goat's milk upholstery cleaner." He glances around, and then wipes his hands on his jeans.

"Oh, Keith," I mutter under my breath. "No. Nonononono." I knock on the window, but he doesn't look back. Trisha has retreated, a look of horror on her face. Keith staggers to Portia's BMW. She had it specially shipped from Germany—the model is not available in the U.S. She is insanely protective of it. I once touched it, and she immediately pulled a special microfiber cloth from her purse and meticulously rubbed at where I'd laid my hand.

"Keith! Shit! *No!*" I run out the front door. Portia, confused, looks up from the divan and follows me out the door. "*Keith!*" I yell again. "*Stop!*"

It's too late. He is bracing himself against the roof of her car. His frayed jeans are around his ankles, and he's letting out a loud, exaggerated sigh of relief. He looks over his shoulder at Portia and sneers. I see the stream of urine splash against the driver's-side door of her car. The crowd points, gasps, titters, laughs. For good measure, he thrusts his hips and traces a loopy pattern of pee down the length of her car. Antonio's jaw drops further. *Yeah, let's see you clean that with goat's milk.*

That has to be the longest pee I have ever witnessed. The sheer mortification of the moment probably made it feel twice as long. Portia gasps in horror and disgust. For the first time since we met, we agree on something.

Without a word, Keith pulls up his pants and zips his fly. He strides up the front walk and pushes past us on his way back into the house. He turns and faces Portia. "Hit me with that bag one more time," he hisses at her. "I dare you." I am at a loss for words. Portia's face grows redder by the second; I know she's going to blow her top. I need to say something. I need to do something.

"I'm just going to go and get the measurements," Antonio says and bolts through the door, closing it behind him. *Great. She's certainly not going to hold anything back, now that her fancy interior-decorator monkey isn't present.*

I frantically grab the hose behind the azalea bush near the front door and turn the water on full blast. "Portia. My God, I am so sorry," I sputter. I spray down the side of her car. Then I get another idea and start a jog toward the garage. I can probably wash her car really quick and still have time to get changed and get to work.

"*TIMOTHY,*" Portia screams at the top of her lungs. "*TIMOTHY, COME DOWN HERE THIS INSTANT!*" Of course, Tim left early this morning: a breakfast meeting with Aria about the script for his radio ads.

I drop the hose and sprint back to her side. "He's not here, Portia," I tell her, trying to muster up as soothing a tone as possible.

"Do not speak to me as if I am a doddering old woman. I have never before witnessed such animal-like behavior. Who are these friends of yours, Brenda?"

"Portia, I am completely horrified at Keith's behavior. Please accept my apology." It's inadequate, but there really isn't anything else I can say at this point.

"Your friend will hear from my attorney," she sputters. "My Birkin will be replaced, and my car will be professionally detailed." She heads toward the house then turns to me. "You and your friend have humiliated me in front of Antonio Diego. I am disgusted with how you live."

I have had it with this woman; I can't hold back anymore. I am trying, but it's not working. I muster up the politest tone I can again, though I am furious. *Who does she think she is?* "Portia, this is *my* home. If you don't like how I live, then maybe you should call before you come over."

Her face turns roughly six shades redder. "Before you came along, Timothy didn't mind if I came over."

"That may be true, but I *do* mind. I would never dream of showing up at *your* place unannounced. It's rude. And despite what you may think, *I* have manners." I turn on my heel and head into the house in front of her, leaving her on the front walk. A leak in the hose lightly sprays the back of her skirt, but I don't bother to tell her about it. As I enter the house, Antonio is exiting. I can tell he's heard the whole exchange, and he flashes me a slight sympathetic smile.

"Let's go, Antonio," she mutters. She scurries to her car and pulls the microfiber cloth from her purse. She holds it over her side of the car, trying to decide how to wipe away the filth. Instead, she covers her hand with it before opening her car door. I watch from my doorway as she locks the car door and pulls her gigantic designer sunglasses onto her gaunt face. She backs out of the driveway, and I hear her rev the engine as she pulls out and speeds away.

I should head her off at the pass and call Tim before he gets back to the shop, but I am sure she's already begun calling him, repeatedly, until he answers his phone. I don't think I'd even get through. Once it's safe to go back outside, I coil up the hose and hang it back onto the wrought iron hanger behind the bush. When I walk back into the house, I see Toni is standing there with her mouth hanging open. Obviously, she has no idea what to say, either.

I shrug and walk past her, up the stairs so I can get changed and head to work. This is definitely one of those situations where I am glad that my mother-in-law prefers to talk only to my husband and not to me. Maybe I'm a coward, but I'll let him deal with his mother's wrath. But boy, did it feel good to tell her what I think for a change.

Chapter 17

"HEY," I SAY, LOOKING UP from the kitchen table as Tim walks in the back door after work. He sets his jaw, walks past me, and doesn't answer. I'm sure his mom has been chewing his ear off all day. "Listen, about this morning…"

"Can we not, please?" He turns and holds his hands up in front of me. "I am pretty tired of talking about this morning." In a way, I am kind of thankful. *What can I possibly have to say that would ease his tension?*

He walks to the front room and gazes for a few moments out the front window; I know he's looking at the fan camp. I also know that his patience is wearing thin. "I knew this would be a mistake," he mutters to himself. "I fucking *knew* it."

"Tim…"

"Just leave me alone. Please." This is awkward. On one hand, I should just give Tim his space. But on the other hand, I know that if I give him too much space, he'll get distant. Once distance is acquired, our marriage will slowly disintegrate. I am not sure what to do here. And I really wish I could talk to someone about this. *But how can I possibly explain Hydra's presence in our house?*

Tim grinds his jaw as he stares out the window.

Even though Erik had corralled the fans, they are growing in number. Just the other day, they came in with signs they'd made. They hold them up now whenever the band's minivans come or go. I try not to look over there, because I don't want to encourage them. But one of the signs reads, *Ben, I'll be your downward dog.* Gross. They barbeque on camp stoves, play Frisbee, and act like every day is a Saturday at the park. One of them has a camera with a really long zoom lens. He's not there every day, and he doesn't seem to participate with the others. I wonder what he's taking pictures of. I am afraid to find out.

"I kind of feel like a prisoner in my house lately," Tim says to me, sighing. *So, does he want to talk to me or not?* I thought I was supposed to be leaving him

113

alone. Just then, the back door bursts open, and hungry band members and entourage flood in. Toni pulls out foil pans that Angela has warming in the oven.

"Stuffed cabbage," she says, pulling the foil off the top of the pans. "Salad's in the fridge. Would you grab it, Jeff?" Jeff pulls a gigantic bowl of salad out of the fridge and sets it on the island. Someone from the crew grabs a stack of plates from the cabinet, and soon band members and crew are lining up to fill their plates. Tim and I manage to score a helping for ourselves, as well. But when we look around for a place to sit, there's no room at the dining room table or the kitchen table. It seems every seat in the house is filled. I shrug at Tim and gesture toward the back door.

I grab a blanket and spread it out on the deck. "Let's make it a picnic. We never do things like this." I'm trying to get Tim to relax and, maybe, start talking to me again. He sits across from me, but from the look on his face, I can tell he's not amused. The deck furniture had been taken inside to accommodate Hydra's crew, so we sit cross-legged and balance our plates on our laps. I swat a mosquito. Then I light a citronella candle and place it on the deck between us. The sun hasn't set yet, but maybe I can turn this into a romantic setting and change his mood.

"My mom called me, like, ten times today," he says. "She's very upset. What the hell happened this morning? What did you say to her?"

"Well, she shows up this morning. Keith was passed out on the divan, and she freaked the fuck out on him."

"Okay, I got that," he says. "But why did you tell her she was rude?"

"What?" I set my plate aside and sit up straighter. "I didn't call her rude. I told her that showing up here unannounced was rude."

"So, basically, you told her she was being rude? Brenda, she's redecorating our house. She's hired the best in the industry. How can you call her rude?"

"Tim, who the hell asked her to hire Antonio Diego to redecorate our house? I know *I* didn't. Did you? Why does she think she can just show up here any time with swatches and start changing our house? She doesn't even live here. Don't I *ever* get a say?"

"We've been over this, and I thought you agreed. My mom is really lonely since Dad died. Redoing our house gives her something to do."

"Well, I am over it, Tim. I am over tiptoeing around her. She needs to get a life of her own. I can't have her walking in here whenever she pleases. It is rude of her to do that. And what if I don't want her snooty furniture? Do we live in a home or a museum?"

Tim doesn't respond. *How can he possibly think that his relationship with his mother is healthy? At what point will he put me first on this subject? Will I spend our entire marriage taking a back seat to his mom?* We hear the band shouting and laughing from inside. They cheer over something we didn't hear. One of the crewmembers opens the back door and tosses an empty beer bottle into the recycling bin.

Beside the Music

"I could ask you the same thing, Brenda." He gestures toward the house. "Do we live in a home or on a tour bus? With the amount of beer these people drink, the garbage men are going to think we're alcoholics. Hell, Mitch Goldstein could just take a picture of our bin on trash day and use that in an ad. I can just see it— 'Take a look at Tim Dunkirk's habits. Do you want a drunk in the state Senate? Vote Goldstein, the sober choice.'"

"I don't think I've ever seen a state Senate candidate run an ad like that," I point out. "Besides, beer isn't illegal, Tim. You could turn it to your advantage and talk about how recycling creates jobs. And you could also say that Mitch Goldstein has nothing better to do but snoop in the garbage." But I know he's still worried about how the state of our home life looks right now. All it takes is one "Tim Dunkirk can't control his house guests—do you think he can control the state Senate? Vote Mitch Goldstein and get a man who's in control" ad to derail Tim's progress in the polls. He's making waves with his campaign, lately. As much as I don't like Aria, I have to admit that she's getting him some amazing exposure. He's done a debate with Mitch Goldstein on NPR's *Political 360*, and he had ol' Mitch scrambling for rebuttals a few times.

But my fear isn't just Hydra derailing Tim in the polls; I just couldn't live with the idea that I was the one to derail his dream. Running for office is something he's wanted to do since we met. He always talks about what he'd do differently, and he has great ideas for making Rhode Island a friendlier state for small businesses. He wants the state to pay more attention to hiring Rhode Island-based companies for state contracts, for example. I really hope he gets his chance to be voted in and implement some of those ideas. I honestly believe Tim could change the world—or, at least, our little part of it.

He picks apart his stuffed cabbage; I can tell he's done with our conversation. *So now what?* He's pissed at me about so many things—his mom, the band. And right now, it feels impossible to get back into his good graces. I don't even feel like trying anymore, at this moment. And I know that this feeling is what sends couples to divorce. But right now, I just can't deal with his mood. Where is the Tim who used to say he loved me, even when he was mad at me?

I spot Keith through the kitchen window. He stops and looks at me; instinctively, I sit a bit straighter. Keith rubs his eyes and makes his way toward the dining room. Tim watches me as my eyes follow Keith through the window.

"Look at you—you're like a lost puppy over him," he says.

"I am not."

"If you weren't married, you'd be all over him."

"Well, I *am* married. So I have no need to be all over him."

"So, how much longer are they going to be here? It's been, what, three weeks? Four weeks? I've lost count."

"I don't know," I murmur. I watch Keith stare out the kitchen window at

115

something behind me. I don't think he's looking at Tim and me; it's more like he's looking through us. He has his plate in his hand, but he's not eating. I wonder why he isn't participating in the conversation. His eyes are far off. I can't tell what he's thinking. *Maybe he's hashing out some lyrics? Thinking about his family? Maybe the pressure of this album is getting to him, and he's getting tired?*

He never seems to participate when the rest of the band and crew are doing something together. Isn't the whole point of all of them living here to get them to bond? I wish I could tell him that this behavior is precisely why the American audience has moved on from him, regardless of how talented he is. This, right here, is why he's often called "unapproachable" on social media. If only I could record his behavior and play it back to him, then he could see what he looks like and change his ways.

"Bren," Tim says, breaking my train of thought. "As much as I love you in that tank top, I don't think you should wear it anymore while the band's here. It's a bit revealing, don't you think?" I look down. He's right: my shirt did slip down a bit in the front when I straightened my back. "He was just looking at you through the window like you're a piece of meat."

"No, he wasn't" I say, brushing him off. "Stop it."

"Oh, my God, Bren. He so was! You are so blinded by these people. I don't get it. We can't even eat in our own house anymore, and we have freaks camped out on the front lawn. I am so fucking *sick* of this." He stands and takes his plate in through the back door. Ben is loading the dishwasher; Tim plunks his plate in, too, but doesn't say a word. *I am so over this mood of his. Why do I need to deal with his bullshit?* I get it: he's frustrated. But does it always have to be such a nightmare to live with him when we have guests?

"Full service rock star, eh?" I joke, as I hand Ben my plate.

Tim wanders off to the living room and picks up his laptop for his meeting with Aria on Skype. Aria, Aria, Aria. A couple of minutes later, I can hear him laughing at something she's said. He saves all his lively conversation for her and none of it for me. I know she knows about Hydra, but does she know about the freaks on the front lawn? Tim's done a great job of keeping her out of the house the last few weeks. They've been meeting at the shop or on Skype. I know that Hydra's timing isn't the best for him—which is probably why he is so annoyed with them. But there's never a good time for a disruption to Tim's life, of any kind. I stand in the doorway of the living room and watch him as he starts his meeting. He rifles through his backpack and pulls out a few file folders.

Tim doesn't look up at me; he's already engrossed in his conversation. I leave my perch in the doorway and head back into the kitchen, where Ben and Jeff are washing the rest of the dishes by hand. I raise my eyebrows in surprise.

"What, you thought we didn't wash dishes?" Jeff asks. "What do you think we do in our own homes?"

Beside the Music

"I just assumed you guys had butlers and staff," I say, laughing.

"A butler? Rock drummers don't have butlers." Jeff smiles. "We have topless women cleaning our homes."

"Perhaps you could suggest it to Angela, so you'll feel more at home," I say.

"No way," Ben says. "I am terrified of that woman." We all laugh until Keith comes into the kitchen, and then we grow quiet. I've noticed that Keith has that effect on the rest of the band. I don't know if it's because he's really the serious-minded one of the bunch or because nobody really knows what to say around him. Either way, it's weird. These are the people he's been around for his entire adult life, and he seems like a stranger to them. It's fascinating and odd, all at the same time.

"Am I interrupting? Well, don't stop on my account." He's obviously offended that we didn't include him, and I feel a little bad. He looks at me. "Brenda, may I speak to you?" He gestures out the back door to the deck. I throw a curious glance at Ben; he only shrugs. I wipe my hands on a dishtowel and follow Keith out the backdoor. I look back at Tim, but he is so locked in to his computer screen that he doesn't notice us going outside. I'll just go out for a minute and talk to Keith; it's probably no big deal. Maybe he has rock-star demands for more creature comforts. Still, I feel a bit funny being alone with Keith, especially in light of Tim's mood tonight.

I wait as Keith watches a hummingbird drink from one of Tim's feeders. He runs his hands through his wavy hair and tucks it behind his ears. "They are such beautiful creatures," he says before turning to face me. *Really? We're out here to talk about the birds?* I resist the urge to look back at Tim through the window and try to be patient. "Brenda, I heard you talking about my lyrics a week ago, and I think you're spot on with what you said. I appreciate your honesty and would like to impose on it one more time."

"Sure," I say cautiously. Usually when people ask for honesty, they really don't mean it. I wonder if this is a moment where I am supposed to be an adoring fan, or if I am really supposed to be honest.

"What do you think of me?" he asks.

Oh, boy. What a loaded question. Is he going to next ask me if he looks fat? "What do you mean?"

"I mean, what is your impression of me as a person?"

"Why do you want to know?" I figure this is a good question to ask; I can formulate a more tactful response if I know why he's asking me.

"According to market research, I am distant and unapproachable. A cold fish."

I pause to collect my thoughts. He's not completely clueless, apparently. He's probably read the nasty things that people have been saying about him online, and

I'm sure it's hurt his feelings on some level. But to get that report in a formal market research study? *Ouch! Poor guy.* No wonder he mopes around the house all the time. Anyone would, right?

I wonder what else the market research has said about him. I wish I could see it all and formulate a more thoughtful response. I need to stop thinking like a publicist, though, and start thinking like a friend. I really don't know what he expects out of this conversation. Yeah, I suppose I could go all the way and tell him exactly what I think. I look over my shoulder; Tim's still in his meeting. *How much time do I have?*

When I imagined giving the band my opinion, I never thought I'd be telling Keith what I honestly thought of him. *But he did open the door, right?*

"Why are you asking me now? Is it because of what I said that day? I'm sorry if I was insensitive," I blurt out. Now I'm not sure where I'm taking this conversation. I hate talking when I feel unprepared. The last thing I want to do is hurt this man's feelings after all he's been through.

"I have made a career out of trying to produce the best music and pack arenas, year after year. But recently I've learned that the music is not enough. I have learned that listeners want to like the people who write the music, too. I am trying to get a sense of whether I am even likeable or not. You are a listener. Now's your chance to tell me what you think. Bring it." He laughs a little bit but then regains his composure. He leans against the railing of the deck and gazes over Tent City.

I've noticed he spends a lot of time with that far-off look in his eyes, and I wonder if it's because he's a creative person, constantly trying to keep himself open to whatever stray idea pops into his head. Or is it that he never wants to be in social situations? I'm still not sure exactly what I should say to "bring it." *Does he even want me to bring it at all?* Yes, his job is to produce the best music possible, but I still don't think he really cares about his ability to be liked.

"You know," he says, "I have read my reviews on Amazon.com, and I've seen the hashtag #KutKeith trend when they thought I went missing last month. I am not completely blind." He pauses. "…And I know that there are a lot of people who do not like me. I would like to change that somehow."

I wonder why, exactly, he wants to change that. Is it because he genuinely wants people to like him? Or do they need to just like him enough so he can sell more tickets? Maybe he's focusing on what I said about making more of an effort with Damien. This probably isn't really about his fans. *Could it be about his family?* I can tell he feels sad and lost without his wife and son. I know I would be devastated if Tim wasn't in my life anymore.

The sun is grazing the tree line of the forest behind the house, and the clouds glow orange. He looks up at the clouds to take it all in, but I notice the tension in his hands. He is bracing himself against the railing as he waits for my response. "You've made a career of making other people likeable, right? Isn't that what PR is all about?" He pauses again. "So, pretend I am a client. What is your impression of me?" In all my years working in PR, I don't think I've ever had a client ask me that question. Usually it's the case that I have to butter up to my clients and tell them I like them first, and *then* I have to make other people like them. They don't actually care about what I, personally, think about them.

"Well." I chew my lip. "If we're being completely honest here, I am sure you're a nice guy, but I kinda think you act like an asshole." I wince after I say it. It's probably one of the meaner things I've ever said to anyone, especially if he's trying to become more likeable. It's one thing to joke and call someone an asshole; it's entirely another to be serious about it. But it does feel a bit of a relief to actually say it out loud. I've watched him sulk and brood around my house since he got here. I have kind of wanted to tell him to get over himself. *Maybe I should. After all, he did ask.*

"So long as you're not holding anything back," he says, and laughs, but his grip on the rail is still tight. He's obviously tense; this is probably a hard conversation for him, as well. "Tamsen thought I was an asshole, too. She told me so when we first met. I fell in love with her right away." He stares off at something across the back yard. A faint smile hangs on his lips; he's probably remembering. Then he turns to me. "She thought I was an asshole because we'd just signed our first record deal and were out celebrating. I was drunk and trying to get her to come home with me. I can see why she thought so at the time, but I want to know why *you* think I act like one now."

"Are you sure you want to know?" I ask.

He nods but doesn't face me.

"You come off as an asshole because people can't relate to you. Remember how awkward that dinner at the Stone Yacht Club was at first? You don't do well with meeting new people and making them feel comfortable with you. You're all about what people can do for you, and not necessarily what you can do for them." I pause, and he nods. "You've lost touch with how life really is. When you met Tamsen, you were a twenty-something guy who was on the verge of becoming a big star, and you were trying to score. Of course you're going to look like an asshole in that situation. But you should have grown up since then. And you didn't. You were wildly successful and played in arenas packed with screaming fans that loved you. You have handlers that cater to your every whim. You have every privilege—"

"I worked hard for those privileges," he interrupts.

"Yes, you did. But you also took advantage of them. Did you think that nothing would happen when you got behind the wheel after that barbeque? Did you think at the time that if you got pulled over, they'd let you go because you're Keith Kutter?"

119

I wait for him to respond. He pauses and then slowly nods in response, and I know it's an unguarded moment of honesty.

"Then that's what makes you an asshole, Keith. You should have been thrown in jail. Anyone else would have been. Getting behind the wheel after drinking is the ultimate act of selfishness. You don't care what happens, so long as you have your good time, right?"

He leans against the deck railing and holds his face in his hands.

"Is that all?" he asks.

"No," I continue. He flinches. *Should I continue? Oh, well, he* is *the one who asked. Might as well go all the way.* "I can't decide if you just *look* like an asshole or if you actually are one. After the accident, you spent your life perpetually high because you'd paralyzed your son. You left Tamsen to deal with that situation, which I am sure was damned hard on her. She had to deal with the sudden paralysis of her child. That's not the behavior of a supportive partner. That's classic asshole behavior. What the hell were you thinking? That everyone would understand because you're Keith Kutter?"

"You have no idea what it's like," he hisses.

"You're right, I have no idea what it's like to almost kill my family and expect to walk away from the fallout. I don't know what it's like to have the world handed to me just because I'm famous. And I certainly don't know what it's like to take off on my yacht to escape it all and leave my mess for someone else to clean up."

"So, what do I need to do so people like you don't think I am an asshole?"

"Well, for starters, you need to get over yourself. I know you've had so much tragedy. But you've caused all of it. Do you claim any responsibility for it?"

"Yes."

"Really? How? As far as I can see, you've decided to get over it by scoring with a bunch of hookers and passing out drunk on my couch. And then you pissed on my mother-in-law's car. What are you? A dog? I mean, you're a guest in my home, Keith. You are a grown man. You have been the worst houseguest ever." I am really on a roll now. I didn't realize how affected I'd been by having him and the band stay here. *Maybe it's starting to get on my nerves more than I'd realized, because I am really letting it fly now. Honestly, it's a relief to get this all out. I need to stop and catch my breath for a moment.*

"Okay, first of all, your mother-in-law was screeching at me and smacking me with that purse. What the hell does she keep in there? A brick?"

"I can't defend Portia's outburst," I say. *I shouldn't have to. Who the hell gives her the right to storm into my house and assault my guest?* "I am sorry that happened, and I am sorry I was a bit harsh with you right now. But Keith, since you've been here, you've only been in three states: drunk, passed out, or brooding. Do you really want to live like that?"

He's staring at me. *Is this seriously a question for him? He wants to live a miserable life?*

Beside the Music

"So, what do I need to do?" he asks. "How do I fix this asshole persona I project?" I can tell that I went way deeper than he'd expected. I'm not sure if that's a good thing or not. *Did I just hurt his feelings?* Maybe I should dial it back a bit, focus on being more clinical than emotional.

I kick into public-relations-specialist mode. "Well, for starters, your public is demanding an explanation. They think you are a spoiled brat for the way you behaved after the accident, and that is bad for your image. You have done nothing to convince them otherwise." I pause, and he rolls his eyes a bit. "Hey, you asked me for my opinion, and I am giving it to you. I have nothing to gain by being dishonest with you. If you don't like it, then go back inside and back to brooding over your life." I am still being harsh; he looks stricken. *But he asked me to be honest, right?* I take a breath; *I need to slow down a bit.* "What is it that you want, Keith?"

He answers me with a brief silence as he thinks about it. I wonder if anyone's asked him this question since things ended with Tamsen. "I want to enjoy my life again, he says, finally. "I know that things are over with Tamsen, and I accept that. But I want to have someone in my life. I want to feel that connection again." He paces a bit; when he stops, I realize he is standing closer. I try to back off a bit, but the railing on the deck is digging into the small of my back. "I feel like I can talk to you about anything, and you won't let me get away with being dishonest about anything. Nobody in my life does that for me, not even my mother. I've been missing that in my life."

I'm sure this honest conversation is very intimate for Keith; but now I'm not sure how I feel about standing this close to him. On one hand, it is pretty exciting, I admit. His eyes are trained on mine; he's staring intently at me. Maybe Tim was right. Maybe Keith *has* been looking at me like I am a piece of meat. I reach down and pull up my tank top. But honestly, I don't really want to cover myself up in this moment. And I know it's so wrong to feel this way. My heart is pounding. I never thought I'd ever again experience a first kiss. I feel an almost electric current in the air as I face Keith, who has now moved even closer to me. On the other hand, what I should do is say something like how he's taking advantage of the situation and showing his asshole tendencies again. But I don't. I just stand there, probably with my mouth hanging open.

He's so close to me—close enough that his lips are just a few inches away from mine. I should just step away and break the moment. But I don't. I don't know why, but I feel like I am glued to this spot on my deck. I feel like I know him now, and that I've known him for a long time. It's like I've seen inside of him. I feel him brush the hair off my forehead, and I don't make a move to stop him. He sweeps his thumb across my brow, and I close my eyes for a moment. It feels familiar, even though this is the first time he's ever touched me so intimately. I never imagined anything like this would ever happen when Hydra moved in. *I can't believe it's happening now.*

"Brenda, I want to thank you for being truthful with me. Nobody's done that in a long time. And you are absolutely right."

I try to compose myself, but the warmth of his hand on my cheek is making it hard to stay focused. I need to say something. I clear my throat, my mouth is so dry. "They don't know who you are," I say, "like I do right now." I can't break the eye contact. *They don't know him like I do? Where the hell did that come from?*

I can tell by his facial expression that he isn't paying attention to what I am saying anymore. Instead, his hand slips through my hair, and he cups the back of my neck. Before I realize what's happening, he leans in toward me, and our lips touch. I know I have to say something, but what? I have to do it quick, before something happens that I am going to regret.

"Keith, I..." His hand is back to cupping my cheek. It's warm; he's stroking my cheekbone with his fingertips. I close my eyes and tilt my head into his hand; I can feel the pulse from his wrist lightly throb against my jaw.

I sense him leaning in closer, and before I know it, we are deep in a kiss. I feel his tongue slide against mine; I keep my arms frozen at my sides. It is all wrong, but I let his hand slide from my cheek and behind my neck to hold my head in place. His other hand slides behind my back and pulls me closer to him. I can feel his belt buckle press against my stomach and his breath exhaling near my ear. I give in to it all and slide my hands around his waist and up his back. I can feel the lumps from his vertebrae and his shoulder blades under my palms. I trace my hands back down again and grip his T-shirt near the small of his back. I am fighting the urge to pull it up and slip my hands beneath it so I can feel the warmth of his skin.

I don't know why I am kissing him. But I am. And it's exhilarating to be doing something and not know why I am doing it. With Keith, I feel that light-headed buzz of a first kiss wash over me while his stubble rubs against my chin and his tongue expertly plays with mine. It's foreign, yet completely familiar at the same time.

I am so drawn in that I don't hear the back door slide open. It's Tim's voice that brings me back to reality.

"Brenda? What the hell is going on?"

Chapter 18

IT ALL HAPPENS SO FAST. Tim shoves Keith backward. "What the hell are you doing with my wife?" Keith stumbles a bit and grabs the railing to steady himself.

"Hey, easy. Are you trying to knock me off the deck?" Keith protests. *Seriously? Tim catches us kissing, and that's what he's worried about?* I don't think I've ever seen Tim get physical with anyone. It really is shocking to see the man you love rabidly angry to the point of violence.

"Tim..." I trail off.

"What?" He turns to me with his teeth clenched. "What could you possibly say to me right now?" His fists are curled into tight balls at his side; it looks like it's taking all of his strength for him to keep them at his side and to not haul off and start punching me. He kicks the wicker chair with so much force that it flies backward, and one of the legs breaks off.

It's a good question. *What could I possibly say?* I don't come up with much. I am stammering. I am scared. I don't even know how to react right now. His expression changes from expectant to beyond disappointment. He's so far beyond it that his eyes are dark and his fists are still clenched. I don't think I've ever seen him look this angry. I wonder if he's going to slug Keith. I hope not.

"I can't be around you right now," he mutters. He reaches inside the back door and grabs his keys off the hook and heads down the deck stairs toward his car.

"Tim, wait!" I call after him. I run down the stairs and grab his arm. "Where are you going? Will you *please* wait?"

"Bren, I really don't want to talk to you right now." He pulls his arm away and opens the car door.

"I wish you'd let me explain..."

"Brenda, no. I can't right now."

"Tim, I'm sorry," I say, pleading with him.

He opens his mouth to speak, and then closes it again. I can tell he's counting to ten as he stares. His jaw clenches, his teeth pulsing together as he counts. "So, was it some teenage fantasy of yours?" he asks, struggling for composure. "Was it everything you thought it would be, making out with a rock star in our home? You were watching him through the window—were you thinking about kissing him then?"

"Tim, it wasn't like that," I say, trying to explain. But then I realize that I don't know how to explain it. Anything I say at this point won't come out right. *Yes, I enjoyed kissing Keith, but I didn't plan for that to happen. It just did.* Tim's pretty black and white about stuff like this. For Tim, things don't *just happen.* He probably thinks it was premeditated, and how could I possibly prove that it wasn't?

"Then what was it? All I know is I walked out there and saw my wife sucking face with Keith Kutter. So tell me, what *wasn't* it like?"

"I have no excuse. I am sorry, Tim. It was wrong."

He gets into his car and slams the door shut. He grips the wheel and stares straight ahead. I watch his jaw shuffle side to side, and I know he's grinding his teeth; he does that when he's angry. I hope that he'll just sit there for a minute and shut me out until he collects his thoughts. He'll probably come out in a few minutes, and then we'll talk about it. He'll accept my apology, and we'll move on. I am watching him—but he doesn't come out of the car. Instead, he jams the key into the ignition and starts the car, yanks the shifter into drive, and pulls out of the driveway. I need to say something. I need to do something. *But what?* I am frozen to this spot, watching my husband drive away when he's so furious with me.

I stand there and wait for him to turn around and come back. In real life, people don't just drive off when they're mad, right? Surely he'll just drive for a few minutes to calm his nerves. *Should I wait for him out here?* It's pretty awkward. I can hear the voices from the fan corral on the other side of the front yard. They're talking, and I wonder if they've heard us argue. *Do they know about what just happened?*

After a few minutes, it's pretty obvious that Tim's not coming back, and I feel like a loser, standing out here. *Is the crew watching me through the windows?* I don't even want to look back. I turn my head down and shuffle back to the steps to the deck, kicking a few rocks out of my way. I don't want to go back inside; Keith's in there. Eventually, the mosquitos help me make up my mind. I go inside and ignore everyone, closing myself and Vito in the bedroom to wait for Tim to come home. I can hear the band and crew downstairs talking in hushed voices; I'm pretty sure they're talking about me and Keith and Tim.

Beside the Music
***

I doze off after two in the morning and wake to the sun streaming through the window. Tim's side of the bed is empty. I grab the phone off my bedside table and call his cell; it goes straight to voicemail. He probably slept on the couch in the back room at the shop; maybe he just needs some space, and he'll come home today. I hope so.

I dress for work and avoid the band as much as I can when I get downstairs. I don't speak to anyone, and they don't speak to me. A hush falls over the room when I enter the kitchen; it's pretty obvious who the crew was talking about. Without acknowledging anyone, I pack some leftovers into a container for lunch and head for the door.

Of course, Keith arrives just as I am about to go out. He has a camera strapped around his neck; he stomps up the deck stairs and kicks off a pair of hiking boots— *Tim's* hiking boots. I can't help but raise my eyebrows while he claps the mud off the soles over the edge of the deck. *Where is his brain? He borrowed Tim's hikers without asking—after we were caught kissing last night?*

"I didn't think Tim would mind," Keith says when he spies me staring at him with my mouth agape.

I snort in response. "And you wonder why I think you're an asshole," I shoot back at him.

He ignores me. "I heard some birds in the woods and had to go check them out." He gestures to his camera. "You have a hawk nest out there. I got some pictures of some babies."

"*Um*, Keith?" I ask. *Is he really going to talk about birds after what happened last night?*

"You also have some juvenile Canada geese out on the pond. Loads of them. They'll be grown and ready to fly south before we know it."

"Keith. Would you just stop talking about the fucking birds for a minute? Do you have any idea what I am going through right now?"

Instead of listening, he turns and walks into the house without answering my question.

"And you wonder why people don't like you," I call after him. I wait for him to come back, but he doesn't. I go inside and hear his bedroom door close upstairs. *What is it with people walking out on me lately? Doesn't anyone want to talk things out?*

Nope, he's not getting away with this. I stomp up the stairs and pound on his door. "Keith! We need to talk." I get silence in reply from the other side of the door. "Obviously I know you're in there. Remember how you said you want to be more likeable? Well, this is a bad start on that, Keith."

125

He opens the door. "Brenda, can we just not do this right now? I have a lot on my mind."

"Are you kidding me? My husband didn't come home last night after he caught us kissing, and *you* have a lot on your mind?"

"My mother called last night. She has a lump on her breast, and she's waiting for the test results to come back. And I cannot be there with her right now. All I want to do is jump on the next plane and go to Sydney, but I cannot."

I remember when we were at that stage with my mom. Waiting to find out whether your loved one has cancer is agonizing. I was in college then and still living at home; I was able to be there for her. I can't imagine what it must be like for Keith right now.

"Oh, Keith," I say. "I am sorry."

"My mum is my best friend. She's the only one who has no expectations other than my happiness. She doesn't care about my reviews on Amazon or my reputation on Twitter. She is my key to my son. I am not allowed to see him anymore, but she is. She is the one who keeps me abreast of the changes in his life. I do not know what I will ever do without her."

"Keith, a lump isn't always a tumor. Many times it's just a lump. I know that waiting for news on this is very difficult. You really just have to push yourself through your days until you get news."

"I get that. I figured that getting some pictures of the birds this morning and texting them to her would distract me and make her smile."

"I know you're under a lot of stress right now, with the album, your mom, everything. But seriously, taking Tim's boots after last night wasn't cool." I pause. A wounded look crosses his face. "Keith, seriously. You're going to kiss another man's wife and then wear his boots?"

"Well, when you put it that way," he says, and shrugs. "Okay, I am sorry. I won't touch Tim's things again." *Wow, an apology. But am I considered one of Tim's "things?"*

I glance down at my watch; it's time to go to work. Work won't care that my home life is in chaos, but the last thing I want to do is go in today, when really all I want to do is go off somewhere with Tim and reclaim our marriage.

When I get into work, I duck into my cubicle and try to run down the clock. I can't focus on anything, and I watch the number of unanswered emails in my inbox tick higher.

Amanda comes into my office and glances at my phone, which is switched to "do not disturb" mode. She raises her eyebrows at the display that now reads eight new voicemails, but doesn't say anything about it. Instead she asks, "Hey, did you approve the proofs for the brochure?"

"Yes, I did. I left a message for Emily. Did she not get it?" *Oh, shit, this*

Beside the Music

would be bad if we had to expedite the printing because she didn't get the message.

"Oh, she got the message alright." Amanda pulls a brochure out of the box. "Brenda, what the hell?" She holds it up to me; I take it from her fingers and examine it. *Oh, shit. This cannot be happening.* "Boxter?" Amanda says. "Really? We have 50,000 of these things, and they're useless. Expensively useless." She gestures to the box on the floor.

This seriously cannot be happening. I reviewed that proof. I know I did. I clutch my hands to my head.

"No. Fuck. No."

"Yes. Fuck. Yes." She tosses one at me. "This is bad, Brenda. Majorly bad. Didn't you review the proof?"

"Yes, I... Oh, my God. I missed it. I cannot believe I did this."

"You need to fix this. We have these going out to the stores—FedEx just picked them up from the printer's this morning. They are on the trucks going out to the brand new store sites all over the country. You have got to find a way to stop them from getting there. If Baxter corporate sees these, we're sunk." She pauses for effect. "I have to go now to catch a flight to New York. You need to make this happen."

Right there, I can feel the balloon inside me deflate. My hopes for promotion just went down the tubes. She walks out of my cube, and I immediately get on the phone.

"Emily, it's Brenda. Do you have the tracking numbers for the FedEx shipments that went out for Baxter? Will you please email them to me?" Then I tap my fingers on my desk until my incoming email dings, and I start clicking on the links to see where my packages are. Six of them went out. Two of them show that they've already arrived. One was signed for by an E. Miller, and the other one was signed for by G. Lee. *I am sunk.*

I slouch down in my chair. Amanda is going to kill me. *What the hell am I going to do?* I kick into action and call FedEx.

"Please, I am begging you. Don't deliver those boxes."

"Ma'am, there's nothing we can do. They're on the truck. We can't reach the driver."

"It's 2015. You mean to tell me the driver doesn't have a cell phone?" I ask, suddenly beyond irritated. "Or a CB radio? Or anything? What about emergencies?"

"Sorry ma'am. I am afraid it's not possible."

I hang up the phone. *Shit. Shitshitshitshit.* I press my fist against my forehead. Tears well up in my eyes. I can't let anyone see me cry at work. I have to get out

127

of here.

I sneak out of the office, not even acknowledging Joy on my way out. I walk down to the beach and kick off my sandals and walk along the edge of the surf to the rocks at the far end. I am still barefoot, so I don't want to climb onto the barnacle-covered rocks. I want to keep walking, but there's no other option than to turn back. My mind is blissfully blank, and I want it to stay that way.

It's pretty awesome to escape to where I can be completely alone, with no Keith, no Tim, no Hydra, no Amanda. Even thinking of all of them for a moment causes the exhaustion to set in. I can feel it weighing on my shoulders; I feel like I just packed on fifty pounds. My limbs are heavy and my feet ache from walking barefoot on the sand. I can see my shoes where I left them at the other end of the beach, and it suddenly feels like they're miles away. I feel like I will never reach them if I keep walking. So I stop and lie down on the sand; just for a minute to rest. I'll get up in a bit and keep walking. I should go back to work, but I just can't.

***

I must have dozed off. I rub my eyes, not realizing that my hands are covered in sand. I feel the sting in my eyes as I wipe the grit out. When I glance at my watch, I realize that it's seven o'clock. I left work at three. My stomach is growling. I didn't have the heart to eat my lunch today; it's still in the fridge at work with my name written on the bag. I can stop to grab a few burritos on the way home. Maybe Tim will be there, and we can talk this out.

When I get back to the house, I hear Toni talking on the phone in the kitchen. Tim's car isn't there, and I am beyond disappointed. I haven't talked to him all day, and I feel like somebody poked holes in my lungs. Suddenly I can't seem to catch my breath. *Why can't he just come home?*

Toni hangs up the phone and takes one look at me when I come in. She probably knows the answer, but she politely asks anyway, "How was your day, love?" I am pretty sure that she and everyone in the crew know what happened by now.

I wordlessly flop into a chair at the kitchen table while Toni brews a cup of tea. She sets it in front of me. I take a sip and feel the hot tears run down my cheeks. She brushes the hair off my face, and, surprisingly, I feel a bit comforted.

She sits down and takes my hand. "Brenda, it'll be okay. Don't cry, love."

"I don't think it will," I whisper. "He's really mad."

"Well, of course he is. You would be, too. But Tim loves you. He will forgive you."

Toni sits with me for a few minutes more, but I don't know what else to say. I grab a napkin from the holder and blow my nose. I know that she has work to do. I can tell that she's getting antsy; I tell her I am fine.

She squeezes my hand and smiles at me before getting back to work. I wait at the kitchen table until the sun goes down, but Tim doesn't come home. The band comes in from Del's and plunders the kitchen for dinner. Keith walks through the kitchen without glancing my way. I hear his footsteps going up the stairs, and then his bedroom door closing.

I fidget with the salt and pepper shakers until they fall over. I don't bother to right them. I stand up from the table and call Tim's cell—straight to voicemail. So I call the shop. The machine picks up on the sixth ring.

I grab the burritos and my keys and get into my car. *He can't ignore me when we're face to face, can he?* I have shattered the trust of the one person who means the most to me in the entire world. Maybe I can lighten the mood and win him over with a burrito, at first. Surely he's hungry, and he'll laugh that I'd brought one to him. Once he laughs, we can talk again, and I can tell him exactly how sorry I am.

Chapter 19

WHEN I GET TO THE SHOP, the windows in the garage bay doors are dark. I pull around the back where Tim has a separate entrance for his office; I see a faint glow coming from the office window. I walk up to the glass, wipe away the dust, and peer in; I see him sitting at his desk, staring at the wall. I gently tap on the glass and watch him jump up, startled. He turns to face the window. I hold up the cylinder shape covered in foil, the sure sign of a burrito. He looks at me, no expression on his face. I try to smile and wave the burrito up and down, trying to make it more enticing. I try the door, but it's locked. I have a key, but I don't feel right about unlocking the door and barging in. I'd rather he let me in, figuring it's a sign that he actually wants to talk to me.

At first, he doesn't move to get up, just continues to stare at me. I can tell he isn't just angry—he's royally pissed off. Tears fill my eyes as I press my hand against the window pane. "I love you," I mouth. He glares and shakes his head at me—not a good sign. What's great about Tim is that, when we've fought in the past, he's always been able to say he loves me, even when I've pissed him off. Not this time, though.

A mosquito buzzes by my ear; I swat at it then replace my hand on the window. I wonder how long he'll make me wait out here. *How long will he sit there and glare at me? How many mosquito bites will I get out here?* I can't read his poker face. *Is he trying to decide whether he wants to let me in?*

"Tim," I call out, "will you please let me in?" He stands, walks to the door, and opens it. The orange glow from the sulfur light shines on him from above and makes his skin yellow. It casts a shadow on his eyes and makes them look even angrier. He's not saying anything. Not a good sign.

I freeze in the doorway. I don't think I can handle getting into a fight right now. There is a distinct possibility that our marriage could end tonight. Maybe standing outside the window and getting bitten by a thousand mosquitos is better than going into his office and getting divorced. I would do it for him; I owe him that much.

A moth flutters down from the security light and into the open door. I watch

Beside the Music

it fly straight into his desk lamp and hear its body click against the lightbulb repeatedly until Tim speaks.

"You're letting bugs in," he says. "Are you coming in?"

"That depends," I reply. "Are you going to leave me?"

"No, Bren," he says, sighing. "I am not going to leave you. Just come in."

I step into his office. Even though I'm not convinced he's being truthful, I feel a little relieved. At least he's speaking to me, which is a start. It's cleaner than normal in here. A mechanic's office is always grimy. In the past, when I've commented on how grungy it always is in here, he's asked me if I wanted him making money on the shop floor or working in here, cleaning his office. When he's put it that way, I've had to agree. I've always had to fight the urge to clean when I came in here, though. He says that he doesn't want me to, because he'll never find anything I've put away. But really, I think that he doesn't want me to feel like I have to clean up after him, and it's sweet that he thinks that. Now, I see that all of the grimy fingerprints are gone, and his paperwork is filed. His desk is spotless, and the floor has been swept clean.

"Tim, I am so…"

"I don't want to hear about how sorry you are," he interrupts. "I just don't. It's a bullshit thing to say. I mean, would you be sorry if I hadn't walked in?" He takes the phone off its cradle and fidgets with the cord. I watch him meticulously untangle it. He doesn't look up when he speaks again. "The thing that bothers me the most is that I'm wondering if you would have told me about it, if I hadn't walked in on you and Keith." This time he looks up and makes eye contact. "Would you have told me?"

I open my mouth to answer and then close it again. I struggle to find the words so I can gently tell him the truth. I am pretty sure I would have kept the kiss to myself. I mean, what's the point in telling him and intentionally hurting his feelings for no good reason? Talk about pouring gasoline on a fire. But then, if I tell him that I would have told him, I'd be lying to him. And I don't want to lie to my husband. Any way I slice it, I'm screwed.

"So, you wouldn't have told me?" he asks, looking up. He sets the phone back into the cradle, leans back in his chair, and crosses his arms. "Brenda? If I'd asked you whether you'd kissed Keith, would you have told me?"

Tears form in my eyes. *What the hell am I supposed to do? What can I possibly say?*

"Brenda!" His stern voice startles me. "Would you have told me?" His jaw is clenched; he is getting even madder, if that's even possible. I don't think I've ever seen him this mad.

"No!" I blurt out. "No, I would not have told you, okay? Is that what you want to hear?" *Well, at least I've told the truth. He can't hold that against me on top of everything else at this point.*

He leans onto his desk and rests his head in his hands, deflating right in front

131

of me. I hate it when he gets this way; and it's even worse when I know that I've caused it.

"I am not going to lie to you, on top of everything else. I owe you the truth."

"Bren, you don't owe me the truth. What you owe me is not going around kissing other men."

"It was just one time, Tim. It's not like I go around—"

"One time?" he interrupts. "And how the hell should I know that? It's not like you'd tell me anyway."

He has a good point. I look down at the chipped nail polish on my toes and try to formulate a response. *What could I possibly say to make him feel better right now?* Talk about a no-win situation.

"How can I possibly trust you now?" he asks.

"Tim, I've told you the truth—that's gotta be worth something."

"You told me the truth by telling me you'd lie to me. If I flat-out asked you, you would lie to me." I hadn't considered that. *Good point, Tim.* "I want Hydra out of my house by the end of the week."

"Tim, if they leave early, we have to pay to accommodate them until they get into another house and we don't get the money that they're going to pay us."

"I don't care about the fucking money. It's been way too much of a disruption to our lives and our marriage. I don't know how I let you talk me into this. It was a stupid idea, one of the stupider ones you've ever had. I don't have time for this shit right now. I cannot handle this. I can't have my mother calling me to bitch at me about her fucking purse and her car, now, either."

Great. Portia's insinuated herself into the fight now, too.

Tears run down my cheeks again. He runs his hands through his hair. He hates seeing me cry, but I know he won't comfort me. It's my turn to comfort him, but there's no way he'll let me right now.

"I am not coming home until they're out," he says and gestures to the couch. He's put away his pillow and blanket, presumably so the guys in the shop won't know he's staying here.

"Are you serious?" I ask. "That thing is filthy." He raises his eyebrows in response, and I shut up. After a pause, I ask him, "Do you need anything?"

"No." He points to the duffel on the floor—he probably went to pick up a few things while I was at work today. *Great. Now he won't even come into our house when he knows I'll be there.* He walks across the office, opens the door, and gestures for me to leave.

"Okay, well, I guess I'll go?" I set his burrito on his desk and lean in to kiss him, but he pulls away.

"Don't," he says. "I just don't feel that way right now."

The door closes behind me. I stand at the window and watch him pace back and forth a few times. Then he takes the burrito and hurls it at the wall. It splatters and falls to the floor, landing in a puddle of sour cream and salsa. I get back into the car and put it into gear. As I am pulling around the side of the shop, I see a Mercedes pull in. It's driving toward me, so I pull off to the side to let it by.

The driver pulls around back. I do not recognize this car, so I put my car into reverse and watch to see who gets out. The driver pulls down the lighted mirror in the visor, and I can see it's Aria. She fluffs her hair then swipes on a coat of lip gloss and mascara. She gets out of the car, and I can see that she's wearing a short skirt and stiletto pumps.

She pulls out a bag from the Gourmet Chalet, that same place where Portia shops. I can see a loaf of French bread sticking out of it. With her other hand, she retrieves a bottle of wine and her creamy leather tote. *Where the hell does she think she's going, dressed like that? Gee, why would Tim want a burrito served by his wife in jeans and a tank top, when he can get Gourmet Chalet delivered by tall, blonde, sleek Aria?*

She enters his office, and I get out of the car and head to the window. I stand in a shadow, away from the security light, and watch as she spreads out the bread, brie, and fruit—Tim's favorite snack. She sits on the couch, crosses her perfect, long legs, and dangles a shoe from her toe. She swirls her wine and takes a sip from the glass. She tilts her head back and laughs at something he said. As she laughs, her hair bounces on either side of her head, like a woman in a shampoo commercial.

Tim closes the file folder he has on his desk, sips his wine, and props his chin on his fist, intently listening to her as she speaks. Of course, I can't make out what they're saying. They could be talking about the campaign, or they could be talking about something else entirely. Whatever it is, Tim's gaze is zeroed in. I can't remember the last time he looked at me like that.

I can't stand being here anymore. I can't stand sitting here, watching Aria throw herself at my husband for another second. And I *definitely* can't stand watching him lap up the attention. He's got some nerve getting on my case about me and Keith. He's been meeting Aria after work for months. God only knows what the two of them have been up to all this time. *And to think I came here to make peace with him.*

I feel my throat tighten, and I know I am going to burst out crying at any minute. *What happened to our normal life?* I knew that having Hydra move in was going to mean a huge adjustment, but I never imagined it would make our life into a soap opera. She's sitting on the couch tossing her hair like she's auditioning for a Pantene commercial!

I never could pull something like that off. But girls like Aria can. Girls like Aria can toss their hair and smile and get guys to do whatever they want. And Tim is that guy now.

Why doesn't he look at me the way he's looking at Aria? Is she really that much more interesting than me? Apparently so.

I think I've seen enough. I walk back to my car and get in. I immediately start the engine and drive home.

Chapter 20

"BRENDA, YOU SIGNED A CONTRACT," Erik grouses. "We're not leaving here until the record is complete. Moving is absolutely out of the question."

"Erik, I understand that," I say to him. "But my marriage is on the line here."

I didn't sleep a wink last night. All I could do was picture Tim and Aria cozy in his office. I went through the different scenarios, but really, my seeing them together in Tim's office last night was nothing like Tim seeing me kissing Keith.

Around three in the morning, I decided that I really need to keep some perspective here. *Why am I inventing more problems?* I already have enough to deal with. There was no contact between Tim and Aria. Really, all they were doing was talking. Sure, she did spend some time in the car primping before going in, and sure, she did bring him food and wine. *But did that mean he's been sleeping with her? Honestly, probably not.* That's not Tim's style. Above all, Tim is a loyal guy. If he wanted Aria, he'd probably come to me first and tell me what was going on.

Really what it boils down to is that I saw Tim enjoying a conversation with a woman who was not me. *When was the last time we sat down and had a conversation where we really listened to each other and laughed?* I am jealous as hell that Tim was having such a nice time with her, just like he was jealous as hell, watching me kiss Keith so passionately. *When was the last time Tim and I shared a kiss like that? How did our marriage get to this point, where we are seeking flattery from other people?*

I promised Tim I'd try to get Hydra out, and I will. At this point, I'm going to do just about anything I can to get him home. My first task is to try to appeal to Erik's good nature, though I don't know if he has one.

"Well, you should have thought about that before your tryst with Keith, darling."

"Oh my God, it wasn't a tryst. It was just a kiss. Erik, we've been more than accommodating..."

"I'll say," he drawls. "Is that what you Yanks call it? *Accommodating*? Look,

Brenda, I cannot have the boys uprooted right now. We're in the middle of recording an album. Having them move is too much of a disruption to their process, and I will not have it."

"So that's it? You won't leave?"

"Not until this record is done, and not a moment sooner."

"And how long will that take?"

"I don't know. It could go a few more weeks. Could be a few more months. Judging by the crap they were putting down today, I just don't know."

"What do you mean, 'months'?" I ask, incredulous. Erik shrugs in response and turns his attention back to his iPhone—that habit of his now infuriates me. He dismisses me with a few swipes of his thumbs, and the conversation is over.

I stand there for a moment longer and wait for him to look up. He's too engrossed in whatever is on the screen. For all I know, he's playing *Angry Birds*. I fight the urge to yank the phone out of his hand and instead walk toward the stairs. I call out to Vito, who's perched on the cushion on the back of the couch, watching the window that faces the driveway. He likes to hang out there to wait for Tim to get home. He looks at me for a moment and then returns his attention out the window—the doggie equivalent of the iPhone. *He's ignoring me now, too?*

"He's not coming home, Vito." I face Erik. "And he's not coming home until the rock stars leave." Vito cocks his head at me as if he understands then hops down to the floor and follows me up the stairs.

***

In the morning, Vito is under the covers and curled up against the back of my knees. Normally, he would have cuddled with Tim, but in the beagle world, desperate times call for desperate measures, so any source of body heat will suffice. I stretch out my legs, which he takes as a sign to commando-crawl out from under the covers. He slips out at the foot of the bed and shakes his body; his ears flap, and the tags on his collar jingle. I reach my hand out and feel the cold of Tim's side of the bed. Tears fill my eyes. Vito senses my sadness, scoots upward, and rests his head on my stomach. He sighs and thumps his tail gently, as if to say, "It's okay, Bren. Tim will come home, the rock stars will leave, and everything will get back to normal."

I wipe the tears from my eyes and stroke his velvety ears. I remember when he was a puppy and his ears were too big for his head. They dragged in the grass when he sniffed around in the yard; the tips were perpetually wet from the dew. Tim used to joke about tying them back to keep them dry. I smile at the memory while tears continue to stream down my face.

I put on my robe and look out the window onto the back yard. The Hydra army is stirring; crew members emerge from their tents and walk toward the house. Toni and Erik are walking together; she looks up at me and smiles sympathetically. I don't have to guess what they are talking about, and I suspect she's trying to convince him that they need to leave. I hope she's getting further than I did last night; but then Erik whips out the iPhone, and all hope of him listening to Toni is lost.

"Time to start our day, pal." I sigh and Vito thumps his tail faster. I pick up the phone and dial Tim's cell. It rings twice, and I hang up—I don't know what I could possibly say to him; I need time to think it through a bit.

Vito springs onto all fours, barks, and wags his tail harder. I take it as his way of cheering me on and press the redial button. Tim answers on the third ring. I can hear the noise of the shop floor in the background and feel guilty because he has to drop what he's doing to get the phone.

"Hi," he answers in his "I don't have time to talk to you right now" voice.

"Hey, I just wanted to say good morning to you and that I miss you."

"Are there still rock stars in the house?"

"Well, yeah. I mean, it's not like they were going to move out last night."

"Did you at least talk to Erik?"

"Yes, last night. He got bitchy with me about the contract."

"So that's it? You're letting them stay?" I can hear the irritation in his voice.

"Tim, I just got out of bed. I haven't had the chance to talk to Erik again."

"I have to go, Bren." He clicks off the call before I have a chance to say anything. *Okay, so maybe today is not the day for us to be fully engrossed in conversation with each other.* Maybe I need to show up at his office in a short skirt and flip my hair around to get his attention. I can feel my body tense up, and I need to stay positive. He told me nothing is going on with Aria, and I need to believe him. *It's only fair, right?*

I shower and dress for work. When I get downstairs, Keith and Erik are at the kitchen table.

"Just the men I wanted to see," I say and sit down. "We need to talk, guys."

Erik stops me before I can even appeal to his nice guy side. "Brenda, I thought we talked about this last night. You signed a contract. If we move, then you are responsible for all of our expenses. Not only will you be out the fifty thousand we would have paid to you, but you will have to pay for alternate accommodation, cars, food, housekeeping... Need I go on? Never mind the disruption to the band. It's more than you can afford, love."

Keith intently stirs the honey into his tea, pretending that he isn't part of the conversation. I try to do a bit of math. They are paying us $50,000. *How much are they paying for cars, for Angela's services? What it basically comes down to is: what is the price of my marriage?*

"Erik, come on. Be reasonable. There's no way we could afford that."

"Brenda, we've already spent thousands of dollars to be here. Do you think we can afford that?" he asks, sniveling.

Toni walks in with her clipboard; the first time I saw her with it, I joked about her being a rock-and-roll cruise director. But now, it lends her some credibility, and I hope that it will convince Erik to change his mind. "Erik," she begins, "if you'd allow it, I'd like to research other accommodations. Maybe just for Keith?"

"Out of the fucking question. The band stays together."

"Erik, would you please just consider it?" she asks.

"No. We'll lose out on a lot of work if the band members are not under the same roof. I am not going to sacrifice this record because this hussy wants to get into Keith's knickers."

"Erik! It was Keith who kissed *me*."

"Oh, and you had nothing to do with it?" Keith looks up from his tea. "Come on, Mrs. Dunkirk, you had your chance to make out with a rock star. And I distinctly remember you kissing me back."

He's right: I did kiss him back. Not that it's an excuse, but I guess I was just caught up in the moment. And I admit, it was nice to feel—to *know*—that someone wanted to kiss me. I don't think I can ever justify kissing another man in a way that anyone who believes in monogamy can understand. But Keith is right: I was just as responsible. The difference is that he isn't married. I am, and my husband and I agreed that we wouldn't go around kissing other people.

It was such a stupid thing to do. *What was I thinking?* It's not like kissing me is going to help him fix his public persona. To think I could have helped him change who he is. Now I know that that will never happen. Once an arrogant rock star, always an arrogant rock star.

"Keith, stop," Toni pleads.

"No, Toni. It's okay. He's right. I kissed Keith and messed up my marriage. And for what?"

"Gee, thanks, Brenda," Keith grumbles. "You've done wonders for my self-esteem."

"Keith, right now this isn't about you. This is about me and Tim. And the only way he's going to come home is if you guys *leave*." I pound my fist on the table in frustration.

"Well, that's not going to happen," Erik says. "We made an investment to be here. If we have to move, you're paying for it." He stands up from the table and raises his chin. "So, are we done here? The lads need to get to Del's."

At least I was dismissed by his words instead of his iPhone.

I sigh and stand from the table myself. I push my way past Erik to the fridge. I slam a few containers on the counter and pack my lunch. "I have to go to fucking work, and then I will come home to a house where my husband doesn't live anymore. And it's fucking Friday, so now I have an entire weekend without him here and *with* you guys here. Great. Just fucking great!" I stomp out of the kitchen and into the garage, get into my car, and head off to work.

Instead of listening to the problems of the world on NPR, I switch off the radio and will myself to come up with a solution to my own difficulties. I pass a few roadside motels and write down their names on the back of a gas station receipt I find wedged under the seat. Maybe I can convince Erik to let Keith stay in one, if it's not too expensive. If that fails, maybe I can convince Tim that *we* should stay in one. Either way, *it's the beginning of a plan, right?*

Chapter 21

WHEN I GET IN TO WORK, I barrel past the crowd of co-workers congregated at the coffee machine. "Brenda," one of them asks, "where are you going? It's bagel Friday. It's your turn to buy—did you bring them?"

Great, just some more people I've let down. I've forgotten to bring bagels for our Friday tradition. But I can't be bothered with that right now. When I get around the corner from the conference room door, I hear another one of them say, "What is her problem lately?" *Gee, where should I begin?*

Work is escaping me. I have got to figure this out. I want to be the one Tim looks at with rapt attention. I want to be the one standing beside him when he gets elected. *I have got to get Hydra out of my house. Think. I have got to think.*

Joy pops her head into my cube. "Staff meeting, three minutes," she chirps. I check my calendar on Outlook: three back-to-back meetings today. *How the hell am I supposed to solve the Hydra problem if I'm stuck in meetings for three hours?* I need more time.

The meetings blur by. I have next to no idea what was said. For all I know, I've agreed to a salary decrease. After the third meeting, Amanda calls me on my extension—she called into the meeting while en route from JFK Airport to a pitch meeting in New York City. I can tell she's still in a car: I can hear honking horns in the background.

"Brenda," she says, "what is going on with you lately? After your big fuck up with the brochures, I thought for sure you'd be trying to redeem yourself, but you barely participated in those meetings. The last few press releases you wrote were absolute crap. I had to rewrite a few of them." She pauses. "Is everything okay?"

I hold my fist against my forehead and try to come up with a reason why my work sucks lately. It's not like I can tell her that my home has been taken over by rock stars and that Tim has left me. I hate the sound of that: *Tim left me. Is that really what he did?* Tears fill my eyes and my chest feels like it's filled with ice. I can't get air into my lungs, and I gasp, trying to fill them. I duck my head onto my lap and try to breathe for a moment, but I feel like I am collapsing from within.

"Brenda? Are you there?"

I stand up and feel light headed. "I have to go. I'm taking the afternoon off."

Before I hang up the phone, I get to listen to how angry she is. "Wait a minute!" she barks. "Where are you going? Weren't you paying attention in that meeting? We have to redo the whole campaign for the Baxter account. Baxter is pissed about those brochures, and *we* have to eat the cost. You're not going anywhere, Brenda. You do, and you're history." I leave her with the dial tone.

"I don't fucking care anymore," I mutter to myself. I grab my keys and my bag and head for the door. I sprint down the stairs to the parking lot with tears streaming down my cheeks by the time I make it out to my car. I run the stop sign at the end of the block and then realize, as I'm squinting into the sun, that I've left my sunglasses on my desk.

It is a bit liberating, at first, to just leave my job in the middle of the morning. Most people in their right minds would be terrified, receiving that kind of threat from their boss. Normally, I would be too. But right now, I am not normal. I've forgotten what normal feels like. Life right now is nowhere near normal. It's amazing how drastically things can change in just a few short weeks, and how many complications can arise in that time. Problems are always fast to develop but seem to take forever to solve. I can't imagine living without Tim for however many months until Hydra leaves. It seems impossible.

I turn on the radio for a little distraction. "*In case you are wondering where they are now,*" the announcer drones, "*they're recording a new album at an undisclosed studio right here in Rhode Island. Look for it to hit the stores and iTunes next summer. It's Hydra...*" The opening chords of "Battleground Zero" blast out of the speakers.

"Fucking hell!" I snap and click off the radio; the knob comes off in my hand, and I toss it out the window. I pound my fists into the steering wheel until my wrists ache. I ride in silence and come home to an empty house. I pace through the house, trying to find something to occupy me, but I am too keyed up. I dial Tim's phone; he answers on the second ring.

"Hey, it's me."

"What's going on? Are you at work?"

"No, I left early. Just too much going on right now. I can't focus on anything."

"I have the opposite going on here. I can distract myself with my work." I hear his office door close; the noise of the shop is silenced. He's in his office. "So, how's it going with Hydra? Any ideas?"

"Well, why don't we just go to a hotel while they're here? Won't that make

Beside the Music

it easier?" I already know he won't go for it, but I figure I might as well try.

"Bren, you mean to tell me that you want us to move out until the rock stars see fit to leave? I will not be driven out of my home by these assholes."

"Tim, you're already out of your home. Where did you sleep last night?"

"That's not the point. I stayed here not because they're there. I stayed here because I saw my wife kissing one of them."

"Well, these are our options. We can't afford to pay for all of these people to live somewhere else."

"Then I don't want to see you until they're gone, Bren."

"Tim, come on. You can't be serious."

"Look, I did this for you. I knew that letting you live out your little teenage fantasy would make you happy. But you're the one who took it too far. I need you to make a decision about this. How important am I to you? How important is our marriage?"

I sit quietly for a moment. I know he's right. I have to find a way to get out of this. *But how?*

"Are you there?" he asks.

"Yeah," I say, tears streaming down my cheeks again.

"You didn't say anything. So I guess I know my answer."

"Tim..."

"Just go do whatever you want, Bren. I am done with this." He hangs up the phone, and I sob into the dial tone until the robotic voice tells me to hang up. And then I get mad and call him back.

"What," he grunts into the phone.

"What exactly are you done with, Tim? If you can't trust me, then fine, I understand. But I don't think I want to be married to someone who doesn't trust me and won't even try to forgive me. It was a mistake, Tim. A stupid fucking mistake. And if I apologize to you for the rest of my life, I will never live it down. So, if you want to play the poor husband whose wife kissed another man, then you go right ahead. Stay at your shop and move the fuck out. I am sure that Aria would be happy to have you." I slam down the phone, but that's not good enough. I throw it at the wall and the plastic casing shatters. The wires and microchip guts scatter all over the floor. I sit on the floor and lean against Tim's side of the bed, sobbing into my hands. I hear a soft knock, and then the door opens.

"Brenda?" Keith asks. "I heard a noise. Are you okay?" He walks in and sits on the floor beside me. He brushes my hair off my face, takes a tissue from the box on Tim's night table, and hands it to me.

"Okay, so here are my options," I say, exhaling. "Plan A, leave things the way they are. Plan B, try to get you to stay in a motel. Plan C, move to a motel myself, knowing that Tim won't go with me." I dab at my eyes. "Any way I slice it, my marriage is over."

"Brenda, Tim is just very angry right now. Surely he'll come around."

141

"I don't think so. Not until you guys leave. How long does it really take to record an album?"

"Well, that depends on how well rehearsed we are. I've seen it take a week, and I've seen it take a year."

"A year?" I leap off the floor. "A fucking year?"

"These are brand new songs, Brenda. We haven't had the time to work out the kinks. We're writing them as we go. It takes a bit of time for them to tighten the songs up before we record them."

"So, dare I ask how far along you are?" I wipe my eyes with the back of my hands and start pacing. *There is no way Tim and I can withstand a year of Hydra in the house.*

"We've completed four songs so far. Nine more to go."

"*Nine* more? That'll take, what, two months?"

"That's entirely possible," he replies. "Sometimes we listen to them later and re-do them, too."

"Keith, please listen to me." I wipe the tears off my face and turn toward him. "I need you out of this house, whether it's the whole band or just you. Will you please do that for me?"

"You know that Erik won't allow that," he replies.

"So you aren't even going to try? What happened to being more likeable?" Now I'm just getting pissed. "Tell me, Keith, does Erik work for you, or do you work for Erik?"

"He doesn't like to lose, Brenda. He will dig in on principle. That's what makes him such a great band manager. He will not bend for anything."

"Keith, I am begging you. Will you please try?"

He doesn't even try to answer. He shuffles out, and I clean up the pile of phone guts and try to figure out what the hell I am going to do for the rest of the weekend.

Chapter 22

I WAKE UP ON SATURDAY MORNING sprawled across the center of the bed with my head on Tim's pillow. I press my face into it and smell him on it; I feel a dull ache in my chest just from missing him. I roll over and see that it's 11 a.m. I am thankful that I've slept the morning away and wish I was tired enough to sleep all of Saturday, too. Vito paces at the bedroom door; he needs to go out. I throw on a pair of shorts and a T-shirt and say, "So let's go for a walk. A long one that takes all day!" He wags his tail excitedly.

The kitchen is empty; hopefully everyone's at Del's. It's nice to know that rock stars don't take weekends off. For the moment, I have the house to myself, and I wish Tim was here to share the quiet with me. I imagine us eating a leisurely brunch and then deciding what to do with the rest of the day. A visit to Mystic Aquarium? Even better, a day in Boston? I wonder if we'll ever again hold hands and stroll through the narrow winding streets of Boston's North End. I can almost smell the garlic and the bread baking, just thinking about it. *When did I last eat?*

Due to Angela's diligence, there aren't any chores to do other than the laundry. I throw a load into the washer and grab Vito's leash. "Let's go, Buddy Dog!"

We walk on the trail from our back yard into the woods. Vito immediately puts his nose to the ground, tracking something or someone that walked there before we did. When he does that, I always wish that he could tell me what he smells. I think it would be fun to solve a mystery with him. He could say something like, "It smells like peaches," and then I could try to guess anything that might smell like peaches that walked there ahead of us.

"Who is it, Vito? Do you know?" I ask. He doesn't look up and instead remains focused. Beagles are excellent trackers in the woods, and once his instincts take over, he cannot be distracted for anything.

He stops and raises his front leg, bent at the knee; he's pointing with it off the trail to the right. He can't tell me what it smells like, but at least he can tell me where it's going. *Should I follow him?* For all I know, he'll lead me into a rabbit hole. But he isn't baying the way he normally does when chasing a rabbit. He calmly and methodically sniffs at the unseen trail before him and ignores everything else. *What else am I going to do today? Might as well let my dog take me on a tour of the woods, right?*

We take a right and head off the trail; I walk quietly behind so I won't distract him. And then I hear the leaves rustle ahead. There's something moving just beyond a cluster of low trees, but the foliage is too thick; I can't make out what it is. It might just be a deer.

Vito cocks his head and listens. I am holding my breath. It's not at all like the sound of a bounding deer or the rustle of a squirrel or rabbit. The footsteps get progressively louder and my heart races. Our woods aren't accessible to the public, so it's unlikely that hikers would be roaming around out here. I feel my pockets and realize that I've left my cell phone at home.

I can barely make out a man walking toward me—and then I realize it's *Keith*. When he spots me, he calls to me, and I see that he has his camera strapped around his neck. I am annoyed; he's out here sightseeing when he should be in the studio, working toward getting out of my house.

"Hello, Brenda." He bends to scratch Vito's ears. The dog arches his back in pleasure; I silently call him a traitor. "And hello, little beagle. Sniffing around, are you?" Vito tips his head to coax Keith to scratch his favorite spot on his neck.

"Actually, I think he followed your trail. We don't normally go this way."

"I came upon a hummingbird nest back that way," he says. He points to the clump of trees.

"Really? I don't think I've ever seen one." I forget that I am annoyed with him. *It would be cool to see an actual hummingbird nest.* "Will you show me?"

I know I should be mad at him. He's supposed to be working, not spying on hummingbirds. *And how on earth would he have found a hummingbird nest?* There are miles and miles of forest out here. But then I figure I'll never get this chance again. I leash Vito and tie him to a tree; he whimpers at being left behind. I shush him and follow Keith to the clump of trees. I'll have him show me, and then I'll lay down the law and tell him he needs to get back to work. He places his finger over his lips to warn me to be quiet. *How does Keith manage to do this to me every time I should be mad at him?* He insists on showing me some loveable sensitive side that makes my insides go all gooey. If only he could exert this influence on the American listening audience.

He points to a small cup fashioned out of twigs and grass. Then he gestures to a log, and I step on it to get a better view. The opening is about the diameter of a quarter, and there is a single tiny egg inside. I gasp.

He tilts his head upward and whispers, "The mother is up there, watching us. See her?" He holds out his hand to steady me as I step off the log. "We'd better leave her be. Don't want to stress her out and cause her to abandon her nest." I want to stay longer and stare. Maybe I can stand here and wait for the tiny egg to hatch. I look around to spot a few landmarks so I can come back and check on the baby hummingbird's progress.

I untie Vito, and we walk back to the trail. Keith holds out his camera to me. "I got some great shots of her sitting on the egg." We stop so I can check out his pictures. He's right: they are great. *How the hell did he find this nest way out here? Just how much time is he spending in the woods, when he should be working?* I consider asking him but decide not to. I think I need to become friends with him again, and then maybe he can help me to get the band out of my house.

"You could probably sell these to *National Geographic,* if this whole rock-star thing doesn't work out," I say and hand his camera back to him.

"Actually, I am just going to send them to my mum. She can send them to *National Geographic* if she wants. Hummingbirds are her favorite."

"So, any word yet on her lump?"

"Actually, yes. She called me this morning. Turns out it's benign. She's fine."

"Really? Oh, Keith, that's great news." I throw my arms around him. "You must be so relieved."

"Yes, I really am. I truly could not face the prospect of life without Mum."

We are standing on the trail at the edge of my lawn with our arms still around each other. I am happy that his mom is okay, but yet somehow I cannot pull away from him. He doesn't pull away, either. He brushes the hair off my face and tucks it behind my ear then caresses my cheek. My pulse is racing in all the right places. *Is it possible to feel so right and know I am so wrong at the same time?*

"Brenda, I have never met anyone like you. You had the courage to put me in my place and be honest with me. Honestly, it's refreshing and sexy."

"Keith, you are so infuriating." It doesn't escape my attention that Keith Kutter called me sexy. He pulls me closer, so close that I take in his spicy, sweaty scent. I remember picking up on that the day he'd helped me take in the laundry from the rain. The smell of him goes right to my head. All I want to do now is press my face into his neck and stay there for the entire afternoon, letting whatever happens, happen.

It would be so easy to just go with it. *What it would be like to go on tour with him?* I don't think I would need to worry about groupies anymore, as the band's now older than the talent that the average groupie considers. Other than Trisha, that is. I would stand in the wings night after night and watch them play for thousands of screaming fans.

Never mind being backstage with the band—*what about getting to see the whole world one city at a time for months on end? How amazing would that be?* While he's rehearsing, I can go walk along the Seine in Paris or take a gondola ride through Venice or hike in Red Rocks. London. Moscow. Tokyo. But when I

145

think about it a bit longer, I realize that I'll probably be seeing those places alone. I'll be there only because Keith is there working, not because I am on a trip around the world with someone I love. I don't really want to see those places with Keith.

I can picture standing in front of the Kremlin with Tim, watching the colorful domes change as the sun hangs lower in the sky. I can imagine a long deep kiss with Tim while a gondolier expertly navigates through the canals of Venice. Really, *it's with Tim that I want to see those places.* He's the one I sat up with to the wee hours of the morning, talking about all the places in the world we wanted to go. Tim's the one who would make sure I had a blanket to keep warm on the plane. Tim's the one who would learn how to say, "No onions," in several different languages, so I wouldn't have to deal with having them on my plate. I don't see Keith doing any of that for me. With Keith, I'd be the one tagging along behind him, rather than walking beside him. And that's really how life with Tim is: we stand beside each other. We support one another. *My God, I really am being a shitty wife. What the hell is wrong with me?* I pull myself away from Keith's embrace.

"You need to get out of the woods and back into the studio, Keith. Get back to work." I really have to get the idea of being Keith Kutter's girlfriend *out* of my brain. But there's still that little voice that asks me why I need to do that. *When will I ever have this kind of chance again?* It probably wouldn't last, but it would probably be a lot of fun. *But then, what would happen when it eventually ends?* Which it will. End it before it starts.

We walk toward the house. I bend down and unclip Vito from the leash. He bolts across the lawn, past Tent City and up the deck stairs to the door. He taps on the glass with his claws until the door opens. I wonder who is inside to let him in. When Keith and I get to the door, we see Tim standing just inside. He glares at me then at Keith and then at me again. I can see the look of disappointment in his eyes.

"Tim…" I begin.

"You are unbelievable, Brenda." He pushes past me and walks toward the deck stairs.

"Tim, would you wait a second?"

He turns to face me. "Why should I?" He lunges at Keith, and for a second, I am afraid that Tim is going to deck him. Keith flinches and takes a step back. "And you! You are a guest in my home, and now you're trying to get into my wife's pants."

Keith turns to face Tim. He's about to say something that'll probably piss off Tim, but then cocks his head to the side and says, "Okay, I am off to work then." *Classic Keith: stir up the drama and then slip out the back door.* But he doesn't leave yet. He's cleaning the lens on his camera and placing it into its case.

"That's not it at all," I try to explain to Tim.

Beside the Music

"Then what is it? Looks like my wife and my dog went for a romp in the woods with Keith Kutter. Did you fuck him out there, too?"

"It wasn't like that at all. Will you please listen?" But he won't listen. Instead he's pacing around the deck, and I am starting to get a bit scared. I feel like, any second, he's going to haul off and punch Keith. Frustration radiates from Tim; *I need to get control of this situation. Fast.*

And then I notice a red BMW pulling into the driveway. "Oh, shit," I mutter. Any hope of controlling the situation is now gone. Keith spots her, turns on his heel, and goes back into the house. I wish I could, too.

"Be nice," Tim warns.

"Did you call her?"

"Yes, I did."

"Are you fucking crazy?"

"Brenda, she's my mother. I should be able to call her when I'm going through a tough time."

"And have her hate me even more?"

"She doesn't hate you."

"Just watch." I plaster a smile on my face; I figure I should lay on the charm a bit, seeing as how she thinks I called her rude. "Portia! How lovely to see you," I call out as she emerges from behind the wheel. She's wearing one of her Chanel suits. She never seems to sweat in them, even on the hottest of days—another way I can tell that she's not human. Out of the corner of my eye, I catch Keith in the window, jumping back so he can dodge her view. *Lucky.* Wish I could do the same. Portia, as usual, doesn't acknowledge that I've even spoken to her.

"Timothy, I've called Albert, and we'll have you out of this mess in no time flat," she says, breezing by me.

"Mess? What mess?" I ask. She ignores me. I haven't talked to Tim about the shop in about a week; *is he in some kind of legal trouble?* Portia has this friend, Albert Sharpley, from her club. He's pretty famous in Rhode Island for being a legal shark. Whatever the problem is, this guy will get results for Tim. That's actually a good thing about Portia: she's pretty well connected.

"Albert is brilliant with divorce, dear. You'll be out of this," she gestures toward me, "in no time."

"And hello to you, too, Portia." I plaster on an even wider, faker smile. *I am so over this bitch.* "How lovely of you to stop by, unannounced. Again."

Tim glares at me for a moment, and I look back as if to say, "What?" Then he turns his attention to Portia. "Mother, I don't want to get a divorce. Would you please be nice?"

"Then darling, why on earth did you tell me you'd moved out?" she asks.

"*Um*, Tim?" I ask, tugging on his arm. "May I please have a moment in

147

private with you—darling?" I smile at Portia. "Would you excuse us for one moment?"

Tim scowls at me but agrees to walk out of earshot of his mother. "Are you fucking crazy?" I hiss. "You told her that we're getting divorced?"

"No, I didn't. She called me on my cell and came and met me at the shop one night, and she figured out that I was staying there. She got onto this divorce stuff on her own."

"Tim," I say, sighing, "is she going to sic her crazy lawyer on me now?"

"No, I'll ask her not to. She'll listen to me."

I don't really want to come between Tim and his mom. It's great that he's so close to her; but she does need to get a life of her own. I had always figured that, if I ignored it long enough, eventually she'd warm to me. After thirteen years, it hasn't happened yet, as evidenced by her willingness to help Tim divorce me— even when he says he doesn't want a divorce. Something has got to change, and it's obvious that Tim won't be the one to make it happen.

"Will you please tell her to go home?" I ask. I don't want to give Portia even more of a reason to hate me, but the last thing I need is her involvement in this mess. "Don't take this the wrong way, but we have enough going on here without her getting involved."

"You're right." He runs his hands though his hair. "I'll get rid of her. But Brenda, you gotta tell me what's going on here."

"What do you mean?"

"You're acting like a fucking groupie, Bren. I saw you guys come out of the woods together, and you were fawning all over him."

"What? No, he was fawning over *me*, Tim."

"Well then, maybe he'll write a song about you, and then you can get over it—" He's cut off by Portia Interruptus.

"Is there a problem here?" She came up behind me as Tim and I were talking. I bristle at the sound of her voice; she is skilled at sneaking up on me when I least expect it, like some kind of snooty ninja. Tim doesn't acknowledge her, but raises his eyebrows at me. *So, he's chickening out and not telling her to get the hell out of here? Nice.*

"No, Portia, there's no problem here. Just having a private discussion with my husband." I sigh, hoping she'll take the hint and back off. I wish I could add, "But if there were, your presence would only be making it worse."

"Well then, *who* could be fawning over you, dear?" She raises her eyebrow, not one crease shows on her Botoxed forehead. She looks me up and down as if it's impossible that any man would find me attractive. "Are you threatening my son?"

"I'm not threatening anyone," I say, glowering at her. *Where the hell would she get that idea? God, she's so infuriating. I wish I could just tell her to go fuck herself. Maybe next time.*

Beside the Music

Tim would absolutely kill me—kissing another man and telling his mother to fuck off in the same week would push him right over the edge. Though I am pretty sure the look on her face after she registers that I've said "go fuck yourself" would be absolutely priceless. That is, if her face is still capable of expressing emotion, what with all the Botox. I wonder if anyone's ever said it to her before; I can't see how she's gotten this far in her life, acting the way she does, without someone saying that to her. But I don't really see the ladies she lunches with talking to her like that.

"Mother, Brenda and I have a lot to talk about. Can I call you tomorrow?" Tim kisses her on the cheek and nudges her toward her car. *Good, Tim's stepping up. Now I don't have to cuss her out.* She lingers on the driveway, tapping her foot; she's probably thinking I'm rude for not asking her in for a gin and tonic. *Sorry, honey, fresh out of gin and Newport niceties.* She sighs and reaches up to air kiss Tim on the cheek.

"Timothy, shall I set up a meeting with Albert for tomorrow?" she asks before heading to her car.

"Mother, please, it's not necessary," he calls out after her. I look up at him, thankful that he doesn't find her bulldog divorce attorney necessary. She dismisses him with a wave, and we watch her slip her probably very expensive sunglasses onto her face and back the car out of the driveway. I can't help but smirk a bit because nothing's going to change the fact that Keith peed on Portia's car.

"Well, I just came to get some clean clothes," Tim says, shrugging. "See ya around, Bren." And then I watch him get into his car and pull out of the driveway, too. I briefly wonder what he'd done with the dirty ones. Angela's going to have to wash them; no way in hell I will, at this point.

I stand on the driveway and try to process exactly what just happened. This morning when I woke up, I tried to be angry with Tim. Even when I tried to imagine going on tour with Keith, I really couldn't be angry at him. Imagining being Keith's girlfriend just felt all wrong. But now, as I watch Tim pull out of the driveway, I can kind of picture it. I mean, it's not like Tim wants me to be his wife right now.

I wonder what the hell he told Portia about us. Whatever it was, it was not cool for him to do that. Though, to be fair, he could probably tell her that I buy my underwear at Target instead of Nordstrom, and she'd insist he divorce me. As I walk up the deck stairs, I wipe the tears from my cheeks and wonder when the hell I'm going to stop crying.

When I get inside, Keith is at the table with a cup of tea. I notice that there isn't any paper or pen in front of him. He's not writing. *Why isn't he writing?* He doesn't say anything at first; I bend down to stroke Vito. He gives my hand a sincere lick and thumps his tail on the kitchen floor; he knows exactly how to soothe me. I tell him he's a good dog.

149

"Off to the studio, then." Keith sighs and opens the back door. "Thought I'd ought to make myself scarce, seeing as how my last meeting with your mother-in-law went terribly." Thankfully, Keith knows when to exit a scene—surely pissing on Portia's very rare and very expensive BMW did not endear him to her, anyway. He pauses, thinking maybe to say something before walking out the backdoor. He has a look of concern on his face, and I wonder if he overheard the scene play out on the driveway. How embarrassing to have Portia show up, on top of everything else. But he doesn't say anything else, just walks out the door and closes it behind him.

After Keith leaves I pace around the house for an hour or two until I get bored. I try to read, but then I realize that though my eyes are moving across the page, they're not absorbing any of the words. I can't fathom another month of this without Tim.

I need to see for myself. *Are they really working as hard as they say? Will it really be a month?* Before I know it, I am behind the wheel of my car and a few minutes later, I am pulling in to Del's driveway. I let myself in and open the door to the basement then I tiptoe down to the bottom step where I can listen undetected.

Chapter 23

WHEN I FIRST SIT DOWN, I hear Erik shout over the band, "No, no, no, stop! It's not right. Start again."

Gill rips out a scorching riff on his guitar to release his frustration. He's on his acoustic, so it comes off a bit stilted; I can hear the band members groan.

"Come on then, let's get it right," Erik says. "These tracks won't record themselves." He's trying to sound cheerful, but I am sensing from my perch on the bottom of the stairs that the guys aren't taking it that way. This is nothing like that afternoon I'd spent watching Keith record the wind-chime song. The tension in the studio is stifling.

The band members grumble and start the song again. First, I hear Jeff tap out four beats on his drum sticks. Then Ben starts to sing, "She says I'm an asshole, but I know she wants me anyway."

My breath catches in my throat; I clamp my hand over my mouth. *Unbelievable*! *Is this seriously about me?* But the song feels all wrong. It's too slow, too mellow. *Why is Gill on the acoustic?* The bass line is soft and fluid, almost jazzy. I hear Erik pipe up, and they stop again. Is this really what their process is like? There's no way in hell they're going to finish this album, ever, at this rate.

"The feeling of this song is all wrong," Erik says "Is this a fucking love song, or is it a 'she doesn't want me, so she can bugger off' kind of song? If it's the latter, then it needs to be faster and a bit bluesy. Not this lame, fluffy love bullshit. We need to re-work this one. Gill, get on your electric guitar."

I listen as Jeff taps out four beats again, this time faster. Gill plays the same riff on his electric but faster. Keith's bass line booms, sounding like a loose rubber band bouncing along to the beat. Ben puts on a raspy voice and sings about a man chasing a woman who says she's not interested but is clearly a tease. I brace my hand over my forehead and wince: *is this how Keith perceives me?* I am being made to look like a tease. *This is bullshit. Man, what if Tim hears this?*

Toni appears on the stairs beside me and raises her eyebrows. "Eavesdropping?" She smiles. I stammer in response. "Don't take the song too personally, Brenda. It's part of the creative process, and we often have to take liberties with our situation to make the song come out right."

"What do you mean?" I ask.

"The story of a man chasing a woman is an age-old rock-and-roll story. And, of course, the man is going to call her a tease, because every man wants to think that, if she's not going to return the affection. It's not personal, Brenda."

"Don't worry, I'm not taking it personally," I lie. *Of* course *I'm taking it personally. Keith wrote a song for me; and it's a song about wooing me.* My heart leaps with excitement. Someday, millions of people will hear that song, and they're going to wish that they were me. They might not know that the song was inspired by Brenda Dunkirk. But I will. When Hydra moved into the house, I never expected Keith to write a song for me. I expected that I would, in a way, help them to produce a great album. But having a whole song just for me is way better.

"So, are you just going to sit here on the steps, or do you want to come in?" Toni asks.

"*Uh*, I don't think I should go in there if they're working on this song right now. I just came here because I wanted to know how far along they are. I keep hearing that this could take months. I want to know if that's true."

"It's too soon to tell, love." And for the first time, I really believe her. *If Erik keeps stopping them every few minutes, how long will it take to finish just this one song?*

Right now it doesn't really matter how long it'll take. Tim won't hear me out, whether it takes a day or a month, anyway. And if Keith is getting over his writer's block by writing songs about me, then who am I to complain, right? So long as he's writing.

152

Chapter 24

ON MONDAY MORNING, I pull into the parking lot and see that Amanda's car is in the spot closest to the door. *How early did she get here?* Then it occurs to me that she probably spent the entire weekend re-doing the campaign for the Baxter account. I didn't even think about Baxter all weekend; this is going to be a bad day. I toy with the idea of calling in sick. But I am here already. It just takes one of my co-workers to see me driving out of the lot, and I'm busted.

I walk as quietly as I can into my cubicle and boot up my computer. Just as I am about to get a cup of tea, my extension rings: it's Amanda. I gulp and pick up the phone.

"Brenda, I need to talk to you right now," she says. No pleasantries, and none of the usual business-but-friendly tone in her voice. I glance at my watch: it's 8:02, and I am already in trouble. I'd kind of hoped that I wouldn't have to actually see her until closer to nine, after I'd had time to prepare a bit more.

When I walk into Amanda's office, I see the dark circles under her eyes. She's been working all weekend, and I instantly feel guilty. "Close the door and sit down," she orders. She's pissed. "Now, what the hell was that about on Friday? I tried to call you on your cell, but I guess you had it turned off. Your leaving early on Friday, after we'd just had that meeting about the Baxter campaign, was unacceptable. Do you have any idea how late we all stayed here on Friday? Do you have any idea how many people had to clean up your mess on this account over the weekend?" She pauses to take a breath and sip her tea. "I want to know what is up with you lately. A month ago, you were in line for a promotion. Hell, I was even thinking about partnership for you in a few years. Give me one good reason why I shouldn't fire you right now."

I stare at her. Nothing I say right now will even come close to an acceptable response.

"Really?" She pauses to bore her ice-blue-eyed stare into my forehead. "God, Brenda, what the hell is going on with you?"

The dilemma races through my mind. If I tell her what is really going on, I'll break the non-disclosure agreement with the band and be in even more hot water. The walls in this office have ears. The ceilings in here are high, and the individual office walls don't go all the way up to the ceiling. I usually walk up to the roof if I want to have a private conversation.

My mind fast-forwards to the eventual article in the *Tattle Tale.* I picture thousands of screaming fans on my front lawn instead of the few dozen we currently have. I imagine people trying to get into my house and more women like Trisha, insisting that Keith's lyrics are for them. *Will they actually fling their panties onto my front steps?* I don't think Amanda would tell, would she? Though these days, I don't really feel as if I could trust anyone with the knowledge that Hydra is living in my house. I am paranoid that someone else will overhear. I involuntarily shudder.

Amanda raises her eyebrows. She's waiting for a response. In the grand scheme of things, having a rock band crashing at my house isn't any of Amanda's concern. She doesn't care if I have the entire Russian army staying there. The only thing she cares about is that I am not producing at work anymore. I need to come up with a response, and I need to come up with it fast.

"Brenda? I'm waiting." She looks irritated and impatient. I need to say something. Anything. *Here goes nothing.*

"Amanda, I have a few things going on in my personal life right now that are kind of difficult. I know that everyone here had to work really hard because I left on Friday, and I am sorry."

"That's it?" She raises her eyebrows. "You're sorry?" She glares at me from behind her desk. She switches into what I call her Nordic ice princess mode. It's moments like these that a glare from her eyes just might burn though my skin. She clenches her chiseled jaw and stares. *When is she going to blink?* I brace for the next sentence that will ultimately end in, "you're fired."

The possibility of hearing that makes me shrink into my seat. Amanda has been my mentor all these years; the fact that I have disappointed her is absolute torture for me. I want to be Amanda when I grow up, and it's not going to happen if she fires me.

She takes another sip of her tea and then a deep breath before speaking again. "Look, the CEO of Baxter and one of our competitors are golf buddies. On Sunday afternoon, I got called into a meeting about this campaign because they're very pissed off about how this has been handled. It used to be that I could give you these sensitive accounts and you'd hit them out of the park. You've royally fucked this one up." She pauses for a moment and then pulls a document out of her top desk drawer and hands it to me.

I begin to read, and then stop. "Amanda, is this what I think it is?" It's on Amanda Dixon PR letterhead. It's signed by her. It's addressed to Ms. Dunkirk; very formal. Too formal.

"This is a written warning," she replies in a calm and deliberate tone. "After that golf game on Sunday, I was this close to firing you." She holds up her pinched thumb and index finger. There's not much space between them at all. "You have thirty days to pull your head out of your ass and get back to work, or you're out of here. We will have meetings every morning in which I will monitor your progress on this campaign. I don't have time to babysit you, Brenda. But it looks as if that's what we need to do right now. Get it together. I vouched for you with the client. Don't make me regret it," she warns.

I wait for her to dismiss me, but she keeps talking. "You are way better than this, Brenda. I saw a spark in you, and I invested in you." She's right: she paid for my MBA. I should be grateful. Amanda doesn't give second chances; nor does she finance advanced degrees. I have a long future at this company, and I need to buck up. I mutter a meager apology, and she continues to stare. "Now, get back to work and show me how good I know you are."

I practically leap out of the chair and burst out her office door. Once I am standing out in the hall, I feel as if I can breathe again. Everyone is looking out over their cubicle walls at me; I avoid making eye contact with any of my co-workers while I go back to my desk. I am completely humiliated.

What's worse? Getting fired or getting a warning? At least if I'd been fired, I wouldn't have to see my boss and my co-workers every day while I grovel so I can keep my job. I look over my shoulder at the walkway between the rows of cubicles. *How many of my co-workers know that I am riding the thirty-day warning?* I've seen it happen to others, and word about it travels fast, especially with the lack of privacy in this place. Surely someone heard her voice echoing over the wall, bouncing off the ceiling, and landing in an upturned ear. I remember hearing others whisper about it and then stop when the victim entered the room; that will probably happen to me, too. I don't think Amanda would tell anyone; she typically avoids the office gossip and gets on everyone's case about spreading rumors. But all it takes is one person to know, and then everyone else knows within hours. If Joy at the front desk finds out, that time is cut down to mere minutes.

It is now 8:30, and I have an entire day to prove myself. Hydra may have taken away my marriage, but there is no way I am going to let them take my job away, too. I pull up the Baxter account on the server and look over all the changes that were made to the campaign over the weekend. I read over the notes and check out the mockups for the ads. I figure that if Tim can bury himself in work to get through all of this, then so can I.

Chapter 25

I FINALLY LISTEN to my growling stomach. It's been complaining for a while now, and I've ignored it. I put a sticky note over the bottom corner of my monitor so that I wouldn't be focused on the time, and then I cranked on Baxter tasks. When I peel it away, I realize that it's already two o'clock. I lean back in my chair, stretch my arms over my head, and groan a little like Vito does when he first wakes up. He's on to something: the stretch and groan is pretty satisfying. For most of the day, Hydra and Tim have not crossed my mind, which is a good thing.

I grab my purse and keys and walk to the beach to get some air. I look over my shoulder as I leave. I don't think I should go, seeing as how I am on the thirty-day warning. But honestly, I need to get outside for a bit. And this morning wanted to get out of the house as quickly as possible and avoid Keith, so I didn't bother to pack a lunch.

Since I heard the song on Saturday, I've been steering clear of Keith. On Sunday, Vito and I spent most of the day driving around. We went to the dog park, and then to a dog-friendly beach. It was nice to have the day to myself, but I missed Tim horribly. Vito was a fun distraction; it was a blast to see him romp with the other dogs at the park. Still, Sunday dragged on as if it had no intention of ending. I never thought I'd so look forward to a Monday.

The beach is just a few blocks away from the office. The thing that's great about this beach is that it's not such a popular spot for tourists, which surprises me, because it's adjacent to an idyllic New England waterfront area. The main drag, which extends along the beach front, is lined with funky little indie shops and a café that serves the best homemade croissants I've ever had. I could spend an entire afternoon sitting at one of the sidewalk tables and sampling every pastry in the case. Just over the rocks at the south end of the beach is a bustling dock where a fleet of fishing boats is tied up. The fish market at the docks is popular with chefs from as far away as Boston; they fill the small streets to buy the catch of the day at dawn. The food is fresh at the Red Canoe Crab Shack, and now that it's past the lunch rush, there's no line.

Beside the Music

I grab an order of fried clams from the Portuguese couple who run the shack right on the beach. They taught me how to say "thank you" in Portuguese. *"Obrigado!"* I call through the take-out window before walking over to my favorite bench in the shade, set at the perfect angle to watch the waves crash onto the rocky sand.

I take my iPhone out of my purse and open up Facebook for a bit of distraction, sending Annie an instant message and hoping that she has a moment to chat. It's been awhile, as I've been living on Planet Hydra. It'll be nice to hear how she's doing. She doesn't write back right away, so I put my phone aside and dig into my fried clams platter. The Red Canoe's fried clams are the best—I can't quite place the spicy and sweet flavors in the breading, but it's amazing. I close my eyes and focus on trying to guess what it is. Of course, I've asked about it, but the owners won't tell me.

The Facebook messenger app on my phone chirps at me. It's a message back from Annie.

Hey girl! What's going on? We need to have a phone date. I met this guy at a bar in the Village.

I pick up the phone and write back.

Sorry I've been out of touch. So busy these days. I hate being too busy to get caught up with you.

I hear you. I feel like all you and I talk about anymore is work. How's Tim?

Just seeing her ask about him makes me ache. *How the heck am I supposed to answer that question?* I don't want to tell people. Yet at the same time I feel so alone. Annie's my best friend. *I should be able to tell her anything, right?* I decide to take the chance. I've held this in way too long; I need to get someone else's perspective on it.

Not so good, actually. I messed up. Bad.

What happened? Are you somewhere you can talk? It seems silly to type into a phone when I can just call you.

Yes, please.

I could definitely use a friend right now. Annie and I lived together all four years of college. We used to sit up all night, obsessing about boys, grades, and

157

life in general. I miss having her nearby, as she's in New York City now. Our lives are different, and it's harder to stay connected.

My phone rings. I have no idea how to even begin. I jam a fistful of fried clams into my mouth, finish chewing, and answer on the third ring.

"Hey" I say.

"So, what's going on? Are you okay?" Annie sounds breathless. I think she's doing her lunchtime power walk.

"Yes," I begin, out of habit. Then, "No, actually. Things aren't so great right now."

"What's wrong?"

"It's kind of a long story. Do you have time? And more importantly, can you keep a secret?" I don't even wait for her to respond. This is my oldest friend; of course she can keep a secret. I don't have to worry about voices carrying over chintzy thin office walls.

She listens while I violate the non-disclosure agreement. It feels good to tell someone about everything that's going on—and besides, at this point, what could Erik do to me that hasn't already been done? My job and my marriage are falling apart. At least I can confide in an old friend and try to get some perspective on it. I tell her the whole story about how Keith came over the day after the dinner, and then how Hydra ended up living in my house.

"What do you mean, 'they're living in your house'?" she asks. "Like, you're all under the same roof? How's that working out?"

"We have these tents in the back yard. Not like camping ones, but like ones you'd see in a movie about Bedouins living in the desert. They have a housekeeper who comes in and takes care of the cooking and the cleaning, and Jeff Gilchrist's drum set is in the garage." I leave out the part about Tim leaving me for the moment. At least I got the rest of it off of my chest and feel much better after having told someone.

"So, what does Tim think about all of this?" It feels like we're back in the dorm, talking about a boy. I feel comfortably warm inside, like I've just had a hot bowl of soup on a cold winter day.

"Well, it's gotten old for him, as you can imagine." I pause, not sure how to continue. "I kissed Keith," I say quietly.

"Wow. *Um*. Just, *wow*." She pauses, and I can tell she's not sure how to continue, either. "Okay, so not only is the band now living in your house, but you kissed Keith Kutter." She gasps. "So, what was it like?"

"What?"

"Kissing Keith! What was it like? I really hope he isn't some sloppy, drooly kisser. Is he?"

"No, definitely not sloppy or drooly." I allow myself to reflect on the kiss for a moment and notice that I am suddenly feeling more than warm inside. "Let's just say he knows what he's doing." *Is it wrong to tell her that kissing a man other than my husband was amazing? Probably.*

Beside the Music

"So, when's he coming back?"

"Keith?" I snap back from my daydream.

"No, Tim. When is he coming back?" she asks.

"Honestly, I don't know. The band has no idea how long it'll take to record the album, and Tim won't come back until they're moved out."

"Are you serious? That could take months, I imagine."

"I know. Annie, I am so lost. I don't know what to do. I thought I wanted to start a family with Tim. But he is always saying it isn't the right time. And now I am so confused. Living with the band has made me see that there is so much more to life than being married, living in the burbs, and my career." I pause. "I feel like Tim and I will never have kids. He's waiting for some perfect moment, and meanwhile, a million moments have passed us by. Have I wasted all these years being married to him? I feel like every year that goes by that we don't finally decide to start our family puts a wedge between is. And the wedge, I feel, is getting thicker and thicker. I hate that I have to wait for him to make a decision that will make my life change."

"I'm sure that sucks, Bren," she says.

"It's just hard right now. And it was hard enough with him working so much on the election. Now we have Hydra living with us, which he was so cool about because he knew it would make me happy, but I kind of wonder if he agreed to it just to shut me up about a baby. And now they won't fucking leave, and he's gone. I just don't know what to do."

"There's only one answer, Bren. They need to go. What's more important, Tim or Keith?" That's the thing about Annie. She has this knack for stripping away all the bullshit of a problem and getting right to the point of it. And she's right. "Well, I hate to cut this short, but I have to get back for a staff meeting. Are you going to be okay? Want to talk later tonight?"

"I'm okay." I take a deep breath, like a sigh, and notice that I don't feel that ache in my gut when I do. "I think talking about it helped. I've been walking around with all of this in my head, and it's nice to just get it out." Tears fill my eyes; I don't want to hang up. I feel lighter inside after talking to her. *Maybe I should hop a train to New York this weekend and get out of the house.* I could use a girlfriend right now.

But for the moment, I have to get back to work, too. Getting things off my chest has definitely helped. I race-walk back to the office with a renewed sense of purpose. Now I need to get my job back, and next I'll get my husband back. I just need to come up with a plan. *How hard can it be to kick a squatting rock band out of my house?*

159

Chapter 26

"OH GOOD, YOU'RE BACK," Joy says as I walk past the reception desk. "Amanda wants everyone in the conference room. Baxter status meeting."

I grab a fresh cup of tea, a new notepad, and a few different-colored pens before heading into the conference room. I perch myself on the edge of a seat at the end of the table, where I can have an unobstructed view of everyone. I am ready to rock this campaign and get at least part of my life back on track. *Let's do this.*

Amanda is already at the head of the table, talking to several of my co-workers about the pitch she did in New York last week. I can tell by the tone of her voice that she doesn't think it went well; she was probably distracted by the impending disaster that is Baxter.

"Amanda, you say that all the time, though," I remind her. "You said that after you pitched Baxter, too."

"Yeah, and look where we are now. They're probably shopping for a new agency right now." She sighs heavily. "Well, let's keep that from happening, guys." She looks at me. "What do you have for me?"

"Here are the changes I made on the media plan," I say. "The publicity for the Factory Tour show is getting some traction. We have interviews lined up with local TV stations in every town that will have a store."

"Nice. I like it. Great work." She throws me a look that says, "And this is why I haven't fired you." I am thankful that she acknowledges my work. My confidence is boosted, and I feel as though riding the thirty-day warning will be a breeze. "But remember, they don't need a product campaign—they've got to do some damage control before they go national. Their quality has declined over the last few years, and people bitch about them on Twitter. They need to improve their image, and we need to make it happen fast. We need some opinion leaders talking them up out there."

"What if we could get Antonio Diego on board?" I ask her.

"Are you kidding me? That would be a huge win. How on earth would you

Beside the Music

do that?" *Good question. Maybe I can ask Portia to put me in direct contact with him. After all, he's going to redecorate my house—whether I like it or not.*

"Okay," I say, scratching a note on my pad, "let me see if I can get Antonio Diego. That'll definitely help boost Baxter's quality image."

Amanda continues talking, but I tune her out for a bit. It occurs to me that Baxter's image problems sound all too familiar: the perception of their product doesn't have the allure it once had. *Who else do I know that has the same problem?* For the first time today, I allow my mind wander to Hydra. I try to fight it, but I feel like I am on to something. Maybe if I just allow myself to think about it for a minute or two, I'll get it out of my system, and then I can focus on Baxter again.

Hydra's product also doesn't have the allure it once had either, so they've decided to counteract their declining popularity with this "Meet the American fans" campaign. Their publicist was looking for opinion leaders, as well: longtime fans who could vouch for the coolness of Hydra. *How can I help them with that?* Maybe I can work out a deal with Erik.

I feel the gears in my brain start to turn, and I zone out in the meeting. I make a few notes to myself in the margin of my notepad and will myself to stay in the present. Then I start fidgeting in my seat, because I've just now stumbled upon a brilliant solution to my Hydra problem. I pinch myself on the thigh to keep myself sitting upright and giving the impression that I am even remotely interested in the Baxter Corporation problem. I contribute a few meager ideas so I can keep my job, but my brain is definitely spiraling in another direction.

Once the meeting is over, I bolt from the conference room, back into my cubicle. I log into my computer and launch the campaign manager software. I check over my shoulder to make sure the coast is clear, and then I start my own brainstorming session. I draft tweets, press releases, and media alerts. If I can find a way to improve Hydra's image in the U.S., then maybe I can bribe them into moving out of my house. After all, I already have a lot of the media contacts in the U.S. that they need.

I pull together a list of entertainment website and news magazine editors and draft an email to Annie at MTV News. Next, I come up with a media release schedule, and then I print everything out on letterhead and tuck it into a folder.

In the time it takes me to work on my new campaign, two hours of billable time goes by. I have to put it away now and swear to myself that I will focus my attention on the Baxter campaign for the rest of the day. I am back into the throes of Baxter when Joy knocks on my cubicle doorway.

"Hi, Brenda," she says, and tosses a newspaper on my desk. "Just thought you'd want to see the *Tattle Tale* page." She lingers for a bit and looks at my computer screen. Joy is notoriously nosy, and I'm relieved that I've already put away my work on my Hydra idea and appear to be hard at work on Baxter.

I thank her, and then thumb through the *Tattle Tale,* just to make sure none of our clients have embarrassing pictures in there. But mostly, I think it's funny to see the indiscreet pictures that this rag publishes. It normally includes high-profile people getting caught in seedy-looking situations with other people who are not their spouse, and the like. I am about to set the paper down again when I see a familiar face on page six.

The picture was taken at a fundraiser last week. I squint at the picture, trying to remember where I've seen her lately. She looks like a teenager at the prom. Her hair is pulled back into a French twist, and she's wearing an understated peach strapless gown with a corsage pinned above her breast. Clearly bored, she's gazing off into the distance, not even remotely interested in whatever cause *du jour* she's supporting. A clean-cut-looking college boy is on her arm and shaking hands with someone off camera—probably trying to make connections for his already-budding political career.

I let my mind wander while I doodle on the newspaper; I know that if I stop thinking so hard about where I've seen her, it will come to me. While I'm doodling, I end up drawing heavy eyeliner on her face and darken her lips; I do that sometimes to magazine pictures. For a while there, I was obsessed with making everyone look like Robert Smith from The Cure. But I don't do that with her. I just give her a ballpoint makeover.

Then it dawns on me. I look at her face with the inked-in makeup and realize that I saw her the night Keith and Ben brought the hookers home. She was the young one who looked so familiar to me at the time. I start to laugh. It hadn't occurred to me to use my public relations powers for evil when I started creating my Hydra campaign. This little revelation changes everything.

"I knew it!" I pound my fist on the table. "Joy! Do you have another copy of the *Tattle Tale*?" I call out through the office.

"What did you do with the one I gave you?" she asks.

"I, *um*, defiled it," I say, holding up the picture.

She hands me a clean copy, and I tuck both pictures into my folder. The butterflies in my stomach are alive and well. My mind is reeling, but I need to get back to work.

I pound away at my to-do list from the Baxter meeting until five o'clock rolls around, but my heart's not in it at all. *I cannot wait to get home.* Erik has no idea what he's in for; I can't focus on anything else other than taking Hydra down. At the end of the day, I drop the drafts on Amanda's desk. Thankfully, she's not in her office, so I sneak out and make it to my car undetected, before she can ask me to do anything else. I feel like I'll explode if I don't get my Hydra campaign out of my brain.

When I get home, the house is empty and Tent City is a ghost town. I assume everyone is at Del's, which is great, because I can take advantage of the quiet and formulate my plan. I take out the folder I brought home from work and arrange the contents on the dining room table. I pull out my laptop and re-write some of

Beside the Music

the work I've done—this time to accommodate my discovery of the photo. I print them out on some extra letterhead.

When I go into the kitchen to get a snack, I get another idea. I grab the whiteboard eraser and mutter a quiet "Fuck you... fuck you... fuck you..." with each swipe over the once-highly-debated shower schedule. Then I write my own schedule in place of the band's daily schedule. "It's my house now, bitches," I say out loud to the empty room. "Nobody tells *me* what time to shower." I was so screwed on that day I overslept: I couldn't take a shower before work because I'd missed my "scheduled" time. At least I managed to wash my face and brush my teeth in between others getting *their* showers.

After I'm done getting set up, I rifle through the fridge for something to settle the butterflies in my stomach, but I don't find anything I want to eat. Instead, I brew a cup of peppermint tea but let it go cold while I pace in the dining room, practicing my speech. Then I realize I'm only making myself more nervous, so I take Vito outside to play. Maybe I just need to stop thinking about it and relax with him.

Of course, I can't take him out in the front, with the fan corral. I can't believe they're all still out there, barbecuing and playing Frisbee. I can see Trisha doing yoga. *Is she trying to impress Ben now?* In the back yard, I don't scold Vito for dropping a bomb near Tent City. I don't scoop it, either. I am so over trying to accommodate these people. *Maybe I should just have him continue to shit there so they get fed up and leave on their own.* I laugh to myself. If only a beagle soiling their camp could make a difference, I would have allowed him to do it weeks ago.

But seriously, the thing I need to remember is what I learned in my negotiation seminar in grad school: ask for what you want and then shut your mouth. The silence will make the other person so uncomfortable that they'll find themselves saying just about anything to break it. I actually tried that when Tim and I bought my car. It worked, and we paid way less than the sticker price. That's also what I need to do right now: bolster my confidence by remembering past victories.

Just after dark, Erik and Toni come in through the back door and heat up the dinner that Angela left earlier in the day. After they start eating at the kitchen table, I walk in with Vito and chat with them awhile—until Erik notices the whiteboard.

"What's this?" he asks. Toni wipes her mouth and stands beside Erik to examine my work.

"Looks like some sort of media communications schedule," Toni murmurs as she reads. "Whoa." She is taken aback at the end.

"Did you do this?" Erik turns on Toni, gesturing to the board. "Are you

163

fucking with me right now?"

"Of course not," she replies. "Why on earth would I do any of this?" They stand shoulder to shoulder and read it all again.

"Un-fucking-believable," Erik mutters.

It's obvious that they've forgotten that I am still in the room. I clear my throat from where I'm still sitting at the kitchen table. Both of them turn to face me, their mouths hanging open.

"It would seem that you have forgotten," I say, "that I am a public relations specialist at one of the top firms in the state. Until you guys moved in, I was in line for a promotion to vice president at that firm, that's how good my work is. I might even be a partner in the firm someday. Though my specialty is building a reputation, not tearing it down. But in your case, I'll make an exception."

"Congratulations," Erik says, with a slight sneer to his voice. But I can't help noticing that he doesn't terminate the conversation with his iPhone: he knows this is important.

I stand up from the table and walk over to the whiteboard. "What you see here is a schedule of proposed communications that I will release to national media outlets if my demands are not met."

"And what would those demands be?" Erik asks. Even though he knows what I have to say is important, I can tell he's trying to make me feel weak. I'm sure he knows what my demands are. *What the hell have I been asking him for this last week? Is he going to say next that the band doesn't negotiate with terrorists?* I smirk.

"I want Hydra and the entire entourage out of my house by the end of the week. If they are not out, I will start off with letting the media know where they are staying and where they are recording. Once the press gets here, I will introduce myself, and then I will fill them in on the last few weeks of life here at the Dunkirk residence. As you are aware, Erik, prostitution is illegal in the state of Rhode Island. I am sure those hookers would love to have their fifteen minutes of fame."

"Oh, who cares? Do you think it's big news that a rock band is into hookers?" Erik sneers. "Stop the presses!" He waves his hands in mock hysteria.

"Erik, the presses would stop for Vincent D'Amico's daughter," I reply.

"*Ooooh*, Vincent D'Amico," Erik sneers. "Who the fuck is that?"

I hold up the picture of Molly D'Amico taken at the fundraiser and raise my eyebrows. He rolls his eyes; obviously he has no idea who she is when at one of her daddy's fundraisers. Then I hold up the other picture, the one I doodled on at work today, and watch the recognition register on Erik's face.

"Read the caption," I say, pointing. I watch his eyes move across the page, but they apparently fail to recognize the gravity of the situation.

"Erik, who is that girl?" Toni takes the pictures from my hand and examines them.

Beside the Music

"So, she's the governor's daughter. Who cares? Surely she isn't the first politician's daughter to pursue a dodgy line of work."

"Toni, she is the *fifteen-year-old* daughter of Governor D'Amico. I believe Erik is familiar with her. Erik, how exactly do you know her again?" I smile thinly.

"She said she was nineteen," Erik croaks.

"Of course she did," I reply. "And you believed her. And why would you even care to check? Oh, and why would you break the law and hire prostitutes in the first place?"

"Brenda, this story," Erik gestures to Molly's picture, "hasn't got any legs. Nobody will care that a bunch of rockers hired a call girl."

"All it takes is one phone call to the editor at the *Providence Tattle Tale,* and this story will go viral. You'll be busted for contributing to the delinquency of a minor. And if you'd thought the band's image was bad enough, just wait until this hits the wire. Oh, and need I mention the rumors about Governor D'Amico's ties to the unions? You're in for a world of trouble if you don't give me what I want."

"And what exactly would that be?" Toni asks, all the while glaring at Erik. I can tell she's starting to weigh the options—*what will it take to keep me quiet? Again,* I ask, *where the hell has she been all week? She knows exactly what I want.*

"If you give me the money owed to Tim and me and move out of here within the week, then I will not breathe a word of this to the media. If not, then the whole world will know what assholes you all are, and your tour here in the U.S. will be over." I gesture toward the dining room. "In the other room, you will find drafts of all the communications I will use to expose Hydra."

"If you do," Erik spouts, "we will sue you for breaching your contract."

"Go right ahead, Erik. I assure you that my publicity campaign will be far more damaging than your lawsuit. Who has more at stake here? Me or you?" I hold up one of the pieces of paper on the table, and I can feel the adrenaline surge through my body; it's making my fingers tingle. "I know that Toni is taking over your publicity, but I don't think that even she can get you out of a mess like this. Piss off D'Amico, and you're done. Once he talks to the unions, you'll never play an arena in the U.S. again."

"I have given my life to this band," Erik hisses. "I will not have this." He curls his hand around one of the perpetually-tarnished silver candlesticks on the table and points it at me for emphasis. Then—and I never thought I'd ever see somebody do this in real life—he actually throws it through the dining room window. It falls into the lilac bush near the front door of the house, the shattered glass sprinkled around it.

"And now you've gone and broken a window in my house, on top of everything else," I say calmly. *I will not let his temper tantrum make me lose control of this situation. I need to stay cool.* "Now you'll have to pay me for my window, or you'll have to deal with the lovely headline, 'Hydra Manager Throws

Temper Tantrum and Destroys Window Belonging to Longtime Fan,' in addition to everything else. The online tabloids *love* stories like that. So, is there anything else you'd like to destroy today? Or are you done?" I smile tightly. Erik runs his hand through his hair; inwardly, I brace for him to throw the other candlestick out the window.

Toni turns on him. "Erik, how could you let this happen?"

Erik clenches his jaw and is silent.

"I want you out Thursday night by the time I get home from work. If you aren't out, then this…," I gesture toward the table, "all hits the wire on Friday morning. I went to college with an editor at MTV News. We keep in touch. One phone call and you're history."

And with that, I leave them to their uncomfortable silence. I scoop up my papers and go up the stairs to my bedroom. I've said what I needed to say, and I feel great about leaving the room without letting Erik intimidate me or rile me up. I wish I'd had my iPhone beside me so that I could have used it to dismiss *him* with a few swipes. I'll call tomorrow and have the window fixed, so Tim won't even know it happened.

I don't emerge from my room for the rest of the night. It's nice to snuggle with Vito and watch mindless TV. At ten o'clock, the band gets home, and I can hear their muffled voices through my closed door. I mute the TV, but I still can't make out what they're saying.

The voices grow louder, and I know that things are heating up downstairs. "Erik, it was *you* who hired those girls, not me," I hear Keith argue. "This is your fault, not mine."

"I hired them because *you* demanded it of me," Erik replies. "And Mr. Rock Star is supposed to get whatever he wants or else you'll throw one of your epic temper tantrums!"

"Don't you dare pin this on me. If you can't do your job and make sure that I am not in a compromising position, then what good are you, really?" Keith asks.

"You tell *me*," Erik says. "You're broke, if we can't get this tour off the ground. This is our only option. If we don't leave, she alerts the media, and we're sunk."

"Erik," Keith says, "she's bluffing. Are you going to buckle under? That's not what we pay you for. You keep saying we can't afford to move, so what are you going to do about it? Have you gone soft on us? Where are your balls?"

I pace nervously in my room and hear my stomach growl. I didn't eat dinner, but there's no way in hell I'm going down there now. I consider calling Tim, but I don't want to jinx anything so decide not to. I get back into bed and feel Vito settle into a tight circle against the back of my knees. I hear the voices downstairs, but I can't make out what they're saying anymore. Even though my stomach is still growling, I doze off clutching Tim's pillow. The ball's in their court now. *What are they going to do with it tomorrow?*

Chapter 27

SINCE HYDRA MOVED INTO OUR HOUSE, the kitchen has always been a beehive of activity at any time of day. In the mornings, members of the crew come and go while Angela cooks breakfast to order, and countless mugs of tea go in and out of the kitchen sink. I remember that, when the band Boston released the album *Third Stage,* they wrote in the liner notes things like how many lightbulbs they'd gone through while recording that album. At the time, I thought it was interesting; now I wish I'd counted how many tea bags we've gone through in the two months that Hydra has lived in my house. When I wake up on Tuesday, it's dead silent in the kitchen; none of the band or crew eating there acknowledges my existence. It would seem that news travels fast. Angela is the only one who says good morning; she flashes me a sympathetic smile. Obviously, she knows about my discussion with Erik, and that, by the end of the week, she'll have to find another housekeeping-for-hire gig. Yet she still manages to smile at me, and I am thankful for that.

She follows me into the pantry and whispers, "Honestly, I can't blame you. That Erik guy is horrible. You have to do what is right for you and Tim, honey." I thank her and pack my lunch. I decide I'll grab breakfast from the drive-thru on the way to work, since being in the kitchen with these people is now way too awkward.

When I get into my office, I see that Amanda has marked up the drafts I left on her desk last night. She made a note in the margin about researching Baxter's claims of product superiority a bit more. I let out an irritated sigh and toss the draft aside. The last thing I want to think about is Baxter, since I don't know yet if Hydra's going to leave. I check my cell phone again for messages, even though I know there aren't any.

"Well, good morning to you, too." Amanda smiles from my doorway.

"*Um,* hi," I say, trying to wipe the irritation off my face. *Great. Now she probably thinks I find her revisions annoying; I am on thin ice as it is.*

"You did a great job on those drafts. You really don't need to change much

167

on there. I just want a bit more meat to back up our claims. It shouldn't be hard; we have access to industry studies. Nice job and welcome back." She hands me a cup of tea. Amanda and I are the only ones here who don't drink coffee. We informally take turns getting tea for each other, depending on which one of us gets in first. "So, what were you really working on so furiously yesterday?"

"What?" I ask, hoping to appear innocent.

"There's no way those drafts took you all afternoon. You're faster than that. And you only logged about ninety minutes of billable time for Baxter yesterday. What else were you working on?" she presses. She's doing her ice-princess glare thing again; I feel as if her eyes are boring holes in my forehead. *Does she think I'm screwing around now, too?* I can't help but feel the paranoia creep in; I'm riding the thirty-day warning, and she's supposed to know everything I'm working on until the thirty days are up, when I will once again be deemed worthy to work here.

I search my mind for a suitable answer that won't get me fired. She braces her hands on her hips, an impatient posture. *Screw it, sooner or later I am going to have to explain my behavior somehow.* "Remember how last week I had some personal stuff going on? Yesterday I came to the conclusion on how to solve my problem. If it doesn't work out as I planned, then you will know everything on Friday, as my life as I know it will be over. If it does work out, then you'll never hear a word about it, and it won't be a problem anymore."

"I need you to stay focused, Brenda. You have a lot riding on the next thirty days here. I need to know right now if this personal problem is going to be an issue. If it is, I will find someone else to work on Baxter. Joy's been chomping at the bit for more responsibility. She wants more than anything to prove herself and get the chance to sit in your chair."

"It won't be a problem. Really." I smile back at her. I hope it comes off as a confident, can-do attitude. She turns on her heel and strides back to her office, chin up, chest out, Nordic princess warrior ready for battle.

I get to work on revising the drafts when Joy rings my extension from the reception area. "Brenda, you have a visitor." *Odd, I'm not expecting anyone.* I check my calendar on Outlook just to be sure. Nope, my calendar is wide open for the morning.

"Who is it?"

"Your mother-in-law."

Oh, shit. What the hell is she doing here? I'm going to strangle her with her stupid triple-strand Mikimoto pearls. And if she's still alive, I'm going to make her watch as I feed them to her stupid teacup Chihuahua. I take a deep breath and stand up from my desk. I need to conjure the confidence from my confrontation with Erik last night and tell this joker where to go. *Past victories. Game face.*

I see her standing in the waiting room, appearing afraid to contract a disease if she touches anything. Which is ridiculous, because Amanda is a neat freak who has hired what appear to be a surgical team to clean this office twice each week.

"Hello, Portia," I say without any expression in my voice. "How about we sit down in here?" I gesture to the conference room. I don't know why she's here, and I want her to know she's not welcome. It's one thing to show up unannounced at my house; it's entirely another to show up like this at my workplace. She knows what she's doing and figures I'll do anything to make her leave, to avoid a scene. I see Joy trying not to look like she's spying, but she totally is.

Portia assesses the conference room and then selects a chair. *Is she seriously looking for the most advantageous chair in the room?* Before I can ask her why she's here, she sets a leather folio in front of me.

"Brenda, given the current situation, I have a proposal for you." She nods at the folio, encouraging me to open it. I don't comply and shove it back toward her just a few inches. "I've taken the liberty of drawing up an agreement between the two of us." She pauses. "We both know that Timothy is unhappy in his marriage to you. I want us to agree to make it easy for him to move on. And, of course, you stand to benefit as well."

"Portia, what the hell are you talking about?"

"If you cared to look," she says, pushing the folio back toward me, "you'll see that you will be provided with a generous stipend. Enough for you to afford a new home and a few extras. Agree to divorce Tim, and you will be well-provided for, darling."

"Are you kidding me with this? Portia, you have got some nerve, coming to my workplace and pulling this." *Okay, it is seriously time to smack this bitch down for good. I have had enough of her crap.* "Since the day I met you, you have gone out of your way to make me feel inferior. I tolerated it, figuring that maybe you'd come around after Tim and I got married. But you only got worse. Do you have any idea how awful you've been to me?" I pause for her to answer; she returns a steely gaze.

"It's one thing to show up at my house, unannounced, but to come here and do this while I'm at work? You are a conniving bitch, Portia. Don't you understand that I love Tim? I thought you'd have gotten the hint when you tried to pay me off before the wedding—your money doesn't matter to me. If you'd bothered to get to know me at all, then you would have learned that I am not a gold digger. You would have learned that I am a good person who is in love with your son and wants more than anything for him to be happy." I pause to collect myself. "Tell me. Why do you think so little of me?" I pause to allow her to answer. She doesn't.

"See? You can't think of one thing, can you? I have kissed your ass since the first time we met. And you can't see who I really am. Your mind was made up about me a long time ago. But, *darling...*" I put a sarcastic twist on "darling." "...you have gotten the wrong idea about me. And at this point, I don't give a shit if you ever change your mind about me. But get a fucking life, Portia. And stop interfering with Tim's. Because some day, you'll go too far with him, and you'll lose him, too."

"Well, I *never*—, "she begins, her face beet-red.

"And that's the problem, Portia," I interrupt. "You throw your weight around, and nobody dares put you in your place. Well, not anymore." I stand up and walk to the door. "We are done here. I would appreciate it if you would show yourself out."

Her mouth is hanging open. I turn my back on her and throw the door open. I don't want her to catch me looking, so I straighten my shoulders and walk out the door, trying to mimic Amanda's bad-ass Viking warrior walk. I carefully step over the area rug in front of Joy's desk; nothing messes up the warrior walk like tripping on the rug.

When Joy sees me come out, she tips her head down, obviously pretending to be working instead of snooping. I know that the conference room isn't completely soundproof, and Joy's a pretty notorious busybody. She probably heard everything, but I don't bother to look her way. I stride past her desk and fight the urge to run out of the office. I feel like a huge weight has been lifted off of my shoulders. I finally got the courage to tell Portia what I really think. This feels even better than I imagined—until I realize that she's going to call Tim and freak out on him.

I get back to my desk, grab my cell phone, and head to the stairwell. I climb the stairs two at a time and then open the door to the roof, where I am sure that I can be alone. I dial Tim's cell. He picks up after three rings. My heart starts to beat a little faster. *What if he's asked his mother to do this for him? What if the stipend was his idea, so that he'd know I would be taken care of? What if he really* does *want to divorce me?* I'd like to think that he would have discussed it with me first, before siccing his mother on me.

When he says "Hello," I realize that I have no clue what to say. *Maybe the direct approach will be best.*

"Tim, you'll never guess who came to visit me at work today."

"Mick Jagger?" he asks. "Did you send him a letter, too?" *Good, he's in a good mood today. Maybe he didn't get his mom to do this after all.*

"Your mother."

"Why? Is it about redoing the house? I'll tell her not to bug you about it at work." *Shit. I guess I just blew my chance to get Antonio Diego on board for Baxter. Oh, well, I'll have to come up with something else now. There's no way I can say to her, "I know I just called you a conniving bitch, but can you give me his number?"*

"Not exactly. Tim, she's really gone too far this time. She showed up here with some legal agreement. Apparently, she's going to pay me off if I leave you."

"What?"

"I don't know the specifics—I didn't look at the papers. But Tim, she's gone too far. She showed up at my office and pulled this shit."

"Are you serious?" I can hear a door close in the background, and I know that he went into his office for some privacy. "Bren, that's terrible. I am so sorry. You're right. She totally crossed the line." He pauses. "So, what did you do?"

"Well, she's probably going to call you and freak out. I have had it with her, Tim. She has treated me like shit ever since I met you. I, *um...*" I stutter, bracing myself for his reaction. "I kind of told her off—and called her a bitch."

"You did *what?*"

"Tim, I am done with her. What she did today was inexcusable."

"Bren, just calm down, okay?" *Don't even tell me he's taking her side.*

"Did you ask her to do this?"

"Oh, God. No, Brenda," he says. "Do you honestly think I'd ask her to do that without even discussing it first?"

"Well, no. I would hope not." I feel my eyes fill with tears. "Tim, you have got to do something about your mother. You won't stand up to her, and as a result, she walks all over me. Don't you see that your relationship with her is pretty fucked up? Do you have any idea how embarrassing it is to have her show up at work? I am on a thirty-day warning as it is."

"I know, Bren. I'm sorry. I thought I could talk to her about the problems we've been having and that she'd actually, you know, be supportive." *I'm surprised he didn't pick up on me riding the thirty days thing. I'm glad he's focusing on our marriage and not that. Normally, he'd freak out about the possibility of my losing my job, and what that would do to our retirement portfolio.*

"Tim, I'm sorry, but what were you thinking? She's hated me from the moment she met me. Of *course* she's going to try to get you to divorce me. I mean, what did you expect? Maybe she has dates lined up for you as well. She has got to be stopped."

"I never thought she'd go that far. It's one thing to try to keep you in the kitchen at a fundraiser. It's entirely another to try to pay you off."

"Twice, Tim. She's now tried to pay me off twice."

"Yes, I know." He pauses, and I can tell he's trying to wrap his head around what his mother has done. "I am so sorry, Brenda. She crossed the line, and I am going to call her right now and tell her that what she's done is unacceptable."

"Thank you, Tim." I tip my face up to the sun, elated. For the first time, he's going to stand up to his mother for me. Until now, he's taken the "Just let it go" approach, because he doesn't want to confront her, either. There was a time when I tried to be friendly with her, hoping that she would get to know me and see that I really am the daughter-in-law she's always imagined. And she's always made me feel as if I've fallen short somehow. Those days are over; and it's liberating to feel that her approval doesn't matter anymore. *I am so over her. Done.*

We don't really say anything else on the call; I don't tell him about my confrontation with Erik, because I don't yet know whether they're actually leaving. I also don't want to tell him about how the governor's daughter is a hooker. He doesn't even know that we had hookers in the house. At this point, it'll just make him believe, again, that if I hadn't been forced to tell him something, I wouldn't have told him. *Someday, a long time from now, I'll tell him about it.* We say our goodbyes, and of course I'm hoping he'll say he loves me, but he doesn't. My heart breaks just a little bit more.

I look out over the other rooftops; it's such a beautiful day, I just want to hang out on the roof for the rest of the morning. But I need to get back downstairs. I'm sure Amanda's looking for me. I sneak back into my cubicle and spend the rest of the day puttering around on Baxter stuff, then leave the office at six.

I try to call Tim on his cell, but it goes to voice mail. I want to see how things went with his mother, and I also just want to hear his voice again. Living without him is getting pretty unbearable. I tell his voice mail that I miss him and ask him to have dinner with me tomorrow night, hoping that I'll have good news for him.

When I walk in the back door of the house, Erik and Toni are at the kitchen table. Erik smiles when I walk in, and the hairs on the back of my neck stand up. It's never a good thing when Erik smiles.

Erik stares at me with his eyebrows raised and his smile still in place. Behind him, I notice that my media schedule has been wiped clean from the whiteboard and replaced with the shower schedule. Apparently, Ben is now showering in Tim's time slot. *Sunrise yoga wins. Okay, this is over, and it's over now.* I straighten up my shoulders and my cheek stops twitching. He hands me a stack of 8x10 photos.

"What are these?" I ask as I shuffle through them. They are pictures of our house, complete with the crowd of fans. Also, pictures of the day Tim and I came home and found the fan brigade. Pictures of me kissing Keith. *Oh, shit. There was that guy in the fan crowd with the camera with the giant zoom lens.* He's not a fan; he's been developing the band's insurance policy.

"I didn't want to have to do this, Brenda," Erik sneers. "But you've left me with no choice." He pauses for dramatic effect; my cheek starts twitching again. "I've taken an interest in the local state Senate campaign. What was the name of your husband's competitor? Mitch Goldstein? It would seem that Mr. Goldstein's campaign could stand for a boost, don't you think?"

Oh, shit, again. Tim will absolutely kill me if Hydra jeopardized his campaign. Erik stands there with his arms across his chest; it would seem he's employing my negotiation tactic—silence until I can't stand it anymore, so I say something like, "Oh, never mind, you can stay."

"Are we agreed that the band stays, then?" *Wow, that's kind of presumptuous.*
There is no way they can stay here anymore. But there's also no way that I

Beside the Music

will allow Tim to lose the election because of Hydra. *What the hell do I do now?* Toni is watching me expectantly; I wonder what she really thinks about Erik's latest move. I wish I had someone I could confer with right now. *How do I make this decision on my own?*

To take a page from Annie's book, I need to strip away all the extraneous stuff and get down to the bare facts. If they stay, there's no Tim. If they leave, then there's no state Senate for Tim, either. And then who knows if he'll be willing to even be with me after I've just wrecked his chance of holding office. So, any way I slice it, there's a chance of me and Tim not staying together. It's just a matter of which choice is the sure thing that Tim will leave me. *Okay, chin up and put my game face on. It's time to take down Erik.* If I can leave Portia with her mouth hanging open, then surely I can at least try to smack Erik Murtaugh down. *Time to bring it again.*

"Erik." I pause to clear my throat—I need to focus on keeping my tone calm and even. "Do you really think the band can afford the bad publicity? I mean, how would it look if you sued Keith's 'long time' fan? Can you imagine that trending on Twitter? You guys have lost a lot of ground here in the U.S. How's planning the U.S. tour going for you, Erik? Filling up any arenas yet? If you sue me, you better believe that the first person I will call is my friend at MTV. And then I'll move on to VH1, and then I'll hit *People Magazine*, then *Us Weekly*, and before you know it, every single American will read about Hydra's indiscretions, while they're waiting in line at the supermarket. Is that really in the band's best interests?"

Then I match his smile with my own tight I-am-an-asshole smile. *I am so over this creep. All the crap that's happened since the band entered my life has got to stop.*

"If Tim loses, he could always run again. His livelihood doesn't depend on his term as a state senator." I pause and let it sink in. "The livelihood of all those people," I point to Tent City, "depends on *you* right now. If you don't leave, I expose you. You stand to lose much more than we do. So, am I calling MTV, or are you leaving?"

"Oh, please, like MTV will care that I hired call girls for them."

"Yeah, but Governor D'Amico will care. And if he cares, then the unions will care. And who do you think sets up the stages in all those arenas, Erik? Little green fairies?"

"The band simply cannot risk the new album. Moving is out of the fucking question."

"If this gets out, Governor D'Amico will shut you down faster than you can blink. Isn't that out of the fucking question, as well?" I stand straighter. "So, you'll be moved out by Thursday night, yes?"

173

"Don't be ridiculous, Brenda," Erik protests. "I cannot possibly move all these people out in two days."

He's not hearing me; time to up the drama quotient. I grab the cordless phone off the kitchen counter and reach for my work tote bag, "Now, where is that phone number for MTV..." I mutter aloud. "Nope, not in that pocket. Darn it, I know it's in here...." I pretend to rifle through my bag until I pull out a business card. "Ah yes. Annie Wilkins, MTV. Did I ever tell you that Annie and I go way back? We were roommates in college and we worked together at the campus radio station. She went to MTV, but I went on to work in PR. She's been able to count on me for a juicy story now and then, and I am sure she'll love this one. Oh, look at the time—I'll have to call her at home...." I ramble on.

"Okay, enough already," Erik groans. "God, Brenda, just fucking stop already. We're moving. Are you happy?"

"I will not be happy until every single tent is off my back lawn, every single member of the Hydra entourage is out of my house, and those losers are off our front lawn." I point out the front window, newly replaced after Erik's tantrum the day before. I open the back door and step out; Vito follows me, wagging his tail. He looks up as is to say, "Yeah, you go girl!" I turn back to Erik. "I am sure you have a lot of work to do right now. Don't let me keep you." I look down. "Come on, Vito, let's go for a walk and give the big rock stars a chance to move out of our house." He wags his tail harder at the use of his favorite word. I smile at Erik one more time before stepping off the deck and walking into the woods with my dog.

We walk the trail that leads to the pond. There's a huge tree at the edge of the pond that fell in a windstorm a few summers ago, and it sits exactly the way Tim and I would have placed a bench, at a perfect angle to stare out at the water and watch the sun go down. I try to let the sunset relax me, but the adrenaline is still coursing through me right now. I am also a little nervous: I've just left a pissed off Erik in my house. I should have hidden the other candlestick.

But leaving the house was the right idea. He needs to know that I am not afraid and I mean business. If I'd stayed, I would have looked desperate, hanging around waiting for him to tell me that he'll move the band out. Instead, I'll hang around out here for about an hour, then I'll go back, and hopefully, by then, he'll have a plan for moving out.

To kill time, I throw a stick just beyond the water's edge. Vito likes to fetch sticks, but he doesn't like to go into the water beyond where he can touch the bottom with his feet. He stretches his snout toward the stick, hoping to retrieve it without having to walk deeper in the water. He inches his nose out until he can grab it with the tips of his front teeth and then pulls it closer, so he can get a better grip on it. The lengths he'll go so he doesn't have to go into the water always cracks me up.

He carries the stick back to me and drops it at my feet then wags his tail as

174

his way of asking me to throw it again. When I don't throw it again, he jumps up onto the log beside me. I stroke his velvety ears, and we watch as the sun reflects onto the clouds, making them glow pink.

The mosquitos start to hum near my ears; I swat them away and look at my watch. I can't believe an hour and a half has gone by already. My mind had just blissfully gone blank, and it's nice to know that I can let go and not worry. Vito is beside me, licking the mud off his front paws. He's pretty good about keeping himself occupied while I daydream. I feel like, for the first time in a month, I am in control again. It feels great.

"Let's go home, Buddy Dog. Want some dinner?" At the mention of his other favorite word, he jumps off the log, and we walk home before the sun finishes setting. We have just enough light to navigate the trail back to the house.

When we walk in the back door, the band and entourage are having a meeting in the kitchen. I can't help but smile when I see that the whiteboard is filled with a packing and moving schedule. I feel victorious—until every head in the room turns to face me. Some of them scowl at the inconvenience of having to move; some, like Toni, flash a sympathetic smile, instead. It's nice to know I have a few friends; they're the ones who will keep the pissed-off ones from trashing my house before they leave.

"Sorry to interrupt," I mutter. "I'll just get out of your way." I walk through the kitchen toward the stairs.

"No," Erik says, bristling. "You should stay. This concerns you. After all, we're getting out of your house. You ought to know how we plan on doing that."

"Honestly, I don't care how you do it," I say, walking toward the stairs. "I just want you out by Thursday night."

"Thursday night?" Ben sputters. "What do you mean, Thursday night?"

"Didn't Erik tell you?" I put on an innocent tone and step back into the room. "Erik agreed to have you all out of here by Thursday night. Isn't that right, Erik?"

"Erik, what does she mean?" Keith asks, objecting. "Where are we all going? You've just told us that our new house won't be ready for over a week."

I can hear the low din of whispers among the crew; I feel the drama brewing. It's fascinating: Erik's lying to the band and the crew about where they're going to stay. *Does he think they're not going to find out?* "On second thought, this meeting looks interesting," I say, smiling. "I think I'll stay." I slide myself up onto the last available spot on the counter. Just like on the first night, a bag of Oreos is open. I grab a few and twist one apart so I can lick the white stuff out of the center.

"Yes, I did say that our new house won't be ready until the week after next," Erik says. "And yes, I did agree with Brenda that we'd be out on Thursday." I dip my cookie into a nearby glass of milk and loudly slurp the soggy Oreo. "God, Brenda," Erik says, "would you please stop doing that?" I smile back at him and bite into another cookie defiantly.

175

"Then where the hell are we going to sleep between Thursday night and when we move into the new house?" Keith asks.

"Well, it would seem that Westwood, Rhode Island offers few options for accommodations," Erik says. "There is a Motel 6 along the highway. I've rented out the whole thing until our new house is ready."

"Surely there's a Marriot or a Westin," Keith says, incredulous.

"This is preposterous!" Ben says. "We are all working damn hard on this new record. Why do we all have to suffer because of Keith?"

"Suffer?" I ask. I set down the glass of milk. "You're kidding, right? Staying in a motel is suffering? Wow, you guys really have lost touch with reality. There are people out there who don't have jobs, and you have the nerve to say *you're* suffering? Big fucking deal—you have to sleep in a motel for a week. God, you guys really love being the spoiled rock stars, huh? You think that just because you put out a few albums in the '80s that everyone should bow down to you. You guys really are assholes. All of you." I point my finger at every person sitting in the room then slide off the counter and storm out of the room.

From upstairs, I can hear them continue to argue. Ben and Keith protest loudly while Erik struggles to maintain his composure. I can distinctly hear Erik say, "I am so fucking sick of having to clean up your messes. It's been nonstop for thirty years, and you guys just won't fucking grow up."

"Well, if that's how you really feel about it then *perhaps you ought to step down then!*" I hear Keith shout downstairs.

"Do you have any idea what I do for you? *Do you?* Everything I do in my life is for you. Every fucking thing I do is to stroke your precious egos so you can feel like you can produce good music. You see that crowd of people out there? Paid for. Every last one of them is a paid actor hired to make you feel like rock and roll gods so you can produce a new album."

"What on earth are you talking about?" Ben asks.

"Trisha doesn't give a shit about your lyrics, Keith. She's only there to make you feel like your lyrics matter. But you know what? It's all shit! This new album sucks, and you're all going to go down. And I am not going to be there when it happens. I am through with the lot of you."

Chapter 28

IT'S THURSDAY NIGHT, and I am scared to go straight home from work. I've stayed out of their way since the meeting on Tuesday night, while the crew has been hard at work packing. I can picture the storm of activity in my home, seeing as it's the last night that Hydra will be there. *What if they change their minds and decide they're going to stay?* I imagine Erik looking up from his iPhone long enough to tell me to go fuck myself. I try to get the image out of my mind, but I'm afraid it's still a real possibility. I mean, at this point, what could I do if they decided they wanted to stay? I would have to call the police and get them out, I guess. What a mess that would be, on many levels.

To kill time, I pull into the parking lot at the movie theatre. Without giving it much thought, I go inside and buy a ticket for whatever is showing next. And the movie is absolute garbage. Pop-Tart Jamie Fire is the star, and she is the world's worst actress. I read in the gossip mags that she was constantly drunk on set. I can't even tell you what the plot was; I think the point of the movie was so Jamie could walk around in a hundred different bikinis and suggestively suck on lollipops throughout.

But still, going to a trashy movie by myself was actually kind of nice. I don't know why I don't do it more often. People always say it's weird to go to the movies by yourself, but it's not like you're going to talk to the person that you go with, anyway. You're both just sitting there, watching. *So why don't more people go alone?* It's nice to watch whatever I want to see and have a tub of popcorn to myself without Tim globbing it with that weird butter-oil stuff.

It's dark when I leave the theater, and while the movie wasn't exactly a cinematic masterpiece, at least I managed to kill some time when I wasn't obsessing about whether or not Hydra had moved out of my house. I considered texting Toni to check on their status, but then talked myself out of it.

When I get home, the house is dark. I pause in the middle of the driveway and look over to the fan corral; it's empty, and the yellow caution tape and stakes are gone. It makes sense, seeing as how they weren't even real fans, but paid actors. I am amazed at the lengths Erik went to so that the band felt worshipped. No wonder they're broke.

I press the button on the remote clipped to the visor; the garage is empty of Jeff's drum set, and I easily pull in to my side. Tim's side is still vacant, and it makes me a bit sad; I wonder when he'll come home. I pause before opening the door into the kitchen from the garage; I am so afraid that they've trashed my house before leaving, and now I won't have Angela to help me clean it up. My mind goes back to Erik throwing the candlestick through the window. I can just picture him and the band blasting some heavy metal on the stereo and stabbing the rest of the windows with their guitars then deciding it wasn't enough and knifing my walls with Tim's meat cleaver.

I feel for the light switch when I enter, but decide that, for the moment, I am better off not knowing. I call out to Vito and let him out the back door; again, I don't turn on the lights, afraid to see what they've done to the lawn as they dismantled Tent City. My mind goes to them turning donuts in the grass, also with death metal blaring through the speakers of the minivans.

Vito starts yelping. I'm scared that he's injured. *What the hell did they leave on my lawn that hurt my dog?* I flip on the outside lights and am relieved to see Vito chasing a rabbit into the woods. I never thought I'd ever be thankful to have him chase a rabbit. I am even more grateful when I see that all the tents are gone, and the crew hasn't trashed the lawn. I am momentarily distracted by how great the back yard looks without all those tents, and I nearly forget about Vito. He's probably hell and gone, deep into the woods. I call out to him from the deck, but he ignores me. He's on the chase, and he'll go as far as the rabbit takes him. Tim and I have heard stories about beagles going for miles after a bunny, and it's always been a fear of mine that one day he won't come back.

"Vito, *no!*" I call out after him. I run down the stairs and sprint across the back yard where Tent City used to be. By the time I get to the trail leading into the woods, he's sniffing his way back to me; his prey likely dived into a rabbit hole. He looks up at me, as if to say, "What? I'm right here."

With an air of nonchalance, he lopes beside me as we cross the yard toward the house. I can see where the grass is matted in the spots where each tent stood. The ground is still scorched from where they set that fire the first night. Vito sniffs around each tent's ghostly footprint, and I wonder what he must think. He looks up at me and wags his tail. Looks like he's happy they're gone, too.

Back in the house, I muster the courage to turn on the lights. I wince when I flip the switch and see that the kitchen is surgically clean. In the fridge are the last of Angela's leftovers; she labeled them and even stocked the freezer with single-serve containers of lasagna, her crock pot chicken, and the barbecue ribs she made on Monday. I will miss her cooking the most. In the entire time that Hydra was here, I didn't touch a pot or pan. I scoop some kibble into Vito's bowl and toss

Beside the Music

some leftover lasagna into the microwave. I plop down on the couch, turn on the TV, and watch some senseless reality show until I realize my plate is empty.

The house is quiet without Tim; I need to formulate a plan. My job is getting back on track, the band's out of the house, and now I need to get him to move back in. I call Tim's cell, but it goes right to voice mail. *When will he ever call me? Doesn't he want to come home?* I think this is what bothers me the most: he hasn't called me to tell me that he misses me and that he wants to come home. At this point, Tim still doesn't even know that Hydra is gone, and I don't know if he's talked to his mom yet.

I try his cell again, and this time I leave a message. "Tim, they're gone. Call me back. I love you." It's not exactly how I wanted to tell him, but it's what I have to do.

I turn off the TV and feel the silence descend on me. Just one night earlier, my house was still basecamp for a once-great band trying to make their comeback. I got the chance to offer my opinion on one of their songs, and a song on the album was written for me. I was part of something that will be important to millions of people, but it ended so abruptly, so badly. I think back to Tim telling me to let it go, the night that we'd first met Keith, and how I get obsessed with stupid shit. *But it's not stupid to me.* This was important to me, and while I know that Hydra needed to leave for me to get my husband back, I am sad that they had to leave and that I am not a part of it anymore. I wish it all could have gone differently.

"Vito, I could have handled this so much better," I say, sighing. He jumps onto the couch and thumps his tail against the cushion; I ignore the fact that Tim doesn't want him on the furniture. He rests his head on my thigh and lets out one of his long "this too shall pass" sighs. "You're right, it will pass," I say, and then smile as I stroke his ears. Tears are still streaming down my cheeks, but I try to feel positive. *Eventually, Tim's gotta come home.*

Before heading up to bed, I put my plate into the dishwasher, instead of the sink. It always bugged Tim when I'd leave dishes in the sink.

***

Friday morning at work, Amanda pops into my cube and hands me a cup of tea. "Well? It's Friday. Has your problem been resolved?"

"Yes," I smile. "All is well."

"Great. Welcome back to the land of the living. I need to see the new mockups for the Baxter ads by the end of day."

I spend the rest of the day putting the finishing touches on the drafts I put together a few days ago and review the mock ups that the graphic artist gave me. I welcome the distraction of work and am actually a bit bummed that the day flies

179

by; before I know, it I am walking out of the office at five. Tim still hasn't called. *Hasn't he heard the message I left him last night?* You'd think he would have called back by now. I wonder if I should call him or not.

After Hydra invaded my home, I couldn't stand to listen to the radio. It had become a minefield. I never knew when a DJ was going to mention the band or speculate about where in Rhode Island they were recording and sleeping. I never knew when I'd hear one of their songs. But now I don't care. *Bring it on*! Now that I don't have to live in fear of the public discovering that they were at my house, I don't care anymore.

Still, the actors were pretty convincing: it was pretty terrifying pulling up to my house that day. I wonder if the band ever did have real fans camped out in front of their houses or if it had always been Erik's doing. Toni said that they'd all gotten used to it; but I'm sure she's relieved that there never was any real threat from a truly psychotic fan. Before I left for work this morning, I walked out to the fan corral area. There were rake tracks in the dirt. It's nice that the actors cleaned up after themselves.

Tim's truck is in the driveway when I pull in, and I park my car beside it. I can feel the adrenaline surge through my body as I run up the stairs to the deck. I stop halfway up when I realize that he could just be home to get clean clothes, and then he'll be gone again. After all that has happened, maybe he doesn't want to come home to me at all. I will myself to steady my breathing, and I'm relieved when I see him sitting on the deck with a beer. And there's another one on the table beside his. I can't help but smile, but I still don't know what to say when I sit down beside him.

"It looks so much better without all those tents," he says, gazing out across the back yard. "How'd you get them out?"

"I used the magic of public relations. But this time I used my powers for evil instead of good." I tell him the story, and then I go and get the drafts of the press releases from inside. I figure having a visual aid will make more sense to him. When the mosquitos force us into the house, we sit at the kitchen table. He reads my work.

"You know, it's funny," he says. "I never fully understood your job. With mine, someone brings in a car that doesn't work, and I fix it and give it back to them. With yours, it's all information that you're putting out. You never really know who's reading it or what will happen, after they've read it." He gestures to one of my media alerts. "But this definitely would have been read, and it would have caused a lot of trouble for them."

"That's what Erik was afraid of. We're still getting all of our money."

"Okay, you are doing all the negotiating the next time we buy a house. You got them out *and* managed to get all our money, too?"

"Yup." I beam with pride. "Bribery is a powerful tool. Basically, we can't talk to the media about why they left, and honestly, I don't even care to talk about it."

Beside the Music

"So, was it all you thought it would be? Having rock stars in the house?"

"Some of it." I take a swig of my beer while I reflect. "I mean, I did like the part where I got to offer my opinion about the new songs. That was very cool. But the other stuff sucked."

"I know, Bren. It was fun to watch you get so excited about reading their new lyrics."

"Really? Because you just seemed pissed off the whole time they were here. And that's the part that sucked, Tim. It came between us in the worst way. Will you ever be able to forgive me for kissing Keith?"

He doesn't answer my question, and I feel like he's just slapped me in the face. Then he changes the subject. "So, do you know where they're staying?"

"For the moment, they're at the Motel 6 until their new house is ready."

"The big rock stars are staying at the Motel 6?" He laughs.

"Yeah, you should have seen it. They were all, like, 'surely there's a Marriot or a Westin.'" I put on a posh Australian accent, and he laughs. "I guess Erik rented out the whole place so they wouldn't have to deal with any other guests." I laugh again. "There was a big argument about it, and I think they might have fired Erik." I pause. "And guess what else? Those rabid fans out there? They were paid actors."

"You have got to be kidding me," he says. "But then, it kinda makes sense. Erik was pretty nonchalant about them being here."

"But that's a good thing. Imagine what could have happened if they'd been real rabid fans? It could have gotten very ugly."

"True. You hungry? I see that Angela's stocked the freezer. While I heat something up for you and me, will you please explain the press release about the fifteen-year-old prostitute, and why you never told me about it at the time?" He raises his eyebrows.

I sheepishly smile back at him.

"Goddam rock stars drank all the beer!" he calls out from the fridge a moment later.

"Of course they did," I say and laugh. "What did you expect?"

Chapter 29

THAT NIGHT, TIM MOVED BACK IN. It was nice to feel his warmth on his side of the bed, and Vito stayed glued to him the first weekend he was home. After that night in the kitchen, we didn't talk about the Hydra experience for a few days; I think we were both needed to deal with it on our own, first.

It's been a month now, and we're trying to get back to normal as best as we can. Tim's been blowing off Portia's Sunday night dinner invites. He told her that he's not going to speak to her unless she apologizes to me. I have yet to get a call, and I'm not waiting by the phone.

To be completely honest, since Tim came home, it feels like we're roommates who share a bed. Sex is still out of the question; I think Tim is still getting over the kiss. He doesn't appear outwardly angry anymore, but he also doesn't touch me or chase me around, like he used to. I figure I'll let it go for a while, until he gets over it, but I can't seem to figure out how to broach the topic. Like, do I start out with, "I know you saw me kiss Keith and all, but when are we going to get it on again?" Obviously, I need to come up with a better opener; the search continues.

We both get up every day and go to work; we come home and have dinner together in front of the TV. Then he works on election stuff while I read. We barely talk about anything, let alone all of the things that really matter to our marriage. Something has got to change, or we'll never get back on track again.

One Friday night in early October, while it is still warm out, I get home before he does and set out a picnic blanket under the oak tree in the back yard. I light some citronella candles; Tim likes the scent. I put together a few of his favorite things to eat: a fresh loaf of French bread, brie, fresh fruit, and some cold leftover chicken that I made from one of Angela's recipes.

He joins me in the backyard; it's nice to lounge on the blanket and eat. We don't talk at first, until I finally say something. "Tim, I really want to get back on track here."

"What do you mean?"

Beside the Music

"You know exactly what I mean. We're walking around here like we're on our first date. It's awkward. I want to get back to how we used to be."

"Bren, I'm still having some trouble with that. I need some time to get over the fact that you kissed Keith."

"Well, how much time will you need?"

"I don't know." He clenches his jaw. "I feel very betrayed by you. It's like, when Hydra was here, you weren't you anymore. You kept secrets from me, and you kissed Keith. I didn't like the person that you became, Bren. And we'd already had our share of problems before they even entered the picture."

"I agree. I feel like we weren't connecting anymore."

"We were on a treadmill to nowhere, Bren. That's why I wanted to run for the Senate. I wanted to do something different. I was getting bored. Is that why you kissed Keith? Were you bored, too?"

The truth is I know exactly how he feels. I felt the same way. I wanted some excitement in our life. And his running for the Senate just made me even more bored with our marriage. This is why people cheat and get divorced: they need pizazz. I think back to how exciting it was to kiss Keith and how compelling it was to entertain the possibility of going on tour with him. If I'd been weaker, this could have ended very differently. "So, what do we do now?"

"I don't know. But I don't think I can just pick up where we left off."

"Tim, what do I need to do to convince you that nothing like that will ever happen again?"

"I don't know, Bren. It's just a feeling that I need to have, and I'm not feeling it right now."

We eat the rest of the brie and talk about our days. Throughout the conversation, I try to come up with the one thing I could say that would make Tim "feel it" again. But then it dawns on me that there really isn't one magic sentence that will make everything alright again. I have to rebuild our marriage, brick by brick. And that means I have to get creative and even woo him a bit until we get back to where we were before. I need to give him a reason not to get bored again.

All through October, I start putting that extra effort into planning fun things for us to do, though it's kind of hard, because we're leading up to the election. So I go with him to his campaign events and help out wherever I can with coordinating volunteers.

One Sunday morning, we wake up a bit late. Tim has decided to take the day off from campaigning so we can do something together.

"I have a surprise for you," I tell him. "Come on, get dressed. Let's go." We get into his truck, and I drive us to the southwestern part of Rhode Island. This part of the state has dense forest with a few small lakes and rivers. I pull into a canoe rental.

"We're going canoeing?" He smiles at me. We used to go frequently, back when we were first married. But things got busy, and we haven't gone in years.

The guide directs us to our canoe. I arranged for it to be stocked with a picnic basket filled with his favorites: of course, brie and grapes. But a few other things, too, like a bottle of red and even some gummy bears. While Tim is checking out the basket, I confer with the guide over the map of the Wood River.

"You'll want to go upstream for about two miles, and then you'll see a small path on the left. Look for the blue dot on the trees."

I get into the front, and Tim gets into the back because he's better at steering than I am. We paddle upstream, as the guide directed, until I see the blue dots, and then we pull the canoe onto the river bank.

"I'll take the blanket," I say. "Will you carry the basket?"

"Where are you taking me?" he asks. It's so hard to surprise Tim, and I am so excited I can barely contain myself.

We walk for maybe a quarter of a mile; the trail opens up to a meadow. We cross the meadow and end up at the top of a ridge that looks over the entire river valley. The view extends for miles.

"Look, you can see the water tower over there. I think that's the one in Mystic," I point out.

"How did you find this place? This is incredible!"

"Well, I've been doing some research on different places we can go together. I wanted to take you somewhere where neither of us has ever been." I like the idea of our going to new places together. It makes me feel as if we are starting over by experiencing new things together. I have plans tonight to take him to try Ethiopian food, as well; again, something neither of us has tried.

While I've been researching new places to go, I've also been right alongside of him, throwing myself into planning a huge fundraiser for the end of October. We are actually having fun together again. We laugh together more and more. He holds my hand when we walk in the woods. He kisses me goodnight now and tells me he loves me before leaving for work. I can feel our marriage getting just a tiny bit stronger by the day.

***

Tonight is Friday, and it's the week before the fundraiser. Tim and I have just seen a great movie, and as we leave the movie theater, I feel like listening to some music, so I turn on the radio in the car.

"*Here's the new one from Hydra,*" the DJ is saying. "*They've been in Rhode Island all summer long, recording a new album. Look for it to hit stores and iTunes for Christmas. But, until then, here's the first single, called 'She Thinks.'*"

The song starts with brash electric guitars and a bluesy bass line, similar to what I remember when I eavesdropped on them in Del's basement. Then Ben starts to sing, "*She thinks I'm an asshole, but she wants me anyway...,*" and I can't switch off the radio fast enough.

"You don't want to hear the rest of the song Keith wrote for you?" Tim asks.

"Nope."

"Have you heard it before?"

"Nope. Well, a little. I went to the studio after you moved out to see for myself how far along they were, and I heard a little bit of it. I've never heard it all the way, through."

It's quiet in the car for the rest of the way home. The tension between us makes my skin feel tight; it start to feel as if all the progress we've made in the last few weeks went right out the window when that stupid song came on. The radio still is kind of a minefield; I never know when I'll stumble upon a reminder of how I let Hydra wreck my marriage. Each time, it's just another reminder of how I'd failed my husband.

"Now I feel like I can't listen to the radio anymore," Tim says, breaking the silence. "I guess I'll have to tune in to NPR for the rest of my life."

"I was just thinking that, myself," I say. "And just watch—the one time you turn on NPR, they'll be interviewing Hydra." I laugh, even though it really isn't funny.

"Well, how does it feel to have a big rock star write a song about you?"

"Not as good as you'd think," I reply.

"Why?"

"Because now I feel like you'll be reminded every time you hear it on the radio, and we'll never get to move on from it. I mean, how is it for you, knowing that another man wrote a song about your wife? God, what if that's the big song that gets played everywhere you go?"

"I'll get over it. It's not like I've forgotten that it happened. But I want to try to fix our marriage. We've been doing so great lately, and we've been having a lot of fun. I don't want to wreck all the progress we've made in the last month. I love you, Brenda. And I don't want to lose you again. I was so miserable without you."

"I was miserable without you, too. I am so sorry for everything that happened."

"I know you are. Me, too." He takes my hand as I drive and holds it until we pull my car into the garage. I can hear Vito in the living room, jumping from the couch to the floor. Tim nods toward the door to the house. "I don't think we worked hard enough to keep him off the couch."

"I don't think he gave us much of a choice. He's pretty much claimed the furniture for his own anyway. It doesn't matter. He's happy."

"Are you happy, even though you're not a rock-and-roll muse anymore?"

I wrap my arms around his waist and kiss him deeply. "Yes. Being a rock-

and-roll muse is not all it's cracked up to be. Maybe I'll get to be a state senator's wife, instead."

We leave a trail of our clothes through the house on the way to the bedroom. I can't remember the last time sex was this hot. I look into his eyes and know that our connection has, finally, been re-established. It makes me feel warm inside, and I paw my hands through his hair.

Afterward, our bed looks like a tornado hit it: sheets, blanket, and pillows are tangled and strewn at the foot. Tim wipes the sweat from his face and leans in to kiss the back of my neck as he spoons me. "God, I missed you," he whispers into my shoulder.

"I missed you, too," I whisper back then sigh. "You're the only one, Tim. Do you believe me?"

"If we keep doing it like this, I will believe everything you say," he says, chuckling softly.

Chapter 30

THE VERY THING THAT WE JOKED ABOUT a month ago happens almost exactly as I described it. I stopped listening to the rock stations weeks ago, and since then, I've kept the dial fixed on NPR—until tonight, when they begin their usual pledge drive. After already donating a hundred bucks to the cause, I'm not in the mood to listen to them try to convince me to chip in, so I switch over to satellite radio. I'm tuned into my favorite station, The Edge, which has obscure recordings from '90s artists and interviews.

Tonight—of course—they're interviewing Hydra. My first instinct is to turn it off. Listening to it would be disloyal to Tim and can only undo all the progress we've made in repairing the damage to our marriage. But—of course—I'm curious to hear what they have to say. *How could I not be? Will they talk about me and Tim?* I tell myself that I'll listen just this once; I pull the car over so I can listen without distraction. Tim doesn't have to know, and *I don't think it's that big of a deal to listen to one measly radio interview, is it?*

Moira Black, the velvet-voiced interviewer on this show, is quite possibly one of my favorite rock-and-roll interviewers. I guess you could call her my girl-crush. I Googled her once, to see what she looks like. I imagined her looking like an '80s metal sex kitten, with the big hair and low-cut top. But instead, she has cropped gray hair, wears little makeup under her heavy-rimmed glasses, and is usually wearing a plain white T-shirt and jeans. Not at all sexy, the way she sounds on the radio, and definitely not the way a woman who knows her way around rock and roll typically looks.

She asks why they decided to record in Rhode Island, and Keith tells the whole story about how he came here to meet me. Moira lets out some intimate *um-hmms* as he speaks, sounding as if she's almost purring. Then Keith talks about how he got the idea for a song while at my house, hearing wind chimes. Moira asks if those were the same chimes as on the track "Green Sky."

"*Yes, they are. And I am afraid I still owe the Dunkirks a set. They were nice enough to let me dismantle them for the record*," he says and laughs.

"*Maybe someday they can put them up in the Rock and Roll Hall of Fame,*" Ben chimes in and laughs. I giggle and cover my mouth; it would *definitely* be cool to have my wind chimes hanging in the Rock and Roll Hall of Fame.

I don't even know how long I've been parked in the breakdown lane on I-95; I am completely sucked into this interview. Any guilt about listening to it is completely gone. I've laughed out loud at a few of the things the guys said. Then Moira asks about the inspiration behind all the songs. She asks about "She Thinks." I hold my breath; I can feel my heart beating in my throat.

"*So, what was the inspiration behind that one?*" she asks.

"*That would be Brenda Dunkirk,*" Keith replies.

"*Brenda Dunkirk, the fan from Rhode Island you came to meet in July?*" Moira asks, skillfully pressing. "*So, does she know about it?*"

"*Yes. And, you know, I feel kind of awful about the way that turned out,*" Keith says. "*See, the Dunkirks were nice enough to let us stay in their house while we recorded at Del Riccio's studio.*"

"*Really? You lived in their home? What was that like? Maybe we should have invited the Dunkirks to this interview.*" She lets out a deep, sexy giggle, and I have to laugh because I know that she looks a bit like a younger Judi Dench. I wonder, *what was their impression of living with us?* At the time, it didn't really seem to matter to them that my marriage was falling apart.

"*I guess for Brenda and Tim, it was about what you'd expect when you have rock stars and their entourage descend upon your home,*" Keith says, chuckling. "*I don't think it went so well for the Dunkirks. We haven't spoken to them at all since we moved out. I know it put a great deal of stress on them, and I hope that, now, all is well with them.*"

"*Well, let's play Mrs. Dunkirk's song,*" Moira says and switches over to the opening chords of "She Thinks."

It is the first time I've ever heard it all the way through, and it's not at all what I expected. For starters, I thought I'd love hearing a song written for me on the radio. But I am sitting here in the car and my stomach is lurching. I want to turn off the radio, but I need to listen to it all the way through at least once. I really hope that this isn't the big hit song that I'll hear everywhere I go: I don't think I could deal with all that nausea until the next big thing comes out.

"*'She still thinks I'm an asshole, but I want to be her lover...,'*" Ben sings, with a bluesy voice that, I have to admit, is very sexy. I think this song alone will get Ben the distinction of *People* magazine's sexiest man alive. The song sounds very different than what I heard in Del's basement that day. Somehow it sounds more modern than the traditional Hydra sound.

The song starts off with me thinking that Keith's an asshole, and throughout the song he's chasing me around and trying to convince me that he's not. It's nice

Beside the Music

to see that he hasn't taken any poetic license with the story—for the most part: whereas, in reality, I still think he's an asshole, the end of the song actually has my character coming around. I know that someday Tim's going to hear this; I wonder what the hell that will do to our recovery efforts in our marriage. *Will he think that I'm secretly in contact with him and haven't told him? Will it be the same scene all over again, where I'll have to tell him that I wouldn't have told him, the way I did with the kiss?*

I hate to say it, but the song is amazing. The arrangement is absolutely perfect. It has the loose, bluesy feel of a rock song that you'd hear from a band like The Rolling Stones or even Stone Temple Pilots. After the song ends, I imagine Moira fanning herself off and is likely swooning over Ben Taylor, sitting with her in the studio. I probably would be, too.

The ensuing silence is a little too long for radio, until she finally clears her throat and continues with the interview. She asks about the upcoming tour and about their reaction to the fact that they're selling out arenas all over the U.S. again.

"The human interest story behind this album is lighting up the Internet right now," she says.

"Yes, our publicists are quite busy," Ben says, laughing.

"You're now outselling Jamie Fire left and right, even with her feature film in theaters right now," she adds. Somehow, even with all the promise of hot teenage-girl promiscuity, Jamie Fire's getting out-sold by a bunch of old guys from Australia. Her publicists must be livid that these same old guys are actually beating out Jamie's well-planned public deflowering for media coverage. Erik must be dancing in the streets.

"Yes, I guess we are," Ben says with a hint of modesty. And Moira eats it up. She comments on how approachable the band has become, as they get older, and I picture Erik popping open a champagne bottle, his brilliant marketing scheme having worked according to plan. After all that has happened, I can't help but still feel a bit happy for the band. It can't be easy to compete with Jamie Fire.

"Now tell me," Moira continues, changing the subject, *"you've had a shakeup in the band's management as a result of the release of this album."*

"Yes, we have as well." This time, it's Keith who answers. *"We parted ways with Erik Murtaugh as this album was being recorded. You know, creative differences and all that."* He chuckles. *"Our former publicist, Toni Wallace, has taken over management of the band. Her first order of business was to hire her boyfriend, Nick Fenton. Nick is a composer and a brilliant arranger. He took over the arrangement of all the songs on this album and gave our sound a much-needed face lift."*

My mind goes back to the night of the great Motel 6 debacle. I am amazed

189

that they really did go through with firing Erik. That must have been a brutal divorce. Still, it's such great news for Toni and Nick. I've seen how hard Toni works for Keith and the rest of the band—she deserves this promotion. I wonder if I should call her to congratulate her, but then think better of it. I need to *not* contact the band at all, ever again.

"*You're right, it's more upbeat than your former albums,*" Moira chimes in. "*It has a younger feel to it.*"

"*Exactly,*" Ben replies. "*A more modern sound has helped us to compete with the likes of Jamie Fire.*"

Compete? Try annihilate. I can't help but smile. They sound so cool, so modest. I am proud of their success, even if it means that the whole world now knows that Keith wants to be my lover—and that I think he's an asshole.

They are winding down the interview. It's getting close to the top of the hour when Keith speaks up. "*Moira, if I may say something?*" He pauses. "*I feel awful about how things ended with us and the Dunkirks. Brenda, if you're out there and you're listening, will you please give us a call? I am sure you still have Toni's number. Please. I hate that things ended that way with you.*"

A public plea? Yup, he's still an asshole. What if Tim hears?

When the interview ends, I pull out of the breakdown lane and back into traffic. I turn the radio off, afraid that I'll hear "She Thinks" on every station. I let the quiet in my car surround me. Listening to the interview has me feeling empty, and now I kind of wish that I hadn't listened to it. I mean, I'm glad that everything turned out so well for them, but I hate the way that living with the band had affected my life.

I also hate that it didn't work out. All I'd wanted was to be a part of the creative process and to help them make something fantastic. But, in a way, I guess I did. If I hadn't kicked the band out, then they wouldn't have fired Erik and hired Toni and Nick. Now they're on top again. So, in a way, I did help them—just not in the way I'd initially hoped.

But now there's a whole other dilemma. *Should I call Keith? Should I give him another chance to explain himself?*

My gut instinct says, *hell no.* But I, too, hate the way things ended with them. It's just that I wish we could have stayed friends with the band after they moved out. Still, I'm pretty sure that, if I try to explain myself to Tim, he won't get it. And Keith does sound more approachable on a radio interview; but I don't really think he's changed all that much. I know I should leave well enough alone.

Hearing the song has had a different effect on me than I'd thought it would, too. Secretly, I really like being the rock-and-roll muse. I liked reading Keith's lyrics over my kitchen table and telling him what I thought. I liked having that frank discussion about what I thought about him, and I think I started to get through to him. I also liked that I was able to contribute something to the band's creativity. I will never forget that morning when I got to read the lyrics for "Green

Beside the Music

Sky" and told Ben and Erik what I really thought. I was part of something bigger than me.

Some days, I wonder what the point is, when I'm working to improve the reputation of some faceless corporation. In the grand scheme of things, *does it really matter? Will I look back on my career and think that I've wasted my time on media campaigns to help corporations sell more crap that nobody really needs?* Helping Keith with his lyrics, and even with his personal life, made me feel like I had a purpose. I wish I could have found a way, but apparently it is impossible to be one man's muse and another man's wife.

When I get home, I pay close attention to Tim, and I'm pretty sure he hasn't heard the interview. He normally listens to the comedy stations on satellite radio, while I'm the news junkie—it's an occupational hazard of mine. The last thing our marriage needs is a rock song written about how another man wants to be my lover. I need to put it behind me and focus on the present.

Tim is setting the dining room table; we've been making more of an effort to eat at the table and not in front of the TV, as part of Operation Reclaim Marriage. We always start off asking each other about something good that happened during the day. Today is no different. "So," he says, over dinner, "anything interesting happened during your day?"

"Oh, just the usual," I answer, but I can see by the look on his face that he can tell I'm distracted. *Putting the radio interview behind me is clearly not working.*

"You seem a bit out of it," he says, prompting me while he pokes his salad with his fork.

"Just tired, I guess." I push my dinner around. I am in a complete funk after hearing the interview, no matter how hard I try not to think about it. I should have just turned it off. I don't know how I'm going to shake this mood. *How could I possibly tell Tim how I feel about hearing the interview?* I imagine saying, "Honey, I heard Keith on the radio, and I miss the band, and I miss being a part of that." *There is no way in hell he'd be okay with that.* And there is no way in hell that I should even be thinking it, as the mere mention of it could destroy the fragile ecosystem of our marriage. Annie was right: Tim is way more important to me than Hydra.

"Okay," he says, setting his fork down. "But listen to me. If we're going to make this work, then we need to be completely honest with each other. If something is bothering you, you've got to tell me, okay?"

"Yes, I will," I say, putting on a fake smile and forcing down the rest of my dinner—even though "She Thinks" still has my stomach lurching. Tim watches me from his side of the table, and I can tell he's concerned. I try to smile wider, hoping that I'll be more convincing, but I know I'm really only kidding myself.

Chapter 31

"UGH." **I'M PAWING MY WAY** through my closet. It's the night before Halloween; Tim's fundraiser is tonight. *What the hell do I wear to this one?* It's being held at a funky club in downtown Providence. He's going to have bands playing, a tequila tasting, and a few other fun activities, like cigar rolling. He's trying to appeal to younger voters with the bands, but older ones, too, with the cigar rolling. I think it'll be a great night, if only I can get dressed and get there. I don't want to look like a dowdy candidate's wife, but I also don't want to dress in slutty club clothes, either.

I pull out my standby club outfit: a black tank top and the dark skinny jeans that I know Tim won't be able to keep his eyes off of. I pull on my black knee-high stiletto boots and snake on a few chunky silver bangle bracelets. After I throw on a bit of eyeliner and maroon lipstick, I'm ready to rock. Of course, I have to take off the boots once I get into my car, because I've never mastered the art of driving a stick shift in high heels.

The valet waits while I pull on my boots and hand him the keys. When I walk in, I see Portia standing with two other women I don't recall having seen at any of her endless Chanel-suit fundraiser brunches. She looks me up and down, and I do the same to her. I've never seen her wear jeans. She's still wearing a suit jacket and her three strands of pearls, but the dark-wash jeans are surprisingly up to date, belted just below her waist with a silver chain belt. I approach her, and she air kisses both of my cheeks. Also a first. I peer into her glass and wonder how many tequilas she's tasted.

"Brenda, I want to introduce you to my new friends, Marianne and Paula." I turn to shake their hands. "I met them at the Newport chapter of Widows with Style."

What? She's going to a widow support group? Now I'm starting to wonder if she's taken to tequila-tasting at home, as well.

Aria ushers us in. "Tim's speech is about to start. Brenda, you need to get backstage so you can make an entrance with Tim." As she leads me through the

Beside the Music

club, I notice that Tim has an excellent turnout. The front of the stage is thick with people dancing to a Pearl Jam cover band. We go through a door just to the right of the stage, and I see Tim poring over his index cards. He looks up and smiles at me, then glances at his watch. *Is he—ever the cool cucumber—actually nervous?*

"You ready?" I ask him and squeeze his arm. Just as I turn my attention away from him for a second, I see a familiar face duck into a doorway down the hall. "If I didn't know better," I say, "I'd swear I just saw Ben Taylor." Tim shrugs and smiles. His eyes shine bright in an "I just got you the single best Christmas present ever" expression. "Are you serious? They're *here*? Why? Are you okay?"

"Bren, we have to go on soon. I'll explain everything tonight after the show, okay?"

It's not okay. I want to know what the hell Hydra is doing here. *How on earth are they in the same room as Tim?* I've thought for sure that Tim would never, ever want to associate with them again. *And why is he so calm about it?*

We're ushered onto the stage, and the roar of applause is deafening. I stand beside Tim as he thanks everyone for coming, and then I step off to the side a bit while the spotlight focuses on him. He talks about his bid for state Senate and why he's the right man for the job.

As he's speaking about job creation and incentives for small businesses, I scan the crowd while trying to keep my eyes mostly on Tim. I spot Portia and her friends; she waves to me and flashes a thumbs up. I nod back. Now I am starting to wonder whether someone slipped a roofie into her drink.

The crowd cheers at something Tim said. *Shit, I really need to be paying more attention. Is it obvious that I am not completely listening?* I flick my eyes back to the crowd again and spot Annie off to the left, near the edge of the stage. Tim must have invited her, too. I can't help but beam when she jumps up and down and waves at me.

Tim finishes speaking, and he turns to me and kisses me as the cameras flash. We raise our clasped hands and wave at the crowd, exiting the stage just as the crew is setting up for another band. I spot Toni in the wings with a headset on and her clipboard in her arms.

"Always the rock-and-roll cruise director, *eh*?" I ask, laughing.

"Brenda!" She throws her arms around me for a hug. "I'd love to chat, but the boys are about to go on."

"I understand." I smile back at her. "Congrats on the promotion! You so deserve it!"

She smiles back at me and listens to her headset. She shrugs apologetically, and I wave her off. "Go! You have rock stars to control."

I decide to get out of the way of all the frantic pre-show stage setting, so I make my way back out to the crowd at the front of the stage. Annie throws her arms around me when I get over to where she's standing. It's so noisy in the club that it's hard to talk.

At last, I can hear Jeff's bass drum begin to pound over the noise of the crowd, and I know they're opening with "Battleground Zero." The crowd goes wild with applause and cheers.

Portia and her friends materialize to the left of me, and she hands me a drink. "It's a tequila spritzer, darling," she gushes. "It's divine."

I take a sip. She's not kidding—it's delicious. I need to pace myself with these, or I'll end up bombed at Tim's big fundraiser. Portia clinks her glass to mine and smiles at me. She and her friends bob their heads to the music. *Who the hell is this woman, and what has she done with my mother-in-law?*

Chapter 32

"OH, BY THE WAY, I'm totally crashing at your house tonight," Annie informs me, while she and I lounge backstage. "I'm doing a story on Hydra, and I want to get some background on how they came to stay at your house."

"The exclusive is all yours." I really don't care to talk about it much. I'll tell Annie so that she can get her story, but I don't want to hold a press conference or anything.

I am still reeling from the whole evening. Tim. Hydra. And—*holy crap*—Portia. She and her friends hung out for a little while backstage with us, and I got a bit more information from her about her transformation. Apparently, one night, while I was working late on the Baxter campaign, she and Tim had dinner together.

"I was so angry with you after I met you at your office," she said. "Nobody had ever spoken to me that way before. But then Timothy laid out some very harsh truths to me at dinner that night. Showing up at your workplace like that was unforgivable, Brenda. I understand if you are angry with me for doing that. I behaved horribly." *That's possibly the closest I will get to an apology from her. And that's okay.*

"He was right, though," she continued. "I haven't had any fun since Charles passed. I had heard about Widows with Style but never thought I'd actually go to an event." She paused to sip her drink. "All of us there understand each other." She nodded at Marianne and Paula.

"Portia knows how to have a good time," Paula chimed in. *Really? Portia? With her microfiber car cloths and snooty furniture?*

Now that she knows how to have fun, I wonder if this means that I can finally redecorate my house the way I like it. Maybe now I can find out what those Louis XIV chaises will fetch on Craigslist.

I am walking to the bar when Keith corners me. "Now will you please stop calling me an asshole?"

"Maybe so, maybe not," I throw back at him. "It was a great show, but I still want to know what the hell you're doing here."

"When Tim calls, we deliver," he says. He takes a sip from his drink. I raise my eyebrows at his glass, and he holds it up for me to inspect. "Seltzer with lime," he says. "I am trying to clean up my act a bit. I am working to get supervised visits with Damien, and I need to pass the random drug tests."

"Wow, Keith, that's huge!" I take a sip of my tequila spritzer and suddenly feel self-conscious, drinking in front of him. The pause between us is awkward.

"Brenda," he begins, "I owe you an apology. I behaved terribly while in your home. I nearly ended your marriage, and that was inexcusable."

I'm not going to say it's okay. He's still got some explaining to do. *Why on earth is he even here?*

I swear he's reading my mind. "It was Tim who called, you know."

"What do you mean?"

"After the Moira Black interview. Tim called me. He was not happy that I asked you to call me in front of the entire world, and he let me have it."

"Are you serious?"

"Yes. That man called and defended your honor in a way I'd never seen. He ripped me apart on the phone for about ten minutes."

"Wow, Keith, I'm..." *Am I seriously going to apologize? I need to shut my mouth.* Thankfully, Keith keeps talking.

"Every word of what he said was true. It was Tim who told me that I need to make things right with you. I have learned so much from you both about getting over myself and being a good person. But I didn't know how to start. You probably would not have accepted a phone call from me. I needed to do something bigger to show you that I can be a good man."

"And here you are, at Tim's fundraiser."

"Yes, here I am. I arranged the whole thing with Tim as a surprise for you. I am sure it helps support his Bars to Cars foundation." Tim's starting a foundation that will help ex-cons get jobs as mechanics. "I have also agreed to an exclusive interview with your friend Annie, as well."

She must be psyched about that. She'll probably get a serious promotion at MTV News, with all these exclusives she's racking up tonight.

I don't even know what to say. I suppose I should start out polite. "Keith, thanks for doing this tonight. I am sure it means the world to Tim that you guys supported him on his campaign."

"Brenda, I was a terrible houseguest. But I hope that we can be friends." He shrugs and bows his head slightly.

"I have to think about it, Keith." And, really, that's the most I can promise him right now.

"I have to get back," he says and tips his head toward the stage. "Apparently we're doing a cigar-rolling-with-Hydra thing over there."

Beside the Music

I gesture to him to go, but my mouth is left hanging open. *Did Keith seriously arrange to play a show for free, for Tim's foundation and for me?* I have to admit, that's pretty un-asshole-like behavior. I watch him pose for a picture with one of Portia's new friends. I always thought that it takes so much longer to fix problems than to create them, but now I am not so sure. Portia and her friends clink their glasses and laugh, and I can't help but smile.

***

After we get home, Annie's already taking notes when I walk with her into the guest room. "Which one slept in here?" she asks, running her hand across the duvet.

"Keith." I sit down on the bed beside her. She gapes when I tell her the truth about Jeff and Gill. "But you seriously cannot use that. I don't think they want to be out to the media." I want to sit up all night with her to gossip and giggle, but I still need answers from Tim. I cut the girl-talk short, tell Annie goodnight, and head to our bedroom.

We're totally having a long and leisurely brunch tomorrow morning.

"So, Hydra was there," I say. "What was that all about?"

"Remember that night you came home and I could tell you were bummed out?" He pauses. "I knew you'd heard the interview on The Edge, because I'd heard it, too. You looked so sad, and you tried so hard not to show it. I knew I had to do something."

My heart is racing. *He heard the song, he heard Keith ask me to call him.* "Tim, you gotta believe me, I didn't call him. I swear."

"I know you didn't. And I knew you wouldn't." Tim pauses. "So I did. I was pretty pissed at the nerve of that guy, asking you on the air to call him. I told him so, too, and called him a few choice names."

"Keith actually told me that tonight. I cannot believe you called him. He said you pretty much read him the riot act."

"I didn't really let him talk in that phone call. I slammed the phone down on him. Then the next day he shows up at the shop with a six-pack. I threw him out at first. But he asked me to hear him out." That's Tim: always at the ready with the second chance. "He's actually pretty easy to talk to when he isn't focusing all the attention on himself."

I am sure that Keith was probably the last person Tim wanted to discuss our marriage with. But then, Keith is the reason why his own marriage failed. Despite his "detached rock star in an ivory tower" persona, surely he's done his share of soul searching, with everything that has happened to him in his lifetime.

197

"He was pretty insightful, you know." He pauses a moment to collect his thoughts. "Brenda, I know that things have been a bit hard for you. Keith helped me to see that. My mom showing up at your job was probably pretty awful for you, too. I'm sorry that happened. But what he said to me that night made a lot of sense." *What? Keith is giving someone else sensible life advice?* "Bren, he really laid it out for me and stripped away all of the bullshit. Nobody's ever presented my life in that way before. Ultimately, it's you and me that matters. Not the band, not the election, not my mom. It's us and our future as a family that matters here. I'd forgotten that, and I am so sorry."

"You're not the only one who forgot," I whisper.

"I know that having Hydra here really messed things up. But, in a way, it shook us up in just the right way. If it weren't for Keith, I wouldn't have had that reminder of what's really important. It's you." He kisses the back of my hand and holds it to his chest. "It was Keith who got me to talk to my mom about her behavior toward you."

"You mean, after I told her to get a fucking life?" I laugh.

"Oh my God. I said that, too. I literally said to her to get a fucking life or else."

"You didn't!"

"I did. And then she actually listened. She's not going to change, but at least she'll chill out a bit. Tonight she had a good time with her new friends. And she knows that I am going to put you before her from now on."

"Thank you." I kiss him. "It was fun to watch her actually having fun," I say, laughing. *I also liked that she didn't scowl at me the whole night.*

"You know what else he said that was pretty interesting?" he asks. I shrug. "He wanted to wait before he and Tamsen had a baby. He wanted to wait until their first big tour was over. Then he wanted to wait until they went platinum or whatever. He always had some reason to wait. Then they had a mishap with their birth control, and Tamsen got pregnant."

"I wonder if the 'mishap' was her not taking her pills," I joke.

"Well, he said that when she got pregnant, it suddenly became the right time. Nothing else mattered—only Tamsen and their child."

"I am sure it was hard, though. He was touring, she was left on her own with a baby…" I trail off.

"I'm sure it was, too. But somehow it worked. He said that there is no right time. There's just a time, and it's as good as any other mythical right time we could ever come up with. And he's right. I don't want to wait anymore. If we're together, and if we're going to stay that way, then it's the right time."

"Really? But what about the election? My promotion?"

"If we wait for those, then we'll only have another thing to wait for after those things come up. Then another, and then another."

Beside the Music

"So, does this mean we're trying?"

"Sure. Starting now." He waggles his eyebrows at me.

I am so surprised, relieved, and optimistic.

Now on to bigger things. Like redecorating. And buying things, like cribs. There is no way I am letting Portia buy this kid's crib.

Chapter 33

THE INAUGURATION OF A STATE SENATOR really is not that big a deal. It's not really even that much of an inauguration. After he won the election, Tim was basically told, "Congratulations. You're a state senator. See you in January." He had to pick out a few committees that he wanted to join and work on; all of the paperwork relating to all of them is spread out on our dining room table.

Annie and her new boyfriend are coming up from New York for the weekend. Tim's going to go pick them up at the train station, while I finish cleaning up. Since the fundraiser, we've made a plan to get together once per month. We take turns hosting. We went to New York just before Christmas so we could see the city all done up in lights for the holidays. She and Sean decorated the hell out of their apartment, as well. Sean is an interior designer. The window treatments were festooned with tasteful white lights, and a single candle glowed in every window. An actual candle: not those cheesy lightbulb things. He even served us drinks with cranberries and spiced orange slices frozen into the ice cubes.

They came up in January, and then we went back to the city for Sean's Valentine-themed decor. It's been so great to have them back in my life. Between visits, we call and Facebook. I didn't realize how badly I'd missed having a girlfriend in my life until now, and I am so thankful to have Annie again.

Keith and I have been emailing and Facebooking each other since their tour began at the Sydney Opera House in early December. For a little while after the tour started, reporters were calling Tim and me at the house to get the scoop about Hydra living in our home for nearly two months, since Keith had already spilled the beans about it during the interview on The Edge. We blew them off, and eventually they lost interest. Toni took over and issued a statement on our behalf, and that seemed to satisfy the tabloids.

Keith, Tim, and I are now good friends. A few times, I've come home from work to find them actually Skyping with each other. If you had asked me back in August if I ever thought *that* would happen, I would have asked you to share your drugs with me.

Right now, Hydra's in Europe, and then they'll make their way to Asia. After

Beside the Music

that, the North American part will start in Montreal, Canada and then extend west to Vancouver before trickling downward and eastward, across the U.S., ending in Providence, Rhode Island. Keith sounds like he's having a lot of fun on this tour, and the screaming crowd of fans night after night isn't wearing him down yet. But I think that's probably because it doesn't feel like work to him. In the '80s and '90s, when they were touring constantly, he got burnt out with it all, to the point that he dreaded going back on the road. It's nice to see him enjoying his job again; maybe this is how he envisioned the life of a rock star, and now it's finally come to fruition.

I can hear them Skyping right now. "No way," says Tim. "You're in Prague? Don't tell Brenda. She's been dying to go there."

"Oh, let me see!" I holler out, as I enter the range of the webcam. "Point the camera out the window."

"It's still dark here, Bren. You're not going to see much." He points the camera out the window, and I see the skyline lit up. *"You'll have to come see it for real. Trust me, it's stunning."*

"So, Prague then where? Was it Warsaw?"

"Yes. Warsaw! There is this café that makes amazing stuffed cabbages. Legit Polish golumpki. Cannot wait!" Keith smiles.

"So, any word on Damien?" I ask. Tamsen and Damien are no longer on the forbidden topic list. Keith's been trying to get supervised visits.

"I just finished Skyping him, too, which is why I am up so late. We try to Skype every few days, which is a wonderful start. When the tour is over, I get to see him in person. He's starting high school now, even though he's getting home-schooled. So smart," he gushes.

"Must take after Tamsen," Tim says and laughs.

"True story," Keith replies. We sign off, and I smile at Tim.

The timer on the oven dings. I am a bit on edge tonight, trying to make our entertaining skills appear as flawless and skillfully executed as Sean's. Tim's committee papers are all over the dining room, and the smell of the roast he put in the oven is suddenly making me want to throw up.

Tim opens the oven, and a cloud of steam escapes. He catches sight of me as I cover my mouth and run to the toilet; he waits for me outside and hands me a glass of water and a hand towel. "Are you okay?"

"I don't know. I wonder if I caught that stomach bug that has been going around at work. I don't know how I'm going to make it through the night. I hate to say it, but the thought of eating that roast makes me want to hurl."

"Bren, do you think you could be…" he begins.

"No way," I tell him. "I think it's just a stomach bug. But now I'm wondering if we should cancel tonight. I don't want to make Annie and Sean sick, too." Tim and I haven't really called it "trying for a baby" anymore. Right now it's "whatever happens, happens, and let's have fun in the process." I like that method a lot better; I was afraid Tim might whip out some crazy, color-coded ovulation calendar. Nothing says sexy like your husband jamming a thermometer into your mouth every morning.

And honestly, getting pregnant has been the furthest thing from my mind lately. The Baxter launch went great, and now I am on to the next project at work. This one is more interesting. I get to work on a band that is trying to get national recognition. Once Amanda learned that Hydra had been living in my house, she gave me this launch—it's actually her nephew's band. So far, I am having a blast with it, and it's fun to not work on something corporate for a little while.

The fall and winter so far have been so busy, with Tim winning the election, then the insanity of Christmas and work heating up again, now that the New Year has passed. In this last week, I've had a few twinges of nausea, but it never occurred to me that I might be pregnant.

Tim's rooting around under the sink and finds a pregnancy test from the last time we actually called it trying. "Do these expire?" he asks, examining the box.

"It's not like it's going to blow up if I pee on it, will it?" I laugh and walk to the bathroom. He follows. "Out." I shove him back into the hall.

"What do you mean?"

"You're not going to watch me pee, are you?"

He pauses at the door, uncertain. I know that, if I am, he wants to experience every minute of it with me. But I have to draw the line.

I sit down and take a breath. Right here is the moment where my life might change drastically. If I sit here for a few minutes, I can keep my life exactly the same for just a bit longer. If I am pregnant, then life will change because there will be a baby on the way. But if I am not, then will things also change? Will we go back to where we were before? Will we get bored with each other, because not being pregnant isn't enough of a change? Will we silently point our fingers at each other and retreat into ourselves once again?

"Brenda?" he calls through the bathroom door. "Come on, you're killing me."

"Hold on." I zip up and wash my hands before opening the door.

"Well?" He barges into the bathroom when he hears the water run in the sink. I hold the test stick behind my back and smile at him.

"Really?" he asks, trying to reach behind me to see for himself. "Come on, you're killing me. Did you look yet?"

"No, not yet." And I haven't. Part of me likes not knowing. I kind of want to prolong that for a bit longer, to keep things the same for a few more minutes.

"Well, are you going to show me?"

I draw my hands from behind my back and hold the stick out to him. The window glows with a + sign.

"Wow. Oh, my God. Bren, we're going to be parents!" He throws his arms around me. "I love you."

"I love you, too." I can feel my eyes filling with tears. I've been weepy for a couple of weeks now, too—a sure sign that my hormones are starting to flare up.

"And I love you, too," Tim says, bending to kiss my still-flat stomach. "I can't wait to see you."

We pace around the house a bit; we don't know what to do with the news that we're expecting a baby. I sit down at the computer and pull up a pregnancy website. We read it together for a few minutes, and then Tim proposes we go to the bookstore and buy every book on the shelf.

"Maybe we should go to the library. After all, we have a college fund to build now," I point out, absently rubbing my belly.

"I wonder when it was. Maybe our little tryst under the Christmas tree did the trick, *huh*? Or was it on New Year's Eve?"

"Not a word to Annie and Sean tonight, okay? I want this to just stay between us until I've at least had the chance to go to the doctor. And don't tell Keith either, okay?"

Tim agrees.

"By the time they play Providence, I'll be seven months along. I don't know how I'll keep this a secret from him until then."

The emails from Keith are more consistent than the phone calls and Skype sessions; we write to each other once per week. Over the months of the tour, my pregnancy will begin to show, and I will have to get creative with positioning the webcam so he won't see that I'm expecting; I want it to be a surprise.

What I like the most about his emails are the photos he sends of all the cities the band has played. I have them printed on matte photo paper, and I paste them into a scrapbook that I plan to give to him when he gets to Providence. I know he'll love it.

I'll have to start another scrapbook for the baby. Tim and I will take a picture of ourselves and our friends tonight, and I'll paste that in the first page, because it's the night we found out that this little life inside of me had already begun. It's also the night where mine became complete.

And I can't wait to fill the rest of the pages.

About the Author

As a former college radio station DJ, BJ was inspired to write this book after asking herself, "Whatever happened to all those '80s rock stars and one-hit wonders?" In addition to devising her own answer to her question in this novel, she also contributed to *RI Fit Magazine*. But her prouder achievements are her original angry-chick rock songs, usually about bad ex-boyfriends, accompanied by her out-of-tune guitar.

BJ resides in Rhode Island with her husband, Todd, and dogs, Nemo and Potter. She is an avid sailor and scuba diver and also enjoys pretty much any outdoor activity, including hiking and geocaching. She has also single-handedly orchestrated hundreds of failed attempts at cooking.

Thank you for reading Beside the Music. I hope that you enjoyed it. Please don't forget to leave a review on Amazon.com and Goodreads.com. Reviews from readers like you are extremely beneficial to indie authors like me.

Here is the link for Amazon.com: http://bjknapp.com/amazon
Here is the link for Goodreads.com:
https://www.goodreads.com/book/show/27899974-beside-the-music

Also, please sign up for my mailing list so I can keep you updated on my new books, events and of course dog pictures at http://bjknapp.com

Thank you. ~BJ

Beside the Music
Acknowledgments

William Campbell, my amazing editor, has challenged me to always do better and has not accepted any crap from me. Greg Simanson, my cover designer, and Kathryn Galán, my proofreader. Thank you all for all you guys did to make this happen.

Stuart Horwitz, the book architect, has given me the chance to sit there for hours and gossip about my characters like they are actual people—which was key to helping me understand them better and get their actions to make more sense. Your keen insight changed the course of this book for the better.

Susan Breen, my group leader at the Algonkian Pitch Conference, took a critical eye to this book. It's always hard to know whether a novel is even interesting anymore, when the process to write it has taken five years. Thank you for your fine-tuning. Viva Group C: Celine Keating, and Nicole Waggoner, that means you!

And now for the family that helped, in one way or another, to make this book happen. Mom, you always said that I could do anything I set my mind to. I wish you were here to see me set my mind to this. I miss you every single day.

Dad and Ania, thanks for the extra encouragement just when I needed it.

Tina and Craig, your subtle little stocking-stuffer gifts to express your support helped keep me going. Best in-laws ever

I have an enormous quantity of siblings, nieces, and nephews--all of whom frequently asked, "So, how's the book going?" and let me blather on about it. Just for that, you all get your names printed in a book. I love you all: Margaret, Bruce, Maya, Walter, Debbi, Janina, Robert, Grace, Christine, Rachael, Maddie, Spencer, Cassidy, Kaz, Melissa, Maggie, Krystian, Hali, Emily, Shawn, Cayden, Collin, and Alex.

To Sean Keene, thanks for keeping Todd occupied in the workshop all those winter weekends when I wanted to write. And thanks for letting me bounce plot ideas off of you and for being a spectacular friend in the process.

Glenn Turner, thank you for making me look and feel like a supermodel when you shot my photo. If weren't for you and your magic camera I would have given up and used the photo on my driver's license.

Jeremy Girard, thank you for your design expertise and keen insight for the awesome web site you made for me.

Nemo, thanks for providing the inspiration for Vito. Potter, thanks for demanding I get up from the chair and go out for a run.

To Todd, I could literally write a whole other book expressing my gratitude for you. You have no idea how much I appreciate your constant support for whatever hare-brained scheme I embark on. You are always the loudest voice in my cheering section. I meant it when I said that none of this would have ever happened without you.

Made in the USA
Columbia, SC
25 August 2017